"Brandy Heineman has knocked it out of the park in her dual timeline *Like Honey for the Bones*. A century-old murder and an intriguing hero and heroine with major problems to overcome kept me flipping the pages to find answers. It's a story the reader will remember long past 'The End.'"

Patricia Bradley, USA Today Best-Selling author of *Counter Attack, Pearl River Series, Book 1*

Like Honey for the Bones

A Novel

Blessings !

Brandy Heineman

BRANDY HEINEMAN

Published 2023
Printed in the United States of America

ISBN-13: 979-8-9883074-1-9 (paperback)
ISBN-13: 979-8-9883074-3-3 (e-book)

Brandy Heineman
PO Box 943
Kennesaw, Georgia 30156
https://brandyheineman.com/

Edited by Irene Chambers, Onward Editing

Cover design by Kristen Ingebretson

Interior art credit: Adobe Stock File # 390009850. Mountain silhouette icon vector set for logo, by kirania.

Author photo credit: Copyright Emilie Hendryx of E. A. Creative Photography, 2014.

To Michael.
Thank you for always
cheering me on, honey.
I love you.

Pleasant words are a honeycomb,
Sweet to the soul and healing to the bones.
-Proverbs 16:24 (NASB)

One

She should have shipped his body to Norway.

The idle wish plumed and vanished with a huff into the bitter morning air. Solveig Borja dismissed it as she paced the squeaky planks of her grandfather's front porch. He wouldn't have wanted that. To him, Cross Keys, Virginia, was home.

Headlamps flashed at the top of the long driveway and burned twin spots into her vision. The vehicle threw gravel with a too-sharp left turn, and an indistinct roar plundered the stillness. She turned her good ear toward the approaching vehicle. The blare grew, and she tightened her lips. Apparently, the local funeral home had upfitted its hearse with a substantial sound system.

The vehicle lurched to a stop in front of the barn, and exhaust billowed gloom over the pastures. As she stepped from the porch, the harsh music subsided and the horn honked twice.

Solveig flinched. The funeral director had hesitated to accommodate her request for a ride to the service. Even so, she hadn't expected him to stoop to petty rudeness.

What choice was there but to find some steel for her spine and get on with it? After today, at least this dreaded goodbye would be done. The last of her family gone; her final tie to Virginia cut. Six thousand kilometers stood between here and Oslo and eleven days until her return flight. If she survived the next few hours, they would take her halfway home.

As she opened the hearse's door, a fervid newscast hit her ear. "Police have identified the victim as twenty-eight-year-old Trevor Roberts of Bridgewater. Authorities advise the public to be vigilant . . ."

"Excuse me." Lemon air freshener and leather upholstery choked her as she leaned in, but the sight of the driver stopped her cold. She expected a suit, not a faded Mötley Crüe hoodie and jeans. A patchy goatee failed to compete with his acne. "Are you . . ." *here for me*, she nearly asked, but that was no question for this low-rent reaper. "Um, are you my ride?"

He peeled a sticky note from the dashboard. "Sal-veeg?"

"Sol-vay."

"Then yeah." He crumpled the note and dropped it into the dirty ashtray.

She gripped the door handle. In theory, this arrangement had seemed more straightforward than a ride-share service, with less risk of an awkward run-in or a familiar face. But now? Every instinct urged her not to get into the car.

The driver scowled. "C'mon, lady, you're letting the heat out."

He evidently found her trepidation ridiculous. Maybe even insulting. As little as his opinion should matter, it nudged her doubts. She swallowed hard and settled into the hearse.

The news report prattled on as he gestured at the digital display. "Murder. Pretty wild, huh? Don't know the last time something big as that happened 'round here."

His eyes traveled down the scars at her neck. Oh, he knew. Everyone did. Wasn't that why she'd left?

She adjusted her loosely knotted scarf. "Will you please switch it off?"

He glared and twisted the dial. "There. Ready?"

Never. She straightened her coat, smoothed the gray wool dress over her lap, and fastened her seatbelt. "Regardless, it's time."

He stifled a belch. She hadn't expected this to be pleasant, but really?

She leaned against the cool window as these last minutes of darkness shrouded the Shenandoah Valley. The black mountain silhouette, cradle and grave for some, murmured terse warnings to her. *Get out. And don't come back again.*

Yes. She and the mountain agreed.

Her grandfather would have argued the point, but Bestepappa rode behind her, sealed inside his casket till kingdom come. Always she put off a visit as too expensive, too far, too hard—and it was all those things now, but here she was.

Though the funeral would begin at nine o'clock, she coveted the extra moments to breathe. The church on the hill where they'd attended had been her first choice for the service, but its office manager refused her. After two fines from the fire marshal for crowds that exceeded capacity, its congregation had moved to the pastor's barn four miles up the road. The chapel hadn't opened its doors in more than a year. That left nowhere to have the service but the funeral home in town. A short ride but a long walk, especially under threat of snow.

In the mirror, a police cruiser appeared and gained quickly, sirens wailing, light bar ablaze. She lowered her eyes but not fast enough. Was Officer Dade at the wheel or one of the others? As her driver pulled over to let the cruiser pass, the blue flashes stole her breath, whirled her thoughts. Would there ever come a time when they didn't?

Get out, get out, get out. Not the mountains but her heart, clamoring for escape. Solveig focused on her breath and let the thrum of the roadway strike a lull. Two years without a panic attack. She could do this.

An echo of the past stirred unbidden. *Hold it together.*

The best road to Harrisonburg came into view. The car plowed through the intersection.

"Wasn't that the turn?" She craned her neck. Her scarf slipped. "I thought we were headed for—"

"Guess you shouldn't assume things." The driver wove in and out of the opposite lane along the empty highway.

Solveig's stomach knotted. Was she being kidnapped? Trafficked? Or worse?

"I want you to turn this car around." Her shaky voice robbed strength from the words. "Right now."

"Relax, will ya?" He wore a rancid smirk. "The backhoe operator called. He needs the spare key. If you want to keep this dog-and-pony show on the move, we gotta make a detour."

She stared at him. "I'm sorry, what?"

"The gravedigger." He spoke to the rearview mirror. "Can't avoid him, my dude. He's got a pair of yardsticks for everyone."

Tightness gripped her lungs. Her peripheral vision pressed in, and her skin buzzed and crawled. The voice branded in her memory broke through again. *Stay with me, now.*

Panic had her as surely as the driver did. Both would take her wherever they wished.

Indeterminate minutes passed. The hearse crested a hill, and the Leyland cypress and Douglas fir trees that flanked the cemetery gate appeared at last.

He slowed as they approached the entrance. A dual-axle pickup with a trailer half-full of garden refuse blocked access to the main way through the cemetery. The driver turned instead down a narrow service road. In the distance, an industrial work lamp illuminated her father's headstone and Bestemamma's. The diesel engine sputtered along as the heavy machinery hollowed out the earth beside them. In its cab, the figure of a heavyset man worked the controls.

Her mouth was dry. "I guess he found the key."

"I like a chick with a brain." The driver's lips curled in a sneer.

Get out, get out, get out.

He steered through the gravel paths slowly enough that crazy ideas peeked out—but no. Movie heroines might jump from vehicles in motion, but what did they know about the smell of mingled blood and earth?

The sky had blued with the promise of morning, but the hearse's headlamps were the strongest light source. Their beams spilled over the rows of grave markers and rested on one as the car jerked to a halt. The lichen at the edges of the stone hadn't yet obscured the name cut into its face.

Reeve Wilkeson.

"Hey, buddy. How's life?" The driver turned to Solveig. "I didn't know him. A friend of mine says he was a real tool."

His words barely registered. That name—the dates below it—washed out everything else.

Solveig released her seat belt and fled the car. Stumbled, hard. Her hands and knees struck a flat grave marker, but she scrambled to her feet. The driver shouted obscenities after her. She looked back as he got out of the car. Would he close the passenger door and leave, or continue whatever awful game he'd started?

She ran toward the wooded edge of the cemetery. The tang of snow hung in the air. At the tree line, the thorny underbrush embraced her, a condition of her temporary refuge.

Muscles taut, mouth dry. Her pace faltered, and her foot caught on a root. A pained cry escaped as she went down a second time. Somewhere behind her, heavy steps crackled in the thickets.

"Hey. Hey, you!" Was this a deeper voice, or did the trees deaden the driver's tones? She couldn't be sure.

Spots swam across her vision, and the past floated forward once more. *Look at me. Eyes on me.*

She leaned into a large oak, hugging herself. Shaking. Her breath escaped in white puffs, and cold stung her throat. The pale dawn, hard earth, and jagged thorns threatened to recede into the darkness that closed around her. She clawed them back from the periphery and attempted to pray. A single whispered word broke through her lips. *"Herre."*

She couldn't run forever. She had to *think*.

Solveig pushed herself against the ridged tree trunk and back to her feet. In the branches of the nearby cottonwood, a remnant of the rope swing Bestepappa had hung for her flapped in the wind. It breached the haze. Yes. She knew where she was, and where to go.

Down to the lower part of the cemetery. The older section.

The trick was to get there. Several meters away lay the embankment encased in a stacked-stone retaining wall. If she braved the short drop to lower ground, she might be able to circle the hill unseen. She angled her head to listen for signs of her pursuer, but tinnitus overwhelmed. She'd have to risk it.

Breaking away from the dubious safety of the oak, she hurried toward the embankment, perched on its edge, and pushed off.

The landing jammed her knees and she yelped. Not as springy as she'd been as a ten-year-old, but she picked herself up and pressed on. If he'd seen or heard, escape would come down to a footrace.

Solveig crept along the retaining wall. Where it ended, exposed roots twisted out from the erosion of the hillside. She used to imagine she might stumble upon a secret passage to another world. Now she counted on it.

Stealth slowed her steps, but at last she reached the bottom of the hill. There lay the first of nineteen engraved stepping stones that honored Harvey Engelwood's short life. She could probably recite each of the prayerful quotations.

This is the way; walk ye in it. A piece of a memory verse from the Book of Isaiah. The rest wouldn't come. As a child, Solveig had leaped and danced a ghoulish game of hopscotch over the stones while Bestepappa worked, until he chided her to respect the dead.

She cringed, but the memory grounded her. The stones and their pleasant words led the way from the woods' edge to her imaginary friend's funny little house. *Det tomme mausoleet.*

Solveig jogged the path. The trick latch would grant her entrance, the granite walls, sanctuary. But the door of the mausoleum stood open. In her rush, she nearly collided with its lone occupant.

Two

"Oh!"

At the startled cry behind him, Kyle Benton jolted and thwacked his head against a stone ledge. He clapped his gloved hand over the sting and bit off a curse.

"I'm sorry. Are you all right?" A mild accent tinged the feminine voice.

"Never better," he muttered. Nothing like a Monday morning blow to the skull, and he might have said so if he hadn't turned to face the stranger at the Engelwood mausoleum's open door.

Blue lips. Dilated pupils. Blood oozed through the ripped knees of her leggings.

"Whoa, hey." Why did she look familiar? He peeled off the gloves and discarded them on the stone ledge. The icy air zinged the sweat creased in his hands, but he offered one regardless. "Kyle Benton. Do you need help?" The real questions—*What are you on?* and *How much did you take?*—he left unasked.

She ignored his outstretched hand. Leaves clung to her auburn hair. "*Hallo*, Kyle Benton." She glanced over her shoulder. "I, um, needed a moment. I didn't mean to startle you."

"No problem." That lilting cadence. Faint but distinct from the Appalachian accents he heard everywhere else. "You must be Solveig."

Wrong move. She backed away and looked ready to bolt. "Do I know you?"

"No." But at once he wanted to know the granddaughter his late sponsor had bragged about at every chance. Starting with why she looked two clicks shy of completely freaked out. "Mr. Borja kept a photo at the office. I'm sorry for your loss."

She turned aside and swiped her cheek. Puckered flesh peeked over the top of the scarf looped at her neck, but she hunched her shoulders and took a deep breath. "You worked for him, then?"

Now she'd run for sure. Mr. Borja's property management company provided landscaping and maintenance services for his clients, and it played well in the local press as a haven of second chances for the employees. Even so, it hadn't taken Kyle long to find most people's goodwill cooled up close. He stifled a sigh and nodded. "I started right after New Year's. It wasn't a bad gig."

A rapid flutter of lashes and a soft ahem. "What will you do?"

Good question. If she was the trustee, his fate rested in her tremorous hands. He leaned against the mausoleum wall and struck a neutral tone. "Keep showing up until they bolt the doors. Then I don't know."

Her brow furrowed. "Why didn't you close for the service?"

He gestured at the graffiti and the floor partially littered with cigarette butts. "Officially it's a half day, but the county called in this mess."

She looked unconvinced. Well, if she had a problem with Danny's decisions, she could take it up with him herself.

He worked up half a smile. "Nothing like being the new guy."

"Welcome to small-town life." She turned toward the names set in the engraved marble slab.

He followed her gaze. *Victor Engelwood, June 19, 1896–October 2, 1918. Lost at Meuse-Argonne.* And more enigmatic, *Harvey Engelwood, January 10, 1900–October 8, 1919. He is not here.*

She traced the strange epitaph with her index finger. "Anyone newer than Harvey here will always be the new guy."

"Yeah, I get that." His pulse kicked. Nothing ventured, right? "Maybe us outsiders should stick together."

The wind blustered. Leaves swirled at her feet, and she tugged her coat tighter. A bramble flew free from her hair. "Or go back to where we came from."

Not an option. "Hey, I don't bite, okay? Come in from the wind."

"No, no. I didn't mean to interrupt." Her ruddy cheeks flushed a deeper pink. Winter roses. "I used to read in here while Bestepappa worked. I thought I could come and . . . be alone, I guess."

"Sure," he said, although being alone on purpose sounded incomprehensible even on his best day, which this was not. He slid his hands back inside the gloves. "But some punks found your hideaway. This isn't the safest place these days."

"Nowhere is, apparently." She rubbed her arms. "Considering there's a murderer at large."

He froze. "Beg your pardon?"

She glanced over her shoulder again and stepped toward the brightening daylight. "It's all over the news. Be safe yourself. Take care of Harvey for me."

While he mustered a response, she fled.

Kyle swept the last of the mess and knotted the trash bag. His ears burned. *That went well.*

On his way out, he paused on the monument's granite steps. Mr. Borja's granddaughter powered up the hill as if that killer was gunning for her personally. She had a long stride. Long legs.

Brilliant deduction, Watson.

So she wasn't high. She also wasn't acting like any normal bereaved family member, but going after her was out of the question. She ought to be headed for the service, and why she wasn't there already was none of his business. The last thing he needed was to get tangled in some random woman's problems.

But she wasn't some random woman. She was his employer's next of kin. Her problems already had him by the throat.

Kyle gathered his cleanup kit. A shadow of graffiti outlasted the end of a can of solvent, but it'd come off with more scrubbing. It was a pretty juvenile effort, probably the work of some middle schoolers on their first date with trouble. *Careful, kiddos. She's a cruel mistress.*

The hardware store in town opened at eight. Plenty of time to grab more cleaner and give it another pass before he headed for his next job. Honestly, the walls needed a good power wash, but that had to wait until spring. He'd be here.

Kyle locked the trick latch that kept out literally no one and wrestled grim thoughts as he followed the access road back to his Ford Ranger. He replaced his tools in the bed box and tossed the trash with the dead flowers and memorials in the back. Heavy clouds dropped snowflakes into the subdued gray dawn. Maybe this was the storm the weatherman had promised. Snow to disguise the world until it passed for clean and new.

He climbed into the truck's cabin and popped open the glove box. Among the jumble lay his newest notebook. He plucked his pen from its magnetic clip, flipped to the first blank page, and jotted a few lines. With a moment's thought, he added a title, centered at the top. *Winter Rose.*

If more came, great. If not, fine. It'd been months since he'd finished a song. Longer since he'd written one worth singing.

He stashed the book and used his phone to search local headlines. The *Rockingham Register* site gave the story top coverage.

The victim was a young guy who worked in a machine shop in Harrisonburg. Trevor Roberts. Newlywed, no kids. Left home Friday morning, found dead in his vehicle early Saturday. Strangled. Drugs on him. Parked outside an art gallery in town.

Kyle stared at the words, gut-punched. Coincidence? Couldn't be. The details of the Roberts murder were an open letter addressed directly to him.

The brief report ended with boilerplate from local law enforcement. A plea for information and the tip-line number.

Two facts zinged like pinballs through his brain. First, he knew who had killed Trevor Roberts. And second, Patterson had found him.

Bring it. He clutched his phone. *You're going down, old boy.*

Halfway through dialing, he canceled the call and scrolled through his contacts. Rule one, check with Charlie.

He glanced at the rearview while the call connected. The wind rustled as the snowfall accelerated. Slender trunks swayed and dropped pine cones, while the stouter ones hosted squirrels and maybe hawks.

In spite of the early hour, Charlie answered. Kyle cleared his throat.

"Mr. Lawrence, it's Kyle Benton. I—"

"For the last time, kid. No rescheduling. You miss another appointment, you're done."

What? "Sir, I haven't missed any appointments, and I'll be there Friday morning as usual. I'm calling because—"

"Benton." Shuffling papers whispered confusion into the background. "You're the new guy from California."

"Colorado."

"That's good. I hate Californians."

I'm sure they hate you too, sir. Kyle dismissed the errant thought and spoke quickly. "I know who killed that guy from Bridgewater. What do I do?"

The activity on the other end of the line quieted. "*How* do you know?"

"I figured it out."

"Ah. Amateur detective. Leave this one for the pros." The paper rustling resumed. The guy ran a seriously analog office. "Says here you're one of Borja's crew. How's the job hunt, son?"

Kyle stared at the retreating figure near the top of the hill. "I think I have a lead on something."

"I *think* you'll need to do better than that."

"I know, sir."

"You signed a contract."

The cold leached into his bones. He cranked the truck for the heater, but the engine stuttered. "Yes. Several, sir."

"Then mind your business and don't be late come Thursday."

The line went dead. Kyle slammed his fist on the dash. Whatever. He'd call the tip line anyway. Even ran through what to say.

His name is Glen Patterson. He's done it before. I can't prove anything, but—

He dropped the phone on the seat and kneaded his forehead. Before, it was ruled an accident.

Brother Mike had coached him to look for answers in the Bible, so he started at the beginning a while back. Hadn't made it far yet, but the part about Abel's murder still rattled him. The blood of the slain, crying out voiceless, heard by God.

19

Keith's blood hadn't spilled. Did his scattered ashes cry out? Did Hailey's?

The Ranger started on the second try. The belts kept slipping and it guzzled oil like a barfly in a brewery, but it came with the bed box and he'd had the cash. He liked to work on his truck. Liked to root out problems and fix them.

Patterson needed rooting out and fixing.

Nice and easy up the hill. No icy slicks, no mistakes. He'd move on with the day. Stop by the hardware store, finish the job he started. Later, maybe he'd get a sympathy card for Solveig. Flowers, even. Or maybe not.

The CCPM utility truck idled at the far end of the parking lot. He pulled in beside it and approached his coworker. Danny's ribbed coat puffed around his barrel chest as he leaned against the cab, arms crossed, watching the distance. Kyle followed his gaze and spied Solveig as she disappeared around the cemetery gate.

Danny nodded after her. "You know what that's about?"

Boy, this day kept getting better. Kyle hedged. "I talked to her for a minute or two. Not sure why she took off like that."

Danny shook his head with a scowl. "Hitting on the boss's grand-daughter on the morning of his funeral. Classy."

"Dude, that's not—"

"Leave her alone." Danny tugged a pack of cigarettes out of his breast pocket. He smacked it on the heel of his hand and withdrew a smoke. The green accents on the box taunted Kyle. Menthol. "Unless you're looking for trouble. She's got it to spare." Danny lit his cigarette and climbed into the utility truck.

The diesel engine rumbled as Kyle returned to the puny Ranger.

As Danny pulled away, Kyle scanned the radio for something familiar. He stopped on a Foo Fighters song Keith used to like, but cut it before the chorus.

Yeah, this wasn't perfect, but he had a home. A truck. A job, at least for the moment. He might lose his mind if he didn't make friends soon, but other than that, he'd washed up on a pretty nice shore. He cleared his throat. "Thank You, Lord."

Cardboard words from a false front of a man.

On the roadway, he passed Solveig. Apparently, she had a past, but who didn't? Hers probably came with fewer than seventeen pages of stipulations.

Danny's warning only sparked questions. Like why would Mr. Borja's granddaughter walk away from the cemetery with scraped knees and dead leaves in her hair?

His heart thudded into his throat. He ought to pull over and offer her a ride, and in another life, he would have already. That alone was reason enough to keep driving.

Three

Solveig crunched through the weedy overgrowth at the highway's edge. Drivers whooshed by her, taking the hilly straightaway too fast. Each levied a toll on her frayed nerves.

After all, accidents happen.

She hugged herself and kept moving. The Realtor from Harrisonburg wasn't due at the house until two o'clock. Plenty of time to strategize. Breathe. Eat. If the listing appointment went well, she might change her flight and go home early. No need to stay eleven days if ten would do.

These thoughts salted her path toward the farmhouse but dissolved on her arrival.

Eggs.

The house had been bombarded. Snotty yolks puddled at the doors, the windows, the siding, everywhere.

She rubbed her temples. Not ideal, but whatever. She'd unearth a ladder, gather shop rags from the barn, and—

Streaks ran down the barn doors. Red streaks, like rivulets on glass. Fresh, dripping, spelling out a message.

Next time you ride SHOTGUN.

She turned away. Just paint. Just words. She'd survived worse, and that was the unforgivable offense. She'd survived.

She draped the barn doors with tarps and scrubbed as much egg as she could, until she found a tiny broken chick cradled among the smashed eggshells. Then she stopped to vomit in the snow-dusted hedges.

By early afternoon, the mess outdoors was marginally handled. Thankfully, the interior was passable. If she'd had the time, she'd have liked to wipe the counters and dust the artificial ficus tree, but the listing agent wouldn't care about such minutiae.

A sharp knock split the silence, and Solveig jumped. She tucked a stray wisp behind her ear and checked the peephole.

Pamela VanGorden had arrived fifteen minutes early. Every detail, from helmet hair and perfectly contoured makeup to the navy pantsuit and red-leather tote, lent the woman an aura of authority.

Solveig opened the door and offered a tentative smile. "Thanks for coming, Mrs.—"

"*Ms.* VanGorden, please and thanks." She sized up Solveig with an odd glance as she brushed past. She rubbed a dusty ficus leaf between her fingertips and made a face. "You must be Saul-vig."

"Sol-vay." Stealing a glance around the living room, Solveig imagined how the agent must see it. Maybe Bestemamma's hand-crocheted throw pillows were more kitschy than cozy. And the stuffed squirrel on the mantel was gruesome, *rett og slett.* "I'd offer you coffee, but—"

"Why is it so dark in here? And cold?"

"Right." Straight to business, then. "The utilities have been turned off. I can get along without since I won't be here long."

"You'll need to reconnect them for showings." Ms. VanGorden snapped a picture of the living room with her mobile. "Buyers want to see everything works."

Solveig responded with a tight smile. Let buyers muster some faith. Bestepappa's attorney had closed his accounts before she arrived, and none of the providers would reopen them without a contract or a deposit or both. "We'll use the generator." Even that rankled. She'd been miserly with the fuel.

The agent continued her inspection. "Late Victorian. Hmm. The fireplace is a nice feature. Bed-and-bathrooms?"

What was she asking? "Yes. Um, four. Four bedrooms, one bath."

"No good. Four-and-one is a hard sell," she said as if she expected a solution.

"There is an outhouse behind the barn. Can we count that?"

Ms. VanGorden placed her fingers on her temples momentarily, then strode into the kitchen, dodging the Formica table and dictating notes into her mobile as she circled the hallway of the main floor. "Butler's pantry . . . tub-shower combo . . . low ceilings . . . no separate dining."

She reemerged in the living room. "These hardwoods look terrible."

What did she expect? "They're old."

The woman stomped up the stairs without waiting for an invitation and gestured to the Borja family gallery displayed on the wall. "These have to go. Buyers don't like to be reminded they're in someone's home."

Solveig followed, pausing over the clustered snapshots of herself as a tiny, wild-haired ruffian, long-memorized prints of her lean, handsome father in the old apple grove, and her grandparents' colorized wedding portrait. Even the one of her mother remained untouched. Each pinged her heart, but this hadn't been home in years.

As they reached the upper landing, Ms. VanGorden fired off questions. How much acreage? Slab or crawlspace? What was the square footage? Where was the attic access? Was the HVAC system up to code? Which appliances stayed with the house?

"It's all staying," Solveig said. "This is an estate sale."

Ms. VanGorden stopped snapping photos and whirled around. "Oh, no. We're not holding some everything-must-go emporium."

"What, then? I can't very well ship everything to Norway."

"That's your problem, missy." The agent slipped her mobile into her tote. "Buyers want one thing, and that's a fresh start. Store, sell, donate, whatever. Rent a dump truck if you have to."

Solveig wrestled with temptation. Satisfying as it would feel to ask the woman to leave, making another appointment with someone else wasted precious time. *Eleven days. You can do this.*

"I can give an excellent deal. What is the expression? 'Priced to move'?"

"Priced to *sell*. You're conflating it with 'move-in ready.'" Ms. VanGorden walked to the window. "See this mottled glass? The seals are broken. You'll need to—" She peered outside at the sill. "Is that a dead baby chick?"

Solveig held her breath until a swell of emotion ebbed. She would *not* cry in front of this woman. "I don't know. Does it look like a dead baby chick?"

"I've seen enough." Ms. VanGorden exited the room and descended the stairs, calling to Solveig on her way down. "Sweetie, you've got work to do before we can list this place."

They hadn't even opened Bestepappa's bedroom. She followed Ms. VanGorden to the main level. "What must I do?"

The agent heaved a theatrical sigh. "I have a list of movers I can send you, but frankly, you're not ready for that. Cut the clutter. Clear out fifty percent of the furniture. Reconnect the utilities." She glanced at the bottle of Akvavit on top of the refrigerator, where it had always been. "And hide your booze, for heaven's sake."

Solveig narrowed her eyes. "You don't seem keen to help me, Ms. VanGorden. Should I find someone who is?"

She sniffed. "Honey, if you want hand-holding and sweet talk, get yourself a boyfriend. No agent who can sell this wreck will tell you anything different."

"This *wreck* used to be my home."

"Then you need to decide whether you're serious about selling." Her voice softened in the slightest measure. "Look, I don't like handling estate sales. I'll send you the name of an auction outfit I've worked with. As for the house itself, a fire sale might work, but I recommend an asking price of one-fifteen if you get it up to par. As is, I can't justify listing it at more than ninety-two."

Solveig pressed her lips together. She needed the exchange rate to fully grasp the difference, but the point was made. It was a lot of money.

"I work at a ten-percent commission. Nonnegotiable. You can pay someone else seven percent on thousands less if you want."

She held out a business card. "My home office, cell, and broker. Call me when you're ready to do business." Solveig took it reluctantly.

As the woman let herself out, she paused in the doorway. "One last thing. There's an *unpleasant* aroma out front. Fewer drunken parties when we start showing the house, m'kay?" Ms. VanGorden flashed a smile and closed the door behind her, leaving Solveig in the living room. The thumb-shaped circle of green on the silk ficus leaf stared, a stranger's eye in search of a fresh start.

She huffed and wiped the leaf clean. Besides snooty and rude, the agent was crazy if she thought fresh starts could be bought and sold. Or that they existed at all.

Solveig slipped into her parents' old bedroom on the first floor. Without the furnace, she'd barely lasted halfway through the first night in her childhood room upstairs, but the fireplace kept the main level fairly comfortable. She'd crept into her parents' long-empty bed and prayed for dreamless sleep.

Now, sleep was far from her mind. She reached into the side pocket of her tote to retrieve the envelope Bestepappa had left with the lawyers. His last words to her, tucked away for a moment when she needed them.

That moment had arrived sooner than expected.

The wing chair beckoned with memories of Bestemamma knitting while she watched evening game shows. Solveig pressed herself against the firm backrest, studied her name on the front of the envelope for a long while, then slid a finger under the flap.

The short letter was written in Norwegian. Bestepappa's familiar block printing had grown unsteady. Her vision blurred, and she blotted her eyes in the crook of her sleeved elbow.

Dear Sunshine,

In spite of my earthly demise, I am glad you are reading these lines. Herr Forrester will send a lesser version of this letter if you cannot come home, but this is the one I am hoping finds its way into your hands. Perhaps he is sitting across from you now, although I imagine you reading it at the house, cozy in Helena's armchair.

She tucked her legs underneath her, never wanting to stir.

Old age confronts me with probability, my dear, not to mention mild surprise every morning upon waking. Among these preparations are certain to be loose ends, so I've laid aside cash specifically for your expenses in that time. You'll find the envelope in the safe. The combination is still the same.

Since you have come so far, I have another gift for you. If you remember some of the local legends we chased once upon a time, then I must send you to see Rice Caverns. One formation in particular. The book on my dresser holds the map that will show you where to go. I hoped to take you there myself, but such is life, ikke sant?

What is left to say? Don't be too sad nor weep as those who have no hope. Kjære godjenta mi, *you are strong and beloved, and you've made me very proud. Most importantly, you are not alone. Let Christ be your comfort, today and always.*

All my love, til vi møtes igjen.

Bestepappa

The words ran together. "You're really g—" Her throat closed mid-word. Every layer of realizing her loss hurt differently. He'd prepared his last goodbye. The chance for hers had ended with the funeral. Why had she let that thug keep her away?

She ached to lean on her faith, but the comfort of heaven was too far off. She *was* alone, dreadfully so.

With effort, she roused herself from the chair and climbed the stairs. *I hoped to take you there myself.* Her reasons for staying away so long crumbled under the weight of that single thought.

On the dresser under a fine fur of dust lay *Landmarks of Rockingham County, Virginia: A Centennial History of Her Civic Progress and*

Pioneers, 1778–1878. The water-spotted blue cover smelled of mildew. She fanned the pages and let them fall slowly. Maps and sketches of pioneers interspersed chapters of dense text.

A line of handwriting flashed for an instant as rough-cut sections passed under her thumb. The slip of thin paper all but disappeared against the weight of the pages. She leafed through the book until she found the note again. *Husk å vise dette til Solveig.*

Remember to show this to Solveig.

She fought tears until they receded.

The marked page showed an outdated map diagramming the then-discovered portions of Rice Caverns, near Massanutten. Question marks and ellipses framed the open edges of the map. A tiny red *X* embellished a point in the northeastern quadrant.

A twinge fluttered in her belly. Unless she missed her guess, Bestepappa had found the fabled prayer wall.

She wanted to go today, this minute, but dwindling daylight held her back. The caverns were too far for a hike, and a solo expedition would be foolish. She'd have to get someone to go with her.

That might prove quite the conundrum.

Still, as she placed the letter between the pages and hugged the book, her heart lightened a smidgen. His last gift. To think she might have missed it. Ms. VanGorden was right. She could hire out the work to settle the estate, but if she left without following Bestepappa's map, another chance was lost.

As for the rest? One thing at a time. Broken window seals, scuffed hardwood floors, furniture, auctions, and dump trucks. She wasn't convinced the utilities were necessary, but everything tallied to one conclusion.

She had not a moment to waste.

Four

Inside the single-wide trailer that housed Community Care Property Management LLC, a secondhand copier in the corner whined and rattled in rhythm like the world's most reliable yet uninspired stage act. Horace and the Rockin' Rackin' Mechanisms. The fluorescent light overhead flickered sporadically, a backup singer coming in on the wrong beat. The coffee maker gurgled its applause.

Kyle wedged paid bills into a packed file cabinet. Karaoke with the copier. Yeah, he needed to get out.

Yesterday's efforts left the Engelwood mausoleum almost good as new. Today he was stuck matching payments to invoices. Grateful as he was for the job, the in-office days proved cemetery duty wasn't the short straw they made it out to be.

The monitor in front of him darkened, so he tapped the space bar and continued the paper shuffle spread across the desk. The local florist's website urged him to "say it with flowers," but bouquets like Serenity Sunrise and Petals of Peace didn't quite cut it.

Sorry for your loss, not giving you a lift, and seeming like I was hitting on you when I kind of was.

Kyle closed the website without ordering. As much as he wanted to do something for Solveig, slinging sixty bucks' worth of flowers at her seemed inane. Unless he was being cheap. That normally didn't pop up in his comprehensive list of faults, but hey, he was a changed man. Anything was possible.

The date on his desk calendar peeked from beneath the stacks of paper. January 20. Twenty days since his last cigarette. Twenty days since he sloughed off the last of his old life in exchange for this new one.

At the desk beside his, Danny pecked at the keyboard. Since Mr. Borja's stroke, he'd taken on his orphaned wards, set himself up as the boss, and kept CCPM's burning ship sailing for now. Whatever he was working on, he made up for low words per minute with maximum PSI. Here was a guy who obviously never applied himself to a computer basics vocational series.

Not much of a talker either, except for yesterday's episode with Solveig. Nothing fishy there. Kyle drummed his fingers in time with the copier. A crush, he guessed. Possibly an older-brother complex. Or maybe Solveig had some dirt on him. There was an entertaining thought.

Danny threw him an irritated glance. "You bored?"

"Not at all." He quit drumming and matched three more payments. He had questions, but so far his interim sponsor hadn't proved a pillar of support. "So. What about that murder?"

Horace kept on rockin'. At length, Danny sighed. "What about it?"

Kyle shrugged. "Seems bizarre. Got any theories?"

"You're the new guy in town. Maybe you killed him."

"Maybe I did," Kyle said. "Did you know him? Trevor Something?"

"Roberts." Danny resumed his two-fingered typing. "Went to school with him. Haven't talked to him since. Real preppy guy."

Spoken like someone who was definitely not a real preppy guy, but Kyle let the subject drop. The odds of Danny telling him anything useful started low and sank with every question.

The guy's desktop offered one clue to his personal life, a photo of a micro-Danny taped to the edge of his monitor. He left early some days to pick up his kid from school and only came back when the kid's mom didn't have to work. If there was any pattern to their schedule, Kyle hadn't sussed it out yet.

He returned to his stack of invoices. Among the typical carbonless copies and printouts sat a register tape stapled to a catering menu from Java Mama's Henhouse. The check stub was easy enough to find. A hundred bucks, even. He inspected the receipt.

"Hey, do you know what we bought twenty dozen organic eggs for?"

Danny continued pecking at the keyboard. "Borja planned a community breakfast. I canceled it when he croaked."

He unfolded the menu and flattened it. "I don't remember hearing about it."

"Guess you should pay attention."

Kyle rolled his eyes but let that slide. "Why didn't we cancel the order?"

Danny stopped typing and turned toward him. "*We* tried, but Gillian balked. So *we* paid and got rid of them. Anything else, Nancy Drew?"

His teeth clenched around words he'd better not say. If this was the result of years of Mr. Borja's mentoring, Kyle would've hated to know him before. "Just learning the ropes, man."

"If I signed it, then you don't worry about it."

Ah. He thought Kyle was questioning his pseudo-authority. Danny did have free rein on the checkbook. Kyle's purchasing power stopped at seventy-five.

Plenty for a sympathy bouquet.

His conscience tugged once, hard. Yeah, Solveig would really appreciate him for spending what was probably *her* money for a basket of daisies. Besides, embezzling was never his style. He marked the egg receipt paid and filed it with the rest.

A movement on Mr. Borja's desk caught his eye. Hook, the betta fish, spread his fins, spoiling for a fight. *I know how you feel, buddy.*

Other than feeding Hook once a day, no one had bothered the boss's desk. Funny how Solveig's picture jumped out since he'd met her. The photographer had chosen the startling topaz blue of her eyes as the focal point of the image. Nice shot.

Kyle made another trip to the copier to disguise his undue interest in the photograph. The fluorescent light flared and dimmed, and only then he noticed the empty paper tray. When had the copier quieted? Regardless, Horace had left the building.

It didn't matter. Danny had turned toward the coat hooks by the door to retrieve his jacket. Break time.

Kyle exhaled. "Have one for me."

"Here." His de facto boss drew two cigarettes out of the pack on his desk and held one out. A friendly gesture, belied by a sneer.

Twenty days. He imagined the smokers' lung poster on the infirmary wall at Sterling. "Nah. I'm on the wagon."

"Suit yourself." Danny pulled a toboggan over his close-cropped scalp and exited the trailer, both cigarettes in hand.

Two smokes. Ten minutes, give or take.

Once the door latched, Kyle fished the tip-line number out of his wallet. Easy, casual. He didn't need anyone's permission. With a deep breath, he dialed.

A robot voice answered. At the sound of the beep, Kyle rushed to explain his brother's death and the similarities to Trevor Roberts's murder. The recording cut him off before he finished. On redial, he got a fast busy signal.

Okay. Plan B. He dialed Detective Mendez's number from memory and listened for the ring-back tone, a violin cover of "Smooth Criminal." A nice little jab, since the guy never answered his calls.

"Mendez."

Kyle almost dropped the phone. "Sir." His throat went dry. "Long time, no talk."

"You don't figure that's on purpose?" One thing about Mendez, he let you know where you stood. "What is it now, Benton?"

"Sir, I have a lead in my brother's case."

"Another one."

"This one's solid, sir. Glen Patterson followed me to Virginia."

"And you know this because he sent you a New Year's card?"

"No, because he killed someone. Trevor Roberts. Call Rockingham County PD. All the details match Keith's case. The choking, the art gallery."

"I'll look into it," Mendez said flatly.

Kyle flexed his jaw. "When?"

"I got a full load of active cases, son. I'll get to it when I get to it."

Son. He squeezed his eyes shut. "Tell me something. Please."

Mendez huffed. "Look, you've been cooperative and you made good. Now you've got two options. Do I need to remind you what they are?"

"No, sir."

"Good." Mendez out. The line went dead.

Kyle swore under his breath. There went Plan B.

The beauty smiling from the frame on Mr. Borja's desk drew his eye again. He rolled his chair closer. A graduation portrait? Sunbeams backlit a halo into her hair. Trouble, according to Danny, but what kind?

Mr. Borja had said she didn't let one mistake hold her down forever. Nothing on what that mistake was. Instead, he drove home his point that Christ's mercy granted new life, that He empowered His own to turn away from the pull of darkness and walk in the light.

If that weren't true, Kyle wouldn't be here. The more people he knew who believed in second chances, the better.

The desk held few surprises overall. A legal pad, a thick volume embossed with *Bibelen*, a pair of glasses. All things a granddaughter might want.

He returned to his desk, settled at last. He might not have made traction with the authorities, but he'd finally come up with something better than a bouquet.

As Ms. VanGorden had insisted, Solveig worked to organize the house's clutter. She emptied closets and cabinets into the living room, but each pile bled into the next. Her attempt to make more space backfired as she angled the sofa bed away from the wall and into the middle of the room, its permanent home unless she got help. Her initial burst of enthusiasm popped off like a string of firecrackers and to equal effect.

What a mess.

A heavy fist pounded the front door. She froze. Had the vandals returned?

She glimpsed through the peephole. Kyle Benton waited on the stoop, a smile in his eyes and a cardboard box tucked under his arm.

Relief flashed and fled. What was he doing here?

She opened the door and gripped the knob in case she needed to slam it shut again. "*Hallo.* How is your head?"

"Flesh wound." Kyle knocked on his skull with his free hand. His easy manner lightened her suspicions. "Like it never happened."

"Sorry to mention it, then." She eyed the carton. "What is that?"

He sobered somewhat. "Mr. Borja's personal stuff from the office. Photos, his coffee cup, that sort of thing. I forgot Hook, but I can bring him over if you want him."

"Hook?"

"His betta fish. Get it? Betta Hook?"

"Ah. Cute." For the first time in days, Solveig almost felt like smiling. "But if Hook needs a new owner, I nominate you, Mr. Benton."

He made a face. "Call me Kyle. Where do you want this?"

Solveig glanced over her shoulder at the jumble. *Perfekt.* Another box of stuff.

He shifted the carton. "Or I can get rid of it for you if that's easier."

She shook her head. What was wrong with her? He was being kind. And so far, he was the first to bother.

"I will take it. Thank you." He handed off the box, and she set it inside the entryway. "You didn't have to do this. I've given up on hearing from the hospital about his things."

"No problem." He slipped his hands into his coat pockets but made no motion to leave. "I guess it's some hike to get here from the cemetery."

She dropped her gaze. "It's fine."

"If you ever need a ride, say the word. Standing offer. Mr. Borja's extension rolls to my phone."

She forced her eyes to meet his. "That's very generous. I'm sure you won't blame me for being leery of strangers."

"Not at all. So let's not be strangers."

She shook her head. "Really, I—"

"Hey, hold still." He reached forward and she recoiled. He froze, his hand in midair, then gestured toward her. "Sorry. Ah, you have some cobwebs in your hair."

Her cheeks warmed as she brushed them away. The thready tickle crawled over her skin. "I appreciate the offer." She tugged her scarf.

"As you might imagine, it's been a difficult couple of days."

"Right. I'll just . . ." His gaze went wide into the mess behind her. "Out of curiosity, where are you headed with that couch?"

She sucked in a breath like he'd thrown her a lifeline. "Do you want it?"

"No, but it looks like a lot for one person to handle." He stretched into a faux yawn to one side and flexed his bicep on the other, and as if that was too subtle, he capped it off with a wink.

Well, why not? If Bestepappa thought enough of the man to hire him, perhaps he solved more than one of her problems. He might not feel so charitable once the lawyer carried out her instructions, but for now, a good Samaritan was more than welcome.

She relented with a small smile and stepped aside. "All right. Come and see what you've talked yourself into."

Five

Even for two together, maneuvering the sofa bed through the front door, down the porch steps, and to the end of the driveway took over an hour.

Solveig squinted against the brightness of the pure-white cloud cover. Sweat stung the corners of her eyes. Bestepappa's house stood down from the roadway a good clip, and they used to plant big gardens in the front pasture as well as the back—tomatoes and wax beans and cantaloupes.

Now the ground lay fallow under a new blanket of snow. No one had worked it in years, but at least it remained level. Small blessings.

"If I had chains"—Kyle puffed—"for the truck, we could drag it."

"We're okay." Her arms and back ached, but she refused to ask for another break so soon. Why it bothered her whether Kyle thought she was strong, she'd contemplate later. "Almost . . . there."

"So . . . close." He crossed his eyes. "I can see it, Cap'n! Land ho!"

She resisted the laugh that bubbled in her chest. "Don't. I'll drop it."

"'Kay." They shuffled another two meters. He spoke again. "You live around here?"

She was dying, and he was making jokes and small talk. "Not anymore."

"In town long?"

"Until the estate's settled." She lost her grip and jumped back. The sofa crashed down where her toes had been.

Coils and springs gonged. Kyle's end got away from him, along with a curse that resounded across the graded pastures. His ears, ruddy with cold, reddened more when he met her eyes. "Sorry. You all right?"

She nodded quickly. The rough wooden frame had bloodied her fingers on the way down, but Kyle probably got the worst of it. "My fault. Are you—"

"All good."

"When I said I'd drop it, I didn't mean on purpose."

"I know. This thing's a beast." He rolled his shoulders. "As soon as you're ready."

She stifled a groan. "Ready to strike a match and let it burn where it sits."

"If you want." He pulled a lighter from his pocket and flicked the igniter. A tiny orange flame appeared, primed to do her bidding.

Wouldn't that draw the neighbors. She shook her head. "The distant shore awaits."

When at last they made it to the end of the driveway, Kyle stretched both arms and plopped on the couch as if to watch the sparse highway traffic like a big game. "Whew. Made it."

"Hopefully someone will take it." She remained standing. Her muscles screamed to take that same stretch, but she hugged herself instead. In spite of the cold, her lower back and underarms had grown damp. How lovely.

Why did she care? He was sweating too, and he didn't seem embarrassed. Men had it so easy.

His exertion didn't spoil the view. Amazing she'd been so preoccupied this morning as to miss his broad shoulders and the hazel eyes framed with faint smile lines. His ready charm fit a chiseled, clean-shaven jaw with the right amount of ruggedness. Maybe she was wrong to compare, but she considered Lars a little too sophisticated.

Lars. Her cheeks heated. He would not appreciate the trajectory of her thoughts.

Solveig folded her hands and stretched her arms in front of her. Discreetly, she hoped. "Thank you, Kyle Benton." In her head, his full name sounded more formal. Once it hit the air, only the teasing note carried. "I'm grateful you stopped by when you did."

"Getting rid of me already? Let's recharge a minute, then we'll tackle whatever else you've got." He took a deep breath and exhaled with a small cough. "Yep, five minutes, and we'll be set."

How funny, to sprawl on a sofa under a hazy winter sky. She perched on the armrest and tried not to look at him. Their tracks in the snow led back toward the house. Her shuffle of boot prints left a narrower path than his, but otherwise, the tandem trails matched. Wavers and straightaways. Steps and stumbles. Connected by the imprints of the sofa in places where they'd set down the load and where it slipped from their hands.

An inconvenient flutter tickled her belly. She peeled her gaze from the trails and back to him. Not helpful.

"You've worked all day already." At the company she'd elected to shut down, no less. "I shouldn't keep you from the rest of your evening."

"Oh, yeah. Trivia night at Ducky's." His eyes danced, but he didn't budge. "I'll hold out for a better offer."

Was he . . . flirting? Her pulse tripped. "Good luck. The best I have for you is cleaning up eggs and spray paint."

"What?" He sat up. "Someone vandalized your house? When?"

His sudden intensity prickled. She shrugged and looked away. "Yesterday morning."

A vein stood out on his forehead. The vapor of his breath billowed up and dissipated, and he slipped on his easy-going demeanor again. "Lucky for you, I've got solvent in the truck, and I scrub dried egg like a champ."

She chewed her lip. Kyle's camaraderie was worth at least as much as the heavy lifting, but accepting his help without revealing the liquidation plan felt vaguely dishonest.

Then again, Mr. Forrester had probably sent the paperwork already, and she wasn't twisting his arm. "If you're offering—"

"I am." He rubbed his hands on his jeans and stood. "Lead the way."

And she did, wondering all the while at that brief flash of anger. The shouted curse word. The lighter in his pocket. Kyle seemed to have a side he tried not to show.

She brushed her fingers at the edge of her scarf and winced. That made two of them.

By dusk, he'd blotted out the hateful words on the barn with cleaner and covered them with primer. His ice scraper made short work of the nastiness that clung to the windows, and they even sorted the first wave of castoffs. The dusty ficus, wall art, and magazines were relegated to one corner; lamps, throw pillows, and outdated electronics to another. All sorted and ready for someone else's rummage sale.

"Controlled madness." She surveyed the room. "Much better than the total chaos before."

Kyle clicked on a battery-powered Coleman lamp and took stock. "I think the donation center closes at seven, but we can haul in some small furniture if we hurry."

"No 'hurry' left in me for tonight." She checked her mobile. The battery bar showed a worrisome dip. "I'll use Ms. VanGorden's movers once I have a full load."

"Sounds like a plan." He set the lamp on the end table. "Want me to clean out the hearth and build you a fire?"

A cozy idea, and much too tempting. "I will later."

He took his coat off the peg by the door without putting it on. "You know to open the flue."

"Yes." She cut a look at him—not too harsh, but honestly. "I know how to do everything on this farm."

"Ah. Have I blundered this yet?" He paused. "'Cause all I'm after is one more minute with you."

Heat flooded her cheeks. "You're not shy."

"I know it's the worst timing, but we had a great day. Let's stretch it out." The lantern light set off his dimples. "What do you say? Let me take you to dinner."

"I have a boyfriend," she blurted.

His smile faded. "Oh."

"Yes. Lars." As if adding his name made it true.

A doubtful look appeared. "Larsh?"

She huffed. "I suppose you'd Americanize it to Larz, but in Norway—"

"Norway." He shook his head. "The accent. Right."

She rubbed her arms, not quite relieved. This day could not get any stranger. "Over there it's the American accent. People think I sound weird wherever I am."

The conversation halted as high beams flashed in the front window. The thunder of blood pounded in her ears, her chest. Her tormentors, back for another round?

The car followed the curve of the gravel drive and blocked Kyle in. Once she saw it from the side, her throat constricted.

A county patrol car.

Hold it together. Stay with me, now.

Kyle stepped away from the window, but she continued to stare out, frozen. Waiting.

The lights died and the driver's door opened. A long-legged figure emerged. She knew the posture, gait, and frame from ten years of bad dreams. He swung a searchlight around, and she lowered her eyes, afraid the sudden flash might throw her into another full-blown panic attack.

Kyle zipped his coat.

Deep breath. The policeman couldn't hurt her. She opened the door before he knocked. "Good evening, Officer Dade."

"It's 'Sheriff' now." He flicked his badge. Its glint stood out from the shadows. "Missed you at the funeral."

She flinched at his gruff voice. That, too, featured in the nightmares. "The hearse driver took me for a joyride to the cemetery, and by the time I got back, someone had vandalized my barn."

Sheriff Dade looked unimpressed. "You want to file a complaint?"

"No, sir."

"Then there ain't much I can do." He paused a beat. "You know how kids can be."

The dart pierced the tender fourteen-year-old buried in her heart. "I do, indeed."

Leonard Dade never had made a secret of his belief Solveig should have been tried as an adult. He tipped his head toward the road. "That couch violates the dumping ordinance."

Kyle broke in. "Sir, with all due respect—"

"Pipe down, son. Unless you're lobbying for the ticket I'm fixin' to write."

"No," Solveig answered without looking at Kyle. "It is my sofa and my land and my ticket."

Dade's eyebrows flicked. "Your stolen land. This here was the old Rice place 'til your granddaddy showed up."

She clutched the door jamb. "I'll list the property soon, Sheriff Dade. Anyone nursing legends of lost inheritance can make an offer."

His gaze lengthened to the piles behind her. Cataloging, perhaps. "That couch better be gone by morning."

As if that wasn't the point of setting it roadside. "I'm sure someone will take it."

"I'm sure." He took a step back. "You always come out smellin' like a rose, don't you?"

What could she say to that? As he ambled to his cruiser, she kept silent. She watched the window and pretended she couldn't feel Kyle's questions in his stare. *What was that for? How'd you land on his bad side? Do you have a record or something?*

But he didn't breathe a word.

Why had she refused his company? She didn't want to sit alone in this big dark house. "You shouldn't have spoken. Dade won't forget that." Her voice shook. The Bible promised *Herren* would remember her sins no more, but everyone else recalled them with perfect clarity. She herself most of all.

A gust of wind funneled through the chimney. Kyle answered as if she hadn't spoken. "You didn't tell me about the stunt with the hearse."

"That's true, I didn't." She faked a smile. "Aren't you sorry you skipped trivia night?"

"Not at all. Think you might take me up on that ride I offered? Say, a run to the courthouse to settle any lost-inheritance questions?"

The idea wasn't a bad one, but Mr. Forrester had explained that the sale process included a title search. Still, it wouldn't hurt to call him tomorrow. "No need. I will check with the estate attorney."

The slip gonged in her ears, but if Kyle had questions about the rest of Bestepappa's estate, he held them to the chest. "Fair enough, but call me first if you need a partner in crime."

"I will." Good sense would thank him and let the idea drop. "But let's use an app and save your phone bill. Do you have a favorite?"

"Whichever you like." He handed over his mobile with a sheepish look. "I'm not too swift with technology."

She smiled. "The one Bestepappa and I used is very simple."

As she searched for the app, he touched her hand. The brief contact sent a tingle running straight to her core.

"This isn't 'social media,' right?" He accented the question with air quotes.

How odd. "No. Why?"

He dropped his hands. "It's dumb, but I have a thing about it."

She shrugged and finished the download. "There. This way you won't regret answering when I ring you."

"Never." With a final nod, he let himself out, and the house grew colder at once.

Solveig studied her hands. One burned where his fingers had brushed hers. The other was blue-tinted in the nail beds and scraped from dropping the sofa.

Better build that fire she wouldn't let him start.

* * *

Hours later, Solveig lay awake, her stomach full of otters. A boy-friend. *Why* had she said that?

Well, she knew why, but knowing didn't make her less disgusted with herself.

Her mobile chirped and she rolled to grab it. An email notification lit the home screen. Sven Skoglund, director of the Regional State Archives in Oslo. The air caught in her throat. Back home, the clock was five over eight, and he had sent her a message titled *"Gratulerer og velkommen!"*

Her heart thrashed. Had she gotten the job? She tapped the message, but instead of his email, the screen showed a battery alert and blackened.

Perfekt. She held down the power button to no avail. Considering the long day, she ought to lay the dead mobile aside and try to get to sleep.

But she needed to call the estate attorney first thing to ask about Leonard Dade's insinuations. Waiting to recharge in the morning would unnecessarily delay the call, and Mr. Forrester was a busy man. If the deed was a problem, she would need his help sooner than later.

Besides, she wanted to read Herr Skoglund's message.

She dressed quickly. The sliding door off the kitchen led to the mudroom, which Ms. VanGorden insisted was a butler's pantry. Solveig passed through and circled the back of the house toward the pickup.

Moonbeams dusted the farm with a false peace, but inside her a tempest swelled. Bestepappa had tried more than once to coach her for this, but she always put him off, never believing the time would come. And now . . .

Aching, she opened the truck door and leaned across the seat to plug in her mobile. Last week, the scent of aftershave and earth and grandfatherliness could have knocked her over. But today was worse because it was already fading.

Tears welled again, followed by fierce, racking sobs. The pain hid in tiny pockets, Solveig had learned, ambushing her with its force and sting. She climbed into the cab and slammed the door. Might as well. She wouldn't sleep anytime soon.

Eventually, gasps dwindled into gulps and hiccups. She checked the battery's progress. Twenty percent. Enough to look at Herr Skoglund's email. In November, they had met for a final interview for an archive assistant position, a foot in the door for a career with the Ministry of Culture. She'd stopped daring to hope they chose her.

Fingers trembling, she tapped his name again. This time, the message appeared.

Solveig Borja:

On behalf of the Regional State Archives, it's my pleasure to invite you to join our team. Among many qualified candidates, you stand out as one dedicated to preserving our nation's past as we forge ahead into a brilliant future.

The formal offer letter will follow under a separate cover. As we are eager to enjoy the benefit of your talents, we propose 1 February as your start date. We look forward to hearing from you.

Regards,

Sven Skoglund
Direktør, Statsarkivet i Oslo

She closed her eyes and imagined Bestepappa beside her. Telling him the news, receiving his blessing.

It didn't help. Her raw heart had nothing left.

The next email gave particulars, all she'd expected and hoped. The director wrote his messages in Nynorsk, and though she'd been raised using the traditional Bokmål language standard, she wrote her acceptance in kind.

As soon as she sent the response, her heart thundered. Why hadn't she asked for an extra week? Had she forgotten already the colossal task before her?

As her email refreshed, Lars Anker's name appeared at the top of her inbox.

Uff. She hadn't emailed him when her plane landed as she promised. His note was written in Bokmål. Familiar, easy. Rather like Lars himself.

Søte Sol, how goes your trip? Norefjell was perfect—except for long nights alone.

Miss you. Lars

She closed the message. The bolder he got, the more distant their friendship became. And of course, her friend Mette spouted endless advice which orbited the theme that Solveig should stop being a prude. *He's not going to wait forever,* jente.

I'm not asking him to. That answer didn't satisfy her friend, who urged her to "turn the page" after Nils. Mette knew less of that disaster than she realized.

Headlights spilled over the snow. Solveig twisted to see a pickup at the top of the driveway. Its engine revved, shattering the winter night.

The truck spun circles in the front pasture. She stared, cold inside, as the tires cut tracks into the earth.

She ducked down. The vandals again. They only wanted to scare her. If she needed to escape, she could put the key in the ignition and—

Her stomach rolled. No. Driving herself to safety was the last thing she'd ever be able to do.

The light dimmed; the motor faded. Were they leaving?

Holding her breath, she chanced a peek through the window.

Red taillights cast a hazy glow. A figure moved from one side of the sofa to the other, crouched, stood, then climbed back into the truck.

With a monstrous growl, the engine raged. Solveig ducked again. Nothing made sense but her dry mouth and racing heart.

Minutes passed like days until the noise finally ceased, and she lifted her head.

The sofa stood ruined in the middle of the dark and dormant field.

Six

Kyle frowned at the tattered sofa. "You're serious."

"Yes." Solveig's face brooked no argument. "Burn it."

Kyle might have laughed if not for the donuts cut into the muddy snow. "You know, the police—"

"There is no burn ban. I already checked."

This wasn't what he'd expected when she called this morning and asked for help again. So far, she wasn't talking. Either she really hadn't seen the vehicle, or panic threw a haze over her memory.

And another thing. The fact she called at all fueled his growing suspicion that she didn't know the real business of Community Care Property Management.

He splashed kerosene on the cushions—not too much or they'd have Dante's Inferno out here—and lit an old receipt. "I do like a good bonfire."

She offered a weak smile. "So do I. We need marshmallows."

"And hotdogs."

"Nei, ørret." She entered something into her phone. "Sorry, I forgot the English. Trout. Fresh caught."

Interesting. The flame raced along trails of accelerant. "Do you fish?"

"Once in a while. You?"

"Not in ages. I'm taking a survivalist camping trip in the spring. I'll get my fill then."

"Sounds fun." She warmed her hands. "You and some friends?"

"It'd be nice if my dad comes." A pipe dream, but sure. It'd be nice.

"Might have to go it alone, though."

"Don't. You'll get eaten by a bear." So casual she could've been remarking on the weather.

"Not going to happen." He flicked the lighter. "I know what I'm doing."

An unimpressed eyebrow told him what she thought of that. "I'll read it in the news when they find your bones, Kyle Benton. I'll think, 'What a pity. Such a nice guy to end up a grizzly snack.'"

"That hurts, Solveig. I'm like a steak. Not a *snack*."

That got an earnest laugh out of her, and its peal sated a hunger that had been gnawing for a while.

She patted her cheeks. "Once this dies down, will you stay awhile? There's more to do if you're game."

He put the lighter away. "Always."

By the time the sofa bed smoldered to a blackened metal frame and sifting embers, the spark in her eyes had returned. Kyle didn't mind taking the credit.

Solveig unlocked the chains holding the barn's double doors closed. "I must warn you. It's horrible."

From where Kyle stood, Mr. Borja's cache of farm equipment, toolboxes, and work benches looked like a playground. Even the storage clutter—leftover hardware, an upright piano, a whole crate of antique Tillman's Miracle Elixir bottles—probably hid a few gems.

"I'm donating the tools to the American Legion," she announced. "They will send a truck tomorrow, so let's concentrate on that. What time is it?"

He checked his phone. "Three-oh-three. Make a wish."

"Done." The corners of her eyes crinkled. "We have two and a half hours of daylight."

She dove right in, rolling a tool cabinet aside to clear a way, so Kyle grabbed a length of rope and wound it over his shoulder. If she thought they'd finish by dark, they had a war of the wishes between them, because he already hoped for a reason to see her again. Larsh or no Larsh.

Did that count as weasel thinking? Nah. No law against lending a hand, and if the boyfriend issue worked itself out in the meantime, great. Solveig hadn't mentioned how long she planned to stay, but for Keith, probate had been fairly straightforward and took six months to close. A lot could happen in six months.

He tossed the coil of rope into a rusty wheelbarrow and took up the handles. "Pop quiz. Last book you read for fun?"

"Probably not one you know. *Den mørke vinteren.* That translates as *The Dark Winter.*" She colored slightly. "Don't laugh. It's a romance."

"Not laughing. Good story?"

"Yes. True love blooms in the nuclear winter. Sad and hopeful at the same time." She appeared overly interested in the bumper stickers affixed to the tool cabinet. "Your turn. Same question."

"*Cryoseed.* It's a sci-fi about a botanist who has his body frozen—"

"And revives to a world that needs his relatively uncorrupted DNA."

He nearly crashed the wheelbarrow into the lawn mower. "You've read it?" *If she says yes, she's The One.*

"I saw the movie. So corny." Her lips twitched as she imitated the leading lady's whispery delivery. "'When you wake up in the future, come find me.'"

Hiding a grin, he maneuvered his load toward the open barn doors and parked it. "Fair point. They left the good stuff in the book."

In no time, they found an easy rapport. Every time he asked what she wanted to do with some antique, she made a cheeky offer to sell it to him, turning the work into a game of mock appraisals. They valued a broken porch swing at two thousand dollars, a phonograph in perfect condition at three kroner. Kyle didn't know what that amounted to, but it sounded like not much.

"Here's an easy one," he said. "Seventeen mix tapes celebrating the very worst of the late eighties. Can I start the bid at two million?"

"Ah. Priceless." Her voice held a pensive note as she waded through the mess to inspect his find. "These were my father's. I used to play his music to feel close to him." She ran her finger over the cases. "Silly, I know."

Kyle coughed to clear the lump in his throat. "No, I get it."

"It's funny. In Norwegian, 'hearing' is *å høre.* But add *hjemme,* 'at home,' and it becomes an expression for belonging somewhere. That's actually the priceless thing."

She choked up and ran from the barn, leaving Kyle boxed in behind paint cans and a roll of chicken wire.

He extracted himself and followed her. Solveig's eyes sparkled and she laughed at his jokes, but he'd forgotten the rawness of her loss. Maybe for these brief minutes, she had too.

Outside, the cold gripped the bones of his hands, tightening around his knuckles like a prosecutor's handshake. He found her on the porch steps, drying her eyes and facing the mountains. Taking the place beside her, Kyle scrounged for something helpful and came up empty. "We've done what we can for today, I think."

"Our time is ticking down," she agreed.

"Sorry your wish didn't come true."

"It still might." She warmed her hands, cupping one then the other against the cold. "Can I tell you a terrible secret?"

"No."

She glanced at him, eyebrows lifted.

"There's not much you could say I'd call terrible," he amended.

"Don't tempt me." Shadows hollowed out her face. "When I got the call about Bestepappa's stroke, my first thought was, 'Is there nothing he won't do for a visit?'" She covered her eyes.

Kyle placed his hand between her shoulder blades and rubbed circles into her back. "Been a while?"

"Years." A sniffle. "See? Terrible. I didn't mean it. I sent flowers, called the hospital for updates, prayed endlessly. Then after a week he died, and all I can think is how much I wish I'd come for Christmas."

"No. Don't do that to yourself." She trembled under his touch, so he patted her back once more and withdrew. "Why don't you go inside? I'll button up the barn."

"N-no, I'll do it." Her teeth clicked between the words, and Kyle bit his tongue to keep his own from chattering. "This cold is nothing compared to h-home. I don't know why I'm shivering like this." So, Norway was home and her family's farm was not.

"Can I do anything?"

For a long stretch, she didn't answer. Maybe she wasn't going to. He watched with her as the mountains deepened their blues, watched as their icy breath floated away before them.

She dipped her chin. "There is one thing. If you will, you can grant my wish."

~~~

As she waited for sunrise, Solveig brewed lemon-ginger tea on the camping stove and drafted an email to Mr. Forrester since he hadn't yet returned her call, but her daydreams skipped toward Saturday.

She had known Kyle would say yes and felt guilty for asking. He agreed to the cavern excursion without a moment's hesitation, but they had to wait for the weekend. Technically, she had the authority to give him a day off. Would he be as keen to help if he knew that?

A better question: would she have decided to dismantle the firm if she met him before her appointment with Bestepappa's estate attorney?

"It's not as if I have a choice," she murmured, but of course, that wasn't true. For instance, she could stay. Live in the house. Learn the business. See if Kyle's attention survived once the gossip circled his way.

That meant surviving it herself.

She groaned and set her mobile aside in favor of perusing the old map in the *Landmarks* book again. The page header caught her eye.

RICE CAVERNS

Did the caverns share a connection with the same Rices that Sheriff Dade had mentioned? Possibly. She ran her fingers over the textured cloth cover of the book and turned to the biographical sketches.

> *A descendant of the hearty stock of Palatines, SAMUEL ELIAS RICE carved his way into the lush Shenandoah Valley as a young man when he settled on the veritable Eden of Cross Keys. Ever the pioneer, he soon discovered the caverns near Massanutten that now bear his name. To this day, areas of Rice Caverns remain unmapped.*
>
> *Samuel set up housekeeping with his bride, the erstwhile*

Miss Sarah Worley, in 1867. Their home boasts many modern conveniences and proves a favorite perch for the proverbial Stork, which has left several daughters and a strapping lad, Caleb Samuel, to continue the celebrated Rice lineage.

Solveig let out a breath. The house did sit on some of Cross Keys' best farmland.

Stolen land, according to Sheriff Dade.

She tapped out more questions for Mr. Forrester, bringing on a fresh wave of guilt. Kyle went out of his way to offer solutions, and in return, she was about to hand him one enormous problem. At the very least, he deserved fair warning of the decisions she'd made.

But what if she sold the business? That way, at least, he and the others would keep their jobs.

She tacked the question onto the end of the email and hit Send.

The last sip of her tea was cool and oversweet. She set the cup aside and stepped into a living room much different from the one Ms. Van-Gorden had critiqued. A visible disaster, rather than a hidden one. Yet closer to restoration than if she'd worked at it alone.

Scraps of conversation surfaced as she stacked photo albums for safekeeping. Kyle confounded her. His altruism had held even after she refused him for dinner, and he never asked what the graffiti meant or why anyone would try to scare her.

There's not much you could say I'd call terrible.

She inhaled deeply. What would it be like to tell him everything? To not wait for some busybody to air her secrets, but to simply confess and let him decide whether to shoulder the truth of what she'd done?

He might surprise her. Most likely not. He'd said enough in bits and pieces to make his intentions clear. Kyle came here to hit a reset button on his life. The same reason she left. Daydreams aside, she'd made her home east of Eden for a reason. This place was lost to her.

Hours slipped by easily in the work of sorting and packing, until twin chimes pulled her away. Her mobile had switched to low battery mode and batched her messages.

She paused amid the clutter strewn around the living room to read them. The first was Mr. Forrester's email.

> *Got your voice mail late yesterday, my apologies. Give me a day to check on the deed question. I doubt there's a problem, but I'll find out and tell you for certain.*
>
> *For the business, selling is certainly a possibility. It won't be easy to find a buyer willing to champion Mr. Borja's causes, but let me know ASAP if you want to change gears.*

She read the brief message twice, sure she had missed something. What "causes" did anyone need to take up to run a property management company?

But never mind. The other alert was a text from Kyle.

Need help tonight?

She hesitated. It was one thing to accept his kindness and another to take advantage of it. He deserved to hear directly that she'd made moves to close the company.

Tonight, then. She'd tell him and maybe he'd understand. She tapped out her response.

I'd like that very much.

Seven

Among limitless possibilities for ruining his precious second chance, risking a speeding citation was probably the dumbest. Even so, the road to the Borja place flew under Kyle's tires. He watched landmarks, muttering to himself as he downshifted at the gnarled apple grove and braked for the turn. "If you pass the dairy-cow mailbox, you've gone too far. Also if you show up with big plans when you already know the score."

He eased down the gravel drive and parked in front of the house. Whether he should even think of dating yet would make a great question for his therapist. As soon as he found a new one, he'd make sure to ask.

But tonight he had a different question in mind.

For at least an hour, they'd work. Painting, packing, whatever. Anything she wanted. Once dusk settled in, he'd throw out a casual remark about dinner. Feel out the boundaries, play it by ear. If she seemed unsure, he'd turn into Mr. Nice Guy and order pizza.

But they had a spark. If she gave him the least bit of kindling, he would take her out tonight. Food to test the line she'd drawn, wine to dance across it, and candlelight to set it ablaze.

There was no pretending this was anything but full-scale offense on the Larsh situation. He glanced in the mirror. His eyes belonged to someone he wasn't supposed to be anymore.

He sighed and flipped up the visor. "Yep. Still a weasel."

The admission hurt. Brother Mike had warned him.

A movement drew his attention. Solveig peered out through the blinds, her lithe silhouette shadowing the front window. The slats distorted her form with broken edges. Kind of like the scars she tried to cover. What might his own jagged edge look like if displayed for the world?

She stepped away from the window and opened the front door. Oh, but she was a sight. Loose tendrils from her side braid framed her face, and she wore a turquoise tunic sweater and matching scarf that made her eyes into gems. As he reached the front porch, she said, "Come in. I hope you're hungry. Pizza is on the way."

Well, that answered that.

He crossed the threshold. Citrus perfumed the air, but inside was barely warmer than out. "Brr. The fireplace isn't keeping up?"

She sighed and closed the door behind him. "I don't know what I did wrong."

He inspected the hearth. She'd set the grate to the side and repurposed it to hold more firewood. A massive log sat atop a pile of dead, partly blackened coals.

"Easily fixed," he said. "I'll show you if you want."

"Yes, but later." She glanced at the window. "We're losing the light."

He followed her to the kitchen. Other than snuffing out her heat source, it looked as if she'd had a great day. Mountains of boxes lined the living room walls, joining the ones they'd piled up on Tuesday. A rolled-up area rug and a broom leaned into the far corner, leaving the hardwood bare and squeaky. "You've been busy."

She turned. "I'm sorry?"

He gestured to the room. "I'm impressed."

"Oh. I didn't hear you." She chewed her lip. "I have partial hearing loss on the left side. So you'll know."

Everything in her body language begged him not to make a big deal over it, so he flashed a thumbs-up. "Got it."

Her kitchen reminded him of his grandmother's with its olive-green appliances, walnut-brown cabinets, and collection of votive candles by the sink. Half-packed boxes, old newspapers, and rolls of tape crowded every available surface. A package of lemon-ginger tea and a jar of honey near the breadbox identified the sweet scent.

"Are you thirsty?"

He eyed the lone bottle on top of the fridge. "If you are."

She followed his gaze. "Oh. I don't—I mean, feel free, but—"

He lifted his hands. "I'm kidding." Though he hadn't been, not really.

"You can take it with you if you like." She reached for the bottle and held it up to the fading light at the window. Dusty and two-thirds full. "I meant to dump it out." She shrugged, and he knew why she hadn't.

"Sure," he said as if it were nothing. "Thanks."

"If you'll help me in here first, we'll have room to eat." She wrapped a mug in newspaper and put it in the box nearest to her. "Then we must pack the books upstairs."

A tremor beneath the benign words caught his ear. "Hey. You've been going like gangbusters. Are you sure you're up to this?"

"Definitely not, but nonetheless." She gave a weak laugh as she tore a half-sheet of newspaper. "To be honest, I really wanted to bribe you with pizza first."

"Yeah?" Might as well go for broke. "I really wanted to ask you out again tonight."

She abandoned the mug she'd started wrapping. "Kyle—"

"I know. Your boyfriend." He shoved his hands into his pockets. The fit of the silver lighter in his right palm shot him through with craving. "I should head out."

"No, stay. Please." She folded her arms and rubbed them. "I have something to say."

He waited. The deep quiet of a house with no electricity could sure get inside a person. Chatter and a crackling fire had covered it the other day, but now her lips pinched and the coals cooled in stifling silence. Kyle wished for the murmurs of shifting ash, singing pipes, or a humming fridge . . . some whipping wind outside. Anything besides this dead air. He caved first. "Look, I'm sorry—"

"No, listen. For starters, I sort of lied to you about Lars."

She did? He held his breath.

"He isn't my boyfriend. I suppose he thinks he is."

Kyle exhaled. Too bad. He'd dared to hope there was no Larsh. "Sounds complicated."

She traced some invisible pattern on the countertop. "It's not, really. A group of us meets for Taco Fridays, and we ski together some weekends. Sometimes it's only we two for tacos, and one night, he kissed me. The moment charmed my head, but my heart hasn't come along. I keep hinting, but he doesn't get it."

Larsh sounded like a real moron, but in Kyle's experience, comedians solved more problems than critics. "Okay. I'm gonna break the International Guy Code and tell you a secret. Ready?"

She nodded.

"Most of us"—he paused for effect—"don't do hints. You need a billboard and a megaphone. At least."

"Seriously." The air of levity fell flat, though, and the corners of her mouth sagged again. "I might as well be candid. He wants to get physical."

He sobered. "And you don't."

"No." Her cheeks reddened as she fiddled with her scarf and tightened it to rest flush against the left side of her neck. "And I don't know why it's easier to tell you than him."

"Simple. You've got nothing to lose with me." He took some sheets of newspaper and worked on a stack of rooster-patterned plates. She followed suit with the mugs. The deepening darkness carried a weirdly revealing vibe, and that gave him an idea. "Let's call him."

"What? Now?"

"Why not? You call. Say it to me, tell it to him."

"We can't." She shifted from one foot to the other. "Time zones are tricky."

"Yeah. Technically, he's in the future. He should already know."

She gave a courtesy smile at the lame joke but kept her eyes down. "How dumb am I to feel guilty for complaining about him to you?"

"You have nothing to feel guilty about."

"I wish that were true." She muttered the words under her breath. "But this lets one thing off my shoulders."

He snagged a candle from the edge of the sink. "Here's to a *lighter* load." He withdrew his lighter and held it out. After a moment's hesitation, she took it.

"That's a groaner, you know."

"Nope. Happiness is a warm pun."

Finally, a real smile. Solveig flicked the igniter twice to get the hang of it, then held the flame to the candle till it caught. The tiny light filled the room and reflected in the glass of the sliding door, the chrome of the appliances, and the depths of her eyes. When she returned the lighter, she wrinkled her nose. "Why do you carry that thing? You're not a smoker, are you?"

"Nope. Just quit. Happy New Year."

"Why don't you get rid of it?"

"I don't know. I'm used to it."

She raised her chin. "My turn to analyze you. In your heart of hearts, you haven't truly given it up."

"All right. Let's lay it all out there." He gripped it in his fist, rolled it through his fingers, and flicked the igniter. "You call Larsh, I'll pitch my lighter."

"No!"

"Not tonight. We'll call at a decent hour tomorrow—"

"I am not going to break up with him over the phone while I'm out of the country!"

"Then I'll hang onto this." With a sleight of hand, he vanished the lighter up his sleeve. "What about you? New Year's resolutions?"

"None for me." The little flame quaked with the breath of her words and cast its unsteady radiance around them. "Don't get offended, but I think they're kind of silly."

"Aw. Who doesn't like a clean slate?"

"I don't believe in clean slates." She taped the box of coffee mugs shut. "Whatever is ruined, most often stays that way."

That sounded like a sad story. Maybe one that had to do with Leonard Dade. Or the punks bugging her. Or both.

Either way, he didn't feel like asking questions she might volley back his way. Kyle palmed the lighter again and kept his tone easy. "You're right. Guess I'll pick up a pack of menthols on my way home."

"Don't you dare." She cupped her hand over her mouth. "I mean, if you can keep your resolutions, don't let me discourage you."

The open flaps of boxes threw angular shadows around the room, arrows pointing in every direction, but none tempted the eye as much as Solveig herself. The candle's glow danced on her face and gleamed in the highlights of her hair.

"Don't worry. I've been meaning to quit, and this was the right time. New place, new job, new life."

"Speaking of which. I haven't quite managed what I meant to say." A shadow crossed her face. "I wish I knew more about Bestepappa's company, but—"

Kyle jerked his head toward the front window. "Did you hear that?"

Eight

Solveig turned her right ear toward the window. "Probably the pizza."

"No, it sounded like . . ." He paused.

His hardened expression chilled her. She grabbed a sheet of newsprint. "If we don't get to work, this evening will be a wash."

High beams flashed in the window. This time, she heard it.

Splat.

"Not again," she moaned. Kyle jumped from his chair and tromped through the living room. She hurried to follow. "Where are you going?"

"Stay inside," he ordered.

She grabbed his arm as he made for the front door. "Stop. Maybe they'll go away."

"You bet they will."

He swung open the front door. She followed to the porch. "Please don't—"

"Hey!" That bellow hadn't come from Kyle, had it? "Who's there?"

"Aw, Sophie's got a new boyfriend. Ask her what happened to the last one, Romeo." Laughter followed—two or three other voices. A whitish orb whizzed by her head and cracked against the siding behind her. A skinny figure ran toward the car, in front of its square high beams.

Kyle chased him. "Where ya going? If you chicken livers came for a fight, let's go!"

"Hey, that ain't a bad idea." The laughter took an uglier pitch as three shadowy figures drew in, each wearing a grotesque Halloween mask. A scarface, a ghoul, a devil.

A wave of nausea rose. If a fight broke out, Kyle would be pummeled, at best. And then? They'd carry out their threat.

Next time you ride SHOTGUN.

Speaking of bad ideas.

She raced through the house and took the stairs two at a time. Burst into Bestepappa's room. Threw open the door of his closet, where mothballs mingled with the faint scent of gun oil.

"*Herre Gud,* guide my hands," she murmured. She grabbed Bestepappa's hunting rifle and fled to Kyle's aid.

When she stepped onto the porch, the time for taunts and insults was ending. She swallowed hard, aimed carefully at the ground, the way Bestepappa used to scare off coyotes and foxes, and fired.

The recoil kicked into her shoulder. She cried out. And her ears! The blast rang inside her head.

Smoke and gunpowder swirled with the confused shouts of men scattering. The trespassers ran for the car. A red sedan. The car doors slammed. One more egg landed on the porch steps and splattered on her shoes.

Kyle gave up the pursuit and resorted to fist shaking. "Cowards."

They laid on the horn, and their headlights disappeared up the road. She placed the gun on the porch railing with the barrel pointed away from them and the house, as she'd seen Bestepappa do. "No more than I. Resorting to this ugly thing."

He muttered a fluent string of vulgarities that reminded her of the juvenile detention center. "Do you kiss your mother with that mouth?"

"Not lately, but I apologize." His features blurred in the twilight, except for his eyes, sharp and bright. "Who's Sophie?"

Just a girl from JDC, she wanted to say. "My American nickname once upon a time. A schoolteacher thought it was close enough."

Her ears still ached. Did Kyle's hurt, too?

"We should call the cops." His weary tone supplied no encouragement.

And tell them what? She had no details. No names. No real confidence the trolls didn't have Leonard Dade's full approval. She shook her head. "They won't do anything."

The crisp air began to prickle through the heat of adrenaline, and the half-moon peeked from behind fast-moving clouds as he joined her on the darkened porch. He glanced at the gun with a raised eyebrow and a smidgen of disbelief, opened the door, and waited. Ladies first, apparently.

She grasped the gun with both hands and held it with the barrel up as she passed Kyle. She hid it under the guest room bed in case she needed it again. From the kitchen, the candle flickered, unattended and full of its own danger.

When she returned, Kyle was positioning the grate in the fireplace. He took the poker from the rack by the hearth and shuffled ashes around. She hung back and watched. "You don't have to do that."

"I said I would."

"Do you always play hero for girls you just met?"

He shot her a pained grin over his shoulder. "Would you believe me if I said you're the first?"

She didn't want to like the way the remark rippled in her belly, nor how it continued to swell like a tide in her chest. She didn't want an audience when the dam broke. Because when it did—

In an instant, her mind flashed a scene sharp and real as a premonition. Her cracking voice. Tightness in her face. Kyle wrapping her in his arms, kissing away her tears. The salt of kissing him back. His hands cradling her face, her getting lost in fervor for his beautiful mouth, starving for air, unable to get enough and unwilling to break away.

And that was a problem because breaking away was the whole reason she'd come.

She tried to memorize how he stoked the fire. A thread of smoke curled out of the coals, and he blew on it. A spastic little flame jumped out of the ashes, and he fed it some kindling. The smaller branches ignited easily.

That was it. The heavy log left the fire no room to breathe. Now she knew.

She stepped into the kitchen to retrieve his jacket, which hung over one of the chairs. Its woodsy, new-leather scent almost changed her mind. He was keeping his resolution. It didn't smell like cigarettes at all. Behind her, floorboards creaked as Kyle joined her in the kitchen.

"It's late."

"No, it's not. Besides, those cretins might come back. I can't leave you here—"

"It's after one in the morning in Oslo. I'm exhausted." She brushed a loose wisp of hair from her face and caught the stink of iron and gunpowder on her hands. "I will be fine."

He shrugged into the coat, never letting his eyes leave hers. "Tomorrow's kind of sketchy. I have, um, a thing in the morning, so I'm working late to make up time. I can be here around seven."

The impulse to fold herself up in his arms almost overpowered her resolve. But he deserved better than for her to steal favors with lies and omissions.

"I won't take more than you've already given, Kyle. You should spend your time looking for work."

The perpetual smirk extinguished. "No, Solveig. Please don't."

"I was trying to tell you. I met with Bestepappa's lawyer. I decided to dissolve his firm."

He closed his eyes and breathed out another curse, looking gutted.

"I have only a week left to finish everything. It seemed for the best." The explanation sounded limp, worthless. "But I should have told you sooner."

"Yeah." His hands went to his pockets. "One week. Wow."

He stalked out of the kitchen. Solveig stood frozen until the thud of the front door gave her the all clear.

She was a *tosk*, getting twisted up over a man she barely knew. How long until she lost the tenor of his voice and the changing shades of his hazel eyes? Probably not long.

From the kitchen, the candle's unattended flicker taunted its destructive power. She perched on the hearth to wait for a pizza she'd eat alone, her back to a flame she only knew how to crush.

Nine

Charlie worked him in, but he had Kyle down for Friday all along.

Beyond the guardrail at the end of the parking lot, the blue mountains met the torn edge of a paper sky. Kyle sat in his truck outside CCPM. Strategizing. Gripping his lighter so hard his knuckles ached. Good thing he denied himself the luxury of "emergency" cigarettes. If he had one handy, he'd smoke it. If he had two, he'd smoke 'em both.

The streaked windshield distorted the view, but in his mind, vengeance ran cold and clear.

I could kill him.

Where did that come from? Wasn't he different? A new creation? Back at Sterling, he had come forward needy and broken. What about now?

If he could still think murderous thoughts, had he changed at all?

"You laid aside the old self." He turned off the wipers and cut the engine. "You put on the new self. Right? Right."

Fine, don't kill him. But punch him in the face.

"Drop it," he said aloud. "Not gonna happen."

Silence at first. Then, *he warned you.*

He gritted his teeth. The dead man inside was on a tear. "You're right. Now get lost."

Danny had called it. Solveig was trouble.

The anger faded as quickly as it had flared. He'd known he might lose his job. It had seemed distant and unlikely, though, until she said it aloud and made it his reality.

But forget reality. The trouble lay in the pleasure of her company.

Acting normal, feeling free. A dangerous dream state.

Exhibit A, the bottle on top of her fridge. If he'd opted to partake, the surprise pee test would have turned this into a very different kind of day. Same with the eggheads. A fight would have been a disaster. At the time, he hadn't cared.

Now he cared plenty.

How about the rifle? If they'd called the police—and they should've—that wouldn't have gone his way at all.

Despite everything, part of his head was back at the house, loading boxes and starting fires. Sneaking glances. Winking when she caught him and earning a blush for the trouble. Wanting to be wanted. Drunk on the possibilities.

Possibilities sure served a wicked hangover.

Bottom line, the thugs rattled her and she pushed him away, and the dude in the devil mask was going to answer for it.

Danny. Same carriage. Same menthol stink. The eggs. Everything fit.

He got out of the truck and went inside.

The coffee maker gurgled as Kyle hung up his coat and clocked in. Air thick with the scent of dark roast called up Sunday mornings spent lazing with Ashleigh on his apartment balcony in Colorado Springs. Strumming his guitar while she schemed to scale with the grandeur of the Rockies and spun ways to spend all their money and ideas for Patterson to expand markets. Labs, private researchers, foreign buyers. He would tune half an ear to the business stuff and the rest of his focus on her. He didn't want those days. Didn't want to long for them.

The overhead light flickered, bringing him back. Small mercies.

While Danny refilled his cup, Kyle grabbed the mail. Two checks, a tax document, and a heavy manila packet from Forrester, Stein & Barron, Attorneys at Law.

His heart thudded.

In his cover letter, Edward Forrester Jr.—a lawyer name if Kyle ever heard one—named Solveig as the trustee and summarized her decisions in plain language. The property management firm would dissolve upon completion of its contract obligations, or sooner as renegotiations may allow. An asset liquidation sale would be scheduled shortly thereafter. Miss Borja promised reference letters and two weeks' pay as severance for those who stayed to the bitter end.

More than she had to do. Not enough to save him.

Kyle sauntered to Danny's side of the office and leaned on the corner of his desk. Show time.

"You got a problem with me seeing 'the boss's granddaughter,' and meanwhile you're egging her house?"

Danny hurried back, sloshing his coffee. He grabbed up a notepad and stuffed it in a drawer. "I don't know what you're talking about."

"Come off it." He shoved the packet at him. "But hey, nice work. She's dumping us like hot garbage, and who can blame her?"

Danny read the letter, then dropped the packet in his inbox. "Get off my desk."

Kyle didn't budge. "It's the pits, right? But man, I don't even care. She's great. I've been over there every night this week." Let him assume whatever he wanted.

Judging by the snarl, he struck a nerve. "You leave her alone."

"Who drives the rust-bucket Salamander?"

"Move, before I make you."

Deliberately, Kyle stood, facing his coworker and interim sponsor nose to nose. "If those twerps bother her again, they're going to jail."

"You'll go with them."

Kyle lifted his chin. "Yeah. Gladly. Understand?"

The other man snorted. Kyle almost hoped he'd take a swing.

Danny disappeared after lunch. Kyle yo-yoed between irritation at his lack of integrity and temptation to follow suit.

Of course, he spied in the drawer to find the notepad Danny hid. The top sheet was gone, but the pencil shading trick told the tale.

Hera Wise—$$$

Beneath that, a local number.

He replaced the flickering fluorescent bulb and combed the calendar, trying to figure out how much longer he'd be employed. They had the first quarter booked, though for all he knew, Solveig was canceling contracts and outsourcing work at this very moment. Either way, his nice little life was about to grind to a halt.

If only he could call Dad.

His workday was winding down when the door cracked. Kyle glowered. "Did you run out of sand to pound?"

"I deserve that." Solveig poked her head in the trailer. *"Hallo."*

He jumped to his feet. "I thought you were Danny. What are you doing here?"

She let herself in but lingered near the door. A grocery sack dangled from her hooked fingers, and she lifted it toward him. "I brought a peace offering."

Confused, he accepted the bag and looked inside. "MREs and Sterno?"

She twisted her braid. "For your wilderness trip. I found them in a cabinet, and the dates are still okay. I need the camping stove for now, but you can have it, too, after I go."

As if he could feel like more of a jerk. Kyle set the gift down. "Let me pour you a coffee." Her cheeks and nose were as red as in the cemetery. "Tell me you didn't walk the whole way here."

"Not from the house. There's a dance studio south of the 'Burg." She wrapped her fingers around the steamy mug he offered. "They picked up the piano, and I hitched a ride."

He rolled Danny's chair around the desk and gestured for her to sit. "I thought you were giving it to your grandfather's church."

"They didn't need it." She settled into the chair. "I called six churches and three schools before the studio. It shouldn't be so hard to give away a perfectly good piano."

He stared at his computer screen to avoid her eyes. "Glad everything's working out."

She scooted her chair closer to his. "Kyle, I'm sorry. If I could change this, I would."

"It's okay."

She must've prepared a whole speech, because she barely paused for breath. "I don't know anything about running a business. I studied library science and history because I want to be an archivist, and my dream job is waiting for me at the Ministry of Culture. Accounting and contracts and . . . I don't know what else. . . . It'd be hard enough if I stayed, but I can't run an American company from my flat in Oslo."

"I know."

"You became a face for everyone I'm hurting, and still I kept it from you, and I feel awful."

"Don't." He hesitated, deciding how much to say. "This might sound weird, but I prayed for this job."

She covered her eyes. "I am the worst person in the world."

"Nah, I've got you beat for sure." He waited until she peeked through her fingers to continue. "But I don't believe God answered that prayer just to ditch me now."

She lowered her hand and stared as if he'd switched to another language midsentence, and she needed time to catch up. "I wouldn't have guessed you were a praying man."

"Sometimes I am. Depends how bad things get."

She missed the joke or didn't find it funny, because her brow furrowed. "You needed this job badly?"

"Yeah." A slight understatement. Should he tell her? "I don't have the greatest work history."

Lame, if basically true. He drew another breath, but she jumped in.

"Bestepappa believed in giving people another chance." She downed her coffee and rolled the chair backward. The moment was dwindling. "I should leave you to it."

"Right. Ah." He shouldn't. He was going to anyway. "So are we on for tomorrow?"

Her eyes lit. "You still want to go?"

"If you do."

Trembling, she nodded. "The nearest thing he had to a dying wish was that I see this cavern."

"Then it's settled." He grabbed a pen and jotted points on a sticky note. Writing things down used to be gold in his bag of tricks. It sometimes kept watery promises from turning to vapor. "You bring bottled water and the map. I've got flashlights and a compass. Our phones might not be up to the job."

"Smart." She entered her own notes into her phone. "Do we need a first aid kit?"

"Nah, we'll be fine." Kyle grinned. "Famous last words, right? I'll get one."

This time, she smiled back shyly. "We should study the map together. Would you . . . like to take supper with me?"

For an instant, Ashleigh's face flashed in his mind. Their affair had started like this. A scheme and a dinner date.

He ousted the memory. Solveig wasn't Ashleigh. "Definitely. There's an Indian place in the square in Harrisonburg."

"Ooh, I know the one. It was always wonderful. I hope you like curry."

"I do." He fixed his eyes on hers. "I might even be a curry lover."

Her blush lit a fuse attached to his heart and tied his gut in knots. Nicotine cravings were child's play next to the desire to cup those cheeks in his hands. It ached and festered right in the middle of his pockmarked soul.

As she surveyed the office, he washed her cup and dropped a pellet of fish food into Hook's bowl. He was clocking out when she held up the shaded note. "Hera Wise and dollar signs?"

He tried not to scowl. "Something Danny's working on."

It rose on his lips to tell her. The argument, the eggs. Everything.

She handed the note back. "I'm sure it's fine, then. I've known him forever."

He stashed it in his breast pocket. He wanted this date. Enough to hold back. For now.

As she let herself out of the trailer, the soft glance she tossed his way made his stomach clench, and he was glad to lock up for an excuse to turn away.

Fools rush in. She'd be gone in a week. He had no right.

Except none of that mattered. Like it or not (and he did), deserve it or not (definitely no), it appeared Kyle David Benton—property assistant, amateur balladeer, convicted felon—was falling in love.

Later, they strolled past storefronts on Main Street as dusk veiled the distant mountains and the streetlights winked to life. Solveig stole glances at Kyle along the way. A mundane word like *handsome* truly robbed him. English needed something grander. *Kjempekjekk* would have to do.

Though impossible to ignore the way his eyes played tricks with the light and how his well-muscled arms filled out a Henley, she savored most the quick wit that had silvered the edges of gray days. Who knew funny was so sexy?

At the moment, he was all business. "Okay. Tell me what we're looking for exactly."

She blinked twice, hoping he hadn't caught her gawking. "There's a local legend of a cavern wall where people used to go and write their prayers. I pestered Bestepappa to take me to find it, but we never went." She dabbed her eyes with her mittens. "I suppose I'll always be sorry for that."

"I'm sorry you're sorry." His voice was warm, earnest. "But for what it's worth, I'm glad I get to go with you."

"Me too." She meant it.

His stride slowed as they ambled by a high-end smoke shop. She caught his arm and tugged gently. "You've done a great thing for yourself."

"I know." He seemed to weigh his words. "I used to hang with a medical examiner. Believe me, I know."

Solveig shivered. "He carried gruesome stories?"

"She had a dark sense of humor." With a slight maneuver, he linked their arms and flashed a smile that both zinged her heart and locked the door on the subject. "What time were you thinking for tomorrow?"

They rounded the corner at Elizabeth Street since traffic was stacking up on Main. "Can you come at eight o'clock? I'd like to set out early."

He made a face. "Let's say ten. You're on Norway time, but morning is when I miss Colorado the most."

"Ten it is." Finally, a plan. "Thank you for this. I know it seems silly."

"Not a bit," he said. "You might not get another chance."

She pressed her lips together. That was it, exactly, always. "What else do you miss about Colorado? Might you go back?"

"I miss my parents, but no. I have to make this work." His eyes rounded and brightened. "Hey, idea. What if I take over the business?"

She stopped in the middle of the sidewalk. "You want to buy CCPM?"

He paused. "Not outright. But I can manage it . . . and funnel back part of my pay as equity. Us guys stay employed, and you won't have to do anything."

Maybe. Or maybe she ended up back in Rockingham County twice a year trying to salvage a company she knew nothing about. "I'm not sure. I want to help you, but have you ever run a business before?"

His excitement dimmed. "Sort of. It's a long story. But listen, this is a first date, not a sales pitch. Let's go for ice cream before it starts snowing."

Her stomach fluttered. Yes, a first date. Perhaps they'd have time for one more.

A chime interrupted. She slipped her arm free from his and checked the message.

Er du våken? Ring meg!

From across the ocean, Lars wanted to know if she was awake to call him. If he'd met them on the street and demanded an explanation, she could not have felt more exposed.

"I—I'm losing steam." Heat flooded her face. "Still trounced with jet lag."

"Sure." He glanced at the device in her hands. "Time zones are tricky."

Did nothing get by him? The phone dinged twice more, but she put it away. "Then again, let's. We might not get another chance."

The ride home passed too quickly. "Dancing in the Dark" came on the radio, and Kyle belted out ridiculous parody lyrics in perfect time with the song until she couldn't catch her breath from laughter. His singing voice wasn't half-bad, either.

"A man of many talents." She clapped as the song ended.

"Really just one." He signaled for the turn and pulled into the driveway. "Being an idiot. Lots of tricks in that bag, though."

Gravel pinged the truck's undercarriage, echoing her heart. She hated for the evening to end.

Ever the gentleman, Kyle walked her to the door, even shining a keychain flashlight on the darkened porch steps as they approached. "Thank you," she offered. "This was fun. And needed."

"Did us both good, then." An intensity in his demeanor made her breath catch. He searched her eyes, looking for . . . permission? invitation? Long enough to entertain one wild thought.

He's going to kiss me.

The nip of winter caressed bare skin where her scarf had slipped. As she tugged it back into place, his eyes darkened and he looked away.

Ten

A storm front moved in overnight, and Solveig had been sure Kyle would cancel, right up until he parked at the gated dead end and asked her to grab hand warmers from his glove box. She lost a piece of her heart to him in that moment. The half-kilometer trail that led to Rice Caverns posed no serious challenge under clear skies and mild temperatures, but he faced an icy, rocky path without hesitation.

A whip of wind blew needling sleet sideways. Pencil-thin icicles lined the mouth of the cavern, where Kyle observed the storm. Solveig squelched an urge to warn him away as she shed her wet gloves and hat.

Finally, he stepped into the limestone corridor. "It's letting up. We'll be fine on the way back down."

"I'm not worried. We Norwegians have a saying: *Det finnes ikke dårlig vær, bare dårlige klær.*"

He unzipped the weatherproof satchel and raised his eyebrows at her.

Pleasure tickled her face. "It means, 'There is no bad weather, only bad clothing.'"

He volleyed back a smirk and tipped his head her way. "Bad clothing? You mean like that scarf?"

She huffed, refusing to grant him the point, and loosened the damp viscose without removing it entirely. "No. It's my favorite."

"If you get cold and want to stash it, say the word."

"Thanks." She wouldn't, though. "Don't let anything wet touch the book."

"Couldn't be safer. I left it in the truck."

Eyes wide, she stared hard at him.

He shrugged. "What? I looked at it. We're good."

She shook her head. "Incredible."

He gestured toward the path. "Wanna go back for it?"

"No!"

"All right, then." He favored her with that grin of his, and she couldn't help but return it.

"Luray Caverns holds a constant fifty-four degrees Fahrenheit. This one should be similar. Once we're well underground, there truly is no weather."

The smile remained, but it took on an oddly serious cast. "Good thing we brought our own whirlwind."

Her heart thudded. "Much nicer than the snowstorm."

Kyle withdrew two heavy Maglite flashlights and zipped his satchel. "Here. Rule one, stay together. Rule two, if we do get separated, we're not going to wander around getting more lost. You stay put. I come to you."

She gave him a look. "Why do you get to be the rescuer?"

"Echoes make it tough to tell directions. Let's play to our strengths." He tapped his ear. "You be the rescuer when the bear comes after me, okay?"

Relenting, she laughed. "Deal."

"As a backup plan, though . . ." He took her free hand and lightly interlocked their fingers with room for her to tighten the hold—or break it.

Her cheeks warmed. He deserved to know she'd called Lars back, and even so, she let her fingers fold into his.

He squeezed and affected a somber baritone. "'Let us go then, you and I.'"

She gave him a quizzical look. "I don't . . ."

"T. S. Eliot. 'The Love Song of J. Alfred Prufrock.' You probably read it in high school and haven't thought of it since." He clicked on his flashlight, prompting her to do the same. "In a nutshell, Prufrock has 'an overwhelming question,' and he doesn't ask it."

"Why not?"

As they moved toward the cavern's entryway, Kyle took his time answering. "He thinks it's too late to be the man he could have been," he said finally. "That's how I read it, anyway."

She studied his profile. Was that how Kyle saw himself? Surely not.

With several more twists and turns, they traded the safety of daylight for the thrill of flashlights throwing dramatic shadows off the rock. The corridor was wider than she expected and vast overhead. A mineral scent thickened the air, and the ground bore a slight downward incline.

She dawdled a moment, aiming her flashlight into the ridge formations above them and craning her neck to take it all in. "I feel as if I'm falling through time."

"I'll catch you." His grip backed him up. Warm, comfortable, and sure.

"Don't," she said. "I might make changes along the way."

"Yeah? Like what?"

She squirmed. "Never mind."

"It's okay. We're all allowed our secrets." No one around to hear, and still he spoke in low, conspiratorial tones meant for her alone. "What if I tell you one of mine?"

"You don't have to."

"I want to. Here goes nothing." He cleared his throat. "I drove past you after we met in the cemetery. You obviously needed a ride, and I didn't stop."

She turned his hand loose. "I didn't give you much reason to."

"It's not that." His eyes followed her as he twisted the dial on his flashlight, casting a diffused glow around them. "Danny chewed me out for making a pass at you. It shouldn't have mattered, but—"

"What in the world made him think that?"

"I don't know. Never mind. The point is, a better man would have helped."

"I don't think I wanted help." She laughed nervously. "My turn?"

"Up to you."

She fiddled with her own beam, focusing it on the way forward. Which was worse? Refusing to play his game, or admitting her conversation with Lars? Her larger secrets weren't even on the table, but her chest hurt thinking of them.

Tell him. She shivered under the dubious protection of the wet scarf. How she longed to remove it. "I can't think of one."

"Didn't mean to put you on the spot." The passageway narrowed, with stalagmites and stalactites closing around them like dragon's teeth. She missed the comfort of his hand, the cadence of his voice, but as the silence grew awkward, he broke it. "How did we get here, Solveig?"

A light panic iced through her. "You're the one who didn't need the map. You tell me."

"Not 'this tunnel' here. 'You and me' here. Mincing words. Dancing around like Prufrock with his overwhelming question."

"Oh." She shrugged though her heart raced out of control. "Ask it if you want."

He reached for her hand again, but this time he lifted it and brushed her knuckles to his lips. "But you might shoot me down."

She nodded, playing cool but feeling breathless. "I might."

"So maybe we should dance."

"Are we still talking about secrets?"

"I hope not." He pressed his palm to hers, circled his other arm around her waist—awkwardly since he gripped the flashlight—and counted off a simple box step. "Because there's no one I'd rather dance with."

"Flatterer."

"Do me a favor and tell me if it starts working."

Their matched steps echoed off the rock to the tune of thrumming hearts and quiet breaths. Surely the top of her head was still attached. And the sensation telling her otherwise? A shortage of blood to the brain, judging by the heat in her cheeks.

It was totally working.

He gave voice to her thoughts. "This is intense, huh?"

"Far too much so." Her legs quaked. "We'll be quite pressed to break each other's hearts before I leave."

"Nah," he murmured. "What have you got against dramatic airport goodbyes?"

"No more than I have against whirlwind romances." She backed out of the embrace and cast the light around to regain her bearings. "On that note. Lars and I talked this morning."

"Yeah? How did it go?"

"I took your advice and told him directly he's pressuring me. He apologized and said he can wait, and that was that."

Kyle clicked his light on and off a couple of times. "You're kidding, right?"

She kicked a stone. It danced across a table of rock and dropped over a slight edge. "Don't think less of me. He's part of my real life. The life I have to go back to."

"Who says you have to?"

"I—" Her words hitched. "I just do. That's my secret."

Kyle brought them to a forked passage and led her to the right. "Okay. Up ahead. *X* marks the spot. Enjoy."

On the approach, his icy facade cracked as he stopped short and whistled. The diffused beam flooded the smaller space with light, and Bestepappa's notation made sense immediately.

"Oh." Warmth coursed through her body. "Kyle, it's—"

She fell silent, barely breathing. Stone partitioned a small recess, and the smooth concave wall was covered, from the ground to a height of three meters, in handwriting, not like harsh spray-paint graffiti, but an outpouring of humanity in scribbles and lines.

"Can you believe how beautiful it is?" She drew closer to see the words as individual messages. Taken in all at once, they were too much to bear.

A bold-lettered missive caught her eye. "'Please heal Scott.' And this one says, 'Help me find a job.'" She leaned close to examine the faded letters. "'Forgive me, Lord.' The prayer wall. It's real."

"Guess you got what you came for."

She aimed the flashlight carefully and read the messages one at a time. "Some are dated. 1977. 1963. Ooh, 1940." She shook her head in amazement. "It's the history of this town in prayers."

The limestone carried a waxy sheen from the many hands that had touched it. Prayers in chalk, charcoal, lead, and ink cried out to God across the decades. Some were etched into the surface.

Kyle stepped closer and read silently. "This one's really old, and it's signed."

Solveig moved to his side and read it aloud. "'God be merciful to me a sinner. Augusta Elizabeth Rice, October 8, 1919.'"

"Nice." Kyle stepped back from the wall. "This isn't the best place for sinning, but it's not the worst either."

"Don't be gross." Her heart raced. "I can't believe what I'm seeing. That is the day Harvey Engelwood disappeared."

"Who?"

"From the Engelwood mausoleum. Remember?"

"Vaguely. Good recall."

She hid her eyes. "When I was young, I wanted to solve Harvey's mystery. This is the sort of thing preteen geek girls obsess about before the boys-and-makeup phase starts."

He propped his flashlight against the rear wall, a makeshift lantern. "Cool."

The clipped response felt like a shot. She handed him the other light and palmed her mobile. "Hold this."

She snapped photos of the wall of prayers—a half dozen wide shots of the whole scene and more of the individual messages piled on top of one another.

Kyle lit her shots. "So, to clarify, I'm not part of your 'real' life?"

"Please, let it be."

"No can do."

"Fine. One dinner date, no matter how lovely, doesn't bridge an ocean. And weren't you just making rude remarks over someone's prayer?"

"It wasn't *that* rude."

"Why are you being like this?" she retorted.

He huffed into the semidarkness. "Because I'm pretty certain my future 'one who got away' is standing right in front of me."

She stilled. No arguing that. She felt the same. Here in this narrow alcove, only six thousand kilometers stood between them.

She drew a deep breath of the heavy air, hoping to filter it into a light tone. "For the record, I'm not completely against whirlwind romances. I exist because of one, after all."

Kyle groaned. "That was in case I still thought I had a shot, right?"

"You're the best estate-sale assistant I ever had."

"Don't forget egg scraper, fire builder, and cavern navigator. And I can fix anything. Your repairs back at the farm? Piece of cake."

She allowed a small smile. "A flatterer, and now a braggart as well."

"I also play guitar. Open mic nights are my downfall, but I'll embarrass myself among friends. Or to serenade my lady. Either way."

"Kyle, please don't."

The hush around them gave the impression the cavern itself held its breath. Absurd. It was only her because this air betrayed them both. No good words could come from it.

Seconds lengthened before he appealed again, his voice low. "I can keep your secrets."

"I believe you. But this"—she gestured to the space between them—"doesn't work."

"Guess not," he said, his eyes drawn. "Not if you're letting some moron push you into something you don't want."

At his harsh tone, her tears rose and spilled. "What are *you* doing right now, then?"

"Wait, are you crying?" He swore under his breath and lowered the flashlight. "Solveig. I'm sorry. I'm a jerk."

She backed away further, butting against the cavern wall and accidentally knocking the other flashlight askance. A startled squeak escaped as near-total darkness eclipsed the alcove.

"Don't cry. I take it back, every word." He directed the beam upward. "Am I so wrong for wanting you to pick me?" He reached out and found her cheek. Brushed a tear away.

A chill rippled over her skin as icy fingertips traced her earlobe, then slid past her jawline, down the ruined side of her neck. She recoiled as if he'd scraped raw nerves.

"What's wrong?"

"How dare you." She lifted her hand to her scars.

Understanding came over his face. "I'm sorry. I didn't—"

Let him keep his worthless apology. She grabbed the flashlight and yanked it away.

She walked as fast as she dared, stumbling twice on uneven surfaces. Behind her, he scrambled to retrieve the other flashlight.

"Solveig, wait." He held his beam high, but its light was scattered and weak, casting a large shadow ahead of her. "Be mad all you want, but we need to stay together."

Tears coursed freely as she hurried along, not caring if he kept up. Cavern navigator, indeed. The whole way was barely two turns. As she rounded the first, the last traces of his light disappeared.

The space narrowed. A familiar shape in the rock at the fork pointed the way. Daylight would appear in moments. She picked up the pace.

"Solveig?" Kyle kept calling. His footfalls faded and his voice came in echoes.

The mouth of the cavern must be close . . . Maybe three more turns. Yes, definitely. The path only seemed tedious because he'd been so distracting on the way in. Another landmark buoyed her forward, but the passage opened to a narrow underground stream. Not the daylight she expected.

They had crossed no streams on their way to the prayer wall.

Should she try to retrace her steps? The concentrated beam on her flashlight wasn't right for these small spaces. She twisted the dial. Unless she planned to walk back to the farm in the sleet, they'd have to reach a truce, but not before she found some way to brick in her heart, safe from his sly maneuvers.

She turned back toward the crevice she'd come through and saw, laid out before two stalagmites, a grinning brown skeleton.

"Kyle . . . *Kyle!*"

"Solveig, where are you?" His faint voice bounced from the walls. Directionless, haunting. She called again, and his answer came quickly.

A sickening crack and an echoing thud.

Eleven

Monday, May 5, 1919

Gussie Rice stumbled at the crack of a gunshot ringing over Cross Keys' foothills. Rabbit stew for the Marsdons, maybe, or a fox at the Dades' place. No matter.

Today was mail day.

Wisps clung to her neck as she hurried along the hard-packed road home. She'd lost track of the hour, listening to Mrs. Trammel gripe over her catarrh, and even offered to bring her a bottle of Tillman's Miracle Elixir from Daddy's overstock, but the poor woman was inconsolable.

When Gussie realized the time, she had made her excuses. The letter hadn't arrived last week, nor the week before. Certainly, it would be here today.

Corn silos and dilapidated barns dotted a landscape hemmed with the glories of the cobalt mountains. Tough as she found it to imagine the world beyond them, she did try. For Philip's sake. He'd promised to write. Promised so many things. When he finally arrived home, they'd marry and take a grand wedding tour. Maybe to France, since he knew the country. Gussie counted the days.

If only she knew the date she counted toward.

The sun beat down as she hurried past the birches that edged the Baptist churchyard. Not much farther.

"Gussie?" Harvey Engelwood called and ran across the pasture to-

ward her. Absent his customary sack suit, he looked comical in shirtsleeves, trousers, and suspenders. "What's wrong?"

Her longest and dearest friend would worry if she didn't stop to
explain. She took the chance to catch her breath, albeit reluctantly.

"Nothing." The word came out with a puff. "But I'm in a tearing
rush to meet Mr. Wexler."

Harvey adjusted the brim of his straw boater and met her eyes.
"Then I'll let you—"

An idea sparked. "Would it be awful to ask you to drive me the rest
of the way? I know it's not far, but—"

But she could not allow Eloise to see the letter any more than she
could explain the reason to Harvey. He already knew what a goose
Gussie was. No need to molt her feathers. "Would you? Please?"

"Any other day it would be my honor, but I can't shirk the task at
hand." His Adam's apple bobbed. "Dolly broke a leg this morning."

"Oh no." Concern over the letter withered. "Did you send for the
veterinarian? Can I help you tend her?"

His brow furrowed momentarily, then smoothed as he regarded
her. "Ah, no. I put her down."

"What?" His brother's beloved horse? "Harvey, why would you do
that?"

"A horse can't beat a broken leg. It never heals right, and they live
in misery. The only thing for it is a clean shot in the head." He paused
and stared at the ground. "It's—it's a mercy."

His explanation confused her, but she'd be heartless to ask again.
The bright, cloudless sky, so perfect a moment ago, burned with the
spiteful sun's mocking rays. "I'm so sorry. Can I bring a pound cake
later?"

"Thank you. I'm sure we'll enjoy it." His voice cracked slightly. "I
panicked as soon as the shot fired. What if the telegram was a mistake,
and Victor came home with the rest? He'd be incensed. Moronic, I
know."

Her heart squeezed. The sad news had come just weeks before the
Armistice and bittered the victory. The Boys were coming home, but
not all of them.

"If that happened, he'd surely know you'd never have put Dolly

81

down if there were any hope of saving her." How well she knew the foolishness a longing heart manufactured. "Do you need help to bury her?"

"Certainly not." He pulled his narrow shoulders back and drew up to his full gangly height. "I couldn't allow you to exert yourself so."

She patted his arm. "Is there anything I can do?"

Harvey surveyed the hardscrabble that led toward Harrisonburg, wearing a pinched expression. "I'm detaining you."

She glanced up the road. Harvey's trouble had chased her errand from her head. It tugged afresh, but she resisted. "Not at all. What is it?"

His fair cheeks turned ruddy. "The Red Cross will hold a rally at the fire hall on Thursday night, with a community sing to follow. Mother and I would be honored if you'd join us."

"Goodness." Not the sort of request she'd expected, and one she didn't know how to answer. Mama had thrown herself into the Red Cross at the start of the war, but Daddy griped over her time away from home. Even since she died, he claimed the "do-gooder clubs," as he called them, were meant for grandstanding and hen parties. Whether Harvey's mother had caught wind of the remark, Gussie couldn't say, but her pointed scowls of late were inescapable.

She hedged. "Should we amuse ourselves while the Boys are stuck over there?"

"They're not helped by our pining." His face darkened further. "I hear Captain Millard will offer remarks about the Blue Ridge Division."

"Oh!" The chance for real news about Philip instead of rumors and speculation? "On second thought, that sounds charming."

"Very well, then." Perhaps he had a mind to say more, but a familiar clicking and sputtering crested the hillside, followed by the machine that produced it. "Oh, there's—"

"Mr. Wexler!" Gussie turned her face toward home, helpless. "I'm sorry. I'll bring the cake later." She set off again, holding her wide-brimmed hat to keep it from catching the wind.

"You'll never beat him on foot." When she glanced back, he stood thumbing his suspenders and looking perplexed. "Gussie, what's so important?"

She crossed her fingers behind the hat. "I'm expecting a letter from Philip."

The fresh jolt of exhilaration carried her, and during the mail truck's lengthy stop at the Engelwood place, Gussie imagined she might win after all. Harvey, bless him, must have hooked Mr. Wexler with the lure of a bendable ear. Oh, why hadn't she waited to speak to him herself? Anyone with a brain in her head ought to have thought of that.

All too soon, the mail truck gained on her. She shouted and waved, but he only tooted the horn as he passed and left great clouds of dust swirling in his wake.

Still, Gussie pressed forward. Daddy might take to jawing before Mr. Wexler handed off their letters.

But alas. She was within shouting distance of their front porch, had she the breath for it, when Mr. Wexler passed a fistful of envelopes into Eloise's waiting hands.

Momentum carried Gussie another few steps as her sister examined the letters, then set her dark eyes on Gussie, a mean little smile playing at her lips.

She was too late.

⁓

Thursday, May 8, 1919

Come Thursday night, the Engelwoods' Buick bumped over the countryside, practically spilling over with bodies. Gussie had made the mistake of telling Daddy about the rally, and he'd invited himself and Eloise along. To Gussie—wedged in the back seat between her sister and Mrs. Engelwood—the whole ordeal felt like a punishment.

"Mark my words, son," Daddy shouted over the Buick's growling motor. "This economy will crumble like ash. Too much labor flooding the market."

What a thing to say, and in front of Mrs. Engelwood. Harvey's mother stiffened beside her, and the car's vibrations agitated all the more in the stifling lull.

"Begging your pardon, sir, but they are men, not beasts of burden." Harvey maintained his grip on the steering wheel. His peaked knuckles stood out more sharply than the mountains' gentle ridges. "The *Rockingham Register* ran some letters recently. By all accounts, the Boys are wild to get home."

How like Harvey to smooth over the flap so easily. Gussie exhaled lightly. "I hope Captain Millard has good news." Of course, she mainly wanted to hear about one particular soldier.

As Gussie's heart warmed, Eloise raised her pointy chin. "I'm surprised Philip didn't guess at their return in his letter."

"Well, he didn't," she muttered. Must Eloise dredge up the letter at *every* opportunity?

"Doesn't it seem odd for him to be as ignorant as we are?"

"Not if it's a secret." A secret, why? She chewed her lip and tossed out her first thought. "Because of spies."

"Here we go. The pretty one versus the smart one." Daddy's jovial attitude had returned. "Care to pick the winner, Harvey?"

"I could never," he said. "Both of the Misses Rice possess such beauty and wits, I'd never know whom I'd chosen."

Gussie folded her hands and stared at them. Even she realized Harvey's answer was as generous as it was untrue.

Daddy roared with laughter. "You ought to head for the capitol and be a diplomat, my boy. You'll be wasted at seminary."

Money, war, and the whiff of politics. All topics better left to those with the brains for them. At least Philip needn't worry over finding a job. He'd always worked in his father's grocery.

A deep rut in the dirt road jolted the car, tossing everyone inside forward and back. "Is everybody all right?" Harvey called out.

"Best get used to it. The Valley Turnpike Company's selling out to the Commonwealth." Daddy waved an arm out the window. "They'll tax us for roads that never reach us and washed-out horse-cart paths like this one."

"At least we shall soon have more taxpayers 'flooding the market.'" Mrs. Engelwood spoke at last, slowly and loud as Daddy.

For a long moment, the discussion gave way to the din of the

Buick's motor, and from her vantage point, Gussie observed Daddy's reddened cheek.

"Indeed," he said at last. "Why, I might bring on a man myself. Once the Register runs these testimonials, I'll have more business than I know what to do with."

Mrs. Engelwood raised her chin. "I suggest minding it."

Mercifully, the attempts at conversation concluded as the outline of Harrisonburg appeared over the hill.

~~~

Twin bay doors stood open to welcome them to Fire Station One on Water Street, and the scent of manure from the stable across the street shooed them inside. Friends and neighbors traded scuttlebutt and admired the fire engine's gleaming knobs and rivets and impressive four-foot wheels. Around the hall, fire hoses, ladders, and equipment Gussie couldn't name had been stacked to the side to make room for chairs, long benches, and overturned pails, all facing the back, where two stacked pallets formed a makeshift platform. Behind it hung the blue-and-orange banner with the department's emblem and the words WELCOME FIREMEN emblazoned in yellow.

Daddy, Eloise, and Mrs. Engelwood dispersed among the crowd, but Gussie stuck close to Harvey as the two looked for a spot. As usual, Mrs. Engelwood had barely a word for her, but asking Harvey what she'd done to offend his mother seemed unlikely to help matters.

He pointed toward the platform. "I see an open bench up front." By the time they reached it, they had to ask the Trammel sisters and one of the Marsdon boys to let them squeeze in. As long as she didn't miss a word once Captain Millard stood to speak, that suited Gussie fine.

"This is perfect." Harvey gestured to the bench and she settled herself, then he sat tall and stiff beside her. He often seemed on edge these days. She squeezed his forearm. "I imagine they'll start before long."

The Trammels turned to her. Marian and Leona were a few years younger than Gussie, and she'd never quite worked out which sister was which. "Have you joined a committee yet?" the older one asked.

"The hospital fundraiser committee is taking volunteers," the younger added.

The two possessed plenty of zeal. The crowded bench felt even smaller.

"I'm not a Red Cross member." Gussie tried to make this sound like her own choice, but the attempt backfired.

"Whyever not?" Maybe-Marian demanded. "The war may be over, but the work sure isn't."

Gussie folded her hands and lowered her chin. "I'll wait until the Boys come back, then find out where I'm needed."

"That's not smart," Likely-Leona said. "The plum spots will be gone."

"If they're not already," Marian added. "Besides, some of the wounded are already here."

Since when? "Where did you hear that?" Gussie asked.

Leona rolled her eyes. "Through the hospital fundraiser committee. It's why Rockingham Memorial is so crowded."

"How else do you think people stay in the know?" Marian jutted her chin.

"And support our Boys, besides."

"No soldier worth his salt will want a shirker on her duff for a wife."

The two might have continued the dual offensive all night had Gerald Millard not rung the fire bell and stepped onto the platform. "Good evening, folks. I understand some of you want to know where our Boys are."

The room shook. Gussie clapped and stomped along with the rest.

"The latest from General Pershing tells us the Eightieth Division will set sail by midmonth, and the first few units are already on their way."

Her breath caught. On the way? After all this waiting, was it possible mere days remained?

From there, Captain Millard's words came as if through an echoing corridor. "Served with honor . . . Our turn to make sacrifices."

Were the Trammel girls right? She'd never understood Daddy's stance on service clubs, and her cheeks burned as she considered her inaction. What if Philip returned asking what *she'd* done for the World War?

"Red Cross volunteers are going around. Let's show the Blue Ridge Division we're proud of them."

Someone set "When the Boys Come Home" spinning on the Edison. The tune never failed to raise goosebumps. Gussie swallowed the lump in her throat as she turned to Harvey. "Have you thought about any of this?"

"Not beyond Mother's involvement." He spoke with a note of apology as if aware of how much she depended on his opinions. "It's why we bought the Buick."

She eyed the volunteers who roved the hall. Moments ago she'd been blissfully ignorant of "plum spots" or less desirable counterparts. Pressure mounted to choose before only dregs were left.

"We have room on the Ladies Auxiliary committee." Mrs. Marsdon approached and held out a clipboard. "Print your name there at the bottom, sweetie."

"But I'm not a Red Cross member."

"I can collect your subscription fee. Just two dollars for the whole year."

Gussie glanced at Harvey, helpless. In spite of Daddy's boasts, the seven dimes and four quarters in her coin purse had to last until his next triumph.

His eyes were understanding as he reached for his wallet. "Mrs. Marsdon, I believe my renewal is due. No sense asking you to make change." He held out a fiver. "Here's for myself and Miss Augusta, and call the balance a donation."

"Oh, Harvey. You've always been a good boy." Mrs. Marsdon scribbled a note on her clipboard. "All right, young lady. Can we count on your help?"

Yet again, she turned to Harvey. "Do you think it's a good spot for me?"

"I do." His cheeks reddened. "That is, Mother is the chair. She'll be pleased to have you."

Suppressing a sigh, Gussie added her name.

Captain Millard returned to the platform and raised his voice over the din. "That's the spirit. Let's have some fun before we put you to work." He chuckled and light laughter echoed back.

Cheers rose when the familiar notes of a Nora Bayes tune trumpeted over the air. Some of the old folks' faces paled when the assembly lifted the refrain: "How ya gonna keep 'em down on the farm, after they've seen Paree . . ."

Gussie added her voice to the crowd. Maybe Philip wouldn't want to stay and work for his father. Well, that was fine. She'd follow him anywhere.

As the song entered the bridge, she forgot the lyrics and sneaked a glance at Harvey. When their eyes met, he grinned and shrugged. He'd lost the words too, and for some reason, it struck her as awfully funny. She caught a case of the giggles, and it must have been contagious, because soon he was laughing along with her.

When the Engelwoods took them home, playful tunes still tickled Gussie's ears, and she hummed as she waved goodbye. She'd asked them in for refreshments, of course, and they politely declined. Exactly what she'd serve if they ever accepted was a problem for another day.

Daddy retreated to his study to prepare for his trip in the morning, and Eloise sprawled on Mama's fancy fainting couch like a damsel. How weren't they exhilarated with the evening's events, the exciting news?

Gussie sashayed through the front sitting room and sang like Mama would have done. When Gussie and Ellie were just moppets in plaits and matching homemade dresses, Mama would make up silly songs about them, and their home always brimmed with laughter. As much as she missed Mama, she missed "Ellie" too. Her sister insisted on her given name now.

Eloise favored their mother in umber hair, dark eyes, and a narrow face sporting perhaps more pinch at the lips. Gussie took after no one particular with her combination of Daddy's fair hair, light-brown eyes fringed with long lashes, and a nose that both grandmothers had tried to claim. Yet if Gussie could reflect a glimmer of Mama's knack for raising people's spirits, she'd consider that resemblance enough.

"Aren't you the merry miss?" Eloise propped her elbow on the arm of the couch. "I guess you enjoyed yourself."

Her singsong taunt raked Gussie's nerves. "Didn't you?"

"How could I, with my dear sister making a dolt of herself?" She narrowed her eyes. "Fawning over one fella and stepping out with another."

Gussie frowned. "Don't be dippy. You know I've been waiting for Philip for almost two years."

"Good." She stood and smoothed her dress, a drab taffeta that wouldn't suffer from a scrap of lace. "Then you won't mind leaving Harvey for me, like table scraps for a hungry dog."

Pins and needles prickled the back of Gussie's neck. "I didn't know you cared for him."

Eloise fluttered her eyelashes. "A girl has to think of her future, and he did give me a brilliant idea." She produced a familiar envelope and crushed it to her heart. "Everyone loves hearing from the Boys. A real sin to keep this beautiful note from the newspaper, don't you think?"

She whipped out the letter and read aloud. "'To the dearest and best girl in all the world—'"

Gussie tried to snatch it away but missed. "That letter is private."

"Indeed." Eloise fanned herself with the envelope. "So private, not even its author has seen it, unless Philip's penmanship closely resembles that of a certain simp right here in Cross Keys."

"Yes. I wrote it." Gussie's face flamed. "I missed him enough to pretend. Are you happy?"

"Not yet." Her sister's face pinched in victory. "But I have just the solution."

Her shoulders sagged. "Ellie."

Eloise tucked the letter in her sleeve. "You promise to stop distracting Harvey, and I'll promise to keep this safe for you."

Gussie spun on her heel and flew up the staircase. Her sister's rude laugh chased her until she threw the bedroom door shut.

Her heart pounded. What a fix. Harvey was her best friend. And even if she could turn her back on him, what about her commitment to the Red Cross? The Ladies Auxiliary group met every Monday in the Engelwoods' drawing room. If she reneged and Philip found out, it'd be worse than if she'd never signed up.

Foolish tears welled up. Gussie peered out the window, but the Buick had long since receded from view. The truth was, in countless daydreams of her own romance, she'd never considered that her sister might have designs on anyone. Especially not Harvey.

Twelve

Monday, May 12, 1919

The Engelwoods' tastefully appointed drawing room featured walls papered in a smart Imperial Artichoke pattern, an impressive mahogany settee with paws carved into the feet, and a gleaming piano with a stoic white bust atop the case.

The arrangement did not feature a surplus of elbow room.

The need for surgical dressings remained urgent, so Gussie attempted to knit on the piano bench between Mrs. Trammel and Mrs. Marsdon. Their needles clacked, putting her slow stitches to shame. The women chatted back and forth as if Gussie weren't there, and the two of them knew everything about everything, from the latest on the Valley Turnpike Company to the price of cantaloupe.

"It's high at Marcus Mercantile," Mrs. Trammel said.

"They're proud of their produce," Mrs. Marsdon agreed.

Gussie had to take their word for it. Desperate as she was for news of Philip, she wouldn't set foot in his parents' store again until Daddy paid on his account.

Days had passed without two words uttered since Eloise gave her ultimatum, though Daddy paid no heed. He returned from his business trip anxious about his newspapers and ledgers and more critical than ever of civic fervor in every form. She hadn't dared raise the ire of either, so she told Daddy she was visiting Mrs. Engelwood, and Eloise that she had a Red Cross meeting. Given the brooding silence of their household, neither would be the wiser.

"Order." The room settled at once. For a woman of few words, Mrs. Engelwood knew how to wield them. "Welcome. Secretary's report."

Gussie focused her attention as Priscilla Dade read the minutes of the previous meeting. The Ladies Auxiliary worked closely with the nursing committee and the publicity committee. Harvey, Gussie learned, participated as a nonvoting proxy member of the motor committee.

Everything hummed along until the secretary read through plans for a hospital volunteer day. Gussie eyed Mrs. Trammel, mother of Marian and Leona. The sisters did say wounded had come home early. Was there a chance, however slight, she might see Philip on a hospital jaunt?

Gussie raised a tentative hand.

"Hold questions." Mrs. Engelwood's sharp command rebuked her. "Treasurer's report."

She lowered her arm, bumping Mrs. Marsdon and making her drop a stitch in the process. What a spectacle. She felt every eye in the room.

All but Harvey's. He studiously avoided her gaze, taking great interest in Mrs. Millhouse's report and probably thinking of how sorry he was to have encouraged Gussie. These women managed homes, farms, and children alongside their husbands, with stamina left for volunteer work, besides. She didn't belong here.

"New business. We welcome new member Miss Augusta Rice." Mrs. Engelwood locked eyes with Gussie and nodded. "You raised your hand. Have you a question?"

Gussie lowered her chin. "No, ma'am. I was confused for a moment, but I'm happy to be here."

Maybe she'd panicked too soon. After all, Mrs. Engelwood had found her place in the community in spite of her thick accent and funny ways. Because of the war, Harrisonburg voted to change the name of German Street to Liberty Street last year, and ever since, mention of either name whipped people into a patriotic dither. She didn't plan to ask how Harvey's mother felt about Germany's defeat.

"Very well. Next item. Harrisonburg shall host a Home Coming Day for the returning heroes in the fall. The event—"

"In the fall? Does that mean the Boys have been delayed?" Gussie blurted. Mrs. Marsdon nudged her with a sharp elbow to the ribs.

"Order. It means, Miss Rice"—Mrs. Engelwood enunciated each syllable—"that there will be an event in the fall."

Oh, she'd done it again. Gussie resolved silence for the rest of the meeting.

Mrs. Engelwood rattled on about the plans for a banquet, parade, and block party. Most importantly, the county would host a ceremony to present every soldier, sailor, marine, and nurse of Rockingham with a medal of recognition for their service. All of this meant pressing legions of volunteers to show their gratitude. Thanks to her determined silence, Gussie was assigned to the potato-peeling committee.

Mrs. Engelwood nodded briskly. "If there is nothing further, take refreshments and reconvene at Rockingham Memorial Hospital in one hour. Bring completed surgical dressings and clothing donations. Meeting adjourned."

What?

The ladies buttoned their knitting bags and drifted toward the dining room, but Gussie remained on the bench, thoughts racing. She hadn't realized the plans were for today. Would they let her come along? She didn't know the first thing about nursing. How would she get there and home again? Dare she hope for Mrs. Engelwood to suffer her presence?

"Shall we play a send-off duet to rally the ladies?" Harvey took the spot beside her on the piano bench.

She scooted left to make more room. "I'm sure I've embarrassed myself enough for today."

"Forgive me." He fiddled with his straw hat. If he kept it up, the red-white-and-blue ribbon around the band would come loose. "I was selfish to suggest this—"

"Could Philip have been sent home wounded?" She spoke over him, then patted her lips, abashed. "Excuse me. But, could he?"

"Possibly." Harvey's long face contradicted his positive response. "You aren't obligated to visit the hospital, you know. The others pre-arranged it."

"I want to." She blanched. Was he trying to discourage her? "Unless you think I'll be in the way."

"What? Never. You'll be wonderful." Harvey turned three shades of red. "We have room."

"Perfect."

Except if Eloise found out. But she wouldn't if Gussie asked Harvey to let her out at the Baptist church on the hill and walked the rest of the way home. She didn't relish the idea of sneaking around, but her sister had done so first by stealing the letter.

Harvey stood and held out his hand like a gentleman. Gussie accepted it for the show of being assisted to her feet.

He grinned. "Do you care for some lemonade before we leave?"

No, not *like* a gentleman. He *was* a gentleman. An eligible bachelor, as her sister had gleaned, and a wealthy one at that. When Gussie married Philip and Harvey married—well, whomever—they'd no longer play duets or sit together at community sings. Their friendship would change. In any practical sense, it would end.

"Thank you. That'd be lovely."

As he escorted her to join the other ladies, she tried to imagine Eloise on his arm like this. She succeeded in picturing her sister as a mythical Siren singing sweetly until she lured him close for the kill.

She stumbled over the slight step into the kitchen. Thankfully, Harvey kept his balance and restored hers. She giggled to cover her embarrassment. "Oh, Harvey. What would I do without you?"

He murmured something unintelligible through the clink of lemonade glasses and small talk and excused himself to ready the Buick. Mrs. Dade dipped out a glass of lemonade for Gussie with a murmured warning. "Sweetened with a wartime measure, dear. This stuff is where those temperance gals get their pursed lips."

Gussie nodded blankly, not taking her meaning but not wanting to ask either. She rejoined Mrs. Trammel and Mrs. Marsdon's conversation as a silent spectator, sipping lemonade so tart she didn't know whether her teeth were the nails or the chalkboard.

Thirteen

Gussie and the rest in the Engelwoods' carload arrived at the brick hospital on South Mason Street some minutes after the other ladies. As the group entered the foyer, Mrs. Trammel and Mrs. Marsdon filed out of the washroom in bleached and starched volunteer pinnies, looking as neat and professional as the regular nurses. Gussie fell in step behind Mrs. Dade and the others, but eager as she was to see Philip, she somehow ended up the last one to secure a mobcap to her chignon.

Well, never mind. Her reflection was quite the picture. The hot, bumpy car ride had put her favorite ratiné dress in a perfect wrinkle, but the crisp white apron she slipped over it helped enormously. Now, to give her pale cheeks a quick pinch and secure that loose tendril—

"Augusta." Mrs. Engelwood blocked the door. "This is not a place for foolishness."

"Yes, ma'am." She dropped a hairpin. It skittered across the washroom's tile floor. "I am a bit nervous."

"Simply be pleasant and follow instructions. No one expects you to know everything."

Gussie nodded and tucked the wisp of hair. Mrs. Engelwood's stark words cut with a familiar edge. People often found the younger Rice sister pleasant, but no one ever expected "the pretty one" to know anything at all.

She followed Mrs. Engelwood back to the foyer and through heavy double doors. The ward was as long as the school gymnasium, but narrower, and lined with two rows of beds with white wooden frames and tiny rollers on the legs. Daylight streamed through the windows, and electric sconces hung over every headboard. The high ceiling magnified the noise of jabber, wailing, and upon their entrance, catcalls. The ladies from the meeting conferred with a nurse. Before Gussie could join them, they scattered like the dancers in the Christmas ballet she'd seen at the high school last year, breaking in unison and dispersing across the great hall.

Maybe she ought to shadow one of them. She was about to suggest it when Mrs. Engelwood turned to face her.

"The cabinet behind Nurse Metzgar's desk holds a box of postcards." She pointed toward a small desk beside the entrance. "Retrieve so many as you will need for this ward. Greet each man politely and collect what letters he has ready to send. Offer him a blank postcard, but if he acts unbecomingly toward you or does not answer, apologize for the bother and move on. Keep your speech soft and gracious. If you finish before our time fills, ask Nurse Metzgar how you can assist her." Mrs. Engelwood nodded toward a fray of white-capped women who swarmed like bees. "Are you understanding?"

Gussie's head swam. She backed up a step.

A harsh male voice barked behind her. "Watch out!"

She stopped short. A doctor and the undertaker, Albert Fischer, wheeled a gurney carrying a figure beneath a bloodstained sheet.

She clapped her hand over her mouth, but the men paid her no mind once the threat of collision was averted.

Mrs. Engelwood's eyes followed the cart some distance before locking Gussie's once more. "*Nei*, this is too much for you. Wait in the foyer."

Like a shirker on her duff.

Picturing the Trammel sisters feeding her to the gossip mill set her heart thudding, but another memory soothed and persuaded her.

You'll be wonderful.

Gussie starched her spine. "I want to help."

Mrs. Engelwood's nostrils flared briefly. "Very well. You have your assignment."

Gussie nodded curtly and swiveled toward the desk. Her assignment, yes. But death had visited this place today. As if postcards could stand against it.

She opened the cabinet and a heavy book caught her eye: *Index of Patient Records, Vol. 1, A–M*. It looked out of place, but never mind. The box of postcards lay open beside it. She grabbed a fistful, closed the cabinet, and approached the first bed in the first row. According to his chart, the patient was twenty-two-year-old Jack Stebbins from Elkton.

"Hello, Mr. S-Stebbins." She stuttered over her greeting. The man had thick bandages over his eyes. "Have you any letters to send to-day?"

He stirred at the sound of his name. "Do I look like I been writin' letters, sweetheart?"

Did the remark qualify as "unbecoming"? She wasn't sure. "Who would you write to if you could?"

He wasn't going to answer. Flummoxed by her very first charge. "Mr. Stebbins?"

"My girl." His voice cracked. "Minnie."

Gussie checked the drawer of his wicker nightstand and found a pencil inside. She applied her best penmanship to the postcard at the top of the stack. *Dear Minny.* "And what would you say to her?"

His chest convulsed. Could those bandaged eyes make tears? "Nothin'. It's too late."

"Nonsense. If she's been waiting like the rest of us, it's high time she heard something."

His jaw worked as he steadied his breathing. "I'd tell her I sure miss her and to go find a fella who can see 'cuz I ain't goin' home like this."

The words broke Gussie's heart to write, but she recorded them nonetheless. "Say, that wasn't too hard. I've put it on a postcard for you. Will you sign it yourself?"

"I can't."

"Sure, you can." She placed the pencil in his hand and guided him to the blank bottom of the note. His roughened knuckles bore old scars. Farmer's hands. He'd have a time finding work. "There. Write your name. That's it."

She coaxed Minnie's surname and town address for the rural free delivery service out of him, then chirped in her brightest voice. "Turns

97

out you have mail to send after all. I'll see it goes out."

Jack Stebbins nodded and turned his face away. The lump in her throat only loosened when she moved on to the next bed.

Nothing hindered Myers Flannigan's eyesight. He whistled and leered as she approached. Even with his leg plastered past the knee, his coarse bearing angled toward threatening. "Hello, kitten. Have I been waiting for you."

She tightened her lips. "Outgoing mail, Mr. Flannigan?" That fulfilled her instructions in the fewest words possible.

A sneer twisted his face. "Another cold fish. What you need is—"

"Apologies for disturbing you." She moved to her next patient, ignoring the filthy talk spewing to the back of her head. "Good afternoon, Mr. Winsell. Oh, look at you. Three letters, ready to go. Do you need any postcards?"

As she continued down the row, her pulse quickened with every introduction and thudded in guilty relief every time Philip did not greet her. In all the months of pining, none of this had ever entered her head. To think she hoped he got an early reprieve. Until today, injury meant inconvenience, a little pain, and perhaps a trip to the doctor. Of course, some soldiers died at war, like Harvey's brother, but she'd never thought of those who survived. Burns, amputations, disfigurements. What if he returned blind, lame, or scarred? She ought to love him regardless, but well, what if she didn't?

As her collection of letters grew, so did her pride and affection for these dear men. In spite of a few lechers like Flannigan, most of them starved for a sweet word. One fella proposed. She giggled, blushed, and gave him an extra postcard to cover her impression he wasn't kidding.

The last patient in the ward had his eyes closed, so she spoke softly. "Mr. Locke?"

He sat straight up. "Sir, we're outnumbered. What'll we—" Stephen Locke took in his surroundings with wild eyes.

Gussie shrank back. "I'm sorry. I didn't mean to startle you."

"Don't apologize." He wiped his face. "You knocked me out of one humdinger of a nightmare. Is it chow time already?"

"Not yet." No matter their schedule, it wouldn't be long. The brilliant gold of afternoon poured in from the western windows. "I'm collecting letters for the mail."

"Oh." Stephen cracked his neck to one side. "I meant to write my ma. Will you come around tomorrow?"

She glanced back down the row. There could be, by tomorrow, dozens of postcards to send. "I'm afraid not, but I'm sure Nurse Metzgar will assign someone else. Here's a postcard."

"No, thanks." Stephen gestured toward the wicker stand between his bed and the next. "I got some paper."

Gussie wagged her finger in jest. "Then you'd better send your ma a nice long letter."

"I will." A lazy grin spread over his face. "I'll tell her about a pretty girl I met while I was laid up."

Always *the pretty one.* She scarcely kept from cringing. "I'll bet she'd rather hear about you," she said gently. "I hope you feel better real soon, Mr. Locke."

Nurse Metzgar wore a different pinafore than the others, but her air of authority truly set her apart. Gussie struggled to catch her attention. "Ma'am? I've finished gathering the mail. What else can I—"

"Fine." Her lined face and raspy voice effused a harried efficacy. "Drop it in the basket on the corner of the desk in the front."

She nodded and did as the head nurse asked. A small handful of blank postcards remained, so she placed them back in the box on the cabinet shelf.

The large patient record book caught her eye again. What if it held answers to her questions?

Her conscience protested, but her heart had the stronger argument. How many soldiers had she just encouraged to send word home? All because she knew firsthand how wretched the waiting was.

She glanced up. The other volunteers were beginning to deliver supper trays. The opportunity inched away like the long afternoon sunbeams.

What did it hurt to flip to the *M* section in the back and peruse the list? She searched for his name and nonetheless gasped when she found it.

Marcus, P. L., 80th Inf. Admitted Mch 10, '19. Discharged Mch 12,

99

'19. Transferred to Byberry. File 59, Box 8.

She closed the book and replaced it carefully, ignoring the prickling sensation that unfurled over her skin. The single line entry revealed one thing. Not the location of Box 8 or what Byberry meant. Only that Philip had been back from France since March or longer, and she'd never known.

Dazed, she sought a place among the other volunteers, but she only got in the way. Mrs. Trammel especially seemed not to want her help. She approached Mrs. Engelwood again. "Ma'am? Should I wait outside?" Oh, she hated the sound of defeat in her voice.

"You may." But Mrs. Engelwood held her gaze for a few seconds and seemed to make a decision. She brought out a slender hardback volume from her skirt pocket and waved it toward a man who had not responded to Gussie's coaxing. "But if you wish, take this and read to Lieutenant Jansen. He's catatonic. Perhaps it will help."

Gussie didn't see how, but she accepted the offered book and hurried to the chair by the officer's bedside. "Hello again, sir."

Though his eyes were open, the lieutenant was far away from the commotion around him. She pressed her lips together and thumbed the pages. A book of plays? Well, she'd take the distraction.

In the section called *Hedda Gabler*, she skipped the list of characters, setting, and stage directions and went straight to the dialogue. "'Upon my word, I don't believe they are stirring yet.'"

Lieutenant Jansen dramatized the line perfectly.

After a few pages, Mrs. Engelwood startled her from behind. "Augusta, come. It is time to leave."

Gussie nearly dropped the book. "Already?"

"Yes. We must get you home before dusk."

"Of course." Reluctantly, she closed the book and patted the man's hand. "Get well soon, Lieutenant."

Mrs. Engelwood herded them to the washroom, where they returned the borrowed aprons and caps and scrubbed their hands. By the time they met Harvey on the side street designated for private cars, Gussie's stomach burned and her brain beat with a clandestine cadence. *March, Byberry. Byberry, March.*

She'd been better off before, innocent and ignorant. Now she was no better than Eloise, snooping to find what wasn't hers to know. The thought sank her spirits.

As Harvey helped the other women into the Buick, Mrs. Engelwood leaned forward. "Well done, Augusta."

She blushed, not least because Harvey glanced up with an expression both bright and open. She didn't deserve a speck of admiration, not from either of them. "Thank you. I'd like to help again."

"We go every Monday." Mrs. Engelwood left no room for discussion.

They finished climbing aboard the auto. The other ladies swapped stories and nudged Gussie into sharing her "proposal," but the loud engine made it easy to slip out of the conversation and become lost in her thoughts. She passed most of the ride watching the buildings grow farther apart and the distant mountains darken.

Here came the trick. If Eloise found out about the volunteer shifts, she'd send the humiliating letter to the newspaper that very hour. Gussie had no options other than to find either the letter—as if Eloise would be so careless—or Philip himself. Surely the newspaper had no use for it once he returned.

Above all else, then, she must discover what Byberry meant.

Gussie lifted her head, suddenly aware of how close they were to home. "Harvey? Let me out at the church, please. I can walk the rest of the way."

"Nonsense." He shouted to make himself heard over the engine. "We'll see you straight to your doorstep, safe and sound."

"But—of course. Thank you." Senseless to argue as they rolled past the little churchyard. Within minutes, the Engelwoods' car coughed to a rest outside her home, and thoughts of stealing into the house unnoticed fled away.

In one of the front-porch rockers, with a book in her hands and eyes fixed like a bird of prey, sat Eloise.

Fourteen

Solveig.

Kyle blinked heavily. He didn't know that word.

A void let him slip and dropped him . . . where? Someplace cold. Cold and dark. Something hard jabbed him in the back, and his head burned. A whiff of warmth dodged and flitted. Faint and sweet, but he couldn't name it.

"Thank God." A murmuring presence lingered nearby. An angel with an accent. "Kyle? Kyle, wake up."

"Ahm awah." His voice came out mushy. The angel tucked a roll of fabric under his head. "Ow."

She shined a light into his eyes, one and the other, and then disappeared, taking the summery scent with her and leaving spots in his vision. He groaned and struggled. His *head.*

Soft sloshes glugged. She returned and brushed an icy cloth over his face. The cold jolted his senses, and he moaned as she raked the crown of his head. "I'm sorry. I'm being as gentle as I can. You're a hardheaded one, aren't you? First at the cemetery, and now this."

"Don't wanna go to the cemetery."

"We're not." She took the cloth from his head and inspected it. Golden threads glimmered under the flashlight. "The bleeding has slowed, but you need to listen."

At first, the water on his face bothered him, but now it felt nice. He closed his eyes.

She stopped dabbing. "Wake up. Eyes on me. Tell me your name."

Okay. This was a hard one. "David."

A pause. "No."

Oh. His other name. "Kyle."

Her caresses to his face resumed. "And what is my name?"

That word. He did know it. He knew *her.* "You're Solveig."

The furrow between her brows eased but didn't disappear. "You hit your head. We have to get to a hospital."

That got his attention. "Don't tell Patterson I'm there," he slurred. "Promise."

She took his hand in both of hers and patted it firmly. "I promise. Now look at me."

He thought he was looking. "'Kay."

"Kyle. Focus. Hold it together."

For her, he strained to think through the haze. Not all the pieces fit, but he knew for sure Solveig was important. "We're in a cave."

"A cavern, yes."

"We're looking for a . . . a wall."

"We found it."

She looked pleased with the effort, so he searched for more details. "You're pretty."

A sheen lit her eyes. "Sweet of you to say, but we're still going to the hospital."

That sounded hard. This cave—cavern—seemed all right. The rock in his back was okay. And his angel showed up. Must be time to go.

"Kyle. Wake up." Her voice anchored him against the drift. "You cannot go to sleep. Put it out of your mind."

Aw. He made her mad. Again? Yeah, because she was mad before. That wasn't good. "I'm tired."

"I know. Just keep talking with me." She moved away again. This time he tracked with her, rolling his head slowly. She was crouched low, rummaging through a white plastic box. The first aid kit. That probably meant bad news. "Can you believe we found Harvey?"

"Who?"

"Harvey Engelwood. We found him."

His head swam as she chattered on. Hard to follow. She kept quizzing him to make sure he was listening. He bluffed his way through by repeating back her last three or four words, but as the fog started to break up, she sprang another toughie. "What do you think we should do about him?"

"Do about . . . Harvey?" Okay. Concentrate. He could make an intelligent response if he tried. "Ask him if he needs a ride to the hospital."

She giggled. The sound tugged his heart. "It's a bit late for him." She laid the wet cloth across his head. "Oh, I'm terrible. I'll leave the wisecracking to y—wait, what are you doing?"

He struggled to sit. Nausea toyed with him like a bored cat with a dead bug. "Trying to keep up."

Solveig helped him lean into the cavern wall. The sore spot in his back remained, but it didn't much compete with the top of his head. He touched under the cloth lightly. His fingers came away tinged, although she'd stemmed the bleeding for the most part. "What happened?"

"I ran." She dropped her eyes and he wanted to touch her arm, but then he'd smear his blood on her. Not that she wasn't up to her elbows in it already. "Harvey startled me. I screamed, and you came after me, or tried to. But you plowed into a stone arch." She pointed. "I found you here."

His temples pounded. He groaned. "Genius."

"I'm sorry."

Patchy bits of memory began to knit together, itching like a scab. "No, I'm sorry. I made you mad."

She didn't speak right away. "You touched my scar."

"Didn't mean to. I was aiming for your lips." He winced. Too much.

She smiled and dabbed the corner of her eye with her sleeve. "You sound more like yourself, at least. Think you can walk?"

The pounding intensified. "Where's the fire?"

"There's no signal down here to call an ambulance. I'm worried about you."

"I'm okay. You go and I'll catch up."

"No. You'll go to sleep."

"I promise I won't."

"Kyle." She looked straight into his eyes. Hers were large and scared. "Do you want to end up like the skeleton?"

Water or blood trickled behind his ear. His arm felt heavy as he reached to wipe it away. "What skeleton?"

"Harvey. I found his bones." She grabbed his boot and jostled his leg back and forth. "I know you're tired and confused, but if I have to drag you by your feet, I'm not leaving you here like this."

A hard chill ran over his skin. Keith should have had someone to drag him by his feet. "I wish you met my brother," he murmured. His eyelids drooped.

She shook his shoulder. That scent wafted close again, and suddenly he recognized it. Pears. "Hey. Kyle, stay with me."

He nodded. Even the minor movement reverberated through his skull. "Yeah. Good idea."

Fifteen

"I'm fine." Kyle's protest barely rose over the din of sirens and diesel and EMTs' reassuring instructions. "Toss me a couple aspirin, and it'll be like it never happened."

Solveig didn't hear whether Sean responded. She was too busy with Mea, who insisted on a thorough scrub and antiseptic wash for her hands and arms. At first she thought this was a kindness, but then Mea lowered her voice.

"Have you and your boyfriend already discussed—"

Solveig twisted her hands. "Oh, he's not my—"

"I see." Mea veered easily. "Here's what we'll do. Sean's going to ask him some questions, including whether he will consent to a blood test. If he does, that will tell us whether we need to treat you for blood-borne pathogens. If not, we'll follow the protocol to be on the safe side. Immediate treatment reduces the odds of infection dramatically, so stay calm. Can you do that for me?"

Solveig nodded dumbly, but her thoughts ran wild and the abrasions on her hands stung afresh. Blood exposure. Of course.

Sean's confidential tone got lost in the road noise, but Kyle didn't modulate as well as the EMT. She caught fragments of his answers. "Not lately . . . Not sure . . . Well, yeah."

Solveig stopped listening, instead imagining her own line of questions. *Mr. Benton, in your studied opinion, what* is *the best place for sinning? Do you actually have any inhibitions for alcohol to lower? And as for all the women you've surely charmed, have you been safe with at least half of them?*

Her cheeks burned. That was none of her business, and unfair, too, considering her sad romantic history. She pressed her hand to the side of her neck. The acerbic light inside the ambulance left her nowhere to hide.

Not since her sentencing had she been so scared.

A radio crackled, and she let its noise distract her toxic thoughts. Easier to cast blame at him for recklessness than to admit her own, but she tried to do the right thing. To protect the people she cared for—and she did care for Kyle. Same as she had cared for Heather. Jonathan. Reeve. And when had it ever mattered?

Never. I have always had blood on my hands. It's been waiting for me all this time.

～～

As soon as the ambulance arrived at Rockingham Memorial Hospital, the EMTs whisked Kyle to another part of the ER and shuffled Solveig into a hard-backed chair in the hallway. Not the general waiting room, but not an exam room either. "Sit tight," Mea said, "and let the ER nurses tell you what's what." That was a nice way to put it.

Gurneys rolled past. People in scrubs and stethoscopes went in and out of rooms, drawing curtains and pushing them aside. An overhead monitor showed partial names and statuses. *BENTK 0407 — SPARRO*, it read. Beneath that, *BORJS 1007 — PENDING*.

One thousand seven? No—ten seven, October 7. She looked again. That meant his birthday was April 7, exactly six months from hers. It would have been nice to discover that fun fact the normal way. She fussed with her cuticles. The antiseptic wash left her skin papery.

She prayed in Norwegian for the sake of her concentration. Otherwise, her thoughts looped back to poetry and portals, secrets and real life. As if there were anything to discuss. She couldn't fall for a man who lived six thousand kilometers from her doorstep. Full stop.

And there, the loop began anew. Finally, she heard her name.

"Miss Borja?" Solveig jumped up. A petite woman in blue scrubs and a red lanyard approached with a clipboard. "I've got discharge paperwork for you."

Every muscle in her body turned to gelatin. *"Pris Herren,"* she breathed. *"Takk, Jesus."*

"Lo siento, no hablo español." The woman patted her shoulder and enunciated loudly. "I'll get you some *water*. Just *sign* these for me, and you're free to *go*."

She smiled back, too relieved to bother correcting her. "Not necessary, but thanks. Here." She signed the highlighted blanks in a shaky scribble and handed the forms back. Free to go.

But also free to stay.

First things first. She found the gift shop and added a new scarf to her collection, a soft poly blend with a blue ribbon pattern which she wore to the register. Next, her logical bent took command. She organized the accumulated chaos of the last few hours and listed needs in order of importance. Food. Two rides home. A tow for Kyle's truck.

And since she was here, Bestepappa's personal items.

Warm colors and funky wall art in the hospital cafeteria created a city-café vibe, an unexpected pocket of comfort. The bistro chairs and tables lent a chic feel, and the fluorescent headache that had gathered in her temples yielded under the softer light.

The first bite of tuna melt went soul deep. The rest was okay. She ate quickly and made her calls from a quiet corner in the back. She needed to regroup. To organize broken pieces and see what fit back together. The day wasn't a total loss. Some days were, but not this one.

She squared her shoulders. Onward. To the business office.

Navigating the newly renovated campus was straightforward, as was explaining her request to the sympathetic office assistant. The manager had gone out on maternity leave the same day Bestepappa died. After a brief check in the computer system and profuse apologies, the assistant returned from the back office with a small plastic bin.

Solveig thanked her and carried it back to the waiting area. Something rattled in the bottom. Here waited another layer of grief to peel back. Best to leave it for a private moment in the pink sanctuary of her old bedroom. No reason to open it here, but even so, the hospital bustle and antiseptic smell receded as she snapped off the lid.

Except these were not Bestepappa's things.

A peach knit top. White shorts. Sandals. The paisley wristlet Bestemamma had given her when she turned twelve. She unzipped it. Inside were two petrified sticks of foil-wrapped gum and a ten-dollar bill. A small shard of glass explained the rattling. It must have shaken loose from the fabric. A leftover piece from a total loss.

Cold prickled from the top of her head down. The clothes she'd worn that night. Forgotten in storage. Flecked with blood. Waiting all this time.

Hold it together. Stay with me, now. Look at me. Eyes on me.

She replaced the lid hastily. How often she'd begged God to do the same. To box up the memories. To wipe them away.

Potpourri air freshener clouded the restroom. Solveig dumped the clothes in the trash and abandoned the wristlet on a hook in one of the stalls, with a prayer that someone who needed the ten inside would find it. The plastic bin fit under the recessed sinks. Out of sight, out of mind. She soaped her hands twice, three times. The headache from earlier was returning, and it reminded her of Kyle.

Free to go. Free to stay.

She dried her hands and tapped out a text as she started back the way she came. *I will be in the cafeteria.*

Her finger flicked Send and she regretted it immediately. The words seemed as sterile as the hospital itself. Without much thought, she softened them with another message.

Is it the future yet? Come find me.

Sixteen

Kyle stood in the doorway of the cafeteria and scanned the room, hope dimming. While weaving the corridors he'd racked his brains, or what was left of them, to recall the answering line to her *Cryoseed* reference. After the wife made him promise to find her, the botanist said—what?

But the time stamp was hours ago. Solveig must have given up on him by now.

The dinner rush was over. Empty stainless steel food bins gleamed under glass at the hot line. A refrigerator case next to the cash register housed a decent selection of salads and sandwiches, and though chatter and laughter wafted from the kitchen in the back, the dining room was a cell block for the prisoners of patients. At tables across the room, folks chained to coffee cups and cell phones waited for their verdicts.

But there. At a corner table near the commercial-grade coffee maker, Solveig dozed against the wall. The sight of her replenished his depleted stores of optimism. How did she do it? He wasn't strong, or brave, or good, but those things seemed near around her. Attainable and worth desiring.

She didn't stir, not even when he came within arm's reach. Although, that was how all this mess had started. Better keep his hands to himself. "Solveig," he called quietly.

Her head snapped up. "Oh!" She rubbed her eyes and stood. "What did they say? Are you all right?"

"Bunch of comedians back there." He prodded his scalp lightly. "Had me in stitches the whole time."

Her brow furrowed and she swatted the air, shooing the joke like a gnat. "Seriously, though?"

He shoved his hands into his jacket pockets. "Seriously, a grade-two concussion."

"How do you feel?"

He could ask her the same, except her swollen, bleary eyes pretty well answered it. "Like a mountain cracked me in the skull."

"Of course." She twisted her neck one way and the other, stretching. "The *mountain* should have been more careful."

"I hear mountains aren't too bright. They never think a-*head*."

There. A ghost of a smile on her face put one in his heart.

She met his eyes. "Minutes out of the ER and punning already."

"Looks like I'm gonna make it."

She covered a yawn, then shook her paper cup and tossed it into the trash. "Do you need to call your family? Anyone who needs to know you're okay? Or who might want to pick you up?"

"Nope." He'd already left a message with Charlie.

"Okay." She gave her phone a few taps and swipes. "Done. You'll be pleased to know I had your truck towed back to your place, and I arranged us both rides home."

"Great. Tell me what I owe you. I want to pay your cab fare too."

"Not necessary." She bit her lip. "I called Danny."

The low thrum in his skull surged. "Solveig, of all the people in the *whole world*—"

"He's one of the few on this continent I knew how to reach." She frowned. "I know you don't get on well, but—"

"No. He's one of your vandals. Not only that, he bought the eggs with CCPM money."

Her eyes widened for a moment, but then she crossed her arms. "I don't believe that. We've always been friends."

"I confronted him. He didn't deny it."

"Fantastisk." Solveig's phone dinged. She glanced at the message and rubbed her eyes. "If he also didn't confess, can we please accept the help and get out of here?"

They waited on the benches at either end of the main entrance vestibule. The stilted atmosphere was his own doing, and Kyle didn't know how to fix it. Solveig craned her neck at every pair of headlights. "He drives a white Buick Regal," he finally said.

"He told me." Had she changed her scarf since this morning? "I'm restless. I don't mean to make you nervous."

"You're not. Listen, I was out of line earlier. Thanks for all this. Calling for help. Waiting around. Not leaving me back there like I deserved."

A shudder quaked through her body. "Like Harvey," she whispered.

He squinted. "Who?"

"I told you when you woke up. Remember?" *The bones*, she mouthed, widening her eyes.

That bizarre dream really happened? "I sort of remember. Did you tell the EMTs?"

She shook her head. "We have to go back."

"Tell me you're kidding."

"Not tonight. As soon as we can, though. Augusta Rice is the key. She wrote her confession the day he vanished. If we find out what happened to her, she'll lead us to Harvey."

He lowered his voice. "Maybe just report it to the authorities and go on our merry way?"

She shook her head. "Not before I figure out why Bestepappa sent us there in the first place. Remember what Sheriff Dade said? My house is 'the old Rice place.' There must be a connection."

"Right, right." He didn't like where this was going. "This may be the head injury talking, but how do you know it's Harvey?"

"Who else?"

"Literally anyone. Solveig, we're talking about bones in a cave."

"Cavern."

"Whatever. The point is, this was someone with nowhere else to go. A prostitute. A thief." His throat tightened. "A drug dealer, maybe."

"Then I still don't want to leave them lost in the dark." Her eyes were bright with unshed tears. "Not if I can solve this mystery and bring someone home again."

Incredible. "The real mystery here is why you'd lift a finger for anyone in this town. I can tell you which one I'd raise."

Her gaze lengthened toward the parking lot. "There's Danny." She massaged her neck. "I will tell you the whole terrible story. Just say you'll help me."

Danny honked twice.

"Come on. We'll talk more later."

They stepped out of the vestibule and into the bluster. Flurries whizzed past the orange street lamps, but it wasn't snowing hard, not now. Kyle opened the rear passenger door for Solveig, partly to be a gentleman and mostly to make sure she sat beside him and not up front. Then he circled to the other side.

Of all the people whose help he didn't want, Danny Calhoun was king.

He eased into the back seat. The scent of menthol dialed up old ghosts, but he shoved them away. "Thanks for the ride, buddy. Didn't know you cared."

Danny answered to the rearview mirror. "No problem. Sorry to hear you bumped your widdle head."

Solveig leaned forward. "Thank you for coming." As she resettled and buckled up, she lobbed a warning with her eyes. Kyle winked back just to see her cheeks pink. And they did.

Danny took the speed breakers and peeled out of the parking lot as if he didn't have two ER patients riding along. At least if he drove this fast the whole way, they'd both be home that much quicker.

Solveig made a valiant attempt at small talk, but Danny didn't play along, and when the fragmented conversation lapsed, she let it. Kyle sat with his hands braced on his knees, head down and eyes closed. Cravings washed over him, worse than pain. Maybe if he thought of something else.

Yeah. Like the bones.

Temptation trawled his soul. A terrible, genius idea.

Solveig wouldn't speak to him again if she knew what entered his mind, and who'd blame her? Moments like these made him want to resurrect his alias and divorce himself from his darkness.

Was it possible, from the midst of that darkness, to lure Patterson into the light?

A hard right jarred his neck, and he groaned. Solveig brushed his hand. "Still okay?" she whispered.

He turned to her. "Hanging on by a Percocet." He kept his voice low and tapped his ear, questioning. She nodded. Good. He was loud enough. "Don't know about you, but I want a do-over for today."

She sighed. "It wasn't what we planned, but—"

Danny interrupted. "Which road to your place, Benton?"

Kyle glanced out the window to get his bearings. "Take her home first."

"I said, which road?"

Solveig bristled. "Gentlemen, please." She cut her eyes his way and gave her head an almost imperceptible shake. *Stop. Don't fight.*

He tipped forward slightly in Danny's direction. *What about him?*

From her, an exasperated face and an upturned hand. *What do you want me to do?*

Without breaking eye contact, he huffed a sigh. *Whatever you want, then.* He addressed the rearview mirror. "First right after you cross over North River."

The remaining miles passed in tense silence. Danny turned hard into the driveway, throwing gravel. The locks popped up.

"That's my cue," Kyle muttered. Solveig pled with her eyes, and they about killed him. "I'll call you in a couple days."

He escaped the car and slammed the door harder than necessary. Immediately, her door unlatched, and she chased him up the porch of his cabin. "Kyle, wait."

He jingled his keys. "Need something?"

"Oh, let's see." She counted on her fingers. "Since this morning, we flirted, danced, bickered, and split an *ambulance*, not to mention I prayed for you all day only to call your greatest nemesis for help in the end. You tell me. Was there anything we missed?"

"Guess not." There was that look again. He glanced away. "But I've got a decent excuse for selective memory. Which way do you want it to go?"

She rubbed her arms. "You didn't answer me before. Will you take me back to the cavern?"

"I'm not supposed to drive for a few days."

"When you feel up to it, then?"

"You don't need me." He glanced at the idling Buick. "Anyone can take you."

Her lower lip plumped in a pout. "But I want it to be you."

He grumbled his assent. "Well played. Bet you cheat at cards too."

She threw her arms around him. "I'm glad you're okay. When I found you . . . I would not have forgiven myself if—"

"Don't." Why did she have to feel so right? The high beams flickered pointedly and reminded him they had an audience. He gave a brief squeeze and broke the embrace. "We're all good here. And for the record, Danny's not my greatest nemesis. He'd like that too much."

"Kyle—"

"I hate saying this, but go. Before Mr. Personality leaves you here. Unless that's your endgame." He wagged his eyebrows and finally, she laughed.

"Promise you'll call me sooner than in a couple of days."

Like a gift, the *Cryoseed* line he couldn't remember to save his life an hour ago came to him. "'You'll be my first thought when I open my eyes.'"

Seventeen

As Solveig climbed back into the Buick, ingrained smoke again overwhelmed the faded pine air freshener hanging from the mirror. He threw the car into reverse before she finished buckling up.

She resisted the urge to turn and watch the cabin recede as the car pulled away. "I'm sorry to hold you up."

"No sweat." Even in the low light, Danny's scowl made his opinion clear. Where was the boy she'd once known? He'd picked up some weight, but the difference went deeper, beyond dull eyes and a hardened face. Although obviously, she had changed too. "Good to see you, Soph. It's been too long."

Solveig looked out the window, hoping he hadn't decided he wanted to talk. She had too much to think about.

My first thought when I open my eyes. Amazing how Kyle had plucked a line from a movie she found ridiculous and turned it into a valentine. Or how he tapped his ear, a small gesture that spoke volumes. Even the brief, wordless argument in the back seat had tugged the heart. Given time, the two of them could build a private lexicon of signs, quirks, and bywords. A language of their own.

She opened their growing thread of messages and started a new note.

I don't think I said thank y—

The screen went black. She held down the power button to reset it. Nothing.

She put her mobile away. Just as well. They didn't have time, and she must stop thinking as if they did.

Danny cracked his window and lit a cigarette. "The packet from your lawyer came yesterday."

Solveig tried not to squirm. The treacherous road stretched ahead. She'd called Danny a friend, but alone in the car with him, that amounted to a gross overstatement. "I feel terrible. I didn't think much beyond the quickest solution."

"You're cheating yourself, closing down. You ought to sell to me," he said. "You get a chunk of change, and I keep doing what I'm doing. Plus, the guys don't have to lose their jobs."

She stammered. "I'm sorry, Danny. Kyle had a similar idea, and—"

He blew smoke in a huff. "What's his bid?"

Her stomach flip-flopped. "He didn't offer to buy, exactly, but—"

"Did you sign anything?"

"No."

"Then we can negotiate. I figure the whole thing is worth fifty grand. I got twenty in my back pocket, and the rest is in the works. You get out clean."

Her head spun at his jargon. She had no idea what Bestepappa's company was worth and once again needed a conversion calculator to fully understand the offer, though any price bested liquidation.

Maybe this solved it. Kyle had groped for a scenario that kept him employed. Danny's version sounded more like a plan.

She bit her lip. "You'd become Kyle's boss."

He took a quick draw from the cig. "For a minute."

"Oh." Kyle's betrayed look on learning she was the trustee flashed to mind. "I'm sorry, Danny. I won't do that to him."

"You *are* doing that to him. Plus, me and fourteen other guys. But whatever. I can make Larry Tillman an offer for his smoke shop, but that won't help you." Danny ashed out the window, sending an orange trail of sparks into the wind. "Say yes, Soph. The farm won't go this easy."

The hated American nickname again. "You don't know that."

"Call it an educated guess. People don't like how y'all got that tract in the first place. But squatting was and is legal if you do it right."

"Squatting? You're implying my grandfather stole the land out from under someone?"

Another puff. The smell was nauseating. "Yep."

"And as long as you knew him, you believe he'd do a thing like that?"

He snorted. "Anyone'll do anything if they're desperate."

Her knuckles ached. She'd balled both fists so tight that bone strained flesh. "Who said he was desperate?"

"Don't be naive. Your granddad shows up from halfway around the world and nabs a lost farm property instead of buying. Something's rotten in Denmark there."

She narrowed her eyes. "Good thing *we* are Norwegian." Still, this was an idea of Bestepappa she didn't care to contemplate. He'd once joked he left Stavanger because he didn't fancy working in an oil rig. Was that true? She'd never asked. "The lawyer sent over boatloads of paperwork. He would have told me if he'd found a problem."

"Sure. Like I said, it's tough to swallow." He shrugged. "But legit."

"Then why the controversy? Who thinks they've been cheated?" She dreaded the answer.

"Amanda Marsdon, for sure," he said. "And Tillman. I've heard rumors of a Dade claim. And plenty others think that land ought to be auctioned off the courthouse steps."

"And what do you think?"

"I think Benton's working the only con that might take you in, and you should stay away from him."

She blinked, taken aback. "Really? Because he said you were part of the crew that egged my house. I told him that was impossible because you and I are friends, and I'm telling you the same."

For the first time, Danny's stone facade cracked. He tossed the cigarette out the window. "Look, you need to understand—"

She closed her eyes. "Danny. Why?"

"They were going regardless, and they needed a DD. You of all people ought to—" He cut himself off, but not soon enough.

"I of all people, what?"

"Never mind, Soph. I didn't mean it."

"Then you shouldn't have said it. Did you buy the eggs? Or rather, did I?"

"No. We did get some for an event, but we canceled and chucked them."

He gave himself away. They'd only thrown a few on the night in question. The funeral egging had been the event-level mess.

Prickly silence lengthened the remaining kilometers. Miles. Whatever.

When they arrived at the farm, she gripped the door handle. "Thanks for the ride."

"Wait." He grasped her arm. She glared at his hand until he withdrew it. "Look, I'll warn those guys off. You have my word. But think about my offer, all right? If it helps, I'll guarantee Benton three months' severance. Send him down the road happy. He doesn't like me either, in case you missed that."

"Because you're both so subtle." No use arguing, though. "I will consider it."

And she did, from the moment she exited his car until she reached the porch steps. She fumbled for her keys, then dropped them.

The front door stood open, half off its hinges.

∽

Kyle breathed the scent of home. Cedar planks and eucalyptus branches. Everything hurt, from his head to—yeah, mostly his head.

He grabbed some ramen from the cabinet and started the water boiling. Eat. Sleep. Plot Patterson's downfall. Everything in its time.

The stove clock read 9:53. His dying habit of automatically converting to mountain time twitched. It wasn't too late to place a call to Colorado.

Tiny bubbles formed at the bottom of the pot, waiting to erupt. They dared him to stand and watch.

No point running it through his scrambled hash of brains. He picked up his phone and dialed.

"Mendez."

He rolled his shoulders and mimicked the detective's terse delivery. "Benton, sir. Calling to see how our case is going."

"*We* don't have a case." Mendez muffled the phone and barked orders, then returned to the conversation. "And I don't answer to you, son."

Kyle bristled. "Look, I get that everyone thinks Keith overdosed. But he was clean. The Roberts murder has the same signature."

"Wrong. It has a couple of coincidences. The main one being proximity to you."

He stopped cold. "You don't think *I'm* the one—"

"Don't flatter yourself. You aren't smart enough to get away with murder. But listen up. I can't investigate coincidences, and I can't waste my budget chasing a bogey."

Nerves gave him cotton mouth. A side effect of guilt and painkillers. "That 'bogey' killed my brother."

"Keep going and he'll have a clear shot at you." Mendez exhaled heavily. "That's it. It's rough, but you got a second chance. Better keep your head down and make the most of it. *¿Comprendes?*"

Kyle rubbed his face. The antiseptic smell clinging to his hand almost gagged him. *"Sí, señor."*

His stomach clenched as he disconnected. He ought to ask Solveig how to say "Yes, sir" in Norwegian. The more languages he could grovel in, the better.

He twisted the dial to high and tried to think. Steam wafted up from the pot.

What if Mendez works for Patterson?

Crazy. And impossible. Mendez couldn't be dirty. If Kyle wanted to get to Patterson, he needed someone who was.

He dropped in the noodle brick and set the timer. Trevor Roberts's murder was linked to Keith's, whether Mendez agreed or not. That meant decision time.

New self and old wrestled. On the one hand, his freedom. Parole appointments, clean living, cold sheets.

He dumped in the seasoning packet.

And the other hand, justice for his brother. What did he have to lose besides his faith, his job, and his delusions about a woman who was leaving anyway?

He groaned. The day was mostly horrible, and he had the stitches and purple goose egg to prove it. But dancing with Solveig in the cavern? Holding her on the front porch in that all-too-brief embrace?

As good as it gets.

He ate, popped four Tylenol tablets, and chased them with a cupped handful of water straight from the tap. The metallic aftertaste reminded him of the water at Sterling. Showering in it, brushing his teeth. Never feeling clean. Having no right to.

His faith in Christ was supposed to make him a new man, but he didn't feel new. He felt like dirt.

He muttered a curse and stepped onto his porch, provoking a latent urge to smoke even though the physical addiction was supposedly gone. Through his sleeve, he poked his IV site from the ER. The ripening bruise responded with its predictable ache.

Pain cinched cords around Kyle's cranium. They knotted and writhed under his favorite ball cap. Pulling and raveling and tangling.

But pain brought clarity.

From behind the railing, he soaked up the stillness. The porch light glittered in the fresh snowfall. The temperature was falling, and low clouds blocked the moon. Heaven probably smelled like snow in the air all the time. Either that or pears. Someday he'd find out. Or maybe not.

Solveig had her ideas about what should happen with the bones, but so did he.

Eighteen

The wind rattled the darkened eaves of the farmhouse, drowning out any sounds from within. Not that Solveig dared trust her hearing. The intruders might still be inside.

She stood several meters off the porch, taking in the wrecked door by dim moonlight peeking through cloud cover.

Stay with me, now.

The snowstorm had erased the trail. The steps were buried under a pile of powder, and the driveway showed only Danny's tracks in and out.

She ducked around the side of the house, trusting shadows to hide her. She needed help, but who? Police, 9-1-1. The thought of blue lights reflecting off the snow made her palms sweat inside their mittens. Besides, the unfinished message to Kyle had used up her mobile. Getting into the truck to plug it in risked too much noise and made her an easy target.

Alone. Solveig shivered. Always, and now completely.

You are never alone.

The words from Bestepappa's letter were just that. Words. They didn't change the broken door or her broken family.

Let Christ be your comfort.

The wind gusted, and she shielded her face with the scarf from the hospital gift shop. He meant comfort from grief, not the biting cold and whatever might emerge from the dark. Yet which was harder to relieve?

Herre, *I need You. Please.*

The answer stirred in her soul, silent and unmistakable.

Barn.

The double meaning pressed into her heart. In English, He told her where to go. *På norsk*, He reminded her she was His child.

Far, she prayed silently, but this dual meaning provoked a pang. He was the only Father she had, and He seemed far indeed.

She shuffled across the driveway, hiding her footprints as best she could in the tire tracks. The chains over the doors were undisturbed, and padlock yielded to key. She let herself in quickly, watching over her shoulder. Too bad there was no way to lock up from inside. If the intruder checked the barn, she'd be found. *Rett og slett.*

As she reached for the flashlight on top of the workbench, the wooden doors clapped into place, and a long-ago memory verse floated forward in her mind. *For the kingdom of God is not in word, but in power.*

Power. The generator. Of course.

All she had to do was start it and flip the switch to make the house come alive. The humming fridge and whistling vents. The lamps. If this prowler was like the others, he was a coward and would run from the light.

Solveig checked the fuel gauge. A quarter tank remained. Plenty to start it, but after that?

The motor rolled over with a heavy cough, and a caged bulb overhead cut the darkness. Her heart raced as she peeked out the doors. As much as she wanted to hide, the generator was loud. Besides, if she remained in the barn, how would she know whether the plan had worked?

In the house, an upstairs window glowed. Bestepappa's bedroom. She'd hardly been in there, and never in the mornings while she ran the generator.

Never mind. She held her breath and watched the doors. The windows. The shadows.

Nothing moved. Stillness returned to her mind, her breath. She waited. Cold lengthened the minutes.

Was it safe to return to the house? No less than staying in the wind and snow. Odds were good, the prowler had come and gone. Her teeth chattered. Time to move.

"Thank You for the barn, *Far*," she whispered. "For words and for power."

She thought of keeping to the shadows, staying close to the walls, and sneaking to the back door of the house, but rejected that plan and grabbed the flashlight. Darkness was the advantage of her enemies, never hers. "Whom shall I fear?" she whispered.

She stomped through the snow. "This is my land now. Thank You, *Herre Gud*, for my inheritance." She climbed the porch steps and paused outside. A small snowdrift had gathered on the threshold of the open door. She wasn't asking Him to wave His hand over the house, but to hold hers and not leave her alone in it. With a deep breath, she stepped inside.

After days of squelching the habit, reaching for the light switch felt like reclamation. Words from Harvey's stepping stones at the cemetery returned to her, and she repeated them aloud. "The people that walked in darkness have seen a great light."

The overhead globe lit the room. Whatever she'd expected, all appeared as usual. She went to the converted study and found the open door as she'd left it, to allow the warmer air from the living room to circulate. Still, she peeked inside cautiously, then entered the room and turned on the lights.

The hastily made bed reminded her how eager she'd been to leave with Kyle for the cavern. How was that only this morning? It felt like eons ago. And how would she sleep tonight? She whispered, "You promise to give rest," and kept moving.

Turning to the hallway, she flipped the switch to the wall sconces and called into the corridor. "You make a way. You make my paths straight."

Fear bled away as she opened the mudroom's cabinets and found the antique dishes and cutlery accounted for. "You prepare a table before me in the presence of my enemies."

She checked the bathroom, determined to invite God into every part of the house. "Please give me clean hands and a pure heart."

She continued into the kitchen and turned on the lights as she thought of meals and conversations over the years when Bestepappa had so often blessed their food and prayed for God's presence at their table. "*Takk for maten, Herre.* Thank You . . . for thy words, sweeter than honey to my mouth."

Another phrase appropriated from Harvey's stepping stones. She'd carried a plagiarized faith into this battle, made from sayings and songs and other people's prayers rather than deep study of her own. What if God were not as near as He felt?

She trembled. And what if He were?

Completing the circuit, she reentered from the other side of the hall. "You are the living God." Her voice cracked. "You are the Author of my faith."

No vermin on the first floor. On the stairs, she sang the words of Psalm 121 the way Bestemamma always had. *"Jeg løfter mine øine op til fjellene—"*

Her foot slipped. Broken glass crunched beneath her boot. She grabbed the banister, wrenching her shoulder but avoiding a spill. Her heart thrummed into her ribs.

The family photo gallery lay scattered over the steps. Frames trampled. Glass cracked.

She gathered the photos carefully. Fourteen of them had hung here, images she knew by heart. One was missing. The smashed frame remained, but the portrait of her mother was gone.

She inhaled sharply, letting the cool air sting her teeth. The theft was meant to scare her, and it did, but she continued her prayer. "When I am afraid, I will put my trust in You."

She stacked the pictures at the upper landing and stomped her boots to shake loose the glass. If anyone remained in the house, the noise would have drawn them out or scared them off. She paused outside her childhood bedroom. "Give me the faith of a child," she whispered as she pushed open the door.

The room seemed as untouched as the first floor until she spied the top of her old dresser. She'd neglected it before the listing appointment, apparently. A finger had left a long trail in the dust. A mockery.

She shivered and moved on, leaving the lights burning.

The books, for all their half-packed disarray, appeared undisturbed. She entered to turn on the lamp and the overhead light. "The fear of the Lord is the beginning of wisdom."

Her limbs felt watery and weak. The last room was the master bedroom. Light shone beneath the closed door. Bestepappa had always left a light on for her. "You are the God of yesterday, today, and tomorrow," she murmured. She opened the door.

The room was still. Everything remained as it had been. She exhaled, suddenly aware of her unrealized fears. Whatever the intruder's goal, he'd completed it. "Even so, You are my refuge."

She swept the stairs and dumped the broken glass in the trash. Of everything in the house, why this portrait? She pretended the loss of it didn't bother her, but . . . "You know my heart," she whispered.

Her mother had left no memories and few possessions. Just a lot of questions and a citizenship that came in handy when Solveig needed to run. After six years in Norway, she'd come no closer to her mother than she'd been as a frightened teen in JDC.

"I want her to know what happened." The words came spilling out as she unlaced her boots and set them on a vent to dry. "I want her to hurt over it. Then I think I could let it go."

And if Solveig's story left her unaffected? If she refused to listen or to see her daughter? What if Solveig never found her? Her mother might be remarried, living abroad, or dead. Would God still be Solveig's refuge?

What if He never allowed her to wield the words she'd been saving?

She dragged herself back to the first floor bedroom, aching at her hypocrisy. The sense of holiness had already faded. She knelt by the bed and folded her hands. A posture of prayer, but He seemed to dwell in the spaces between her fingers. She'd known Him deeply in the moments she'd unclenched her fists.

"Please. Please stay." But it was only she who had fled.

Nineteen

Thursday, June 5, 1919

The days continued their irritating habit of dawning, even after "Philip's" letter appeared in print.

Gussie pedaled the whole way into town on Mama's old safety bicycle, begrudging the sun warming her skin, the breeze cooling it, and the air fresh with mown grass tickling her nose. The deep-blue mountains cosseting her home comforted her soul when she let them, but as soon as she took pleasure in them, reality shrouded her again.

Eloise had made good on her threat. The *Register* had run the letter alongside other recent missives. It stood out like a thistle in a melon patch. What a dolt, imagining a wedding tour in war-torn France or supposing Philip might pen such natter from the trenches.

He deserved honor. Instead, she'd made him a fool.

Her quest for Byberry floundered, in spite of asking several church ladies and consulting Daddy's dictionary while he was out calling door-to-door. Her plan to inquire of Nurse Metzgar dissolved once she recognized the question would reveal her snooping.

Worst of all, Eloise's ploys to endear herself to Harvey were nothing short of painful to watch. She found new motivation to attend church, and each week, she buzzed around him like a mosquito, biting him with too many compliments, and high-pitched laughter when he said anything remotely amusing. When that failed, she employed smart-sounding chatter from the business section of the newspaper and then controversial questions of the faith. If any of her tactics succeeded, that would be the one.

The paved road beginning at the city limits banished her musings and prompted more-practical thoughts. Daddy had promised to pay Mr. Marcus before catching the train for his business trip. Their pantry shelves, once lined with Mama's canned wares, stored a meager collection of store-bought tins. She and Eloise could have put up vegetables, but Daddy hadn't planted a single row of peas since Mama's death.

When she approached the familiar storefront, her heart pumped something fierce. Hopefully, Philip's parents hadn't seen the newspaper that day.

Gussie propped the bike against a streetlamp and entered the store. She breathed deeply, savoring the scent of corn husks and muscadines, sunshine and fullness. Propped on the shelves among the stacked jars and tins, signs read, Lowest prices in town!

Saying it didn't make it so. Everything was priced two to five cents higher than the nearest competitor, but Bartoo Grocery didn't extend credit.

Gussie went straight to the produce. Fresh raspberries, green beans. Cucumbers, cabbage, beets, and new potatoes. They even had asparagus tips, little tender ones like she used to snatch fresh from the gardens. After weeks of rice soup, navy beans, and wild dandelion greens, she meant to buy all she could carry.

A phlegmy cough startled her out of her scrutiny. Mr. Marcus perched on his stool. His lips disappeared under his bushy mustache, so she had to rely on his equally impressive eyebrows to read his expressions. Right now, they were drawn and bunched.

"Good afternoon, Mr. Marcus." She steadied her voice. "What a lovely selection today."

He grunted and kept his eyes pinned on her.

Rattled, Gussie turned to inspect the fish case. They had a special on trout. Her favorite. Eloise had an aversion. All the more reason to fill the icebox with it.

She put on a bright smile. "I think I can lug two pounds of trout along with all this."

Mr. Marcus didn't budge. "And how will you be paying?"

Gussie's smile faded. "On account, sir."

The caterpillar eyebrows cinched together. "These prices are cash-and-carry. Besides that, you're topped out."

She widened her eyes. "Daddy said—oh, please, Mr. Marcus, if you'd just—"

"Pardon me, Mr. Marcus." A long-familiar voice interrupted. "I'll cover Miss Rice's bill."

Gussie pivoted. "Har—ah—Mr. Engelwood. What a pleasure." Her face burned.

He inspected her order. "This won't see you through the week. Why don't you finish shopping while Mr. Marcus wraps your fish?"

"Anything else is too heavy." The groceries and his kindness were both too much to bear, but her throat tightened and kept her from saying so.

"That's easily solved if you don't mind a short stop at the train ticket office." He nodded sharply as if the matter were settled. "Mr. Marcus and I will finish our business in the meantime."

Gussie pressed her lips together and took a second pass through the store. A fruit fly buzzed by her ear, but those gorgeous vegetables were untouchable now. Nothing seemed needful enough to spend Harvey's money on. Butter? A luxury. Coffee? A waste.

She settled on dried beans, rice, and tinned meats. Provisions to carry them through this endless dry spell.

In the back corner of the store, the Marcuses kept toiletries and household items—laundry soaps and sewing notions, chintzy flatware and scandalous dice. In the middle, a dressmaker's dummy modeled a yellow silk-and-chiffon tea dress in a collarless style with a beaded bodice. The high waist featured a ruched band, and the sleeves and skirt ruffled demurely. A sheer celadon shoulder drape and a peacock-feather fan shed glamour over the ensemble.

Gussie reached to run her fingers over the magnificent gown.

"Eighteen dollars and forty-five cents." Mrs. Marcus narrowed her eyes as she swept around a crate stacked with flour sacks. "Otherwise, look, don't touch."

Gussie nearly lost her basket. "I'm sorry," she said meekly. Philip's mother used to treat her kindly. Before the letter and their increasing debt, she'd have simply asked her about Byberry.

Mrs. Marcus pursed her lips and gripped her broom. "Peacock feathers. Land's sakes. What stunt you young girls won't pull for attention."

Oh, yes. She'd seen the letter.

"Lovely chatting with you." Gussie swiveled and zipped back to the counter. Harvey and Mr. Marcus had watched the whole exchange, for one more heaping of humiliation. Her two pounds of fish waited on the counter, wrapped in newspaper.

As Mr. Marcus rang up her order, Harvey turned back to look at the dress and then at Gussie. "Do you want it?" he murmured.

"No." A bald lie, but eighteen dollars and forty-five cents bought a lot of overpriced cantaloupe. "This is already—" She choked up.

Mr. Marcus announced her total, and to her horror, Harvey counted out twice the amount. "Put the change on Mr. Rice's account, sir, in case the Misses Rice need anything else."

He thanked the Marcuses, carried her groceries, and held the door for her. He whistled a slightly off-key version of the new Arthur Fields ditty as he tied the bike to the back of the Buick and cranked the engine.

In the confines of his car, she ventured to speak. "Thank you, Harvey. You are too dear."

His Adam's apple bobbed above his starched collar. "I'd never let you or your sister go without while it's in my power to help."

Did that mean he'd noticed Eloise's attention? Was he somehow flattered by it? "How did you know I'd be here?"

"Thank Providence for that. I have a standing appointment with Mr. Marcus." He spoke over the engine, but without being carelessly loud. "They aren't pleased about the letter."

She hid her eyes. "I know."

"Gussie, what happened?"

The story came spilling out. "I wrote it as a lark. So long passed without a word, and my friends had letters from their beaux, and I wanted . . ." Oh, but the admission was mortifying. "I wanted what they had."

His cheek twitched. "You sent it to the *Register* so they would see?"

She shook her head vehemently. "Eloise got it, the day I rushed to meet Mr. Wexler. She sent it."

"But why?"

What could she say? "Jealousy." The word burst forth. "Because I'm marrying Philip. Thanks to her, his parents are cross with me, and he'll be livid whenever he comes back from Byberry."

Harvey jerked, and the Buick with him. "How do you know about that?"

She gripped the seat. "From papers I saw at the hospital. How do *you* know about it?"

"Mr. Marcus enlisted my help. Since I'm breaking his confidence discussing it with you, do handle that secret with more discretion than your forged letters."

She stiffened. "You say that as if it's my fault."

The prominent cords of his neck strained. "The argument can be made."

Was he truly angry with her? "What argument?"

"That letter was a lie, Gussie. Even if you meant only to deceive yourself."

"That's absurd," she said. "I've never told a lie in my whole life."

He cast a skeptical look her way. "Never?"

She lifted her chin. "Not once, and you ought to know. I've been in church as long as you have."

"Then perhaps you've heard all have sinned, and come short of the glory of God."

"Not me." She raised her voice to compete with the road noise. "I'm completely innocent."

This he met with a shake of the head. "You're better than me. Since breakfast today, I've lied, coveted, and wished ill on another."

She crossed her arms. "I don't believe you."

"Believe what you like."

They drove well past the courthouse in silence. Sensing the subject was closed, she nonetheless prodded. "As for your great secret, consider it safe. Byberry could be a cemetery for all I know."

The horror of her words struck her. She'd seen the undertaker at the hospital with her own eyes. Transferred to Byberry might mean exactly that.

"No." Harvey gripped the steering wheel. "It's, well, a type of hospital, up in Philadelphia."

"Philadelphia?" What sense did that make?

"Yes." He sighed. "I'm sorry for snapping at you, but you must not tell one single soul. Mr. and Mrs. Marcus are anxious over his predicament."

Questions tumbled forth. "But why is he in Philadelphia? What predicament? He must be injured, but is it very bad?"

"I can't say," he said firmly. "I'm sorry."

"We've never kept secrets before."

He took his time responding. "No, I suppose not. You've set your heart on Philip, but if you value my view, he's not the one to take you to see France."

Her face burned with the reference to her blasted letter. "I don't care about France. That's Eloise's dream. It sounded romantic."

They came to a stop at the depot. "Then where would you like to go?"

"You're changing the subject."

"Yes," he said mildly. "I am."

She flounced against the seat. "Can I send him a letter?"

"I'll trade that answer for one to my question." No longer competing with the noisy automobile, his voice was gentler as he repeated his query. "If you could go anywhere you wished, where would you choose?"

Her geography lessons were so long ago, and one place like another on Mrs. Winkhoffer's dusty globe. Blue-green for Italy, brick-red for Spain. "I don't know."

"Think on it."

He really wasn't going to answer unless she did first. Silly tears threatened. "Fine. I pick Philadelphia. If I can't send a letter, I'll send myself."

"Please don't." He exhaled heavily. "I will deliver a letter and tell him you'd appreciate a reply. That is all I'll promise."

She threw her arms around him. "You're the best, Harvey."

He stiffened without returning the embrace and disentangled himself. "Ahem. I'll be back in a trice."

In the quiet moment while he attended his errand, her mind raced with what she'd learned. Harvey thought she shouldn't pin her hopes on Philip, but he'd obviously never been in love. No request was too great. She'd already helped dozens of wounded soldiers. Whatever Philip needed, she'd pour herself into providing.

Twenty

The no-name mini-mart and gas station at the edge of Mount Crawford stocked a whole aisle of gadgets. Kyle studied the selection of prepaid phones. The lights drilled his skull.

The ER doc's prescription for "no mental heavy lifting" had sounded doable for a guy on Kyle's end of the brainiac scale. Then they filled him in on the particulars. No work. No TV. No reading. No music if it gave him a headache, which it did. He wasn't even supposed to make important decisions.

"What *can* I do?" he'd asked. "'Cause it sounds like the shorter list."

Dr. Sparro was nerdy, lanky, and around Kyle's age. The product of years of far superior choices. "Take it easy for a few days," he said. "And try not to hit your head again."

Technically, that meant no driving, but he'd go home later and it'd be all the same.

Twenty-four bucks to get connected. Chocolate milk and a bear claw rounded out his haul. He paid cash.

A short drive took him to a grocery store parking lot. The other cars gave him cover to blend in. Perfect.

Kyle swallowed his nerves. No big deal. Just getting in touch with an old friend. People without no-contact clauses in their parole conditions did it every day.

But this line, once crossed, couldn't be uncrossed.

He blocked the caller ID and dialed. The finger tapping the screen belonged to a dead man, yet there it was, attached to his hand.

A hard rock station in the background bit his ear as much as the gruff voice that answered did. "'Lo?"

His throat went dry. "Omar?"

"Who wants to know?"

Yeah, who? "It's David Kyle."

"Davey!" The music dulled a decibel or two. "Where'd you go, man?"

"Getting on my feet. Listen, I've got a forensics problem." Fingers crossed that the expanding-markets idea had panned out. "Can you get a message to Patterson?"

Omar left him dangling for a long moment. "You makin' a better offer than he did?"

Ouch. "Guess I don't have any favors to cash in."

"Nope. But hey, I'll always run my mouth for fun or profit. Might make a buck off you yet."

"Don't do me like that, buddy."

"Like what?" A door slammed, and the abrasive music ceased. "Like you did everybody else?"

"Not everybody." But if there were honor among thieves, a narc surrendered his part in it, and both of them knew it.

"Chill, man. I'm messing with you. Why don't you check with Ashleigh?" No mistaking his mocking tone.

"Better not." He forced a laugh. "If you see her, tell her I said, 'I was here.'"

A spate of keystrokes clacked. "And where's 'here?'"

"Never mind. It was a thing with us." He closed his eyes and pressed his knuckles into his forehead. Stupid, stupid. "She'll get it."

"Sure." The music returned in full force, a backdrop for a man on the move. "I gotta go. Good talking to ya, Davey."

Omar killed the call.

Kyle ached for a cigarette.

All right, new plan. Calling Omar was lazy. To bring Patterson down, he had to get with the times. After all, his parole conditions barred him from social media for a reason.

Creating his first account took two false starts, plus the extra step of creating a throwaway email to link it to, but once that was done, he was in.

In? In what? He tapped icons. This was stupid. He'd end up doing like Mendez said, bringing Patterson straight to his door. Or worse, Sheriff Dade.

The magnifying glass icon brought up a search window. He tried the old slang. *Tango and Cash.*

His screen filled with posts. Too many, too scattered. It took him ten minutes to figure out how to search locally. His hands shook as he scrolled through the nonsense.

Dance the tango and cash the check lol

His instincts stirred, and he clicked the profile. "AgentTangerine19" kept a spotty stream of updates until a month ago, mainly complaints about things that were boring—math class, his mother's SUV, the whole catalog on Netflix.

Down the feed, the posts turned into cryptic bywords. Kyle had sent a coded message or two back in the day. He didn't need to crack the code to know what it was. He keyed a message.

You selling?

He sweated. There was no explaining this away if he were caught.

The response buzzed back.

Who are you lol

Then a follow-up.

Haven't heard the word

His fingers hovered over the screen. Think like a junkie. What would Keith say if he didn't know the code?

He'd only think of his need.

Need H. You got or not?

He counted backward from one hundred with the intent to bail at zero. The answer came at thirty-eight.

Meet at RHS. One hour. Come alone.

Kyle rolled his eyes. Whatever. He got what he wanted.

Loitering at a school ranked high on his list of thou-shalt-nots. Somewhere between setting up a drug deal on social media and losing his head for a woman who lived six time zones across an ocean. Batting a thousand, as usual.

He parked in the teachers' lot and made his way toward a kid dressed in black, waiting on a bench in front of the bus lot. He was all of fifteen, trying to look tough. Kyle remembered how that look felt—the stone jaw and flint eyes it took to survive the school after he'd been suspended for fighting. All because some kid said Keith was a junkie and got the better of him because it was true.

But he figured out how to fix it. How to save his brother. And once Kyle started selling, new "friends" came out of the woodwork. It was easier to breathe for a while.

He guessed Agent Tangerine hadn't found his clientele yet.

Kyle approached cautiously, keeping his distance. A thousand ways for this to go south. The kid could be armed. He could have backup. He could try to rob Kyle or get paranoid Kyle would rob him. Anything could happen.

And if the kid ever looked up from his cell phone, it probably would.

"Hey, man," he said finally.

The kid jumped, startled.

"What's happenin'?"

He scowled. "No fair sneaking up on me."

Kyle shrugged, letting the wide-open lot answer for him. "Got my *X*?"

"You said *H*."

"Changed my mind. I sent a message."

The kid messed with his phone. "I didn't get it," he said triumphantly, as if that forced Kyle back into the original arrangement.

He felt bad for the kid but also wanted to pound some sense into him. "Let's work something out. Who's your supplier?"

"None of your business."

"Is he hiring?"

The kid smirked. "I'm all *she* needs."

"Careful mixing business and pleasure, man." That much, at least, Kyle spoke from the heart.

The kid grabbed his backpack. "Whatever. If you're not buying, I'm outta here."

A whiff of cigarette smoke brought back a trick that had fooled him once. "Hey. Buy you a carton of smokes for a name and address."

The kid made a rude gesture. "Big deal. I got some."

"How long will they last? A week?" He remembered hoarding cigarettes before he was too hooked to resist. "Look, I'm not after your market. I'm running with a different crowd, you know?"

"Yeah, the geriatric ward."

He let the remark roll off. "And I'll pay you for our little misunderstanding. What do you say?"

The kid narrowed his eyes as if he knew he was being played but wasn't sure how. "You need me to set up a meeting."

I was in this game before you were born, kid. The thought provoked a pang. "Don't worry so much. You'll get your finder's fee."

The kid clearly hadn't thought of that but liked the idea. He cracked. "Fine. The boss is Hera Wise."

Kyle affected a bored look. As if the name meant nothing. As if he didn't still have the woman's phone number in his coat pocket. "Address?"

"I pick up the junk at the old depot annex. She says there's an investor calling the shots, but I never seen him."

An investor. A magic word, or at least a familiar one. The old dog was up to the same tricks.

"That's what I needed." Kyle gave a broad smile and stuffed his fists in his pockets. "Thanks, kid."

Agent Tangerine finally stood. "Hey. What about my cigs and my money?"

Kyle's face twisted in David's old sneer. "Word of advice. If you want to be a criminal when you grow up, get used to being double-crossed."

He turned and slogged back to the truck with all the swagger he possessed. Burning the kid with a taste of this life was the most he could do. He hoped it made a difference.

The number in his pocket set his head spinning as he vacated the school property. No wonder Danny tried to hide it. Bad enough if he was buying or selling drugs. If he was peddling information, Kyle had to assume Patterson knew everything. His schedule, his address. His associates.

Solveig.

He parked at a grocery store and messaged her on his real phone. Kept it casual. She was probably fine.

Still know my own name. Happier thinking of yours, though.

Heavy clouds sat low and threatening. He waited. No response. Technology was the worst.

He called her and didn't listen through her Norwegian greeting when it rolled straight to voice mail. Without another thought, he peeled out of the lot and jetted for the farm.

The boxes and crates stood in rows in the barn, almost too organized to move again. Solveig would take a picture if she had her mobile in hand instead of this rake. It seemed better than a broom for knocking down cobwebs, though not so maneuverable in the air as on the ground.

Punchy. That's what she was. She'd given up trying to sleep and brewed coffee at four in the morning. The six o'clock pot was too strong, but no sense wasting that glorious electricity. Then the gas ran out, so she brewed the twelve-thirty pot with water heated on the camping stove, and it had been the best of the three.

Why wouldn't that cobweb hold still?

"Solveig? Knock, knock."

Startled, she whipped around, readying the rake over her shoulder like a bat. "Who's there?"

"Whoa." Kyle put up his hands. "This is one solid swing from being the worst joke I ever heard."

She lowered the rake. "What are you doing here? I didn't think I'd see you today." Her stomach twisted. Caffeine. Nerves. Misgivings.

He wore his leather coat and a baseball cap that covered his stitches. "I tried to call."

"I left my phone in the kitchen to charge."

"You're running the generator?"

"I was until the fuel ran out." The queasiness grew. "You said you weren't allowed to drive."

"I had to make sure you were all right. I was starting to think

139

Danny—"

She narrowed her eyes. "You said a few days, correct?"

"It's just a bad headache."

No. She couldn't listen to him rationalize. She charged through the barn doors and into the snow.

His boots crunched behind her. "Solveig, what's wrong?"

She pivoted. "You're lucky you didn't hurt anyone."

"I'm fine."

"No, you are not." The more he excused himself, the angrier she got. "People are killed every single day by people who say they are 'fine.' You should have known better."

"Okay." He jingled his keys. "Looks like you're good. See you when I see you, I guess." He started toward his truck.

Solveig put her hands on her hips. "Where are you going?"

He exhaled a plume of breath skyward. "Home. You're safe but mad, and I'm ready to see how much Tylenol it takes to match one good shot of whiskey since that's off the menu too."

"No. You cannot leave."

He rubbed his temples. "Why's that?"

"Because you shouldn't have driven here in the first place. You need to go inside and be still until I'm ready to look at you again."

He frowned. "You're not making a ton of sense."

She closed the distance between them and placed her hand on his face. His cheek was ruddy and ice-cold to the touch. "Why don't you understand I'm glad you are here?"

He barked a short laugh and shook his head. "Because you're yelling at me."

She turned aside, abashed. Primer-covered words still seared in her mind. *Next time you ride SHOTGUN.*

Kyle spoke into the void her silence created. "I promise to be careful. And don't argue, because my fingers are going to freeze and break off."

She backed away, her heart staggering under the break-in, the bones, the grief, the growing despair over this doomed affection. Another heavy load escaping her grip, but this time he didn't know she needed help. How could he? He'd never heard the crash that rang and buzzed in her left ear still, never seen the piercing light that tore her seams or the gray afterward, the out-of-body moment. She'd never confessed it to anyone how she remembered looking down on herself with a peculiar tsk-tsk.

The EMT shined a light in one eye and then the other, and whatever separated had rejoined enough to hear the words, as if from a great distance. "Hold it together. Stay with me, now. Look at me. Eyes on me."

Her lips moved around the memory without a sound. *Stay with me, now.*

If she said those words in just the right way, he wouldn't leave. But it wasn't fair to manipulate him. He needed to understand.

"When Danny left last night, the door was ripped off. Still is, if you'd like to see." She pointed. "They broke some glass and stole a portrait of my mother. If they wanted to scare me, it worked. I haven't slept."

He reddened and cursed. "Why didn't you tell me that? Did you call the cops this time?"

"Don't swear at me. And no, I didn't. You saw how interested they are in pranksters." Incidentals. She was buckling, but she wasn't alone.

"This isn't a prank. It's a crime. You don't deserve—"

"Three people are dead because of me." She kicked the snow from her boots. "I know exactly what I deserve."

Twenty-One

Dusk fell, and the temperature with it, but neither of them moved. The crisp air, still and reverent, held its breath. Kyle waited for Solveig to speak.

"When I was fourteen, my crush threw a bash at his house. Reeve Wilkeson. His parents were away overnight at a wedding in Charlottesville." She spoke softly, almost to herself. "I told Bestepappa I was spending the night with my best friend, Heather. It wasn't a lie, technically. She was there."

His pulse pounded.

"I'm awkward at parties. I imagine you own the room."

He shrugged in response, but she was right.

"But Reeve invited me personally." The wind gusted. It stirred the pear scent from her hair.

"Things got pretty crazy?"

An ambivalent look crossed her face. "I suppose it was all very typical. Alcohol. Drugs. Couples slipping behind closed doors."

"I've been to my share of parties like that." The stillness magnified every sound.

"I had one drink. It burned going down, and I have no idea what it was. But what a thrill. For a few minutes, I didn't care about being the too-tall girl with no mother and a name no one could pronounce. Reeve gave me my first kiss, and I could have died happy.

"A senior boy kept bothering Heather. She wanted to leave, but we both knew we'd be in trouble. Reeve offered to take her home, but I'd seen him drink so much. I said I could drive his car, supervised, of course. His friend Jonathan decided to tag along. Heather planned to tell her parents she didn't feel well and had asked Bestepappa to take her home."

"And you were fourteen."

"I thought I knew what to do. Bestepappa had started giving me driving lessons. It was the middle of the night. No traffic. And I was the soberest. Supposedly."

"One drink," he said. "You probably were."

"My only drink, ever," she countered. "I had no tolerance. No driver's license. Not even a permit. No experience on the road. No reason to think I could get behind that wheel."

Not a sound, not a breath.

"You know what happened." Her voice was dry, but her hands trembled. "I wrecked. I took a curve too fast and rolled Reeve's car. And I was the only one to walk away."

"Solveig." He struggled for words.

"It's how this happened." She touched her ear. "The hospital released me into Dade's custody. I was tried as a juvenile, so that kept my name out of the papers, at least.

"I finished high school in JDC, and when I was released, I applied to the University of Oslo. It was an easy decision." She tried for a smile. "Imagine you're eighteen, the entire town hates you, and you are already fluent in Norwegian."

Kyle didn't have to imagine it. With no more than a smattering of Spanish, disappearing to Mexico had been his one backup plan for years. "Sure. What's to decide?"

"I had to apply to retain my Norwegian citizenship, regardless." She spoke to their feet. "But there's nowhere to run from it. I've prayed a thousand times for that night to be blotted out. Living in Oslo, sometimes I forget that girl is still me. That has to be enough."

Finally, she let her eyes meet his. In them, bone-deep loneliness reached, a prisoner's outstretched arm from between iron bars. "And now you know the whole terrible story."

He shook his head. "You left out the part your grandfather remembered, about not letting the past hold you down."

"He had on rose-colored glasses concerning me."

"I don't think so. He held you up as an example for—" He stopped himself. "I mean, as someone who didn't stay down."

She dropped her eyes and didn't answer. He ached to take her hand, but held back, unsure. "Believe me, I know this feels awful. But it's not—"

But the cliché he'd been ready to toss out stuck in his throat. Why should she listen to him? Whatever comfort he offered was walled behind a confession of his own.

For a fleeting moment, he sensed an opening. A chance to speak truth and light.

And he stood frozen until it closed.

"You don't have to carry this," he finally said.

"You're right." Her voice suggested she was less persuaded than simply tired of talking about it. "Thanks for not being horrified. Or if you are, for hiding it."

Tell her, his conscience demanded. But he couldn't. Or wouldn't.

Renegade snowflakes floated to the earth. He'd said he could fix anything. One more lie in a whole blizzardful. Why not add another? "I'd do anything to make this hurt less."

"You do." She surprised him by stepping close and laying her head lightly on his shoulder. He wrapped his arms around her without thinking twice. "So just keep being wonderful until I go."

He tightened his hold. "Bank on it."

This moment tipped the scales, crossed that invisible line between might and must, budding and blooming, dark and dawn.

He loved her.

As much as that meant telling the truth, it also meant trying not to hurt her. Or so he convinced himself.

He found his voice and steadied it. "On that note. You wanted my help, but—"

"Harvey." The name came out muffled against his shoulder, and she broke the embrace before continuing. "When I think of him lying there—he deserves better than to be forgotten in a pit like that."

"Less talk about what anyone deserves." He lightened his tone. "For my sake, if no one else's. I've got some doozies."

Tell her, but the nudge was fainter this time, and easier to ignore.

"For your sake." She stifled a yawn. "I'll try the genealogical society on Tuesday."

"And if you're wrong, and it's not Harvey?"

"Then it's still someone who never made it home." She shivered. "You were right. We should have reported it already."

"If it's been a hundred years, one more night won't hurt him."

"For a hundred years, I didn't know he was there. Now that I know, I have to do something."

"Not tonight. You're cooked." He took her by the hand and led her to the door. "Go lie down."

"But—"

"Rest. If you can't sleep, close your eyes." He had a feeling she'd go out quickly once she got off her feet. "I'll secure the door before I leave."

"I told you earlier. No driving. You, mister, are stuck here."

"I don't think it's a good idea for me to stay, though." He loosed her hand gently. "Appealing as that sounds."

Emotion or cold colored her cheeks. He meant to become the sole expert on making those roses bloom. She shook her head. "I'm not teasing—"

He let a smile into his voice. "Are you sure?"

"I'm not joking, I mean." Her voice wavered. In trying to lift her spirits, he'd crossed a line. She backed away. "You shouldn't—"

"There's a long list of things I shouldn't do, Solveig." On file with the Commonwealth, no less. He studied her lips. "Let's go inside."

He followed her in. The state of the front door gave him an intense desire to smash something. Like the face of whatever punk did this.

She lingered outside the room off the hallway. "I'll feel safer if you're here."

"I will be," he said. "For a while."

The look that crossed her face was a pout if he'd ever seen one. She slipped into the room and left the door partway open. Not an invitation. Not anything. He directed his thoughts. Anywhere but the other side of that cracked door.

He built a fire, then raided Solveig's labeled boxes for leftover hardware. A new-old doorknob and matching key solved one problem.

The broken bench swing sat on a pile of crates, apparently destined for firewood. The damage was superficial, so he repaired it and hung that too. It didn't take long, and it distracted him from the guilt of the day. Not too much distraction, though. He still needed to try Hera's number before he dumped the burner.

When he couldn't find anything else to do, he listened at the door for Solveig's soft, even breaths and left the new key next to her phone. He quietly let himself out, making sure the door locked behind him. Last thing, he made a run to the gas station and bought fuel for the generator.

None of that erased the illicit device or his pseudo-drug deal or the lothario lie that he'd do anything to lighten Solveig's heartache.

Because he was making such a great show of being a good guy, he'd go home and get between those cold sheets. Better that than turn her eyes into ice by telling her the truth. Brother Mike had said he'd be a new creation, but no one who followed him through today would believe it.

Kyle shuttered the barn, then palmed his keys as he headed for his truck. Chunky flakes raced to the earth in sporadic patterns. If he were careful and quick, maybe he could walk between them and stay warm.

Twenty-Two

The kitchen chair under Solveig's feet tottered as she made yet another attempt to position a mirror over the fireplace. Ambient heat from the murmuring orange coals roasted her shins. Careful. No time for a hospital visit today.

She steadied herself, mindful of the bergamot candles and hurricane lamps full of pine cones resting on the mantel, then tried again to align the hooks and wall fasteners. This time they caught.

Things were coming together.

She lifted her fingers from the frame and studied the reflection. Two almost-matching wing chairs draped with knitted lap blankets and a Tiffany lamp on the end table stood ready for afternoon tea. Under the table, a basket of comfort classics. *Charlotte's Web. Matilda. Through the Looking-Glass and What Alice Found There.* A happy blend of childhood memories and adult aesthetics. The mirrored version, presumably free of prowlers and their vendettas, reflected a *koselig* dreamworld.

I'd live there. An errant thought, but a pleasant one. Edging back into the frame, she craned her bare neck. Her doppelgänger had the scars, too, and problems of her own.

She climbed down and dragged the chair back to the kitchen table, then circled the lower floor, preparing for another critique. She affected a nasal tone. "'That's *Ms.* VanGorden, but *buyers* call me Arngunnr the Terrible.'"

She giggled and slapped her wrist for the meanness. The agent's personality was terrible, but her advice was not, and freeing up space did enhance the farmhouse's charm. Some focused web searching had helped to pair her grandparents' orphaned belongings with various charities and ministries. The Salvation Army sent a team of volunteers to pick up the extra furniture. The women's shelter needed all the clothing, blankets, and linens she could give, and though the library system refused her offer to donate the books, the Coffeewood Correctional Center gladly accepted.

For the household items and bric-a-brac, she contracted with a consignment shop in Charlottesville. Their movers had been in and out with the first load. They'd come for the rest after the house sold. Her plan to keep what she could carry had expanded into three large boxes and two small ones. It'd cost the white out of the eye to ship them home, but then, Bestepappa had earmarked the money. Might as well use it.

One phone call, moving box, and confession at a time, the burdens were falling away.

Satisfied with her inspection, Solveig swathed herself in a fleece blanket and stepped outside. The wind was up, and she hugged the fleece closer.

She admired the porch swing for a moment and settled on its bench. Installing a new doorknob and fixing the swing had proved Kyle's handyman claims, but neither compared with the patch he placed on her heart. She flew across the Atlantic running from that night. From herself. But Kyle hadn't run.

He did, a troll inside countered. *You asked him not to leave. Begged him.*

Her fingers twisted around the taut chain bearing her weight. Yes, he went home—after hearing her out and making sure she was safe. Repairing the lock was considerate. Hanging this swing went straight toward his promise to be wonderful until she left.

But what if she stayed?

She smiled in spite of herself. He'd keep his job, and their next date didn't have to be their last. Sledding. Fondue. An open mic night, maybe. They'd let the whirlwind swirl, until . . .

She feathered icy fingers along the knots and ridges on her neck, her smile fading as Nils invaded her thoughts. In her second year at university, he had blitzed into her life during an Easter ski trip to Vestlandet. For six months they had something she assumed was special and real, but when the time seemed right to give herself to it—to him—he'd humiliated her.

She shoved the memory away. The net of hypertrophic scars across her neck, shoulder, and arm disgusted her. Why expect more of anyone else? At this point, she wouldn't know how to broach the subject with Lars if she wanted to.

Lars. Uff.

She hadn't thought of him since . . . when? She planted her foot and stilled the swing. Enough lounging. Her daydreams of staying weren't meant to be, but neither were she and Lars.

As she entered the front room, she draped the blanket back over the chair. Her mobile lay on the kitchen counter. A full charge lasted two hours or less. The conversation needed to be quick.

She retrieved Lars's contact but hesitated. Was she wrong to end it like this? Maybe. It seemed worse to leave him clueless now that she was certain, though. Since he was the gregarious social glue of their group and she the slightly strange fringe dweller, odds were good she'd lose most of their mutual friends in this divorce. Not the ties she was supposed to be cutting.

But never mind. If she overthought it, she'd chicken out. Best to dial and—

Lars answered on the first ring. *"Hallo, søta."* He sounded in high spirits. "I guess you've been busy."

"Hei, Lars." She swallowed her nerves. A megaphone and a billboard. "I'm sorry this cannot wait until I'm home, but we need to talk."

⌒⌒

The depot annex was buried in an old part of town. Kyle parked his truck up the street, as close as he dared to the building. His first stakeout. Although in a strictly legal sense, this probably qualified as stalking.

If he walked in asking to talk to Hera, the alias would melt like a snowflake on his tongue along with the information she might have. Her phone number rang twice and rolled to a recording that the user's voicemail had not been set up. Dead end.

Not a problem. He didn't need a supplier. Just a messenger. Sooner or later, someone would come or go, and Kyle would be ready. Ideally, he'd catch Danny, but he'd get photos regardless. Photos were leverage.

In the meantime, he stewed. The longer Solveig's story soaked in, the madder Kyle got. As if the accident wasn't its own punishment. Who were Danny and his goons to give her grief for it?

The phone rang and he jumped. Solveig's picture appeared on the screen. His heart raced as he grabbed the call.

"Hey. Everything okay?" He almost sounded like Mendez. Terse. Tough.

"Yes, of course," Solveig said. "Tell me I didn't wake you."

Okay, nothing like Mendez. He stifled a groan. "You didn't. I expected to hear from you later."

"Ms. VanGorden will be here shortly, so I can't talk long." Her voice softened. "But I wondered how you were feeling."

He leaned against the bench seat. She assumed he was home, following the doctor's orders and respecting her wish that he avoid driving. As long as he didn't lie outright, why disappoint her? "Stir crazy. Sore. My brain feels like cottage cheese in a Cuisinart." He prodded the injury through his hat. Plenty to say that qualified as true. "Never get stitches if you can help it. They itch like the dickens."

"I'll try to remember." The sound of her smile in the words pushed every button he had.

What a goner.

"Good that you're finally resting."

"Is it?" Another trick with the truth. He had a million of them. "I'd rather be there. The gutters need TLC, and there's a soft board off the back."

"You did all that matters." Emotion laced her words. "That's why I called. To say thank you."

She didn't mean home repairs, but he kept it light. "What did you decide about the window seals?"

"Everything is as good as it's going to get." She sounded resolved.

"And something else I need to tell you. I got another offer for the company."

He exhaled. "That's probably best. As much as I—"

"From Danny. I haven't said yes or talked to him again, but I wanted to tell you before he did."

He struggled to keep his voice neutral. "Do you think you'll accept?"

Her long silence seemed to answer for her, but she surprised him. "Not if you have a better plan," she finally said. "Tell me you do."

He wanted to. Nothing had changed at the depot annex. But as soon as it did, he'd move. And then? No guarantees. He'd have a hard time keeping hasty promises if he got arrested—or worse.

He sighed. "Take it. I've got nothing."

"Well, keep thinking."

His chest felt full to bursting.

Her tone shifted to matter-of-fact. "Ms. VanGorden scheduled an open house in two days, and I will need to disappear. *Buyers* don't like sellers 'skulking' nearby. Her word, not mine."

He laughed. "You should come over. We'll drink cocoa and figure out what's next for ol' Harvey."

"Sounds perfect." She hesitated. "Except I'm not keen after using a ride service."

He sighed. "And you don't want me to drive."

"I'm sorry, Kyle. I cannot be the cause of another tragedy."

He let silence fall, but the lapse didn't sway her.

"I get my head checked next Monday." By then she'd be gone.

"So our time together . . ."

"Has been great." He coughed. The cold and maybe more stung his throat through the lengthy pause. Not often did seven miles of rural highway and the Atlantic Ocean come to the same difference.

Finally, she spoke. "If the headache is *completely* gone."

It will be. "Yes, ma'am."

"Okay." Her tone lightened, but with an odd, apprehensive note. "Speaking of headaches, I spoke to Lars earlier."

Headache? More like whiplash. "Yeah? And how is *Larsh* today?"

"Better off, I hope. I told him how it is." She paused. "More clearly this time."

He waited for the rest, but only a slight crackle filled the silence. "You okay?"

"Yes. Grieving the friendship, but mostly relieved."

"Good." The assurance freed him to let a smile back into his voice. "Can I ask why you're telling me this?"

"Um, I wanted you to know." A shuffle in the background interrupted, followed by a clatter like she dropped the phone. "Kyle? She's here. I must run. If you want, I'll call later and tell you how it went."

"Square deal," he said, and then she was gone.

He added a verse to "Winter Rose," then cranked the truck for the heater. The smart thing was to go home, nuke some canned chili, and call it a day. A glance in the rearview mirror revealed the humble brick outline at the edge of the city. It reminded him of one of Keith's oil paintings: a city skyline viewed through binoculars that showed the faint reflection of the looker's eyes in the lenses. That one was the triumph of his first and only art show. They dubbed his debut "Back from the Brink," and at the time, it was perfect. Providential, even. That night, Kyle had taken a dozen pictures before the gallery owner quietly informed him they prohibited photography. Then he took two dozen more on the sly.

Ah, he missed his brother.

Kyle cut the engine. He wasn't leaving. Not if Hera Wise got him one inch closer to nailing Patterson.

Exhaust billowed around the side of the annex. He tensed and gripped the door release.

A scrawny guy pushed through the annex doors and strode with purpose toward the gathering cloud. He was young, late teens or early twenties. Dog collar, guyliner, combat boots.

What an idiot. At the height of his criminal career, Kyle had gotten a haircut every five weeks and worn name-brand polo shirts. This guy might as well wear a sandwich board that read, Guilty, Your Honor.

Kyle took bursts of pictures on his phone. None showed the punk's face clearly.

Too soon, he disappeared around the corner. Moments later, a hearse pulled out of the lot and zoomed up the street, out into the fog.

Great. So much for catching Danny.

Kyle pulled into the side lot to investigate the annex and spotted a red sedan parked by the dumpster.

The rust-bucket Salamander.

Kyle grabbed the notebook he kept in the glove box and scribbled a message. No point disguising his handwriting. Any expert would see through the attempt. He left the note under the windshield.

How many traffic cameras on this street? Too late to wonder. Every level he descended made the climb out steeper. Every time he took off the new and put on the old, he found the fit more comfortable and familiar.

He drove away, his stomach churning, the foolhardy message looping in his mind.

I want in. Tell Hera David Kyle has a gift for her investor.

Twenty-Three

Solveig trailed Ms. VanGorden's circuit through the house, cheeks burning. *"I wanted you to know"?* Really? How subtle and clever. A prize-winning communiqué there.

No time to dwell on it. The agent kept saying "hmm" and snapping pictures but offered no other feedback. Every dust mote missed on a thousand previous inspections stood out like glitter under strobe lights.

Once they completed the tour, Solveig planted herself in front of the fireplace, hands on her hips. "Well?"

"I'm surprised, considering the steaming pile we had before. The porch swing is a nice touch." So Ms. VanGorden *could* lower her snobby nose a millimeter or two.

Solveig exhaled and eased her bullish posture. "There are still problems, but—"

"Home warranties go a long way toward massaging a 'maybe' into a 'yes.'" The Realtor reached into her leather tote. "I can give you the name of a firm I've worked with—"

"No warranty. Local interest is greater than I first assumed, and I don't think there will be a problem to find a buyer. I want to price it at ninety-nine thousand."

She hid her shock that the agent didn't immediately reject this idea.

"Let's say one-oh-five. Gives you room to come down." The woman's demeanor transformed with talk of hard numbers. "When you say there's interest, does that mean you've received offers?"

Solveig led her to the kitchen. *Drat.* "Unfortunately, no. I've heard rumors that several others feel they have a rightful claim."

Ms. VanGorden arched one oversculpted eyebrow. "Are you telling me there's a lien on the property? Because you know the contract includes a statement guaranteeing you have the right to sell."

"As I said, it's just a rumor."

If that was Ms. VanGorden's most intimidating glare, the woman should meet Sheriff Dade.

Solveig crossed her arms. "I have a scan of the deed on my phone if you wish to see."

The pleasant mask returned. "No, thank you. We'll list it and whatever happens, happens."

Ms. VanGorden brought out page after page of tiny-print forms and agreements, summarizing with smooth phrases like "this only says" and "the important part is." Solveig half listened as a troublesome thought flitted in and out of her head.

I could stay.

In spite of the memories, the vandals. They shrank beside the fondness growing in her heart.

Once the agreements were signed, a dark thought cast a shadow. "When you show houses, do you ever feel . . . unsafe?"

"Never. Most people, I find, engage on the terms I set. For the rest, I carry pepper spray." She produced a set of keys from her suit pocket, and a black vinyl-sheathed minicannister lobbed conspicuously amid their bright jingle. "All right. You have made arrangements for yourself, correct?"

"Yes." Although the plan to visit Kyle's cabin seemed tenuous. She'd compromised on the one thing she thought she never would.

But she wanted to see him.

Ms. VanGorden tucked the signed pages into her tote. "I'll send the scans later this evening." Her smile was fairly convincing. "I suppose you won't wait up, being on Norwegian time."

"I'm adjusting rapidly. It will hurt to return home." In more ways than one. She twisted her hands. "One question. What happens if the house doesn't sell?"

Ms. VanGorden continued packing up. "Simple. We relist until it does. You pay nothing until the closing, of course, and I'm constantly working on your behalf."

"But what if, for instance, I change my mind?"

Her eyes zeroed on Solveig as if targeting. "The term of the agreement you signed is ninety days. You are at liberty to cancel with thirty days' notice, but if you sell within forty-five days after termination, I am entitled to my commission." A thin smile sharpened along with her tone. "Would you like to give your thirty days' notice now?"

Must she be so difficult? "No, no. Random worries. I was thinking how life changes"—she snapped her fingers—"*i øyeblikket.*"

In the blink of an eye. Fast as an almost kiss escaped in a haze of overthinking. Or as hazel eyes might skim the surface, darken, and dart away.

Ms. VanGorden zipped the tote and left it on the table. "I'll see that deed after all. I'd hate for anything preventable to impede our partnership."

Of course. The woman wouldn't play hazards with her time or reputation. Biting her tongue, Solveig grabbed her mobile and navigated to Mr. Forrester's email.

She opened the file and enlarged it, holding it out for Ms. Van-Gorden's benefit. "Here shows the address and description. Below is the part showing my grandfather as the legal owner. At the bottom, the signature of the last seller. No liens. Nothing—"

Her mouth went dry at the signature. With the flowing penmanship of a bygone era, the previous owner had signed away his interests in the property, but Bestepappa had never seen fit to mention he purchased the land from Harvey Engelwood himself.

How is that possible?

Solveig stole a glance at the transfer date, and tremors frosted her spine. It *wasn't* possible. The supposed sale had occurred in 1971, more than fifty years after Harvey's famous disappearance.

"Ahem." She found her voice and stowed the mobile before the agent could spot the fraud. "Nothing out of joint."

Twenty-Four

Wednesday, June 25, 1919

Hadn't the flies of Rockingham County any business besides buzzing Gussie's face? She'd left the back door open to air the blazing kitchen, but even covered, the honeycomb on the sideboard drew pests in droves.

She tossed her head to shoo them and kneaded dough. Eloise begged off her turn to cook with a headache that didn't stop her from lolling over some novel all day. Daddy closed himself off in his study. When the house got quiet like this, Mama had set a record on the phonograph or plunked ragtime tunes on the piano with more enthusiasm than skill. Daddy had banished both the piano and phonograph to the barn, but Gussie hummed that catchy Arthur Fields song with Mama in her heart. *Oh, bring back those wonderful days.*

Wonderful days, before the Great War or the Spanish Flu, when love and laughter had filled their home and keeping up with her lessons was the worst of her troubles. Then came the fever. Endless doses of Tillman's Miracle Elixir. She'd emerged from delirium to learn Mama had succumbed.

Daddy's voice boomed from the front room, and Gussie winced. "Harvey, come in. Thanks for coming. Care for a cigar?"

He always refused. Why did Daddy keep offering?

Never mind. She covered her dough for the rise and wiped her hands. There were a few sugar cookies held over from last week, but no coffee to go with them.

"Say, I haven't thanked you for stepping in at Marcus's shop. Our Gussie, confused as usual. No concept of the value of a dollar."

She stilled. When was she confused? About their grocery account? The air thickened with Daddy's cigar. Harvey stifled a cough. "My pleasure, sir. I'd hoped to speak to you about Miss Augusta."

"No need, young man." Daddy's mirth ebbed, though not completely. "As I recall, you declared your intentions toward my daughter three years ago, when you saw fit to carve them into the wall of my barn."

His . . . intentions? Gussie's heart galloped as she slipped from the kitchen to the hallway, where she stood a better chance of eavesdropping undetected. A dreadful silence stretched out.

"Ah. Yes, sir," Harvey said.

"I well remember being your age, smitten with a pretty face. Sometimes more than one." He laughed. "But listen here. A brainy fella like yourself needs a woman sharp enough to be an asset. Gussie may be easy on the eyes, but she'll never be half as clever as Eloise."

Gussie cringed. Of course, the tired jab was true, but must everything come down to the shape of one's face or the contents of her skull?

"Your daughters excel in their respective charms, Mr. Rice. I'd never wish to prevent either from attaining the fullest measure of happiness."

Through a long pause, the reeking cigar fog grew heavier. "You're cut out for preaching, boy. You turn a pretty phrase." The friendly note had evaporated from Daddy's voice. "Let me put it to you straight. My one aim is to marry these girls off before the likes of Lou Marcus or Joe Tillman can put me in the poorhouse."

Gussie leaned into the paneling. Daddy could lose their home? Why? How?

For his part, Harvey sounded as stunned as she felt. "What can I do, sir?"

"Nothing, I'm afraid. The taxes on that worthless mountain tract will bankrupt me before I find some fool to buy it. Unless I sell a whopping lot of Miracle Elixir this fall, we're done for."

Harvey coughed again. "But if your debts were paid, there'd be no need to rush the Misses Rice into marriages."

"The bills pile up, regardless, son. In another six months, we'll be right back here." He broke off briefly. "If I had a living relative, I'd sign over the house to keep it in the family and get it back when the economy turns around. But never mind. These days, you can't trust anybody, family or not."

"I don't wish to presume, Mr. Rice." Harvey spoke in the careful, slightly overloud manner he'd lately adopted for serious conversations with older men. "And I'm honored you consider me worthy of the elder Miss Rice, but if I might help secure the lesser treasure of your home for *all* your family's benefit—"

"Brilliant, Harvey. I knew I liked you." The floors groaned as the men stood, and Gussie froze. Should she hide in the mudroom or keep still and wait?

"You and your mother should join us on the Fourth of July. We'll eat a fine meal, sign the papers, and head to Harrisonburg in time for the fireworks. And who knows? It may be that you and Ellie take a shine to each other after all."

Another long pause. "I'll pray about it."

The sound of the front door opening signaled her chance. She slipped back into the kitchen and through the open back door to circle the house.

After hiding in the dark hallway, the brightness overwhelmed, but she had to catch Harvey before he left. Her ears burned with what she'd heard. Business and taxes and land and marriages—and bad blood between Daddy and Mr. Marcus putting a crimp in her plans to marry Philip—all paled beside the one thing that changed everything.

Intentions.

Gussie dodged the mud by the downspout and listened for voices. All clear. She peeked. Harvey had parked in front of the barn, and he was already halfway to the Buick.

She waved and hurried toward him, not wanting to call out and catch Daddy's ear. He favored her with a broad grin.

"Gussie, I hadn't realized you were home. Your father had some business to discuss, but I have news for you, and a small token as well."

Her breath hitched. "What news? Is Philip back?"

"Ah, no." He hesitated slightly. "But Mother says Lieutenant Jansen is improving."

"That's wonderful!" Her heart leaped in spite of everything. "You'd never believe it if you'd seen how lost he looked. How did they help him?"

"*They* didn't. It was you, Gussie. Visiting him, talking, and reading that play."

"Hogwash." She dropped her gaze. "He never knew I was there."

"Tell that to his nurses. For three days he's been clamoring for *Hedda Gabler*." His voice gentled. "You don't know what a balm your presence is."

Like Mama. The unstated comparison raised tears, and Gussie fought to squelch them.

She affected a light tone. "As for *Hedda Gabler*, I hardly know what I'm reading."

"No favorite of mine, for all her conniving," Harvey said. "But if you've brought her character to life and convinced Lieutenant Jansen to return to us, who am I to gainsay? All glory to God."

"Amen," Gussie murmured. A gust of wind set the weathervane atop the barn turning, and for a moment, all angles squared. Daddy's business woes and Eloise's schemes and Harvey's "intentions." Anyone needing a husband by fall could do very much worse than marrying her best friend.

Then a blade of grass tickled her leg, and when she shifted, the sun's glare reflected in the Buick's mirror, blinding her. What about Philip? For pity's sake, what kind of girl waited through a whole war only to give up on her sweetheart while he languished in a faraway hospital? Though not so far that he couldn't return any day. "I'm glad he's on the mend. Please thank your mother for me."

"I will." He cleared his throat, cheeks reddening, and retrieved a slim volume from his suit pocket. "In the meantime, your gift."

He passed her the book. The clothbound cover bore gleaming foil-stamped lettering. "*Sweet to the Soul and Health to the Bones: Re-*

flections on the Proverbs, by Harvey Engelwood," she read. "Oh, how marvelous."

"My copies arrived from New York this morning, and I wanted you to have the first." His laugh sounded self-conscious. "Probably not as entertaining as Ibsen, but I hope you like it."

"I'm sure I will." She gingerly lifted the front cover, and he reached out to stop her.

"It's inscribed to you," he said, his color deepening further. "But don't read it in front of me."

"Whyever not?"

"I can't stay. Mother and I are going for portraits today."

"You need a posy for your lapel."

He glanced down. "But I—" A crushed bit of green and white flitted to the earth. "Oh, brother."

"Never mind." She stooped, intending to pick a perky daisy from the yard, but a broad four-leaf clover caught her eye. She plucked it instead, knotted the stem, and tucked it into the buttonhole. "There. For luck."

"And mercy when luck fails." He took a step back and doffed his hat, awkward and charming. "Always a pleasure, Gussie."

She dipped her chin but didn't retreat as he cranked the Buick and started the engine, nor as he tooted the horn and drove away.

Gussie let herself into the barn, not caring that the bread resting on the counter would end up small and dense or that bits of flour dried into her cuticles. She found the plank Harvey had defaced with their initials, and traced the letters—*HE + AR*—and the lopsided oval. Had he started a heart, then decided that was too bold?

Yes, that sounded like Harvey. How brilliant of her to piece it together. Only a few years too late.

But she must have misunderstood. Confused, as always. The carving and the overheard chat couldn't mean what they seemed to. For if so—if Harvey indeed had *intentions* toward her, for years now—then she was more dull-witted than she could bear.

She sat at the forgotten piano for some minutes with Harvey's book in her hands, willing her wild heartbeat to slow and collecting her courage to read his inscription.

Dearest Gussie,

You possess more gifts and graces than you know, and for that, you are far lovelier than anyone suspects.

Always,

Harvey Engelwood

Proverbs 17:22

She'd have to look up the verse later, but she reflected on his assertion until a tear escaped. She closed the book. Always "the pretty one." Even to Harvey.

Not to Lieutenant Jansen, though. Not to blind Jack Stebbins, who got a visit from Minnie as a result of his postcard and was happy as a lark when last she'd seen him.

Gussie rose from the bench, avoiding the carved initials as she straightened her skirt. The light had lengthened enough to remind her she had a meal to prepare. And then? Well, she'd better turn her attention toward her dearest and best patient. There were boatloads to do with any hope for a fall wedding.

Let alone two.

Twenty-Five

In spite of her pounding temples, Gussie smiled as she set a vase of wildflowers on the table. Everything looked perfect. Fried chicken, black-eyed peas, buttermilk biscuits, string beans, cornbread pudding, and individual congealed salads made in Jiffy-Jell fluted molds. And of course, the apple cake. If that didn't win Eloise a husband, nothing would.

Her sister paraded into the kitchen, but in an instant, her shoulders dropped. She too had prepared, coaxing her limp locks into a loose figure eight twist and stealing Gussie's prettiest lace shirtwaist to pair with a plain taffeta skirt. Her gaze swept the array of food, and she scowled. "Showing off for Harvey, I see."

For a moment, Gussie reconsidered her plan. What point was there if her sister insisted on imagining the worst?

But Daddy was right. Eloise had the brains to be a boon to Harvey, and he had the heart to soften hers. They just needed a nudge.

A firm rapping dismissed her doubts. "There they are. Will you get the door?"

Without waiting for a reply, she raced upstairs to blot the shine from her face and exchange her smock for a blue-striped middy. Once presentable, she listened for Eloise's muffled voice, then checked behind a framed watercolor of daisies. Both letters remained safely tucked away.

Gussie leaned against the wall and let her breath escape. Harvey had hand-delivered the first letter the day after his strange appointment with Daddy. "See that this one doesn't go to the *Register*," he said with a wink. He refused her questions and left in a rush, whistling.

The single typewritten page set her middle aflutter. Odd to imagine Philip typing from a hospital corridor like the one at Rockingham Memorial, but nonetheless. The letter was sweet and earnest, and if the lines about gazelles and pomegranates were somewhat oblique, the straightforward declaration had unveiled them.

I have always loved you, Gussie. For all the times I've wished to tell you, this letter is a poor substitute. Call me a coward for leaving these bold words unsigned, yet you deserve to hear them spoken, and I selfishly long to hear them returned.

The next letter had come through the post. Handwritten, signed, and ardent, if not as tender as the first. Still, every thought of the letters made the waiting more unbearable. Philip's words tickled the loose curlicues at her nape as she dreamed through her days.

She returned to the first floor to find Daddy pumping Harvey's hand while Eloise and Mrs. Engelwood searched for pleasantries to exchange.

Oh, that was mean. But true.

Harvey inhaled deeply. "Everything smells terrific. Thanks for inviting us, Mr. Rice."

Gussie fairly threw herself into the mix. "Can you believe what a job Eloise did?"

Her sister's surprised expression might give away the game, so Gussie redoubled her praise. "She's a marvelous cook anyway, but here she's outdone herself."

"That's my girl." Daddy puffed his chest as if *he'd* cooked the meal. "Shall we?"

Though her bleating conscience rivaled the headache while she served plates, Gussie justified herself with the true part. When Eloise did cook, she never plodded over the steps, double- and triple-check-ing measurements and ingredients. Her meals came out quicker than Gussie's and better too.

After a short and rather glib blessing, Daddy let loose a tirade about his testimonials over the polite clink of china and silver. "Buried on page seven with the updates from the do-gooder clubs," he groused. "No one reads that tripe."

Gussie hid a blush with a long sip of her tea. The Red Cross often published recognition for its volunteers, and Gussie's, Harvey's, and Mrs. Engelwood's names had appeared on the same page with Daddy's advert. Apparently, he hadn't noticed.

She attempted to smooth the wrinkle from the conversation. "I thought the testimonial was perfect, Daddy. It fit right in with the regular news."

Philip was listed on page three, of course, along with the other shareholders of the Valley Turnpike Company. Once he cashed them in, those ten shares would start their life together.

Eloise swooped in. "Never mind the newspaper. The best reading in the house is your book, Harvey. I've only started it, though. Gussie's been hoarding it."

Because he gave it to me. Gussie bit back the quip. Eloise had absconded with the volume, but how tempting to mention the dime novels and worn copy of *Les Liasisons dangereuses* parked on top of Harvey's study of the Proverbs on her nightstand.

"You're too kind." Harvey cut into a piece of fried chicken. "All glory to God for letting me write it."

His placid response convicted her. She had meant to help Eloise, not shame her.

She turned a smile toward Harvey and gave the conversation a nudge. "Leave room for dessert. Eloise made apple cake. Your recipe, in fact, Mrs. Engelwood. You must have given it to Mama."

She nodded, suspicion lining her face.

Harvey lit up, though. "Did you know that is my favorite confection?"

Gussie did, but he'd directed the question to Eloise. She lowered her lashes and giggled. Good. Best if she let the cake speak for her.

After dessert and coffee, Daddy pushed away from the table. "Well done, Eloise. Harvey, let's you and I have a cigar while the girls tidy up."

Eloise patted her hair. "Since I cooked everything, you won't mind cleaning up, will you, Gussie?"

"Of course," she muttered. But if her sister had caught on to the ploy, that surely meant Gussie's part was done. As she rose to collect the plates, she massaged her temples. "Daddy, I feel a touch of headache. May I be excused from going to see the fireworks?"

"Take a dose of Tillman's Miracle Elixir, and you'll be right as rain." He tossed the prescription over his shoulder as he herded Harvey away.

As the men retreated and Eloise flounced to her leisure in the parlor, Mrs. Engelwood folded her napkin. "Hedda Gabler comes to a bad end, Augusta. Do you model yourself after her meddlesome ways?" The heavy pronunciation of her Christian name sounded like a warning.

"I don't understand."

"Ibsen's play. It is arrogance and vanity to try to design another's fate." She spoke under her breath, low enough that Eloise wouldn't overhear. "Whether by pistol or apple cake."

Her face grew hot. Everyone had figured her out. "Yes, ma'am."

The older woman's hard expression eased as she rose to help clear the table. "Very well, then."

They had finished the dishes when the muffled sound of Daddy's boisterous laugh carried from behind the closed door of his study. Alongside it, fainter, came Harvey's cough.

Cigars were lit—so, the deal was done.

⌒⌒

Long, perfect rays splayed over the mountains and onto the courthouse lawn. In these golden hours before the fireworks started, a cappella crooners belted out patriotic songs, and suffragists hawked their pamphlets. People milled around the square in Harrisonburg, picnicking and tossing boomerangs and playing games of horseshoes and badminton. Gussie longed for the joy of it to land on her, but it flitted past, a butterfly with a path of its own.

"They're lining up a shooting competition behind the tannery." Daddy clapped Harvey on the back. "Up for a challenge, son?"

Harvey righted himself. "I'll defer, Mr. Rice. I'm no crack shot, I'm afraid." A tight expression undercut the polite words.

"Suit yourself." Daddy barreled into a crowd of good old boys, probably more interested in talking up his miracle drug than whatever prize they offered the winner.

Gussie's heart ached. Wouldn't Philip love to enter a shooting contest. The second letter had made a point of mentioning that the hospital took away his gun.

As soon as Daddy's back turned, Eloise perked up. "I'm glad you decided to stay with us, Harvey. I've been wanting to ask your thoughts on predestination."

His eyebrows raised and lips parted, but his mother interrupted. "Come, Eloise. You and I will discuss it. I have business with the tailor on Liberty Street."

Trapped in her own snare, Eloise trailed Mrs. Engelwood, leaving Gussie and Harvey in the idyllic brouhaha of the town square.

He shook his head and offered his arm. For the smallest moment, she hesitated, and the pinch in his brow said he noticed. "Is your headache much improved?"

"Not really." Tension pressed the edge of pain. "I'm sure the excitement will distract me."

"Let's go see the new soda parlor, and whether a root beer float won't put it to rights." He directed them away from the square. "We'll be back this way long before Mother and Eloise return."

"She has her hopes pinned on you." She spoke in a rush and stared straight ahead to avoid taking in his reaction.

"I know."

"I'm sorry I didn't tell you before."

"Your father thinks we're a match." They walked in step across Elizabeth Street. When she stole a glance at Harvey, his expression was troubled. "What do you think?" he asked.

"Me?" she squeaked. "Mercy, Harvey. That's not for me to say."

"You've asked my opinion on decisions of every stripe," he countered. "I cannot approach this one without yours."

Sweat tickled at her collar. "You should pray, of course."

"I have. When I searched the Scripture, my Bible fell open to say: A virtuous woman is a crown to her husband: but she that maketh ashamed is as rottenness in his bones." He coughed lightly, his face reddening. "After all my studying, the spine is cracked in the Proverbs. But I do wonder if that was God's answer."

"You've never once suggested I pick a verse at random as a guide."

As they neared the soda parlor, a few strapping men in shirtsleeves crowded outside the storefront, passing matches and cigarettes among themselves. They possessed the easy vigor she'd seen in other returned heroes. Philip deserved to be among them, celebrating freedom and victory.

"And besides that," she added, "when did she shame you?"

"She hasn't." In the distance behind them, a bullhorn garbled that the shooting competition was about to begin. "I don't yet understand, but—"

He broke off as his mother and Eloise approached from the opposite direction. Her sister tossed up her hand, fingers wide apart, illustrating some argued point. Both women looked exasperated. They must have cut their walk short to be headed this way so soon.

The bullhorn blared again, and a dozen shots cracked. From there, everything happened in a blur.

One of the men in front of the soda fountain dropped his burning cigarette. Panic contorted his face. "Take cover!"

Eloise swiveled her head toward him. Mrs. Engelwood fell back a step, eyes wide.

"Get down!" The man threw himself at Eloise. They fell over the curb and into the path of an approaching roadster.

"Help!" Her shriek rose above the clacking engine's roar.

The panicking motorist shouted vulgarities.

Harvey dropped Gussie's arm and plowed forward. He yanked the man to his feet and sent him stumbling into a gas streetlamp.

The man threw a wild fist. It knocked Harvey's straw boater into the wind as he scrambled to pull Eloise to safety.

The other men caught their friend by the arms and restrained him. "Vince, get a hold of yourself."

The roadster crushed Harvey's hat as it rolled by.

Vince's friends led him away. He cast a backward glance, his dark eyes darting everywhere. "The guns . . . I thought . . . the Germans . . ."

Harvey had his arms around Eloise, and she hung on him like a ragdoll.

When Mrs. Engelwood rushed to his side, he patted her hand and shook his head. As he caught his breath, she faced Eloise. "Do you need a doctor?"

Gussie stood with her mouth agape. Her sister's hiccuping reply and Harvey's low, raspy response escaped her hearing, but there was no missing the tears shining in both their eyes.

Twenty-Six

July 13, 1919

Dearest Gussie,

I gladly received your charming letter of the 5th inst.

Indeed, I knew a Vince "over there." He died with half my unit at Meuse-Argonne. We were sitting in rifle pits, waiting for relief from the 5th Division. The Germans saw movement through the timber and rained fury on us. A nightmare. I remember nothing of my escape. Perhaps this is the nightmare and I am still there, underground. You'll be disappointed, Darling, but sentiment for the 4th of July fled when "bombs bursting in air" began cracking over the treetops, indistinguishable from bombs bursting in trenches.

How lucky for your sister Saint Harvey happened to be standing by.

Write again soon. Until then, I am,

Truly yours,

Philip

—

July 27, 1919

My own dearest Gussie,

You paint such a pastoral scene of domestic life, yet one that reads to me as a page ripped from another man's diary. I can't let myself think of the Home Coming Day. I have no part in a hero's welcome, nor any home to return to.

The nights pass in fits, cold sweats, and increasingly, restraints. Dr. Hermann has twice placed me in isolation. Too often have I wandered from dormitory to battle, descended from laudanum dreams into terrors of being buried alive.

Our pharmacist knows nothing of the elixir you mentioned. He says if it's a "miracle" I want, to get religion. Of course, Harvey is hard on that case.

Your letters sustain me. Write soon.

Yours faithfully, I am,

Philip

—

Aug. 18, 1919

Gussie—

Forgive my last letter. I didn't intend to frighten you.

How shall I explain? Dreams of home drove me through those months in France. Not the roof overhead but those gathered under it. Not the bread eaten but the hands breaking it. Not the pillow where I'd rest my head but the breath tickling my neck in the night.

Instead, I am here at the behest of a father ashamed of his son, but never mind, darling girl. My home shall be where you are. The whole quarrel is a waste of ink and more than your pretty head needs to bear.

Speaking of wasted ink, I can do without updates on Engelwood's every inspired word. The sooner he's off to Richmond, the better. Perhaps if we're lucky, he'll drag your sister along. It is true harrowing events bind souls as little else can.

For your sake, I've marked the date of the Home Coming Day. Escape is simple in itself, but then comes the trick. I shall need a traveling suit, cash, and my pistol.

Sincerely yours,

Philip

—

Sept. 12, 1919

My sweet Gussie—I beg you to write. I wither and die without you.

Yours in agony—Philip

—

Sept. 26, 1919

Darling—that's a splendid idea—Philip

⁀⌒⌒⌒

Tuesday, September 30, 1919

"Gussie, that's an awful idea."

The music of tea spoons and china tinkled throughout the Engelwoods' parlor, but Harvey's discreet manner offered no song for eavesdroppers.

Today the Ladies Auxiliary settled its preparations for the Home Coming Day. Harvey came for the weekend to help with the plans, and he'd return for the festivities and to accept his brother's medal. Far from the ideal time to make her request, but Gussie didn't expect another chance. Besides, the letters had her thoroughly convinced. Philip wasn't a bit well. He needed her.

"Don't sugarcoat it, of course." She stuck out her lower lip. Yet it felt good to talk to him. From the terrible incident on Independence Day until the start of his university term in Richmond, he'd called on Eloise every week. They went twice to the New Virginia Theatre to look at the pictures. If jealousy bobbed in Gussie's heart, she only dunked it down and tried to be happy. Everyone had hoped for exactly this outcome, hadn't they? But she missed her friend.

Even though he was being a pig-headed oaf at the moment.

"Be reasonable, Gussie. How do you intend to get to the wretched place?"

"By the Chesapeake Western."

He huffed a mirthless laugh. "Certainly. The short line to Elkton, then the afternoon parlor car to Hagerstown, *then* a sleeper car to Philadelphia *via* Harrisburg, *then* hiring a car to finish the trek. You realize this is a two-day trip at minimum."

Her resolve tottered. She admired suffragists who toured the nation making speeches, but Gussie had seldom traveled and certainly didn't know how to buy a train ticket. "You're trying to scare me."

"Because you're courting disaster. Literally." He lowered his voice. "And not to be crass, but how will you afford this excursion?"

Ah. Clever Harvey. "I thought if you might spare it—"

"No." His jaw hardened. "I won't finance your ruin."

She withdrew. Heat rose up her neck. "Don't you care? I think he despairs of his life."

A momentary lull lifted her comment above the din. Priscilla Dade and a few ladies with her gave curious glances, then returned to their conversation.

Wasn't that the natural impulse? To look away? She didn't blame them, but trembled when Harvey refused to meet her eyes. "Mr. Marcus says he is improving."

"I say he is not." Her heart thudded. She didn't dare admit the accumulated letters stirred doubts into her dreams. "You once told me I have 'many gifts and graces.'"

"Gussie—"

"Did you mean it?"

The color drained from his face. "Yes, but—"

"Then help me."

He swirled his lemonade as if that might abate its bite. "I am helping you. Eventually, you'll see that."

Her lips tightened. "You'd do this for Eloise."

She may as well have slapped him. Blotches rose from his neck. "No. Not least because Eloise would never ask."

She shoved her lemonade glass into his hand. "Excuse me." The room's Imperial Artichoke pattern, with regal lines and color reminiscent of Harvey's wealth, left her dizzy and ill.

She would find another way.

*

Friday, October 3, 1919

Though the sun brightened the town square this morning, the

crisp air nettled Gussie's nape. Already the organizers prepared for the Home Coming Day, washing windows and constructing the platform on the courthouse grounds, but she wasn't volunteering, not today. She'd wheedled Mr. Wexler for a ride to town in his mail truck and sent with him a sealed letter, special delivery. When she returned, Harvey would be angry, disappointed, and waiting on the platform when her train met the station. Of that she had no doubt.

Now she stood outside Marcus Mercantile and rehearsed her request one final time like a character in a play. If she delivered the lines perfectly, the scene would unfold as it must.

A cowbell clanked her arrival. Gussie bypassed the merchandise and approached the counter. The beautiful dress had disappeared months earlier, of course. Today the dummy modeled a tricotine suit.

Mr. Marcus claimed his perch on the stool and regarded her with twitchy brows. His specs slid down his nose, and a pencil rested behind his ear, secured in the wiry hairs sticking out around it.

She dipped her chin. "Good afternoon, Mr. Marcus. Fine weather, don't you say?"

"Fine year for aphids, you mean." He crossed his arms. "Can I help you?"

So much for pleasantries. "I hope so," she said brightly. "May I ask where our account with you stands?"

She held her breath. Harvey had continued to fund their groceries, and she'd tried to be careful.

Mr. Marcus heaved a sigh and opened his record book. He felt around until he laid hold of a pencil, seeming to have forgotten the one he had stowed. The silence stretched and stewed as he flipped pages, followed columns, and finally located a balance.

"Twelve seventy." He closed the book. "Will that be all?"

Gussie's heart thudded. Everything hinged on her next few words. She offered her prettiest smile, rested her hands on the counter, and spoke as sweetly as she knew how. "That's keen. I'd like to withdraw the balance, if you please."

The ever-present glower deepened. "I look like a bank to you?"

Her smile faltered. "No, sir. I merely hoped to apply the funds to other obligations." Somewhere between truth and a lie. She did feel an obligation to Philip. One she dared not mention to her future father-in-law.

Her hands went cold. Oh dear. There was a thought she hadn't considered before.

"Tillman, the gas company, Woolworth's—take your pick, eh?" He punched keys on the register, and the drawer flew open. "Don't come in next week looking for credit, hear?"

She nodded quickly, eyes on the bills and coins he counted out before her. As she tucked the money into her coin pouch and thanked Mr. Marcus, a weight settled in her chest. Without his knowledge, Harvey had paid her way after all.

Well, never mind. She had money for the train ticket. In two days, she'd see her darling Philip at last.

Twenty-Seven

The local genealogical society headquartered in a historic home at the edge of Harrisonburg's residential section. Its scalloped shingles and yellow-and-plum paint job stood out from the winter grays. Ten years since Solveig's last visit, it remained as lovely as ever.

Her eyes had crossed at the files from Mr. Forrester, and the search for records related to "the old Rice place" ended in frustration. Only months before Harvey's disappearance, Caleb Rice had signed the property over to his neighbor for one dollar.

It didn't make sense.

She slowed her steps on the approach. This might end up being a waste of time. If the mystery's answer lay inside these walls, someone would have solved it. On the other hand, had anyone who searched for Harvey Engelwood ever thought to look for Augusta Rice?

Beside the front door, a cheerful wooden sign in the shape of a tree read, Don't LEAF! We're open!

The building's familiar charm lingered inside as well, although the displays had been refreshed. Detailed models of early autos decorated a section highlighting books about the Valley Turnpike Company.

The table dedicated to Cross Keys' most famous missing person featured a familiar portrait to accent the reference materials. Young, homely Harvey with a Bible held to his chest and a clover in his buttonhole.

"Hi there. Can I help—you." Amanda Marsdon's smile evaporated. She had gained maybe ten kilograms since Solveig saw her last, and gray peppered her short, spiky haircut, but otherwise she looked the same.

"Hello, Miss Marsdon. I'm looking for records on the Rice family from this area."

"Ah. Let me guess. Title trouble?" She crossed her arms. "Quite a fix, I'll bet, selling land you never rightly owned."

Not this again. She tried to sound confident. "The records are confusing. I hoped information about the previous owners might shed some light."

"You think?" She crossed her arms. "The Marsdons have a Rice connection, you know. My granny used to say we should've owned that land."

Solveig offered a tight smile. "Did she leave you some money to buy it?"

Miss Marsdon narrowed her eyes. "Wait here." The floorboards groaned under her tromping. Solveig exhaled as soon as she cleared the room.

While she waited, she gravitated to the Engelwood display. The stack of resources included a first edition of *Sweet to the Soul and Health to the Bones*, a binder of photocopied newspaper clippings, and embarrassingly, her seventh-grade research project, submitted to the archives by an impressed teacher.

She glanced at the copier. Ten cents per page. Credit cards accepted. Why not?

While the machine ran the copies, Solveig thumbed through Harvey's book. She'd read the public library's copy years ago, but this one bore an inscription.

Her heart quickened. The penmanship was similar, if immature compared to the signature on the deed. The message, addressed to someone called Gussie, was brief but earnest.

How did this beautifully inscribed gift end up a castoff at the genealogical society? And what about the verse? *Proverbs 17:22. Hmm.*

Solveig tapped the reference into her phone. Harvey used the King James Version for his reflections and likely cited the same to this Gussie. "A merry heart doeth good like a medicine," she read, "but a broken spirit drieth the bones."

Chills raced over her skin.

As the copier whined to a halt, she carefully placed the book on the glass plate and captured the signature too.

Miss Marsdon returned with a file folder three centimeters thick. "Here. Copies of all the material we have directly related to the Rices. Nothing that will prove whatever right you think you have to that property. Maybe you'll see that and do the right thing."

Solveig paid for the copies and added them to the Engelwood stack. "Thank—"

"You are so much like your mother."

She froze.

"Did you know she joined our MOPS group? Right after your father died." Miss Marsdon's nostrils flared slightly. "We circled around her, but she didn't want the help, I suppose."

Of a thousand questions she'd longed to ask, not one came to mind.

"His death was tragic. Nothing to do for it. But she chose to run."

It must have seemed like the only option, Solveig wanted to say, but the words hung in her throat. She clutched the papers and fled.

Just like her mother.

Twenty-Eight

Run, run, run.

Solveig bounced from room to room, her bad ear warbling the *Healing Waves* nature sounds just enough to make her seasick. When they'd scheduled the open house, there seemed plenty of time to prepare. Now, Ms. VanGorden would arrive soon, Kyle was on his way, and she'd been chasing "one last thing" for two hours.

Finally, she rubbed her forehead and stilled to catch her breath. "That's it. I can't run anymore."

"Then stop."

She startled and whirled to find Kyle dripping melted snow onto the hardwoods and holding a handful of envelopes. "Sorry. I knocked and texted. Got your mail, by the way."

"Thanks." She grasped the stack and waved it in the direction of the sound. "What do you think? Good enough?"

"Are you kidding? Everything looks great." He followed her into the kitchen and glanced overhead at the light fixture. "You're running the generator for this?"

"I had the power reconnected." She shrugged. "Ms. VanGorden insisted. I had to open a special account. The power company won't auto-draft my bank in Oslo. Oh, I didn't thank you for hanging the porch swing. She specifically liked that. Increases curb appeal, supposedly."

"That's good, I guess." His hands migrated toward his coat pockets, then dropped to his sides instead. "But I did it so you would like it."

She didn't speak right away. "And I do."

The canned waves kept crashing, laden with the gravity that the racing around, the electricity, even this, their day to sneak away together, came down to a fast-approaching goodbye.

He coughed lightly. "Ready?"

"Almost." She pawed through a drawer she'd already checked twice. "There's a loose knob on the cabinet over the sink. I need to check the barn for a screwdriver."

Before she finished, he opened the cabinet, spun the knob, and pulled a hard plastic card from his wallet. He unfolded a tiny screwdriver and secured it while she watched. "There. Ta-da."

Another of his hidden talents. Oh, for time to discover them all.

He tucked the multitool back in its spot, but before he stuffed the wallet back into his pocket, she reached out and gently wrested it from his hands, mostly to see if he'd stop her.

He didn't. "Take anything but my Java Mama loyalty card. I'm almost to my free coffee."

She poked in the folds of the wallet until she found it, took the punched red ticket, and smiled as she slid it into her front pocket.

"Right." He sighed. "No problem. Need a kidney?"

Solveig let the thin smile rest on her lips while she rifled through the contents of his wallet. Cash, but no credit cards. A Virginia driver's license so new the edges were sharp. A few notes and business cards. The logo for Community Care Property Management caught her eye, and the name "Aksel Borja" jumped out, but she swallowed the lump in her throat, unwilling to give up the game. "You have quite a boring wallet, mister."

The words were still on her lips as she turned over a leather flap and discovered a photograph inside. Without asking, she slipped it free of its slot.

A lovely woman in a red-and-black bikini stared out in wide-eyed, tanned perfection. Thoughts nipped like wolf pups fighting for dominance. She did her best to make them heel before she spoke. "Who's this?"

Kyle's face was ashen. "The medical examiner friend I mentioned. Ashleigh."

Far from the white coat she'd imagined. Ashleigh, caught by surprise, faced the camera full on, eyebrows raised, lips parted. A low ponytail bunched thick dark hair at the nape of her neck, the loose strands at her temples floating on the breeze just so.

She glanced at the back and found three little words jotted in a feminine hand.

"'I was here'?"

"Just a thing we used to say."

She didn't ask how long ago. In a wallet full of new things, the picture bore two thumbtack holes and foxed edges. "This was taken at the ocean?"

"Yep. Cozumel."

"By you?"

Kyle raked his lower lip with his teeth. "By me."

As surely as he had touched her scar without meaning to, she'd repaid him in kind, and she didn't know how to smooth the gaff with a flirty quip as he had. *I'm sorry, I was aiming for your lips*, she wanted to say, but he showed no mood for wits. If she didn't miss her guess, he seemed ashamed.

"I didn't mean to pry." She returned the photo and the wallet, letting her hand linger against his in the pass. "Okay, I did, but not like this."

"Forget it." He stowed his wallet and dropped the photograph into the empty trashcan. "Are we staying for Her Majesty's arrival?"

Solveig shook her head. "She can use the lockbox key."

What was left? Other than the stack of mail Kyle brought in, the house was ready. She shuffled the envelopes. "This can't be what it looks like." She tore it open and skimmed the contents briefly.

"What's wrong?"

"These people!" She waved the letter like a lunatic. "The funeral home sent me a bill. A bill!"

He looked perplexed. "I'm sorry, I know it's hard to deal with—"

"No. This was all prepaid. I have receipts."

He reclaimed his jacket from the hook by the door. "Get them. I'll take you there."

She faltered. "I should call first."

"Nope. They'll help you a hundred times faster if you're standing there raising—"

"Concerns." She interrupted to stop him from swearing. "Yes, maybe you're right."

While he waited, Solveig retrieved the files. On her way back down, she slipped into the kitchen and rescued the photograph. She'd mail it back to him later, once their whirlwind inevitably stilled.

Nerves rattled at least as much as the old truck, but Solveig turned down Kyle's offer to accompany her into the funeral home. Disputing a bill was something to shoulder on her own.

She affected a purposeful stride toward the wooden double doors, which lasted until she passed the heavyset woman who plodded along with a large vase cradled in one arm and a box slipping from under the other. The cold whitened her labored breath in puffs.

Solveig slowed to match her steps. "Ma'am, can I help?"

"I hate to—oh, if you'll take this." She balanced the box on her hip and let Solveig take the vase.

Solveig gripped it with both hands. "Goodness. You were juggling a load."

"I didn't want to make a third trip." The woman bettered her grip on the box. "I'm Trevor's mother. Did you know him?"

"I'm sorry, no." Did she, though? Trevor, Trevor. "I have business with the owner. Bad timing, I'm afraid."

"There's no good time to talk to the undertaker." The woman sniffled.

"That is true." Solveig swallowed hard. A fresh tremor of her own grief rattled her, and she tightened her grip on the vase. "I lost my grandfather last week. I know it's not the same, but I'm so sorry about your son."

The woman's eyes filled. "Thanks," she said. "Me, too, about your grandpa."

"We ought to hug, but . . ." Solveig raised the vase slightly, and they laughed through tears.

At the entrance, she held the door for Trevor's mom, then followed her to one of the visitation halls inside. Three others, probably family members, rushed to take over the heavy lifting.

"Thank you, young lady," she said, but her eyes didn't meet Solveig's. The warm gold and brown hues inside the funeral home, the somber music piping through some hidden speaker, and the sprays of flowers everywhere were settling the loss into another layer of the woman's soul. Solveig saw it happening.

She reached for the woman's forearm and squeezed. "This is terrible, I know," she said softly. "But you aren't going through it alone."

The woman nodded. There was nothing else to say.

As the family huddled, Solveig clutched her crinkled receipts and slipped away. Helping the woman dispelled whatever righteous indignation she'd planned to wrap herself in, and now she was vulnerable. Exposed.

Her hands were hot, and she sensed splotches rising on her neck. She adjusted her scarf and proceeded toward the back of the building. On the way, she passed identical reception halls on the right and left. They'd remembered Bestemamma in room three. Which had her father been in? And her friends, after the accident?

Her chest tightened. Here, it became impossible to forget how her life had been marked by death.

A small placard stuck out from the wall at the back office, and the door stood open. Knock or step into the doorway?

Before she made up her mind, a phone inside the office rang and she froze in the hallway.

"Fischer and Son. This is Stu." She remembered the name of the man who had helped her with Bestepappa's arrangements. "What do you mean, 'he's *missing*'?"

Whatever answer he received sent him into a frenzy. She shouldn't eavesdrop, but it wasn't as if she wanted to be here. She coughed politely.

"Call the police! This has never—listen, it's almost two o'clock. I have to tell the family something." A pause. "Keep me informed."

At the clatter of the handset landing in the cradle, she stepped into view and rapped the open door lightly. "Excuse me, Mr. Fischer?"

Last week, her first impression of the kindly funeral director was that he'd make a decent Santa Claus. His white beard was short and neatly groomed, and his eyes, if not the brilliant blue ascribed to the old elf, were at least a passable gray. Now, the veins stood out in his neck and forehead, and he looked like a walking heart attack. He met her eyes without sign of recognition. "Can I help you?"

She swallowed her nerves. "Yes. My name is Solveig Borja. You helped me last week with my grandfather."

"It was our honor," he said hurriedly, getting to his feet. "I'm afraid I have to—"

"You sent me a bill." She held up the envelope featuring the Fischer & Son logo. "But my grandfather prepaid when my grandmother died. I have receipts."

"My dear, I have a crisis to attend to."

Kyle was right. If she had called, she would have sat in a holding queue until she died herself. She crossed her arms. "Me too. I'm being robbed by a funeral home."

He sighed and dropped back into his chair. It wheezed as the vinyl cushion depressed. "No, you're not. Let's have a look."

As Mr. Fischer put on his glasses and inspected her documents, she glanced around the office. P&L binders, file cabinets, and framed photos. A family trip to SeaWorld and a silly shot of a scrawny teenage boy who pretended to shoulder a massive rock formation. No special measures to comfort the bereaved here, she noted. This was probably where he answered email in the morning and paid bills in the afternoon. Business as usual in the death trade.

"I know what happened here." He pecked at the keyboard. Whatever appeared on his screen prompted a polite but tense smile. "Some records were duplicated when we switched our bookkeeping software. The payment applied once, and it appeared to leave a balance that didn't exist." He took a red marker out of his drawer and scrawled PAID across the invoice, initialed it, and handed it back. "I'm sorry about that. Please, if you'll excuse me—"

"Does one of your drivers wear a goatee and listen to heavy metal in the hearse?" The question burst out, raw and unpracticed.

The patient smile faded. Mr. Fischer closed his eyes briefly. "That would be my son. Maxwell."

Her eyes flicked toward the framed photos. Yes, she saw it now.

"You should know, then, that after I arranged for a ride to my grandfather's funeral, he took me instead to the grave of a dead friend for some heartless prank and vandalized my property while I walked back home."

Mr. Fischer gaped at her. "Miss Borja, that should never have happened. Let me assure you—"

"I don't need empty words, Mr. Fischer. I'd think, in your business, you'd know how useless they are." She stalked out of the office, ignoring the rustling footfalls and murmuring voices behind her.

A wail stopped her short at the heavy doors. She paused as a voice echoed through the empty foyer. "You *lost* my son?"

She shivered even before pushing her way back into the cold. Something awful had happened, but Lord forgive her, she didn't want to know.

Kyle had vacated the truck in favor of leaning against it. She slowed to observe him. He frowned intently, apparently caught up in his thoughts. With the ball cap shading his eyes, she couldn't tell whether he directed his gaze at the white Honda and beat-up Salamander parked in the far row or the funeral home's sign by the road. *Fischer & Son, Est. 1909.*

When he spotted her, his demeanor perked. That smile. Why did he have to be so candid? "Hey, that was quick."

She returned his smile and shook off the heaviness of the place. "A software glitch. Mr. Fischer fixed it. I told him what I thought of his son too."

They got in the truck. "Who?"

"The hearse driver." She wrinkled her nose. "Maxwell Fischer."

Kyle nodded slightly before turning the ignition. "Bet that felt good."

She let herself relax against the seat. She'd dealt with Danny, and now the hearse driver, all without involving Sheriff Dade. "It really did."

Lighter topics rallied as he drove. Solveig got the sense Kyle was steering the conversation as much as he was the pickup truck. Navigating rough roads, coasting over icy slicks, and detouring restricted areas.

Defensive dating. The thought entertained her as she spotted the sign at North River.

"Here's something I've been meaning to ask," he said. "Which language came first for you?"

"*Både.* Both." She watched the glinting snowfields and ice-laden birch trees fly past, suddenly missing home. "In our family life, we spoke Norwegian. English for everything else."

"And that wasn't confusing?"

"Never." She reflected a moment. "Don't most people use special words and phrases with those they love? We happened to have a whole language."

"When you put it that way, yeah. Makes sense. Do the two have much in common?"

"Mmm, some." Inspiration struck. "Take the word for 'kiss.' It's spelled *k-y-s-s*, very similar. But in Norwegian, the *K* and *Y* combination makes a *shh* sound. *Kyss.*"

"Shiss," he repeated back.

She giggled. "Close enough for lesson one."

The green flecks in his irises danced. "Wanna help me practice?"

Yes. Yes, she did. When had the truck interior turned into an oven? She affected a breezy tone. "You'll need more than that when you come visit me."

He eased on the brake and pulled into his driveway. "I don't know about that."

She twisted toward him and touched his sleeve. "I'm kidding. Most people speak English. And you don't need words to see Oslo Fjord is the most beautiful place on earth."

A shadow flitted through his brows, so fast she might have imagined it. "My next vacation."

They got out of the truck, and in spite of the cold, she warmed to the idea. "I was thinking the other day how much you'd like it there. The skiing, the boating, the music. We take our weekends seriously."

"Sounds like." There was no mistaking the wistful tinge to his voice, and she knew it would never be.

She forced a smile. "Though why jet across the ocean when you have those already, *ja*?"

"Yeah." He fixed a long gaze on her. "Everything I could ever want, right here."

A thrill curled in her belly as he unlocked the door. *Whatever happens, happens.*

Twenty-Nine

Solveig inhaled deeply as they entered the cabin. A sharp, clean scent danced on the tipping point of recognition. "What is that?"

"Eucalyptus. I heard it helps with nicotine cravings." Kyle's lip twitched. "Turns out that's a lie circulated by the eucalyptus companies to sell more of their stinking weeds. I signed a petition."

Oh, that man could finesse a laugh out of her. She dabbed away a tear. "You, sir, are out of control."

"I'm trying to toe the line. It keeps moving." The inscrutable look on his face quieted her and held her captive for a long moment.

She averted her eyes, suddenly nervous. "The cravings are bad, then?"

"Yep." He ran water into a pair of mugs and set them into the microwave. "They're the worst."

While he heated the water, she hung her coat and discreetly surveyed the small space. A tiny kitchen filled the right side of the cabin, with the island and two barstools serving as the dining area. To the left were a two-seater couch, coffee table, bookshelf, and modest TV. A tight spiral staircase circled up to the loft. She assumed a door toward the back led to the bathroom. The decor was sparse except for the massive painting that hung over the couch.

The canvas had to be at least two meters long, and the image drew her in. The artist painted the figure of a man reflecting in a pair of mirrors and diminishing into infinity. The signature read, Keith Benton.

The microwave dinged. "Decision time. Cocoa or this stuff?" He held up an unopened box of lemon-ginger tea.

Her heart warmed. "You bought the tea I like."

"Honey, too, if you want it." A serious tinge undermined his light tone. He wanted her to be pleased, and she was. Delighted, in fact.

"Yes, thank you." She settled on a barstool. "Good for the bones. Or so I tell myself before every ski trip."

He laughed. "A little insurance?"

"A very little. I like your cabin. So cozy."

He dunked a tea bag into the water and offered it to her. "Yeah. I don't need much, and the price was right."

Accepting the mug, she shook her head. "Time for lesson two. The word I want isn't 'cozy' but *'koselig.'* It's almost the same, but it means more than being snug and nice. Anything warm and inviting can be *koselig.* A room or a meal or a person. It's about contentment." She paused to sweeten the tea. "Connection, even."

"I like it." He lifted his mug. "To being koozley."

"We'll work on your pronunciation later." She giggled and raised her own. "Cheers."

The painting kept drawing her eyes as they chatted over the steamy beverages. Should she study it or force herself to look away? She didn't want to intrude by asking if Keith was the brother he'd mentioned. Kyle made a habit of levity, but the image proclaimed scars as deep as her own.

"Hey, before I forget. I'm back at work tomorrow." He loosed a three-fold pamphlet magneted to his fridge and passed it to her. "So I ran an errand for you earlier."

Curiosity piqued, and she set down the tea to peruse the brochure. *Tillman's Fine Tobaccos.* "Thank you," she said dryly. "I am completely out of fine tobacco."

He laughed. "Look closer. It's the same Tillman's from those old bottles we found in the barn."

"Ah, I see. So you visited their shop." She glanced at the products listed on the inner panels. Loose tobacco, premium cigars, engraved lighters. "How was that?"

"The belly of the beast. But worth it. I chatted up the owner, Larry Tillman. Told him about the bottles to see if he might buy them. He was interested at first."

"But?"

"When I said where we found them, he went off on a rant that any Tillman's bottles on 'the old Rice place' are rightfully his, regardless."

Solveig rolled her eyes. "*Fantastisk.* Is the long-lost heir preparing to step forward?"

"Nope, just carrying some epic grudge against one Caleb Rice."

Solveig's ears perked. "That's interesting."

Kyle nodded. "Way back, Tillman's originally sold patent medicines. Including opium-laced tonics and cocaine tooth drops for kiddos, which explains their change in direction." His eyes drifted to the painting momentarily. "Once Larry got going about his poor granddad, it sounded like a drug ring. Seems ol' Caleb owed for a lot of unsold product."

Solveig drummed her fingers absently. "I wonder when, exactly, because I made a discovery too. The Rice family sold the farm in 1919 to none other than Harvey. Guess what the sales price was."

"A hundred million kroner."

She smiled. "Try one dollar."

"Wait, really?"

"Really. An odd deal for a man with unpaid debts." She bobbed the tea bag. "What's worse, Harvey supposedly sold the land to Bestepappa in 1971."

He studied her. "Then wherever he disappeared to in 1919, he took his bones with him."

"Unless it's a forgery. Danny said Bestepappa stole the land, and you were there when Sheriff Dade said his piece." She curled her fingers to the mug to anchor herself. "What if they're right?"

"What if they are? You didn't do anything wrong."

"But it might mean Bestepappa did. I don't like to imagine him having secrets."

"Solveig. Brace yourself, but your grandfather had secrets." She held her breath, but he continued. "Same as everyone else. You, me. Everyone."

"Point taken," she said too quickly, refolding the brochure and stashing it with her coat. "Thank you for this, but if it's all right, maybe we can, um, lounge around. Relax for a while." Such a transparent suggestion to her own ears that she couldn't believe his nonchalance.

"Sure. Tell me if you're hungry. I'm not proud of the menu here at Casa Benton, but there's bologna, peanut butter, tuna. Cola in the fridge. Burgers in the freezer. And brussels sprouts." He shrugged. "Don't judge. I love those little buggers. Anything I have, whatever you want."

"I want . . ." This was it, the perfect moment. She slid from the barstool, stepped close to him, and snaked her arms to his sides. Pressing her palms to his, she laced their fingers. "I want you to kiss me."

Though his hands warmed to hers, he searched her eyes instead of closing the distance between their lips. His irises were brownish green. Equal parts doubt and hope. "Oh yeah?" His voice dropped to a low, intimate rasp. "When did you decide that?"

"As soon as I met you." She tugged on his hands, affecting a pout.

"At the cemetery?" A half-smile teased. "Must've been the paint thinner."

"If you are going to argue—" Solveig took the risk and kissed him first. That would teach him.

He proved a willing student. His lips firmed against hers, then parted, a playful, curious dance. In those first moments, everything faded but their little world of discovery and mingled breath. With unhurried tenderness, Kyle kissed her not like a man hunting for treasure but like one who had found it.

He squeezed once and loosened his grip. Sorrow needled, but no. His lips stayed true as cautious hands circled her waist. Solveig deepened the kiss, trying like mad to tell him everything in her heart. That he didn't have to be careful, that she wouldn't push him away this time. She let her fingers trace the contours of his back. These muscles moved sofas for her without expecting a thing in return.

The sofa. What an excellent idea.

She glanced toward the loveseat. He took the cue and waltzed her across the room until they tumbled against the cushions with shared laughter.

The tangled embrace quickened her blood. Her lips surveyed the terrain of his face—chin, temples, cheekbones—but his hands kept within invisible boundaries. Of course. After her reaction when he touched her neck, it'd take time before he ventured much.

Time they didn't have.

A pang barged into the moment. There shouldn't be wounds between them already, not during this heart-skipping newness. She broke away to catch her breath.

He stroked her hair. "Okay?"

She leaned into his shoulder to hide her face. Maybe . . . maybe the remedy was to follow the moment wherever it led. "A little warm," she confessed. With trepidation, she unlooped her scarf and discarded it over the arm of the couch. "There. Much better."

He grinned and drew her near again. "You sure? You still look hot."

Yes, because happiness was a warm pun. This one might have been everything she needed to hear, except he was looking into her eyes and not at the exposed scars. He didn't know how bad it was.

Trembling, she let her fingers graze his roughened cheek before returning to his lips. Home had nothing to do with place and everything to do with presence. Nothing to do with language and everything to do with being understood. But she couldn't make that leap toward him without knowing he'd catch her.

Eucalyptus-scented desperation, honey-flavored desire. Time passed as if caught in a looping infinity mirror, both endless and dwindling. Urgent, breathless. Somewhere in the reflection waited the moment when he'd either accept her as is or withdraw in revulsion.

She wanted him to take the lead, though, and he did. Just not the way she expected.

A shift in his posture signaled her to pause, and he straightened slightly with kindness, apology, and longing mixed in his eyes. "Why don't we do like you said earlier and relax for a while." The words posed a question. His tone did not.

Don't move—but the spell was already broken. She nuzzled his neck. "This is not relaxing?"

He chuckled. "Um, no. Not at all."

She pulled away. His red cheeks and swollen lips surely mirrored her own, but the serious pinch around his eyes made her self-conscious. "I thought you'd want—"

His fingers traced her jawline and stole her breath. "Have mercy, Solveig. I'm barely over one addiction. I can't get hooked on you." He reached for a remote on the coffee table. "Which is why we are going to watch the greatest movie of all time—"

He broke off and left the big decision up to her. Solveig settled against his chest. Her good ear had no trouble picking up the runaway beating under his breastbone or its explanations of all he left unsaid.

She cringed inside. The rebuff burned, but not worse than knowing she'd put her feelings over his. "See if you can find *Cryoseed* for us."

He kissed the top of her head. "I thought you didn't like that one."

"It has its moments. Besides, we must watch it together before I go home, *ja?*"

"Sounds like a trick question." The screen flashed as he found the movie and confirmed the rental. "So how would we beat the odds if this was the nuclear winter?"

She recalled the final pages of *Den mørke vinteren.* "We'd take comfort in knowing love is eternal and freeze to death in each other's arms."

"Seriously?" He seemed to chew on that for a long moment. "That's the worst ending I've ever heard."

"I told you it was sad." Yet as the loading screen spooled, their own sad ending weighed down her spirits. "Will you do something for me, Kyle?"

"Name it."

"Will you drive me to Washington Dulles on Friday?"

He was silent as film credits ghosted over a black screen. "I did promise you a dramatic airport goodbye," he said finally. "But for the record, it's gonna be hard to watch that plane take off."

Images flashed on the TV. Not that she'd say so, but boarding it would be hard, too.

Thirty

This can't be right.

The taxi car sputtered away, its tires throwing dust from the hard-packed dirt road. Gussie stared at a house flanked by a creek to one side and a stand of golden rain trees to the other. Beyond them, a cluster of smaller cottages sat back from the road, partly hidden. On the front door hung a hand-painted placard: Byberry Farms, Thornton House. The unmistakable stink of chicken houses hung in the air.

This was nothing like Rockingham Memorial Hospital.

Short of chasing down the driver, she had little choice but to walk up to the house and ask—no, *demand*—to see Philip. She carried Mama's little leather valise, packed with one of Daddy's old suits and the copy of Ibsen's plays borrowed from Mrs. Engelwood. It had helped Lieutenant Jansen, after all.

Gussie knocked twice to no response. She held her breath and twisted the knob.

"Hello?" Inside, a narrow plank table held a lamp, scattered Esterbrook bank pens, and an abandoned copy of *Ladies' Home Journal.* As for the rest of the room, two long wooden benches lined the barren whitewashed walls. A faint dead smell permeated the air.

She called out again, and finally, a stocky woman stomped in from the back of the house. Salt-and-pepper curls escaped her dingy dust cap. She eyed Gussie up and down and said, "You'll do in the kitchens, I suppose. Too pretty for floor duty. Follow me."

"I beg your pardon." Gussie's voice shook. "I've come to see a patient. Philip Marcus, please."

The woman stared. "You're not here for a job?" She heaved a sigh and pulled a small record book from the desk drawer. An interminable moment passed until the woman's finger rested on an entry. "Marcus. Farm Group. Grubb House, third floor. You'll see it past the trees, the gray one on the hill."

Gussie trudged through the high grass past the golden rains, still clutching her valise. Grubb House might once have been white. She didn't bother knocking when she reached it.

Inside, a mixed odor of humanity accosted her. She placed a hand over her face and looked around. This time, sallow men languished on the benches. One fixed her with his gaze. She glanced away instinctively and hurried toward the stairs.

The stairwell was narrow and dark, but at least it provided her nose some relief. Temporary, as it turned out. The third-floor landing smelled of tobacco and unwashed bodies. The two doors at the top of the stairs had labels roughly carved into the boards. To the right stood the Farm Group Dormitory.

Finally. Ignoring the stench, she breathed deep and pushed open the door.

"Philip?" Gussie called. "Hello?"

Shouting and commotion clamored from all sides. Rows of empty cots lined up head to foot in tight rows. Unlike Rockingham Memorial, where the rows were spaced for the doctors and nurses to work, this room was meant to shoehorn as many sleepers as the space allowed.

A few of the beds were occupied. The shouting men in restraints didn't even have chairs at their bedsides for visitors. The ugliness of it etched her heart.

"Someone? I'm looking for Philip Marcus." No one paid her attention. She craned her neck to search the room.

A unified shout went up from the corner. They'd shoved two beds together as a makeshift card table. By it stood a man with familiar chestnut curls framing the fine profile she'd memorized at church years ago, although his face was thin and his whiskers scraggly. *Philip.*

To think she'd feared him changed. He was here, not disfigured or maimed, but handsome as ever.

She hurried toward him. The sticky floor gave her soles some resistance. No matter. They were together at last.

Time stopped when his eyes met hers. "Gussie?"

He broke away from the card game and met her in the maze of cots, crushing her in arms that looked too bony to feel so powerful. He squeezed the air from her lungs, and she tried to cry out but only managed a wheeze. He held the back of her head and mashed her lips with his. She couldn't breathe. She couldn't—

"Darling." He broke the kiss, gasping himself. "Good as your word. You shouldn't have come."

Her free hand flew to her mouth. The valise dangled from the other. "Philip, you're . . . you're hurting me."

He released her at once, his eyes rimmed with red. "Forgive me. You appeared like a vision, sweet girl. I scarcely believe you're real."

She patted her lip and attempted a smile. "Real as can be."

"Indeed." He glanced around the dormitory, frowning. "This is nowhere you should be, love. Come. There's a lockbox under my cot."

As he navigated the crowded ward, she stayed close. The general noise of the room had dimmed, and a smatter of talk focused around them. A catcall raised the hairs on her neck, but Philip turned and glared until a cough and muttered apology came from that direction.

He would protect her. She must believe that.

Beside a rumpled bed, he crouched to fiddle with the lockbox. He eyed the valise. "Did you bring my things?"

"Yes," she said automatically. "I hadn't realized this was a farm. The suit I brought may not be exactly—"

"Never mind, woman." He turned a lock with his thumbnail and revealed sundries—a belt, a small silver button, an engraved cigarette case, another Esterbrook, and a pocket Bible. All but the last, he took, then stowed the box without bothering to secure it again. "My pistol. Give it to me."

He grabbed the valise and rifled through the contents. When he came to the book of plays, he held it up. "What's this?"

She breathed deeply, willing herself not to cry. "Ibsen. I thought I might read—"

He chucked it onto the mattress and donned the jacket over his shirtsleeves. It hung off him like a set of drapes. The button turned out to be a pin, which he fastened to his lapel.

To her horror, he dropped his dungarees and changed his pants as if she weren't there. She looked away, scandalized.

"No matter," he mumbled, sounding distracted. "We'll improvise. Come, we must hurry."

She dared a peek. Rather than securing the sagging suit pants with the belt, he wound it partway around his hand and walked toward the door Gussie had entered.

She grabbed the book and stuffed it into her skirt pocket. "Where are we going?"

"Home."

The word set her heart galloping. "But how—"

"No more questions," he said. "You are to follow me and do as I say."

As Philip flew down the staircase, Gussie struggled to keep up. Why did they keep him here if he had so much strength? He didn't seem to need a hospital—and indeed, Byberry didn't seem to be one.

When they reached the first floor, he led her toward a small room off the back. The door was labeled with crude etching like those upstairs, but this one read, Dispensary.

He grabbed the knob and swore. "Locked. Wait here. I shall have to find a hammer or—"

"What is the meaning of this?" A nurse charged up from the front hall. "Who are you, and why is this man roaming about?"

Gussie raised her chin. She'd come to read a play, but instead, she was to perform one. In her heart, she became Mrs. Engelwood, commanding the Ladies Auxiliary. "I came to see my sweetheart." She mustered a highfalutin note. "As an invited guest, I might add."

She glanced at Philip for approval, but he only wound the loose end of the belt around his free hand. She turned to the nurse again, whose stony expression twisted Gussie's stomach in knots.

The woman's scowl deepened. "Is that so?"

"It is. And to find him and the others in this wretched state—why, this place ought to be reported."

The nurse placed her hands on her hips. "I'll tell you who's going to be reported."

Quick as a snake, Philip looped the belt around Gussie's neck. "I'll kill her."

The nurse's eyes went round as nickels. "There's no call to hurt anyone. Let's put that away, and—"

Air. Gussie's fingers clawed the belt. *Please, God. Air.*

She'd dropped the valise. Philip nudged it with his foot. "Unlock this door," he ordered the nurse, "and fill the case with the laudanum."

She kept her eyes down as she answered. "You know I can't do that."

"I need it."

"But a doctor has to administer medications."

"I will kill her."

His grip. He meant it.

Gussie's chest burned. Faces floated before her eyes. Daddy, Mama, Eloise. The Trammel sisters, Lieutenant Jansen, Mrs. Engelwood. And of course, Harvey. She should have listened. Stars erupted as the nurse unlocked the door.

Philip shoved Gussie through. She gulped a tiny breath. *Not enough.*

He nudged the case with his foot. "Hurry."

Spots crowded Gussie's vision. They burst before her eyes to the tune of clinking bottles. Her knees quaked and she tried to focus. The shelves of medicines lined one wall of the compact space. In the far corner stood the boiler. Her arms flagged to her sides. She was going to die in a boiler room.

She was going to die.

The strap at her neck slid away. She gasped and crumpled to the floor as Philip grabbed the case. "Get up," he said. He grasped her hand and wrenched her to her feet.

Gussie coughed and stumbled, but he held fast with an iron grip. He clamored for the door as she struggled for footing. At the first opportunity, she had to get away from him.

But the valise contained the last of her money. His knuckles strained as he gripped the handle. She doubted he'd let go.

An exhausted gasp escaped her, half-breath, half-sob. "Please, wait."

"No. We must hurry." He kicked open the door, and Gussie registered the listless interest of the men on the benches before he dragged her into the daylight. She squinted, momentarily blind.

He released her hand and pointed to a house down the hill and across some pastures. "We'll take Dr. Hermann's flivver."

Her pulse pounded in the tender flesh bruised by the belt strap. His words echoed in her head. *I will kill her.*

She glanced toward the lonely road. Escaping on her own was impossible. She'd sent a letter asking Harvey to retrieve her at the Harrisonburg train station tomorrow, but how would she get back to Philadelphia's city proper without Philip?

She needed him. Heaven help her.

He slowed, watching her. "My beautiful girl. Once we're away from this dreadful place, everything will be like we planned." He wiped a tear from her cheek with his thumb. "Do you remember when I asked you to wait for me?"

She nodded, not trusting her voice. They'd walked the grove at sunset, and as long beams kissed the tiny green apples, he'd promised to return for her.

"Then you mustn't give up on me." His voice shook. "If you knew what I've seen. What I've suffered."

She blinked rapidly and nodded again. Yes. Hadn't she come for that very reason?

The one-story cottage was well-kept compared to the other buildings. She fell behind again, but Philip bypassed the front stoop and beckoned for her to follow him around the cottage.

In the back sat a Ford Model T, one of the few cars Gussie knew on sight. Did he mean to simply take it?

Philip set the valise behind the seat and fiddled with levers at the steering wheel. "Get in," he said. "They'll soon be onto us."

She stumbled toward the passenger side. How many times had Harvey helped her in and out of his Buick?

Her leaden arms struggled with the latch, and a clapping door and craggy voice interrupted them. "Mr. Marcus."

A portly gentleman had emerged from the back door. His starched shirt and suspenders contrasted with the nasty black revolver he carried.

"Dr. Hermann," Philip said in an amiable tone. "Rather expected you'd be at chapel."

"If you ever attended, you'd know when it lets out." The older man raised the gun.

Gussie's heartbeat filled her ears.

"I'll grant you that." Philip sidled up to Gussie and slid an arm around her shoulders. She shrank from him, and he tightened his hold. "Have you met my girl? We're to be married."

"Splendid." Dr. Hermann took a step closer. "Nothing like young people in love. You'll have to invite me to the wedding."

"I'm afraid not." Philip whipped his arm around her throat. With her body in front of his, he rushed Dr. Hermann. The man wavered under the attack. Philip wrenched his arm. He snared the gun and bashed Dr. Hermann in the head.

He crumpled. Blood gushed onto the porch. Philip tucked the weapon into his waistband.

"Get in the car." His breath was hot in her ear, and she could only obey.

He cranked the engine until the motor sputtered and roared. The nurse at Grubb House had evidently raised the alarm, but the two muscle-bound men running in their direction came too late. Philip jumped into the driver's seat, and the Ford careened down the dirt road. A small crowd of nurses and inmates watched from outside Thornton House too, but none attempted to follow.

"Won't this be a tale for the children someday?" He laughed as if that were a real gas. "When does our train leave, Darling?"

Gussie shook her head. "I don't know."

His mirth dropped in degrees. "You don't know? Which route had you planned to take?"

"The same I used here," she stammered. "Hagerstown and . . ." But the stations and lines Harvey had named with ease wouldn't come to mind.

Philip's eyes narrowed. The gun lay in his lap, ready should he need it. "You didn't check the return schedules?"

She stared at her folded hands. It had never crossed her mind.

He cursed and accelerated the flivver. Lush farmland blurred by. "Woman, how can you be so intolerably stupid?"

Hot tears wet her lashes. How, indeed.

Thirty-One

Gussie's meager funds wouldn't cover passage back to Harrison-burg, of course, but Philip managed to bunco the cash from an elderly woman outside the train station. Tremors nettled Gussie's stomach as they boarded the passenger car. Thank the Lord he only got fare for general cabin seats and not a compartment.

Once they settled on the train, a dose of laudanum put him at ease. Not so for her. Even as he nodded off, her nerves hummed and whined like an electric lamp.

Might she get the gun away from him? She glanced up the aisle and behind them. The train was full and the risk too great. She could never hope to overpower him.

Were she half as clever as Hedda Gabler, she'd simply coax it away, but the book of plays offered no instruction in the art of persuasion beyond the character's mystifying example.

"Darling." His abrupt address startled Gussie from her thoughts. "We need a plan."

Her injuries burned with her pounding heart. "Certainly. Won't your parents be surprised? They'll get you some decent clothes and a good meal."

A bath and a trip to the barber ought to be on that list as well, but he snorted derisively. "My parents have no use for a 'quivering goldbrick.'"

Oh, yes. They were "anxious over his predicament," as Harvey had put it. She shifted in her seat. "Might you board with Harvey and his mother? They have plenty of space."

He scowled and scratched his arm. "That prig. I'd sooner hang myself."

"Don't say things like that." The train whistle blew, signaling some unknown waypoint. Though the journey stretched every minute, they'd arrive home all too soon. "Perhaps if I speak to Nurse Metzgar at Rockingham Memorial?"

He seized her wrist and leaned close. "I don't need another hospital," he said in a low voice.

We're carrying a lot of medicine for a man who isn't sick. But this she daren't say, so she nodded, trembling. "Of course. How stupid of me."

"Good girl." He released her and foraged again in the valise until he withdrew one of the medicine bottles. She inched away as much as possible and stared at the furrowed horizon, trying to think of a plan that didn't rely on heaps of money.

What about his shares in the Valley Turnpike Company? He had to cash them out soon anyway. The same shares that had candied her dreams of marriage now wove hope, delicate as spun sugar. She prayed it would support him until he returned to himself again.

Philip's head snapped up from drowsing. "I have it. We'll hide out at your father's caverns. It's genius."

Gussie had never been accused of genius, but this didn't resemble her notion of it. "But in your letter, you said being underground was like a nightmare. I should think a cavern the last place you'd want to be."

His brow furrowed and he nodded slowly. For one bright moment, she was sure she'd convinced him.

"Nonsense, Darling. Without Germans lobbing bombs at us, we'll be quite snug."

Did he expect her to stay with him? "If I don't go home, Daddy will look for me," she whispered.

He scratched behind his ear. "Nonetheless, he'll never find us, love."

Her lip quivered. "I'm going to rest my eyes."

And so she did, praying all the while that Harvey had gotten her note.

October 6, 1919

Harrisonburg teemed with travelers. Gussie had never seen crowds like these in Rockingham County.

As she and Philip stepped off the train, she half expected a horde of policemen to cart them away. More foolish imaginings. Everywhere, people in their own worlds rushed and lagged, colliding in happy embraces and accidental bumps, ranging the gamut of emotions. Joy, relief, confusion, despair, exhaustion, determination. All of them stewed in her own heart as she scanned the crowd.

He's going to be furious. The thought applied equally to both men, and she didn't bother deciding which she meant.

Harvey must have been waiting. As always, he stood out from the crowd. She recognized his gait first, and his presence, more than ever, comforted her soul.

He lifted his hand to wave as soon as he spotted her, and lowered it again, scowling.

Philip turned to her. The veins at his temples stood out, engorged. "Him? I told you—"

"I asked him to meet me on the return trip, to take me home," she said. "I had no way to know you'd be here too."

Philip's eyes blazed. "So, is that how you play things?"

She fumbled for words as Harvey cut through the crowds and met them on the platform. He regarded the other man warily. "What's this, now?"

Philip's shoulders went taut, and the people gave them wide berth as if a shift in the air signaled them to keep their distance. "Not your concern, Engelwood."

Harvey rose to his full height. "Until she says otherwise, Gussie is my concern. Especially when she's got a fat lip and bruises on her neck."

Her fingers flew to cover the tender spot. No one on the train had looked her straight in the face, or perhaps the injuries weren't so pronounced, but Harvey noticed.

Philip didn't turn his gaze from Harvey. "Gussie, tell him to be on his way."

"But he can help us. Right, Harvey?" She shot a pleading look.

Harvey's eyes flicked in her direction. "I will take him to his parents' house."

"We're not going to them," Philip said. "And we're not going anywhere with you. Gussie, come on."

"Philip, please!" She fought the tears that would agitate him. "We're trying to help you, and you're not letting us. We've left a trail of folks who will be keen to send you back—" But she didn't dare mention the place.

He scratched his face and said nothing.

"Look here." Harvey stared Philip square in the eyes. "The lady's done what she can. Now you'll decide whether you can be reasonable."

"Will I, worm?" He stepped forward, his stance menacing. Though the two were of equal height, Philip outweighed him slightly and had his comportment as a soldier.

"Yes," Harvey said evenly. "Because if we mix it up in the streets, the police will be on us in a minute. I'll pay a fine I can easily afford, and you'll be strapped to a cot in an insane asylum."

Philip's nostrils flared. "Don't test me, Engelwood."

"I'd never." He turned his face slightly without taking his eyes off Philip. "Gussie, can I give you a lift home?"

Home. Was there a sweeter word? "Yes, please."

A short huff escaped Philip as though he'd had the air knocked out of him. "You're choosing him."

"I have to go, Philip. Please understand."

A slight narrowing of his eyes was all the answer he offered. He stalked off, clutching her valise and its stolen contents, and disappeared into the throngs.

A train whistle cried, and the express line chugged into motion. Harvey offered his arm. "What can I do?"

Any number of things, yet she shook her head. "Please take me home."

He nodded and escorted her to the street where the Buick awaited.

"What were you thinking?" On the road, Harvey wasn't so sanguine. "When I saw your note, I'd half a mind to catch the next train after you."

The car's vibrations rattled bones already sore from the train. "I'm glad you didn't, or you wouldn't have been here to meet us."

Haltingly, she recounted all. His lips and knuckles whitened long before the tale was told. "He's nothing like he used to be." She sniffled. "What's wrong with him, Harvey?"

"They call it shell shock. When I first visited, he shook uncontrollably and slipped into memories of battle unawares. He'd made great strides since then. I've never seen him violent before."

She fought a lump in her throat. "I was afraid he wouldn't look the same, but it's much worse than that. Instead of eyes or legs, it's as if his soul is maimed. Maimed and gone."

"Not so," Harvey said. "He's ragged with war and rotten with laudanum, but hold out hope for his soul."

"We quarreled on the way. I was confused about the trains. He said I was 'intolerably stupid.'" She covered her face. "I'm not any brilliant thinker, but why did he h-have to s-say a thing like that?"

Harvey stopped at the church over the hill from their homes and parked by the birch trees at the edge of its yard. "Gussie—"

"You probably think the same! If I'd listened to you, none of this would have happened."

"No use bemoaning what's done," he said gently. "And what I think is that you've tenfold more heart than the brainiest person alive."

Beneath the birch trees was as good a place as any to mourn her dreams. She let the tears come. They were fewer than she might have supposed.

An exhausted peace settled over her as she gazed at the many-layered horizon. "I know where I'd like to go, Harvey. If I could go anywhere."

"Tell me."

"I want to see the fidge-jords."

He gave her a questioning look. "Come again?"

"The fidge-jords. I read about them in some of Ibsen's plays, but I can't imagine them. Jack Stebbins asked me what they looked like, and I had to admit I didn't know."

"Oh, Gussie." The corners of Harvey's mouth twitched. "It's a good dream. I'd like to see the fidge-jords, myself."

She slumped in her seat. "Philip wanted to hide out at the caverns on Daddy's mountain tract. I suppose he'll make his way, but it's going to be cold tonight, isn't it?"

"The cavern depths hold a steady temperature. He won't be comfortable, but he won't freeze." He sighed. "I'll take provisions."

"That's kind, all things considered." Yet she almost told him not to. She wished the cold on Philip, and hunger too. It might help him find some contrition by the time she saw him again.

Harvey took the opposite tack. "Let's hope relieving an ounce of misery will make him listen to reason." He threw a glance in her direction. "On the subject of misery. I intend to end things with Eloise."

"Oh." Gussie swallowed her surprise. "She'll be disappointed."

"Better now than later," he said.

She let a glance toward home be her request, and he obliged, working the pedals and steering wheel to set them on their way.

Few more words passed between them, and Harvey walked her to her doorstep. He stayed another half hour to assuage Eloise with a heavily truncated explanation. Once he escaped, barely enough time remained to take supplies to Philip before dark.

Jitters plagued Gussie throughout the evening. She nursed a cup of tea, and as an afterthought, took a dose of Tillman's Miracle Elixir. The harrowing trip deserved some remedy. Although Daddy's cure-all never eased her complaints, maybe this would be the lucky stroke.

Alas, if anything, the compound stimulated her all the more. She lay awake for hours in a state of nameless dread, but not until the dead of night did she sit up in bed, mouth dry and heart pounding.

She hadn't told Harvey that Philip had the gun.

Thirty-Two

Solveig's old bedroom remained as it had when she and Bestemamma redecorated for her seventh birthday. White-wicker furniture and light-pink walls. Stuffed animals, a dust ruffle, and a handmade quilt on the bed where she used to curl up with cocoa and her library books.

Now it was lemon-ginger tea and the files from the attorney and genealogical society, but the old comforts soothed the less acute aches bundled in her heart. Whatever she found in the stack of papers would distract her from replaying the night before.

Solveig cupped her hands over her face. As if she could stop it.

When the movie had ended, she finally asked Kyle about the painting. He described his brother's art show and showed her pictures on his mobile, mostly of artwork, but some of his family too. He spoke of Keith in the past tense without offering hows and whys, and Solveig didn't press.

On the drive back, she recited how her father's gap year abroad turned into a short-notice wedding, and how the brain aneurysm that killed him sent her mother running home to Norway. Not her favorite story, but he'd earned the right to hear it.

By the time they reached the farm, the sting of rejection had faded. He walked her to the door, and because the porch swing looked so inviting and there probably wouldn't be another chance, they had stayed outside until—

Enough.

She arranged the photocopies into piles on the bed and wrapped herself in a quilt.

Reviewing her own research first seemed wise. Although she cringed at the immature writing, the details were sourced and sound. Over five hundred Rockingham veterans, not to mention their families, had poured into Harrisonburg for the Home Coming Day celebration on October 8, 1919. Harvey was last seen at the high school by his mother, hours before he was to accept his brother's medal. When he failed to appear during or after the ceremony, a search party galvanized, but no one had turned up a single clue.

Until now.

Solveig eyed the next stack. Who was Augusta Elizabeth Rice, and what was she doing in the cavern on the day Harvey disappeared?

The files Amanda Marsdon had copied offered glimpses in clippings, train schedules, and ledger pages. Mr. Caleb Rice had racked up significant debts, so why would he sign his property over to Harvey? The list of accounts ended abruptly in August of 1919, without payoffs and seriously in arrears.

Dead end.

She perused the names. Caleb owed money all over town, particularly with Marcus Mercantile and Tillman's Patented Elixirs. Just as Kyle had said.

Her heart accelerated as she examined the stapled packet among the bundle of Rice files. A crooked typewritten label at the top titled it *Diary of Eloise Rice Marsdon, 1916–1923*.

Pay dirt?

Well, dirt, at least. Her eyes crossed trying to decipher the photocopies of spidery handwriting. Eloise Rice wrote sporadically and veiled her secrets in terrible French. Between a two-year intensive at university and the translation app on her phone, Solveig gleaned small tidbits of vulgar gossip and one chilling line from November 1918.

Gussie brought influenza into our home, and it should have been her that died.

Gussie, like the inscription? *Dearest Gussie. Always, Harvey.*

Yes! Eloise's hated sister had to be Augusta Rice. She reread several entries and scanned for missed clues.

Slowly, fragments emerged. On May 12, 1919, Eloise hadn't cared who knew what she thought of her sister. She wrote the entry in plain English.

> *I warned her. My simpleton sister will learn I mean what I say. Though Harvey might be equally moronic for following her around like a besotted puppy. By this time next week, we won't be hearing the name Philip Marcus every minute, will we?*

The next page included a clipping Eloise had saved.

"'To the dearest and best girl in all the world,'" Solveig read aloud. "Hmm."

The printed letter that followed seemed silly and inauthentic, but at face value, it was a love note from a soldier to his sweetheart.

Interesting, but was it important? Solveig keyed notes into her phone. *Philip Marcus. Connection to Augusta? WWI veteran?*

If so, he would have been honored as a part of the Home Coming Day.

The rest of the diary gave her insight into the family dynamic. The pretty one, the smart one, and the snake oil salesman.

Eloise rounded out the summer with a sketchy plan to marry Harvey although she despised him. She complained about Harvey's domineering mother, but she pegged her sister as the primary obstacle to her scheme.

That certainly meshed with the way Harvey inscribed the book.

The entries went dark for a year and a half and dashed her hopes for a firsthand account of Harvey's disappearance. By the time Eloise picked up her pen, she'd lured Wendell Marsdon down the aisle, and the latter pages of the diary descended into complaints of daily minutiae. Solveig skimmed the final pages but found only the mundane until Eloise lost interest in her chronicles and the journal ceased.

Two sisters. One who left behind a book of rants and schemes. The other whose message to the future was a plea for mercy.

Maybe whatever had happened that day was an accident. That much, Solveig understood.

But what had happened after?

When she finished with the stacks from the genealogical society, Solveig used her phone to search online newspaper archives. One in particular: the *Rockingham Register* from October 9, 1919.

She read the newspaper column by column to take in the mood of the day. The newly formed American Legion post had elected officers, and the shareholders of the Valley Turnpike Company stood to lose their investments if they didn't cash out by January 1, 1920. The mail carrier, Paul Stanley Wexler, passed away in his sleep at age eighty-one the night before the Home Coming Day.

Everything in Rockingham County that week revolved around the celebration. Train schedules had changed and businesses closed. Every account called the event an unqualified success.

And near the bottom of the front page, she found a small and peculiar story.

ASYLUM BREAK!

A local man and decorated veteran, lately an inmate of Byberry Farms in Philadelphia, Pa., is missing after an exciting caper Sunday last. Dr. E. M. Hermann reports Philip Marcus, son of local grocer Louis Marcus, knocked him unconscious and stole his weapon, a Colt single-action revolver. Marcus may be accompanied by a woman aged about twenty years and is considered dangerous.

Solveig's hands shook. Philip Marcus. The same man mentioned in the diary? Likely. And the young woman with him? Augusta—Gussie?

She scoured the internet for anything more on the two, but apart from Philip's name in the list of investors and a small item that recognized Augusta, Harvey, and Mrs. Kristine Engelwood among other valued Red Cross volunteers, she came up short.

She sighed and kicked off the quilt, steeling herself to the frigid morning air. Harvey should have left behind a rich legacy as a man of faith, not an unsolved mystery and a pile of bones still awaiting burial. Stories of remains in situ had never affected her like this, but they never lived in her town or owned the house she once called home. They didn't fall to their fates quite so near anyplace Bestepappa had asked her to go.

Harvey's inscription came to mind again. "A merry heart doeth good like a medicine," she whispered, "but a broken spirit drieth the bones."

The cavern called her. What she wouldn't give to go back. To scrutinize the prayer wall, retrace her steps to Harvey for the authorities. She longed to pave his path home.

Kyle had given the impression he'd rather not go near the cavern again, but maybe she could talk him into it. Solveig peeked out the front blinds to check the weather. Clear skies. Perfect.

The broken surface of the snow stretched across the field in front of the house. Had someone been traipsing around out there? The path was so strange. It looked like . . .

Words.

Yes. Once she saw it, the message was plain.

I WAS HERE.

She shivered. Had he forgotten she knew this was his inside thing with Ashleigh? Another message walked into the snow would have been wildly romantic. This . . . stung.

Never mind. She'd lollygagged long enough. Time to head downstairs, cancel the shuttle she'd arranged to the airport, check in for her flight, and call Ms. VanGorden.

Worst is first. She dialed in speaker mode and paced through the update. At least the news from the open house was encouraging.

"We had a decent turnout from prospective buyers. Of course, the usual train of lookie-loos too," Ms. VanGorden said. "A seasoned eye can tell the difference. Two of them asked about a home warranty. I left a brochure on the table for you."

Solveig sighed. "Yes, I looked at it, but I don't think—"

"That's fine, dear. You have me to think for you."

Solveig stopped short her pacing. "Excuse me?"

A short silence spoke volumes. "Excuse *me.* That was uncalled for. My ex-husband used to say that." Her tone was brusque, businesslike.

"I apologize."

"Thank you," Solveig said, maintaining some edge in her voice. Still, it made a difference where the barb came from, that under the helmet hair and pantsuit, the agent hid hurts of her own.

"I've already had two calls for showings today. One at ten and another at twelve thirty." The agent paused for breath. "Will those times be convenient?"

Not at all, but at least she asked. "I'll stay out of the way. So you know, I will be leaving Friday morning. No need for courtesy calls from then on."

"I'll make a note." Keys clacked in the background. "I will say, your staging was quite good for an amateur."

Solveig rolled her eyes. "Thanks."

As soon as they ended the call, she spruced up for the showings and dialed Forrester to update him. The last-minute list grew longer, but she might as well visit the cemetery to see her family's graves one last time.

Because her plans hadn't changed. Once she left Virginia, she was never coming back.

More snow dumped over the mountains in the night, and Kyle woke to a group text from Danny pushing their start time back until ten. Probably more to do with his kid than concern for the men he managed, but fine. Kyle had no complaints.

He shoveled a path from his door to the truck and pictured Solveig doing the same between the back door and the barn. Or maybe she was stoking coals that hopefully had kept the house warm through the night. She watched closely each time he built a fire and had probably figured out what she was doing wrong.

When he dropped her off last night, he'd almost asked if she wanted help. No problem to get a flame crackling before he left, except that plump pink lips and eyes full of moonlight had given his old self bigger ideas than to end the night with a chaste porch kiss.

Groaning, he squinted his eyes shut. "Stop."

Like Honey for the Bones

Gather ye rosebuds, idiot.

He tossed a shovel load of snow as far as he could. "I'm not discussing this with you."

Dude. She was into it.

"Yeah," he said to the man who wasn't there. "Exactly."

Goodnight had lingered on their lips, but when she brushed his face with icy fingertips, he caught her hand and warmed it between both of his. "It's late, and you're freezing. Go in. Get warm."

"I'm not c-cold." A chill shook her jaw, and she smiled. "Oops. Caught fibbing."

He kissed her knuckles, led her from the porch swing to the front door, and turned loose of her hand. "I'll see you tomorrow, okay?"

"Okay," she whispered. "Kyle . . ." He wished the words into the empty space, but she'd held them back. They weren't true. Not yet, not ever. "Goodnight."

He finished the path and replaced the shovel in the utility room. Why did this sting? He clung to his tattered shred of honor. Didn't invite himself in. Didn't play with fire.

Yes, he probably hurt her feelings by slamming the brakes, but if she was going to fly away with his heart regardless, he might as well do the right thing. Funny that not so long ago, he would have drawn the opposite conclusion.

A text buzzed his phone. The number was unfamiliar, the message direct.

Hera says she's interested. Meet at HQ. Nothing stupid, etc. . . .

How did they get his real number? The traceable one?

Didn't matter. A moment later, another message came.

Don't delay. The girl is here. We start cutting off fingers in 30.

Kyle ran for the truck.

Solveig brooded over the Borja family plot longer than she meant to. Her feet would not step away.

Even knowing she'd see her grandparents again. Even knowing she'd meet her father one day. She stood still as the stones around her until the inscription of the Engelwood mausoleum floated to mind.

He is not here.

True of her family as well. These graves were for bones. Their souls had arrived home, and the reunion would be sweet. Someday.

As she trudged toward the cemetery's gates, the loss and finality dragged along like chains wrapped around her boots. But brilliant sun sparkled over undisturbed shifts of snow. Her very favorite type of day. A good day for not being too sad.

She checked the time. Too early to return to the farm. Kyle's coffee punch card edged out from the folio case of her phone. Stealing it had been for a laugh, but she meant to give it back to him.

Java Mama's stood at the edge of town. Not much farther. Coffee to warm up and lift her spirits. Soup if she felt like eating. And some company, hopefully.

She snapped a picture of the punch card and sent it along with a note.

Kicked out for showings again. I'm headed to Java Mama's. If you can sneak away for lunch, I'll buy you a coffee. ;)

No answer. Probably busy catching up on his work.

Seconds measured in snow tread crunched by without a response, and she fought off disappointment. Maybe he'd see the message in time to meet her. If not, they'd have tonight, tomorrow. Goodbye loomed, but it hadn't come for them yet.

Thirty-Three

Kyle pulled into the empty parking lot at the depot annex. He circled the building to scout the exits. The hearse was parked in the back.

He pounded the front door. His pulse throbbed in his head and balled fists.

The heavy clank of the lock's release spurred him on. He pushed his way in.

The same punk he'd seen on his stakeout leaned into an ancient ticket counter. Maxwell Fischer wore skinny jeans and a black suit jacket over a ragged-out Ramones T-shirt. He took a drag of a short cigarette and flicked it to the cement floor still lit. "Come on in, man. Make yourself at home."

The place stank like chlorine and sawdust. The inside resembled a warehouse, with bare brick walls piped in conduit and ominous pallets covered in tarps. The exits corresponded with the doors outside. No obvious hiding places. No sign of anyone.

Kyle got in Maxwell's face. "Where's Solveig?"

Maxwell jerked his head toward the ceiling. "Smile for the camera, tough guy. You lay a hand on me, she's dead."

A domed mirror occupied the corner of the ceiling. Likely a bluff, but he exhaled and backed off. "Answer the question."

"She's fine. If you want to change that, keep stalling. Otherwise, let's get down to business."

"Fine. Where's Patterson?"

"You're looking at him."

Kyle gaped. *Him?* When "David" and Ashleigh had run the operation, this guy would have been about ten.

Maxwell burst out laughing. "Your face, man. Okay, okay. First, you can't go around using outdated aliases. Makes you sound like the geezer you are. Second, 'Patterson' summons *you.*"

Inside his coat, Kyle's phone buzzed. He ignored it. "Wasn't that what he did when he killed the guy from Bridgewater?"

Maxwell shrugged, nonplussed. "Either way, he's not here."

"Then I want to talk to Hera."

"And I want spinning rims for the hearse. Let's start with what we *need.*" Maxwell nodded toward the door. "You *need* the Norwegian chick to stay alive. If she doesn't, you're out of a job, am I right? That violates your parole, and you get to rot in prison for a few more years."

Kyle gritted his teeth. How did this punk know all that?

"So that's you. Now let's talk about what *I* need. Nothing much. Just some intel for the boss about this so-called gift."

Show time. He tried to find David Kyle's bravado, but the dead man had bailed. "He's still in the pre-owned mortal coil business, right?"

"Here to donate yours?"

Kyle glowered. "If he wanted me dead, I wouldn't be standing here looking at you."

"True, true."

"I've got a set of remains for him."

Maxwell snorted. "He doesn't clean up your messes."

"It's not my mess. I have an open account, and I want to settle it. An apology for how our last business went down."

Maxwell wiped a fake tear. "That's touching, man. Definitely doesn't sound like you're trying to set him up."

The plan wasn't going to work. Sweat ran down the small of his back. "What does he want, then? He killed my brother, followed me here—"

"Cool your jets." Maxwell looked bored. "So, where's the body?"

"You've got enough to see if he wants to dance."

"Maybe." He grabbed a cell from the counter and tapped out a message. In seconds, an answer chimed back. "Okay. You're good. We'll let you know when we're ready to talk again."

Kyle glanced at the phone. A direct line to Patterson? What would it take to get the phone away and take it to the police?

Maxwell waved it at him. "Oh, you want this? It is a pretty sweet phone. But you need Hera to get to the top."

Kyle tried not to react. Patterson structured his operation as before. This snotty kid was Kyle's replacement. "Don't know what you're talking about, but I'm not leaving without Solveig."

"Actually, you are, cuz she's not here and your time's up." He sneered. "Can't blame you. She's hot except for that gross neck."

If he didn't get away from Fischer, he was going to kill him. Kyle pushed his way through the double doors and stalked off, ignoring the laughter at his back.

He jumped in the truck and tried to think. If he didn't get to work, Charlie had every right to report him in violation of his parole conditions and no reason to hesitate, but he couldn't worry about that until he knew Solveig was safe.

He took out his phone to text her and saw the missed message. She had sent it while Fischer taunted him. Did that mean it was a trap?

It looked real—the sweet request, the picture of the punch card. His chest ached. Regardless of the consequences, he had to know for sure.

～～～

The coffee shop lay within sight when Solveig's mobile trilled and the number for CCPM filled the screen. Her heart lightened as she answered. "*Hallo,* handsome. How is your day going?"

"It's Danny." Solveig cringed, but he didn't sound surprised. "Benton's no-show, but that's not why I called. Wanted to see if you'll take my offer."

Kyle hadn't gone to work? Had something happened? A relapse with his concussion? She pressed the button for the crosswalk and the countdown at the signal began. "I'm so sorry, Danny. May I have one more day to think about it?"

"Take two if you want. The money's supposed to come through on my end this week."

Her sigh floated up into the air. "Thank you. I don't mean to be indecisive, but—"

"It's Benton, isn't it?"

"Not . . . entirely." What could she say that wouldn't make trouble? "It's hard to explain."

The signal changed, and she stepped into the street.

"Are you sleeping with him?"

"What? No!" Her face burned. "What makes you think that?"

"'Cause he said you were."

Blood crashed in her head, her ears. On the left side, the whooshing drowned out everything else. "I don't know why he'd say a thing like that. Or why you would ask."

"What you do is your business, but he's trash."

Her spirit battled between the impulse to defend him and the desire to hear more. "I trust him for the same reason I trust you. Because my grandfather did."

Danny laughed, but with a mean edge. "Soph, you're smarter than that. Your granddad made a *ministry* of hiring addicts, parolees, and last-chance losers. He warned me off calling you before you left town, and he would've sooner run Benton out of this state than let him near you."

"My name is *Sol-vay*. It's not that hard," she snapped. "And you don't speak for Bestepappa."

"Oh, I'm not," he said. "But I have it on good authority Benton's going to be brought up on new charges, so I wouldn't factor him into your long-term plans if I were you."

"New . . . charges?"

"He didn't tell you." His laugh was a bitter, broken sound. "Of course not. I thought you two bonded over the whole 'life on the outside' thing, but nope. No, he knew you were upset about your granddad and figured you for an easy lay."

"Stop it."

"You bet." Danny exhaled forcefully. "Go ahead and straighten things out with the scumbag. When you decide about my offer, call me."

She seethed as she stepped inside Java Mama's Henhouse. Her mobile chimed again. Kyle's reply. She knew it before she looked.

On my way. I'm in the field and slammed today but really want to see you.

Her heart tore down the middle, and the halves warred as she keyed her response. *I'll be waiting.*

She struggled to control her breathing, to keep from clenching her teeth as she stepped up to the counter. The dusty glass eyes of the stuffed rooster by the cash register creeped Solveig out. Was there any work more disgusting than taxidermy?

The poultry-themed decor of Java Mama's Henhouse made sense considering "Java Mama" Gillian Christianson was the county's largest producer of grass-fed, free-range organic chickens and eggs. She sold eggs by the case, cheaper than the grocery stores. Perfect for omelets, or egging houses.

As she waited with a double Cockadoodle Brew, Solveig pitted Danny and Kyle against each other. Her *trofaste* childhood friend versus the man she'd fallen *hodestups* for. One playing games with her property. The other toying with her heart.

She consciously relaxed her jaw. He might have an explanation. If he denied the words Danny put in his mouth, she would choose to believe him. And as for the rest?

Addicts, parolees, and last-chance losers, Danny had said.

Which are you, Kyle Benton? Who are you?

She had Wi-Fi. She could ferret out his secrets, confront him with the results, and demand the truth. He'd already admitted Virginia was supposed to be his new start. His clean slate.

"No such thing," she whispered.

She keyed his name into the search bar of her mobile, then backspaced immediately to clear it. She didn't want to google him. She wanted there to be a good reason, and the awful things Danny relayed to be a mistake. That whatever *his* "whole terrible story," Kyle would trust her and she would understand.

But why didn't he already trust her? She'd told *him* everything.

Instead, she tapped in *Aksel Borja* and hit enter. A line she'd never thought to cross. Until his stroke, she could have asked Bestepappa anything with perfect confidence that he'd answer with the truth.

The search screen hung blizzard-white so long she had to refresh. The results loaded on another try. His obituary topped the list, and she purposely scrolled past it. No time for tears now.

"Rockingham man creates haven for ex-cons," read the next result, and the third, "Property management firm launches transitional employment initiative."

She skimmed the articles and winced as the details aligned. Aksel Borja—Norwegian immigrant, farmer-turned-businessman, friend of sinners.

"Why, Bestepappa?" But she knew why. He had started the project while she served her sentence.

One link pointed to an interview, and his voice and inflection echoed in the words as she read them from the screen. "The Bible exhorts us to remember the prisoners," he'd told the reporter. "And to treat the least of these as Christ Himself. These men need to provide for themselves and their families. Many of them need a proper introduction to the dignity of work. A way to set the past behind them."

The reporter interjected. "You believe they deserve a second chance?"

"They do not," he had answered. "Mercy is by definition undeserved. But everyone needs mercy."

He would've sooner run Benton out of this state than let him near you.

Glutton for punishment as she was, she clicked over to page two of the results. Several more articles in a similar vein appeared, but one in the middle of the list stood out.

Scandalous Scandinavian Safer in the Clink!

She tapped the listing. Instead of text, a scanned image of old newsprint filled the tiny screen. It pixelated as she zoomed in, but the words remained legible.

A Swede by the name of Hans Aksel Borja, lately of Harrisonberg, pled guilty today to assault with a deadly weapon and other charges. Sentencing is expected in the near future. His victim, a man named Phil Marcus,

*veteran of the World War, remains at Richmond Charity
Hospital and is little improved, although doctors say he
may recover. As for the dastardly villain, he may find the
hoosegow more hospitable than the streets of Richmond.
Though charged with no capital crime, popular sentiment regarding the foreigner calls for his hanging.*

Impossible.

She suppressed a shudder and skimmed the piece for a date. De-
cember 23, 1919. More than a decade before Bestepappa was born.
Her tense knuckles relaxed. Neither could it be a relative, because they
had no Swedish roots.

Although that was a weak argument. The brief article displayed
sloppy journalism, from the misspelling of Harrisonburg to the
sketchy details to the pointless rabble-rousing. Its writer probably
couldn't have found Sweden on a map, and besides, Richmond was
too close and the name too unique to be a coincidence. Bestepappa
must have had family in Virginia when he came.

And what about "Phil Marcus"? A cold certainty drilled into her
heart. He had to be the same man who had escaped the asylum and
whom the diary tied to Augusta Rice.

Her mind raced. Every new clue made it harder to believe Bestepappa had gotten their land honestly.

The door swung, reflecting the light outside and bringing her back
into the moment. Kyle approached, his stride easy, but the eyes were
tired and his cap was askew.

She laid the loyalty card on the table and leaned into the backrest, arms crossed. His smile faded as he took the other chair. "What's
wrong?"

Everything. Please, say the right thing and make this go away.

"Busy day at work?" She narrowed her eyes.

He hesitated. Too long, too late.

"Because Danny said you didn't show up."

"Yeah." He seemed wary, guarded. "What's this about, Solveig?"

So now he wanted to have it directly. Fine. "Danny asked if you
and I were sleeping together. Tell me, why would he think that?"

Kyle swore. "That guy—"

"I know how to curse in four languages," she snapped, "and I choose not to. You will not speak like that around me again."

"Sorry," he said, reddening. "Forgive me?"

Tension knotted in her shoulders. "I haven't heard an explanation yet, so no, I don't think I do."

"Okay. I told you Danny was with those meatheads bothering you."

"He explained that. Unlike some people."

"I figured they'd stay away if they thought someone else was there."

"So you told him we were *intimate* in order to *help* me." Her voice rose in pitch. "How thoughtful of you."

"All I did was imply you weren't alone." The defensiveness leaked away, and he lowered his eyes. "But yeah. I knew how it sounded."

"And it worked so well, considering the break-in."

He exhaled and his posture loosened as if he thought the worst of the conversation was over. "Don't be mad, Solveig. The road to, uh, good intentions paved the way."

"Good intentions." She pursed her lips and considered him. "Is that also how you ended up needing 'transitional' employment?"

No hint of his trademark humor. Just long shadows and serious lines. "Guess Danny did all my talking for me."

"He didn't," she said. "I didn't ask. I'm asking you."

His arms crossed now too, and he pressed back in his chair. "Fine. I'm a felon. Out on parole. Happy?"

The noise of other patrons dimmed.

Her skin prickled. "I told you everything. Bared my soul."

"And I let you. Guess I'm not who you thought I was." He stood and zipped his jacket. "So that's it, right? Safe trip and all that jazz."

He left her at the table. To think he had made her believe she could stay and face the past instead of forever running from it.

She stared at the tabletop, too cold and spent to watch him go. He'd left the loyalty card behind.

Thirty-Four

The snowplows had cleared the roads, and the drive to Mount Crawford was mindless. The highway to CCPM's office forked before the river and led toward Kyle's cabin. Sunlight glinted off the snow pastures to the right of the highway. Barren trees dappled the left with shadows.

He needed to go to work. His parole officer would have enough to say about his sliding in late. But when he got there, he was going to kill Danny with his bare hands, and that wouldn't thrill Charlie either.

She's leaving regardless. It's a clean break. Take it.

His heart needed convincing, but his head had work to do.

Whenever Patterson or his lackey called, he would have to move quickly. For the first time in ten years, he was close.

Smoke billowed from somewhere up the road. A warning buzzed in his chest.

He glanced at the clock on the dashboard. Ten after eleven. Kind of early for a bonfire. Must be someone had a sofa bed to burn.

When he got to the office, he'd clock in, check the assignment chart, and head out again. What he said about being in the field today wasn't entirely false. He was supposed to be.

The fork was up ahead. The closer he got to it, the thicker the smoke. That was no bonfire. The smell. Plastic, chemicals, and . . . cedar.

When he reached the split, he veered onto the low road. The truck gained speed as he careened down into the hollow.

Someone might need help. He'd check. If not—

He never finished the thought. The smoke blackening the sky poured up and out from his own cabin.

He parked and jumped from the Ranger. Everything he had of Keith's was inside. He tested the front door. Still cool. There might be time to save something.

The roar was deafening. Popping, hissing. Kyle covered his nose and mouth as if it helped. The TV and the stereo were engulfed. No chance of grabbing the crate of records. They had to be melted. Gone.

The painting over the couch was already warped. The figure had darkened, the signature distorted. Keith's brush strokes couldn't be saved.

His lockbox of photos and the few letters his parents had sent him in prison were upstairs. Foolhardy at best, but he grabbed the fire extinguisher under the sink.

Overhead, something split with a loud crack.

The fog in his brain cleared. If the loft collapsed on him, he'd die. And if dying wasn't bad enough, he'd die without bringing Patterson to justice.

He fled the cabin.

In the minutes that followed, he called 9-1-1, Charlie, his landlord, Mendez, and the local police, in that order. His stomach twisted. He breathed deep through the burning in his chest until the nausea mostly passed. Then, he climbed into his truck and called Solveig.

She picked up on the first ring. "I don't want to talk to you."

"I know." Kyle coughed. His eyes still watered and stung. "Solveig, my cabin is on fire."

A sharp intake of breath told him she heard him, but otherwise, she was silent. He tried to focus. Stay in the moment. Not think of the flames licking Keith's painting and curling around the guitar his father had given him before things went bad and devouring every physical remnant of his life before Patterson.

"Are you all right?" she finally asked.

"Yeah." A miserable lie, but true in the sense she meant. "The fire trucks are coming, but I'm headed for the police station. Tell them what happened. See if I'm in trouble."

"Why would you be?" No missing the sarcasm.

"I have things to tell you later if you'll let me." *If I don't get arrested,* he added silently.

She let a long pause stretch. "You may sleep here. *One* night. You'll stay on a cot in the living room. You will not, for any reason, carry tales suggesting otherwise. Understood?"

"Yes. Thank you." His throat, itchy with smoke, tightened. "Solveig?"

She sighed. "Yes?"

I've done too many awful things to be the one who gets to love you. The new-life-in-Christ thing doesn't change that. I'm sorry for thinking it might. But it wasn't the smoke residue catching the words.

"I messed up," he said. "Bad."

The line scratched. "Can I do anything?"

"Yeah. Pray for me." The request escaped unrehearsed, but it was right. Better than what he'd held back. "Please."

Another pause. "I will."

⌒⌒⌒

Solveig did pray, but Kyle never showed.

Why did it help to filter heartbreak out of one language and into another? Maybe some of the anger got lost in translation. Maybe hopes dashed in English still found their Redeemer *på norsk.*

When she ran out of words, she opened the cavern pictures on her mobile and prayed across time over that holy graffiti. She took comfort in believing God knew about her future prayers when these needs were fresh and that He was certainly able to credit them to the correct accounts.

Her throat tightened at Gussie's plea. *I pray she found mercy,* Far. She swiped for the next photo, but Gussie's prayer was the last in the series, taken moments before the argument that led to discovering the bones.

Uff. She'd dreaded his arrival for hours, and now she worried what kept him away. She dozed in Bestemamma's chair by the fire to await his knock and woke to dawn light, a cooling hearth, and no sign he'd come.

He went to the police. He's fine.

After her steadfast refusal to enlist their help, he would have been amused to hear her say that.

She distracted herself with coffee and phone calls, starting with the Realtor. Ms. VanGorden was becoming her new best friend.

"The first showing went well. The second said they want something more modern. I don't know what they think 'Victorian farmhouse' means."

"Not to worry. The right people will find it and have a happy life here."

"Exactly. It won't be long. It's an excellent property."

Solveig wiped a renegade tear. "Thank you. I think so too."

Next, she set a new shuttle reservation and looked for an email from the airline, but it was too early to check in for her flight.

She struggled to write an email to Mette and finally gave up. She didn't feel like the same person her friend knew. For now, God was the only one around who understood Norwegian.

A cheerful confirmation came from Sven Skoglund at Statsarkivet, and she answered promptly without troubling the waters. Her new job was due to start on Monday. She'd have the weekend to recover and then stretch open her hands for the future.

Of course, there was one call she'd been putting off.

Danny.

What to do? Even as she dialed, she weighed one choice versus the other.

"CCPM. Danny Calhoun speak—"

"Danny. It's Solveig. I'll sell." The words spilled out, raw. "I've decided. Let's draw up papers or whatever needs to be done."

"Hey, great. I knew you'd rescue these idiots." He chuckled. "Myself included."

"Kyle too," she said with authority she didn't feel. "I want it added in our agreement that his employment is guaranteed for a full year."

"That's some severance package for a guy who's been here less than a month."

"No." She suspected severance pay wouldn't satisfy his parole conditions. "Full-time work. That is a nonnegotiable point."

"You know he's MIA again today."

"I already spoke to him." She masked her fears behind a firm voice. "Are we settled?"

He laughed. "You're tough, but all right. We've got a deal. I can't promise he'll be on desk duty much, though."

He'd rather work with his hands anyway. "That's fine," she said. "Can we do this quickly? I'm leaving on Friday. I don't want loose ends dangling too long."

"I'll have the money by tomorrow. Once it posts, it's practically a done deal."

A done deal. Was that what she wanted? She fought ambivalence and rattled off her email address. Her task was nearly complete.

It was almost time to go home.

She walked through the house, touching doorways, tracing faded wallpaper where pictures had once hung, savoring memories of Bestepappa and Bestemamma, sleepovers with Heather and the rest of their girlfriends, and even moments with Kyle.

He'd wanted to tell her things. What she wouldn't give for another chance to listen and try to understand, the way he had for her.

She perched on the hearth and bowed her head.

Be kind, Far. Show him mercy. Give him shelter and refuge. A new job sooner than later, a good one where he can thrive. Send him friends. Let him love. Deliver him from his past and give him a hope and a future—

The doorbell rang, three times in rapid succession. She jumped. She didn't think it worked. Another thing Kyle had fixed.

The brunette through the peephole smiled widely, her eyes fixed on the tiny lens. A stranger, so why was she familiar?

Solveig opened the door. "Can I help you?"

"Definitely, yes. I'm new to the area, and my partner, Kyle, told me about this grand old farmhouse. Wow, he wasn't kidding. So amazing. You must be Solveig?" She stuck out a thin hand with long, well-shaped nails. "I'm Ashleigh."

Solveig sucked in a breath as she accepted the handshake. The cold air zinged the nerves in her teeth. The woman in the photograph from Kyle's wallet, his *partner*, stood before her in the flesh.

"Hello." She stumbled over her words. "I'm sorry, I didn't expect you."

"Seriously? That goof. He said he'd meet me here." She rolled her eyes good-naturedly. "I don't mean to intrude or anything, but I hoped to take a peek."

"Oh. Yes. Come in." She stepped aside and studied Ashleigh more carefully. She was older than Kyle. At least five years. Maybe ten. She wore a tailored wool coat. No gloves—the better to show off large rings on both hands.

"I can *so* see us here." Ashleigh stood in the middle of the living room, a rapt expression on her face as if she saw something invisible to Solveig.

Why hadn't Kyle mentioned Ashleigh was back in his life?

I have things to tell you later.

A log in the fireplace popped. The whole room was roasting.

"When you say 'partners'—"

"We were in business together, years ago. Moonlighting, you could say." Ashleigh winked. "The benefits were killer. So, I hear you're from Norway. That's so cool. Say something in Norwegian."

"*Noe på norsk,*" she replied. "That means 'something in Norwegian.'"

Ashleigh laughed. "I knew I'd like you. Oh, wow. This kitchen is a-*dor*-able."

The over-the-top enthusiasm grated. The kitchen was small, functional, clean, outdated, and other less complimentary things before it was adorable.

"It only has one bathroom, I'm afraid." At Ashleigh's odd look, Solveig caught her error. "The house. Not the kitchen. Four bedrooms. Four-and-one."

"Perfect. So great." Ashleigh explored the house, talking a mile a minute. She'd always wanted to visit the Blue Ridge Mountains. When Kyle had moved east, she couldn't let him get away. "Virginia is for lovers, they say."

Solveig let a pinched smile color her response. "It's a catchy slogan."

Ashleigh let loose a laugh. "Sorry to be a weirdo. I'm just overwhelmed. Like everything I've worked my whole life for"—she stretched out her arm and grasped the air with splayed fingers—"is right there."

As they climbed the stairs, Solveig felt the absence of the family photos she'd taken from the wall. "How exciting. I can't imagine."

Ashleigh bubbled over the bedrooms, and Solveig stepped into the hall, trying to get her to follow. "Let me call Kyle. See what's delayed him."

"Good idea. I'll do it." The woman lingered at the doorway to the master bedroom and dialed. When her shoulders dropped, it was obvious she'd gotten his voice mail. "Hey, tiger. I'm here and you're not. Call me."

Tiger. So intimate, so familiar. Ashleigh probably knew everything there was to know about him—his secrets, his *felony*—and remained completely comfortable with him in spite of them.

She hung up and gave Solveig a rueful smile. "I'm the teeniest bit embarrassed for popping over unannounced like this. I really thought he'd be here to make introductions."

"No worries. My asking price is one-oh-five," Solveig said. "I'm sure that seems high—"

"Oh, honey." Ashleigh opened the closet and spread her arms as a measure. "I didn't become a medical examiner to pinch pennies. I've got that in cash."

Kyle, where are you? "You've taken a job with the county?"

"State. I've done my time in county." She laughed. "The district office is in Roanoke, but they want me to spearhead a satellite office here. I'll miss fieldwork. I'm not getting younger, I guess, but there's nothing like the thrill of a cold case."

Solveig tried not to choke. Harvey's case would cross this woman's desk. "Kyle mentioned you worked in forensics."

Ashleigh clapped her bejeweled hands together. "He told you about me? Well, now I have to know everything he said. Girl to girl."

Solveig bit back a groan. Doubtful that Ashleigh wanted to hear he'd dropped her photo in the trash and said to forget her. "He said he'd known you a long time." So lame. "You obviously, um, mean a lot to him."

She preened at the secondhand praise. "Definitely. We were practically kids together. But you know how it is. When you live near the people you love, you take them for granted. Well, not me. Not anymore." Her tone grew soft and serious, and one word rang above the others.

Love. Ashleigh loved him. Casually, openly. Since they were practically kids. What did that mean? She was no kid in the photo at Cozumel.

"He used to romanticize my work," she continued. "Giving answers to families, making way for justice. Heart of gold, that one."

"So true," Solveig answered mildly, as if she wasn't writhing inside. She shook her head. "Honestly, I'm pretty callous. I have to be. But Kyle never let me forget it mattered, finding out the truth for the ones who couldn't speak for themselves."

Solveig hung back and fought a tide of emotion while Ashleigh snapped pictures.

The other woman stood at the window, peered toward the road, then laughed and swore merrily. "You know what? I'll take it."

Chills spidered down Solveig's back. "You'll—I'm sorry?"

"Crazy, right? But I've got to live somewhere, and the fire puts him in a sling. We need something fast. I guess it's not officially official until we do the gymnastics with your real estate agent, right? I'll look her up and email her this afternoon, but you've got yourself a verbal, lady."

Well. A solution for everyone. Hadn't she been breathing the words when Ashleigh arrived? Refuge. Love. It didn't feel like a Sunday school ending, but she couldn't very well amend her prayer now, could she—Nei, Far, *not like this?*

"Wonderful." Shouldn't she be happy? She'd finished what she came to do.

Almost.

All except closure, answers, and justice for Harvey.

And here was someone able to help. What did her misgivings matter if she was an answered prayer? A miraculous answer given as the words had come.

Solveig gathered her courage. "So, you solve murders."

"Technically, the detectives get the glory." She smirked. "Thankfully, it's not all so dramatic. Suspicious deaths, but also mysterious and flat-out weird ones."

Solveig twisted her hands. An answer to prayer. "The reason I ask is—this is hard to explain—I have a problem that might fall under your range of expertise."

Ashleigh lifted her brow and lowered her chin. "I'm listening."

Thirty-Five

The Rockingham County PD's interrogation room had seen some tender loving tax dollars recently. The handcuff bar of the table showed only faint scuffing, and the chair Kyle sat in didn't wobble. The cinder block walls sported a recent paint job, a two-tone white-and-blue combo probably designed to induce perps to tell the truth.

The fluorescent light hummed quietly, unlike the one he'd fixed back at the office. The receptionist brought him a Styrofoam cup of coffee while he waited for Officer Howard to return. That was sort of nice.

Howard reentered the interrogation room with a bottle of Mountain Dew in hand. He twisted the cap and took a long swig, then pulled out the chair and let it scrape the floor.

What a show.

Howard put one foot up on the chair and leaned down to glare across the table. "So, tell me again. You got home—"

"I saw the smoke from a half mile away. Didn't think much of it—"

"But you said earlier you heard an explosion. Just another day in the neighborhood, Benton?"

"That came later." His stomach growled, and the site of his stitches burned and itched. Howard wanted to catch him lying, but Kyle *wasn't* lying, and even if he were, this guy's ham-fisted, nonlinear questioning technique needed work.

"How much later?"

Kyle suppressed a sigh. "Like I said, I heard the explosion after I came back out of the house. I assume it was either the furnace or the water heater. That part is on the 9-1-1 tape, if you're so hot over it."

"Don't get smart with me, son." Howard took his foot off the chair and crossed his arms. "Unless you're looking for a place to stay. We got the room."

"My apologies, sir." He stared straight ahead. Speak when spoken to. No mouthing off. No swearing. Solveig would be proud.

No, Solveig set that as a minimum requirement. He straightened and waited for another question.

"And after the explosion?"

"I called my parole officer, Charlie Lawrence. Then I called my landlord. He was upset. Probably still is." No. No attitude. He cleared his throat. "After that, I called—"

"Yeah, yeah, you made a bunch of calls." The officer narrowed his eyes. "Why didn't you do that first?"

"I wasn't thinking real clearly, sir."

"You entered a burning building because you weren't 'thinking real clearly.'"

Had to get my toothbrush. Don't say it, don't say it. "I wanted to save my brother's music collection, sir."

"Doesn't do streaming, I take it?"

"He's dead, sir." Eyes forward. No swearing. No punching officers in the face. Although in fairness, he'd only done that once.

"Seems like it's going around." The bullish voice entered the room first, its source filling the doorway. Leonard Dade trained his hawk-eyed gaze on Kyle. "I'll take it from here, Howie."

Officer Howard's shoulders slumped. "All yours, boss."

No wonder Solveig thought Dade was intimidating. Six four and impossible to read. Well, Kyle was not guilty. Not this time.

Of course, he was not innocent either. He'd blown that status a long time ago.

Right now, he occupied an awkward in-between—in custody, held on suspicion of parole violation. And he *had* violated his parole. There was that.

Howard left the room. Dade pushed in the chair and remained standing. The man's instincts were unerring. Silence made people nervous. It was making Kyle nervous. "Hello, sir."

Dade never blinked. "Heard you've been missing work."

Breathe. Tell the truth. Don't try to be funny. "Doctor's orders. I took a few days off to recover from a head injury."

"And how did that happen?"

"Spelunking."

"Bad time of year for that, ain't it?"

"I never claimed to have much going on upstairs, Sheriff. Probably less now." There went his goal about not trying to be funny.

Dade tapped a stylus to the screen of a tablet outfitted with a thick black case. Even interrogations had moved into the digital age. "Says here you told your PO you were supposed to be back on duty yesterday. What happened?"

He answered carefully. Flexing his Fifth Amendment rights would stick a pin in his guilt. "We had a late start because of the snowstorm. Then the owner of CCPM texted me to meet her in town. I was on my way to work when I saw the smoke."

"What'd you and Miss Borja discuss?"

Please, God. Don't let them drag her into this. "She dumped me, sir."

Dade lifted an eyebrow. A tiny fissure in the cement. "Tell me everything you did and saw inside the cabin. The truth."

Kyle ignored the insinuation. "I tested the door with my hand. It wasn't hot to the touch, so I figured the inside was still safe. Relatively."

Dade made a hand gesture. *On with it.*

"I had the TV, DVDs, stuff like that, in the living room—"

"And where was that?"

"First floor, left of the entryway. The kitchen was on the right. Bathroom in the back. Bedroom in the loft."

Dade narrowed his eyes. "I'll worry about the floor plan, Benton. You answer the questions I ask."

Kyle took a steadying breath. "The living room was already engulfed. That's when I remembered I should crawl below the smoke, but I thought if I grabbed the fire extinguisher from the kitchen—"

"You'd do what with it?"

"I know how to use one, sir. I thought I could make a dent."

"I've seen a better man than you die for making that mistake."

Sorry to disappoint you, sir. Don't say it, don't say it. "The fire extinguisher was smaller than I remembered. Then I heard a loud crack from one of the beams that supported the loft. The danger level kind of dawned on me. I exited through the front door."

"You risked your life trying to save a pile of old CDs. That's what you want me to believe."

Kyle dropped his eyes to the table. "My brother's collection was all vinyl, but that is basically correct, sir."

"You weren't disposing of evidence."

"Definitely not."

"Did you enter the loft?"

"No, sir."

"You're sure about that."

A shiver rippled Kyle's flesh. Dade was hunting. "Very sure. The smoke was pooled in the ceiling, like the fire was much worse upstairs."

"Probably started in the loft, you think?"

"I don't know. The experts will have to figure that out."

Dade lifted his chin. "How do you know Trevor Roberts?"

Vague nausea lapped over him like a wave. The sudden swerve was a bad sign. "I don't, sir."

"No? Let me fill you in." Dade's face remained granite. "Last week he was your run-of-the-mill murder victim from Bridgewater. Now he's a missing stiff."

He froze. "What did you say?"

"You heard me. If I need to remind you, the Commonwealth of Virginia is doing you a favor letting you breathe our good air, son. My first stolen cadaver case in eighteen years crops up inside a month of you rolling into town. Gonna tell me that's a coincidence?"

No. It was not a coincidence.

"I'm fully prepared to cooperate with your investigation," Kyle muttered. Eight years in Sterling had proved cooperation wouldn't save him.

Dade continued as if Kyle hadn't spoken. "You know what's interesting? They say scent and memory are linked in the brain."

"I've heard that, sir."

"Then let's talk about what you smelled inside the cabin."

Kyle frowned. "Smoke, sir. Cedar. Chemicals. I don't remember anything more specific."

"Nothing familiar? You didn't catch a whiff of anything that reminded you, say, of operating a crematory?"

Bile bittered his throat. "No, sir."

"That's funny, Benton." Dade wasn't laughing. "Because I've got my forensics team telling me Trevor Roberts's corpse burned up in your bed."

Thirty-Six

Dawn would break in an hour. Gussie rose from her restless bed and dressed as quickly as she dared, afraid to make a sound.

Harvey had gone to the lions' den. But like Daniel, his faith preserved him, didn't it?

She hoped so, because her own was failing.

Their pantry offered little to spare. She wrapped meager provisions in a clean flour sack. Corned beef. Their last jar of Mrs. Engelwood's tomato soup. Half a box of National Biscuit Company lemon snaps. The hodgepodge would have to do.

The air cut with a frosty edge, and the softening sky twinkled with lingering stars, cold and clear. The same stars that had stared down on Philip all night and witnessed whatever he had done.

She shivered and touched her lips. He'd injured her to show affection, and again in his anger. What had restrained him against a hated rival?

That prig, her memory taunted.

But Harvey simply had to be safe. And Philip needed her patience. She'd try. It'd be different this time.

She raced over the pastures between their two houses. The Buick ought to be parked under the awning of the Engelwoods' barn. Once she set her mind at ease, she'd figure out how to take the food to Philip and what to say to bring him back to himself.

When she rounded the corner of the barn, a cry escaped her lips. The car was not there.

She spared a glance toward the house. The windows remained dark. Either Mrs. Engelwood still slept, blissfully unaware, or she'd already gone searching.

Gussie let herself into the barn and found her answer. Both the Engelwoods' horses stood in their stalls and nickered softly at her intrusion.

The third stall had belonged to Victor's horse. She'd been flummoxed how death could be a mercy when Harvey put Dolly down. Now she understood.

"Shh, it's okay." She patted Clarence's neck and accepted his nuzzle in return. "It's all right, boy. Feel like a run?"

Nerves trilled. She'd never saddled a horse by herself, but she knew how. If she remembered.

She tucked the food into a saddlebag and arranged a blanket over his back. Yes. Most likely she was in fits over nothing, but she'd ride to the caverns and settle her mind. If it turned out something awful had happened, she'd double back to Harrisonburg and send the police.

The barn door creaked open. "Funny. I never took you for a horse thief."

She whirled around and nearly cried. There in the entryway stood Harvey with her valise in hand.

She threw herself at him. "You're all right. I was so worried."

"Ah, well." He extracted himself from the unseemly embrace and stepped in from the wind. "The hot meal, electric flashlight, and sleeping bag bought me a moment's goodwill. That'll disappear once he misses this." He lifted the valise slightly. "I waited until he dosed himself into a stupor and took it."

"Clever," she said softly, "but he'll be furious."

"Let him be furious, then." The red rims of his eyes and the weariness in small movements suggested he hadn't slept. "If he's as sane as he says, his actions will bear consequences. I'd rather he get himself caught without involving you."

"You mean that." She drew back and her pitch rose. "After everything you wrote about mercy in your book."

His face was flint. "Those who confess their sin and ask for God's mercy in Christ assuredly receive it. Some time in a jail cell may give him the chance to ponder it."

"You honestly care nothing for him?"

Harvey stepped closer and captured her eyes with the emotion blazing in his. "If you doubt my concern, let me assure you," he said roughly. "I pity Philip and the lost souls of strangers and all of suffering Europe, and I'll pray without ceasing for their relief, but not at the expense of one hair of your head, Gussie."

"Lovely." Eloise's intrusion startled them both. "I'm moved practically to tears."

"Ellie? What are you doing here?" The silly question puffed into the crisp air. Neither of them belonged here at this scandalous hour.

"Following you, you little minx." Her eyes narrowed meanly. "Staying out overnight, stealing food, and still so audacious as to play the innocent."

"Don't be ridiculous. I was never away for a night. Those silly novels have turned your mind." The lie hiccuped along, implausible and shameless. Scrambled thoughts settled on the valise, and she wrested it from Harvey's grip. "I merely left this with Mrs. Engelwood last week and wanted to retrieve it before Harvey heads back for school."

The weight of it surprised her. Harvey's eyes rounded. "Gussie, I insist that you—"

"Never mind, it's quite manageable. And didn't you want to speak privately with Eloise?" She flitted toward the door. "I'll let you lovebirds be."

The wind fought her the whole walk home. Her trickery left her stomach in knots. If Eloise felt this way all the time, then no wonder she acted so prickly.

Yet she hadn't threatened to go to Daddy. That was something, and so was the valise. The heft of its illicit contents imparted a sense of power, and rays of sunlight that poured into the basin of the Shenandoah Valley gave Gussie a notion she ought not give up on Philip so readily as Harvey had.

Once safely locked into her bedroom, Gussie unfastened the latch. Of course, the gun drew her attention first, with its long, narrow barrel and oily iron stink. She took several moments to work up the nerve to touch it.

It was heavier than it looked, and E. M. Hermann was engraved on the hand grip. Dr. Hermann. Gussie wondered if the man had recovered.

She trembled and laid the gun aside. Possibly not.

The copy of Ibsen's plays remained safely tucked into the inner pouch of the case. How naive to imagine reading plays might save him. She was no better than Hedda Gabler, thinking she directed fate with her supposed gift.

She removed the bottles of laudanum and hid them in her dresser drawer. Each bore a warning on the pharmacology label. Poison. One was empty.

Obviously, it did not help.

Well, if Tillman's Miracle Elixir did its job, Daddy would have a new testimonial to run in the *Rockingham Register*.

Gussie tromped down the stairs. Daddy kept his main inventory in crates in the barn, but a half dozen bottles took up space in the kitchen cupboards. Two ought to be plenty for Philip, but on second thought, she packed them all.

A door slammed in the next room, and burly shouting arose. When had Daddy gotten home? He complicated her plans, but only a little.

She'd stay out of his way and wait for Paul Wexler to come by in his mail truck, then beg for a ride. If he refused, she'd appeal to him with her plan to write on the prayer wall for the Home Coming Day and make his hometown heart swell with pride.

Gussie latched the valise and hid it in a sideboard, then poured a bowl of Post Toasties. Who'd imagine "the pretty one" could design such a scheme?

⌒⌒⌒

Paul Wexler was happy to take Gussie to the prayer wall.

The mail truck plugged along over the rough roads to Massanutten. Gussie's wrist grew sore from bracing herself against the dashboard panel. The steering wheel kept Mr. Wexler anchored, and he had talked continually since she joined him, besides. "The Good Lord didn't make no mistakes when He set us down in these mountains. What we need these days is young'uns who know where home is. Make sure you pray for that. And to keep from gettin' stars in your eyes over city life. What else you planning to write?"

"Oh." She tugged her coat around her and tried to think. "I have faith it'll come to me."

He nodded. "That's how the preacher does it. Say, I ought to come along and add a word or two of my own." A disaster in the offing.

"I'll be too shy if you're there," she said. "In fact, it may take some time. I don't want to keep you all afternoon."

He glanced toward the back of the truck, loaded with parcels and crates of bundled letters. "I s'pose you're right, Miss Gussie. Awful lot to do before tomorrow. How do you figure on getting home again?"

She pressed her lips together. The thought of being stranded at the cavern with Philip raised her hackles, but then, Harvey knew to look for her there once she was missed. He might not abet her ploys, but he'd never leave her bereft in them.

"The Lord will provide a way," she finally answered.

"Ah." He wasn't as happy with her faith this go-round. "Sure, of course. Amen."

Red-and-yellow leaves near the peak of their glory obscured the way, but Gussie judged they were close to the cavern's entrance. They wound the last few curves in the road, and the truck sputtered to a stop. She leaned across the bench to lay a kiss on his weathered cheek. "Thank you, Mr. Wexler."

He patted the spot, grinning. "My pleasure, Miss Gussie. It gives an old man hope to see young people with respect for tradition."

Her chest knotted. She let herself out of the truck faster than he offered to assist, and tossed a jaunty wave to allay the growing reluctance on his face.

The cool air nipped as she marched through tree litter. The truck's idling grumble roared and coughed and finally receded as Mr. Wexler drove away.

For the moment, she was alone. The broad path toward the cavern's entrance beckoned. The bottles inside the valise clinked against each other and the gun.

Should she wield it from the first? Wait to see his mood? What if he wasn't near the entrance? Mr. Wexler had probably assumed she had a lantern in the case, but of course, she hadn't brought one. A mistake, and she didn't own an electric flashlight.

The darkened maw lay ahead. Gussie starched her spine and called out as she approached. "Hello-o? Philip, come see what I've brought you."

She waited outside the stone entrance. Her heart thundered as Clarence's hooves might've, had her horse thieving been successful. An option she may have to revisit after Harvey went back to sch—

"My darling girl." Philip emerged from the darkness and rushed her for the valise. "You're a saint."

No! The revolver would end up right back in his hands. She grabbed for the handle, but he'd already opened the case and begun rummaging.

His smile faded. "What's all this?"

She swallowed back her nerves. "Tillman's Miracle Elixir. Remember in my letter, where I told you how it cured Daddy's customers? Since the other medicine didn't seem to be helping—"

He tossed the bottle in his hand, and it shattered against the limestone.

"Not helping, you say. What would 'help,' Gussie? Perhaps if I threw myself from the nearest cliff." His eyes were bloodshot and his hands trembled.

"Don't talk like that," she said, voice quavering. "Harvey says—"

"Don't utter his name in front of me again. That worm stole you and he stole my laudanum. If I see him again, I'll kill him."

He cast the valise against the cavern wall, and more glass shattered inside.

Gussie screamed, but Philip only mocked her. "Are you afraid of the dark?"

He stalked away into the deep and muttered to himself. She stood and listened but didn't dare follow.

The sun sought its grave amid the mountain peaks. Yet as dusk sealed its fate, the distant clamor of a car echoed. Not any car. Harvey's Buick.

She collected the ruined case, checked that the gun had escaped damage, and hurried along the footpath. Harvey looked humble as ever, wearing an overloose sack suit and his new straw boater. He carried an oil lamp and the flour sack Gussie had prepared this morning. She pitched herself at him once they met on the way.

She battled down a sob. "You came."

"I shouldn't have." He pulled away from her and adjusted his hat with a frown. "What are you thinking?"

"Never mind. We ought to leave." She grasped his arm. "He says he'll kill you."

"Splendid." He went to the cavern's mouth to deposit the lamp and the sack. "Here's food if you're hungry," he called.

Without ceremony, he doubled back the way they had come, and Gussie followed. He cranked the car for their journey home. Everything she meant to say flew out her ear when he took the driver's seat.

"I'm sorry," she said. "For this, and for earlier."

"As am I," he said. "Eloise and I are to be wed tomorrow."

The breath went out of her. *"What?"*

Harvey took a long time to answer. His face was mottled between pale and ruddy patches. "After you left, she cast all manner of accusations. Not an ideal prelude to my suggestion she and I part company."

"You didn't tell her."

"Oh, I did." He sighed. "She went straight to your father and told him she is, well, in delicate condition."

Gussie's face went aflame. "I see."

He threw a sideways glance toward her. "It's not true, Gussie. At least, not on my account."

"Oh." Still, her sister's schemes bowled her over. "Then you can tell Daddy—"

"Your father is not interested in arguing the point. We're off to Richmond tomorrow."

"You'll miss the Home Coming Day."

"Indeed." A stretch of road passed beneath them before he spoke again. "More importantly, the next time you chase a mirage, I won't be here to run to your rescue."

She stiffened. "No one's ever forced you."

"No. I did it because I love you. Gussie, I've loved you since the schoolyard."

The winding road twisted her head and stomach in opposite directions. "Why didn't you tell me so?"

A strangled noise escaped his throat. "Which day did I not tell you? I explained it with math and science and literature. I carved it in wood and inscribed it on a book and finally typed it in a letter that I've wished every day since I'd had the courage to sign."

Her lips trembled. "And Eloise?"

His knuckles whitened. "She certainly maketh ashamed."

He fell silent. Waiting for her answer? So was she. She cast about for a response but no words came.

Road wind tousled her chignon, and the cold worked its way inward. Harvey had wooed her with a long-suffering heart. The fault lay with her. She'd longed for love so much, she missed its call. His only mistake was underestimating her unfailing stupidity.

Thirty-Seven

"Careful up ahead." Solveig's warning ricocheted off the stone walls. How did Ashleigh keep in front when Solveig was supposed to be leading? "This is the turn."

"I'm so excited." The woman's bubbly personality had probably been a major attraction to Kyle. She was uninhibited, bold, charismatic. He must have adored her. "It's been a long time since I've done CSI work. My first love."

Solveig bristled, unsure why. "I'm anxious to hear from Kyle, though."

Ashleigh swung the beam of her flashlight into the dark. "Have you known him long?"

An impulse to lie gripped Solveig. She shook it away. "Not at all. Fast friends, you might say. I'm only in town until Friday."

"That's plenty of time for him. He's a smooth one." Laughter echoed throughout the cavern's chambers. Ashleigh clearly didn't view Solveig as a threat.

Solveig glanced at her mobile again. No message, of course. No signal down here in the dark. "I have noticed."

Meant as bait, the remark hung in the air. Ashleigh paused at a fork in the corridor. "Which way?"

Solveig indicated to the left with her flashlight. That was how she did it. Ashleigh stayed ahead of Solveig's beam, and her enthusiasm carried them along. At first, it had seemed reasonable to show the skeleton to Kyle's friend in forensics, but with every step, Solveig's doubts grew. "Maybe we should—"

"You're right." Ashleigh doubled back a few steps. "We're wasting valuable debriefing time. Tell me what you know about the subject."

Such a clinical term. "I don't want to bias you."

"You won't."

Sighing, Solveig gave in. "I believe the bones belong to a man named Harvey Engelwood. He went missing in 1919."

"Great. Who wanted him dead?"

Solveig blinked. "No one that I know of. There was a woman—"

"Aha."

"Her name was Augusta Rice, and she wrote a Bible verse in another part of this cavern, dated the same day Harvey disappeared. It reads like a confession to me."

"Irrelevant. Anyone who wanted to pin her to the case could have written it at any time."

Their footfalls filled the large stone hall where she and Kyle had danced. "I never considered that."

"Makes you wonder who had it in for *her*? But back to Harvey. Any reason someone might make him disappear? Legal trouble, gambling debts, maybe?"

"Nothing I can find in the records. He was quite devout."

"Ah. Fleeing the stain of sin." Ashleigh's sarcasm said more than her words.

"I don't think so," Solveig said firmly. "His widowed mother was left to fend for herself."

"He was young?"

"Not even twenty."

"Do we know how tall he was?"

"Not exactly. A journal I found calls him a 'scarecrow.'"

Ashleigh snorted. "Colorful, but not quite useful. Anything else?"

Solveig recited facts fresh from review. "His older brother died in France, but Harvey was too young for the draft. He inherited a good-sized estate, and he had just published his first book when he vanished."

When Ashleigh finally spoke, she sounded apologetic. "I hate to point this out, but young guys are a high-risk group when it comes to bailing at the first sign of trouble. Especially when there's money they can dip into."

"A generalization."

"A small one," she said. "Based on experience." Ah. Ashleigh didn't fear biased conclusions because she had already formed them.

"You don't believe it's him."

"I don't." She surveyed the path with her beam. "Probability. So, you stumbled across a corpse. The odds of correctly guessing its identity are pretty low."

"Then why ask about Harvey?"

"Because it's easier to rule him out than to prove it's him, so we'll start there. And it is a good theory. Just unlikely to pan out." A bitter edge laced Ashleigh's laughter. "Here's my guess. The bones were a homeless person, the graffiti is unconnected, and as for Harvey, he probably got some girl pregnant and ran out on her."

Solveig blanched. Was that a veiled accusation at Kyle? She backed away to lengthen the light. It shone in the waxy sheen of the limestone. "Do you want to see the prayer wall?"

Ashleigh hesitated. "If you think it's important. I'm more excited for the bones."

Solveig pressed her lips together. Yes. It was important.

"It's here." She stepped into the alcove and directed her flashlight to the wall. "Gussie—Augusta, rather—wrote her message there. And—"

Whatever she'd been about to say escaped her. She spied words she must have missed before. A faded graphite prayer. Unremarkable, except for the language.

Vis oss veien.

No name, no date, and no doubt this prayer was exactly what Bestepappa had wanted her to see. She put her fingertips lightly to the stone, careful not to smudge the words.

Show us the way. The sort of plea one might make for a new little family starting out. The handwriting reminded her of the scrawl on the inserts of the collection of old cassette tapes.

Her father must have written it.

Ashleigh snapped a picture of Augusta's prayer. "Okay, got it."

Solveig lingered in the moment of imagined closeness with the father she never knew and sent his words back to the One she did. *Yes, Far. Show us the way.*

"Sorry. We're nearly there." She took a deep breath as the bones came into view. Before, when she'd turned and faced the skeleton, she screamed like a ditz in a cheap horror film. This time, the sensation of ice water circulating through her chest took control. "Here, up ahead."

"I see it." Ashleigh's voice shook with unconcealed giddiness as she handed Solveig her flashlight and whipped out a small pack. "This is the most fun I've had in months. I'm tempted to look around some more. Maybe we'll find another one."

Solveig stared into the vacant eye sockets while Ashleigh donned gloves and collected tools from her field kit. If the bones weren't Harvey's, they had still belonged to a living soul. One who surely didn't deserve this crude final resting place.

"No hair left." Ashleigh took an incessant number of pictures. "That's a bummer."

How could she be so cavalier? "Can I help?"

Ashleigh held a pen in her mouth as she adjusted a measurement tool. "No. I won't be long."

"Oh." Solveig's hands shook, and the lights with them.

"Can you hold that steady? Thanks."

"Sorry."

She watched Ashleigh work through a haze of rising regret. At least she now knew what was worse than taxidermy.

"Okay, we have bullet fragments. There goes my hapless-homeless theory. This is definitely a murder victim." Ashleigh straightened to address Solveig. The flashlight's beam made her look rather skeletal herself. "How much did Augusta hate Harvey? Because if I wanted someone to suffer, I couldn't pick a better place to leave them to die. Can you imagine? The intense pain. Going into shock. Completely alone. Not knowing where life ends and death begins. No light. No sound. No hope."

Solveig shivered. "I'd rather not imagine. Hopefully, death came swiftly."

Ashleigh crouched again and returned to her work. "Maybe so."

This couldn't have been what Bestepappa intended. He wanted her to see the prayer wall, not these bones. If she'd come at Christmas, he would have eagerly shown her. There'd have been no argument, no wrong turn. She'd have a priceless memory in place of this awful burden.

"Worthless." At length, Ashleigh rose and removed her gloves. "It's not him."

"Are you sure?" Solveig asked, but there seemed little point in questioning Ashleigh's bold pronouncement.

"Sorry, hon," she said. "I know it's not the answer you wanted."

"But how can you say for certain?"

"Granted, this was a quick and dirty examination." Ashleigh took back her flashlight and spotlighted the skull. "But Harvey was an adolescent in developmental terms, and these cranial suture sites show fusing consistent with adulthood. Same with the dental wear. The teeth are in good condition overall, but he must have gone through sustained' periods of stress. I see lots of dentin showing through the enamel. He was a grinder."

"There must be room for error."

"Sure. Aging a skeleton has a lot of data points. But if this man was as young as Harvey, I'd see something to suggest that. Chin up. He may have disappeared because he was the one who killed this guy!"

"Ah." Solveig had no answer to that.

"We can say 'he' with relative certainty." Ashleigh tilted the beam downward. "The pelvic bones are larger than you typically see for females, there's no ventral arc, and the greater sciatic notch is unambiguous. Definitely a male.

"Here's the kicker." She scrolled through the pictures on her camera. "Look."

The image showed a silver star emblem emblazoned with the letters *US* and circled with a laurel wreath.

"A button?" Solveig asked.

"Even better. A World War One lapel pin." Ashleigh enlarged the image. "I've seen a couple of these. The army awarded them. Bronze for honorable discharge, silver ones to soldiers wounded in action if I remember right. It'll narrow the candidate field considerably, but it rules out your guy, I'm afraid."

And it begged certain questions about Philip Marcus. The sketchy article claimed he had landed in a hospital in Richmond, but had he? Solveig swallowed hard. "Where did you find it?"

"Lying in the dirt beside him. I'd guess it was fastened to his clothes before everything rotted away."

Solveig's stomach flip-flopped. "Can you tell what the man's war wound was?"

Ashleigh shrugged. "Not here. Maybe in the lab, but just as likely it was a soft tissue injury."

"Then it's circumstantial. The presence of the pin doesn't mean this man owned it."

Ashleigh finished repacking her field kit. "True, but sometimes you have to read the writing on the wall."

The writing on the wall. The strongest evidence these bones involved Harvey was still Gussie's message. What did she mean by it? Did she intend her prayer for God's eyes only? And if so, why sign and date it? Those features aimed at a more temporal audience. But who?

The plea for mercy came under the purview of the God who was able to grant it. But Gussie wanted someone else to know—what? That she was a sinner. That she recognized her failures. That she was sorry and spent and at the end of herself.

Rather like Kyle. *I messed up. Bad.*

"I know you're disappointed." Ashleigh interrupted her musing. "Think you can fake it for a selfie? I want loverboy to know he missed the party."

Solveig barely veiled a shudder as Ashleigh stretched out her arm to snap the picture. The flash seared, blinding her.

"Perfect." She presented the image for inspection. Solveig hated her look of ambivalence. Ashleigh's expression was more sneer than smile, but she didn't ask to retake. "I wish I could see his face when he gets this."

Solveig widened the beam of her flashlight and started back the way they had come. "How long, do you think, before the medical examiner's office will inter the bones?"

"Oh, who knows?" Ashleigh lagged, shining her light around the various rooms and formations of the cavern as if on a walking tour. "I might not open a file on it right away. No use coming in the door with a ton of drama."

How did she do her job without a sense of urgency over victims? "Do you think the state will test for DNA? Or is there some other way to identify him? He's still someone, with a story and a family and—"

"A missing person case," Ashleigh said. "Such fun."

Solveig gripped the passenger door of Ashleigh's Volvo. The woman sped through the mountain curves as if she wasn't scared to die.

Must be nice.

Solveig's mobile vibed, but she left it in her coat pocket. If it was Kyle, she didn't want to say so, and the easiest way to ensure that was to leave it tucked away.

Besides, Ashleigh had hardly paused for breath. "The thing is, the bones have been in darkness and at a constant temperature for a good long time. Not an optimal temperature, mind you, but still, that helps preservation immensely. Mummification would have been more exciting, but there's a great chance of extracting viable DNA if the case grows legs."

"You mean, they might not investigate?"

Ashleigh tapped the steering wheel. "They will, but they might decide it's not worth expensive tests and media hoopla. Speaking of which, I'm curious who else knows about this?"

"Kyle and me," Solveig said. "No one else."

"Fun. I love being in on a secret. I'm sorry it isn't the storybook you wanted—"

"It is." She attempted a smile. "Grimm's, but a fairytale nonetheless."

Ashleigh laughed. "That's the spirit."

"I wish Kyle had caught up with us. I admit I'm concerned about him."

"I'm sure he's fine. If you knew how many times he rescued that brother of his—"

"You knew Keith?"

Ashleigh nodded and kept her eyes on the road. "Unfortunately."

No compassion. Not that Solveig expected any. "Kyle thought he hung the moon."

"And I'll never understand why. At the risk of sounding like a horrible person"—she dropped her voice conspiratorially—"he's better off."

Solveig nodded. "In a better place," she agreed.

Ashleigh snorted. "If you like to think so, but I meant Kyle. Seriously. Keith was his blind spot. Now"—she shrugged—"no more blind spot."

Solveig had no answer for that. When would they ever get home?

Home. She studied her chapped knuckles as if comparing two maps. The house she'd agreed to sell only hours ago, she'd just thought of, once again, as home.

"I'm starving," Ashleigh said. "Feel like a bite?"

Solveig blanched. "I have some calls to make before it gets late. In Norway, I mean. Six hours ahead." She faked a laugh. "My window is closing."

"Why didn't you say so sooner?" Ashleigh accelerated, and Solveig's stomach dropped. "I'll have you home in a jiff."

Ashleigh was as good as her word. When they pulled down the driveway minutes later, she released a small sigh. "Look at that. So peaceful and perfect. I hope your agent comes by with a 'sold' sticker for the sign before the snow melts. I'm dying to get a picture."

"I'll take one and send it if I can." Why did she say that? What was it about this woman that made her so apt to make offers and promises and tell secrets and everything else? "Thanks for the ride. And the consultation, would you call it?"

"Expedition, totally."

She nodded. "I appreciate your help."

"You are so welcome." Ashleigh lengthened her gaze to the house. Rather than the moon-eyed look she'd worn inside, she stared with some sort of calculus in the crinkle of brow and the set of mouth. "Ciao."

Not until she was safely inside the house did Solveig let out a moan. "*Kjære Gud, tilgi meg,*" she said. "Forgive me. I thought You sent her. Truly I did."

She leaned against the front door as if to barricade it and willed her thumping heart to quiet. It took a long time.

She should not have trusted Ashleigh.

Thirty-Eight

Hours in the county lockup passed long and cold and familiar as an old pair of boots. Leonard Dade suspected him of Trevor Roberts's murder. He didn't have evidence to charge him, though. They'd have to release him eventually.

Kyle had to hand it to Patterson. Not only had he seen through Kyle's trap but he'd turned it inside out and laid a better one. The police would never agree to a sting at the cavern now. And sending them to the depot annex meant admitting the rules he'd broken.

He'd done a lot of wrong, some of it recently, but he wasn't a murderer.

His head hurt. He stank. The smoke had permeated his clothes, his hair, his skin.

Better not try to place his one phone call to an international number. Besides, he couldn't face her. Except, when he got out, he had nowhere else to go.

So he lay on the metal bench of the cell, his jacket wadded under his head, and prayed while he waited. He asked for Solveig's forgiveness and justice for Trevor Roberts. For any miracle that kept him out of prison. He had lots to discuss with God, all of which boiled down to begging for one more chance.

He slept a little. Not deep. Just enough to see ghosts in the shadows and startle awake.

The pounding in his head was excruciating. Too many days, too many claims he was fine. Maybe he wasn't fine. Maybe he had a brain bleed. The cherry on top.

When the officer on duty finally called his name, he was surprised to hear "Kyle Benton."

He'd half expected "David Kyle."

⌃⌃

Solveig had said one night. Kyle hoped the offer hadn't expired. He'd texted from the police station, but standing at her door, he lacked the courage to lift his hand and knock. Because when he did—

To say: "I am Lazarus, come from the dead,
Come back to tell you all, I shall tell you all."

The pathetic Prufrock had nothing on him. He pressed his fist against his forehead. His story didn't fit inside lines from a worn-out literature textbook repeatedly checked out of the prison library. No quote from that lame movie fixed this either. If words existed to sum up this train wreck, they were the ones inked on the cavern wall.

"'God be merciful to me,'" he muttered, "'a sinner.'"

Two things were going to happen. First, he'd tell Solveig the truth. Then, she'd throw him out.

Why not save her the trouble? By this time of night, the shelter in Harrisonburg was full, but—the cavern. Yes, once deep enough in, he'd be protected from the frigid temperatures. Midfifties beat the low twenties expected tonight.

The hike might be rough. Besides his truck, what did he have? No change of clothes. No dry socks. His next paycheck would be sparse from missed time. He leaned his back against the door, aching.

His phone, one thing he did have, dinged.

Do you want to come in?

He sighed. "Yes," he said aloud. The door at his back unlatched, and he stepped away as she opened it.

"I got your text," she said quietly, her eyes downcast. "I was watching for you. But you didn't knock."

"I didn't know how to explain. Not after—"

"I'm not as mad as I was." She offered that soft, reserved smile he'd fallen for so hard and so fast, then lowered her chin. "Still a little mad. You still have to sleep on the cot."

"That's fair." He followed her into the refuge of the farmhouse.

When Kyle emerged from the shower wearing borrowed clothes from Mr. Borja's old things, Solveig had already piled blankets in the living room and tossed together a simple supper. She scooped up his smoke-laden clothes and put them in the washing machine.

"Your jacket might be past saving, but the rest will be okay," she said. "I'd rather put you upstairs, but there's no propane. It is too cold. And I hope tomato soup is—"

"It's perfect." If he drowned in her kindness before the wellspring ran dry, that'd be perfect too.

She served the food, dismissing his attempts to help, and bowed her head.

"*Vi takker Deg, Herre*—uff, sorry. We thank you, Lord," she began. This time Kyle bowed too.

"For this our good, but more because of Jesus's blood. Let manna to our souls be given, the Bread of Life sent down from heaven. Amen."

"Amen." He met her eyes. "So. Which four?"

"Pardon?"

"You said you don't swear in four languages."

Her shocked face was priceless. "I don't swear in any languages!"

"Okay, but specifically?" He ticked fingers. "Norwegian, English . . ."

She shook her head, mouth agape. "Danish and French."

"Cool." He drummed the tabletop lightly. "That's all I've got in the icebreaker department."

A short laugh escaped. "That works."

He stirred the soup to make the scent rise. "What's that word again?"

"*Koselig.*"

He nodded and tried to freeze this frame. How she knew what he meant. How the hot liquid soothed his smoky throat, how her topaz-blue eyes almost made him feel he could catch his breath. Too soon, the food was gone and the table cleared. The piper wanted payment; the Reaper had come to collect.

"Solveig, I'm sorry—"

"I'm sorry too." She reddened. "I forget you have a whole life that has nothing to do with me. You don't owe me explanations."

A reprieve. Undeserved. He couldn't accept it. "I want to tell you."

"Then I'm listening," she said softly.

"It's not a good story. Don't hate me when it's done."

"I won't."

We'll see. He exhaled heavily.

"My brother had a drug problem. When I was fifteen, some kid found out and goaded me over it after gym class. Instead of ignoring him like they always say, I pounded him into hamburger meat. I got suspended for two weeks.

"Afterward, everyone knew about Keith. Some were jerks about it, and I've never done real well with jerks. More importantly, I loved my brother and he needed help. I wanted to save him. I wanted to be the *one* to save him."

He searched her eyes for understanding. So far, so good.

"So I became his dealer. I know how dumb that sounds. But my twisted logic went, if I controlled his access, I could ween him off. Bring him back.

"Obviously, it didn't work. What I thought was simple, wasn't. Addiction had its hooks in him. He did what he had to do to get high.

"Then I got hooked too, but not like you'd expect. See, my supplier didn't go for the one-client idea. I had to meet a quota. And that wasn't hard to do. Suddenly, I had a lot of money and a lot of new friends. Bad news all around. And the more I got, the more I wanted. Keith's addiction was chemical, physiological. Mine was plain greed."

"You don't think you're being hard on yourself?"

"Nope," he said. "It went on like that for three years, Solveig. I moved product. Had an alias, code words, and a gun I never needed to use because 'David Kyle' had the golden touch."

He paused for breath, but the air refused to satisfy.

"Then, surprise, Keith did a stint in rehab and got clean. It didn't stick long term that time, but—"

"You had a choice to make."

"Yeah. Mission accomplished. So, did I give up my thriving enterprise or give Keith an attaboy and keep doing my own thing?" He barked a short self-deprecating laugh. "I picked door number two. And I got caught."

"By the police?"

"Worse. My mom." He rubbed his eyes. "I lived at home and worked twelve hours a week as a bouncer at my buddy Omar's nightclub. Mom got suspicious of where the money was coming from. She found my stash, and her and Dad laid down the law. Quit selling, get a real job, and get out of their house or else.

"I asked Omar for more hours. Instead, he got me a job at a crematorium. But here's a tip. Never ask your crooked friends to find you honest work.

"It was an actual business, not a front, but there was a silent partner. An investor, we called him. Glen Patterson. I never met him. I dealt with his assistant. Ashleigh."

Solveig drew a sharp breath. "Your forensics friend. The one you took to the ocean."

"Right." A buzzing sensation tingled at the base of his neck. "Twice a week, she'd show up with paperwork ordering cadavers to be transferred to universities and teaching hospitals. This happened for a month or so, and then she came by with a fat envelope for me. I asked what it was. She called it my bonus for the transfers and asked if I wanted to earn a lot more."

He left out the details of that night, how Ashleigh had asked him to dinner and sketched out the plans. How enraptured he'd been with her charms. Solveig didn't need to hear that part, and he didn't want to dwell on it.

"You went from selling drugs to selling . . . people." This was it. The gears were turning. She was going to throw him out.

"Their bodies, yes."

"And you got romantically involved with the woman who helped you *traffic cadavers*?"

"Is it that hard to believe?" His stomach turned. "She was the one person I could love without hiding my dirtbag secret life."

Solveig's face was unreadable. "You loved her."

"Whatever love is." He swallowed hard. No lies. "Yeah. I loved her."

The wind outside howled. Solveig lowered her eyes and stilled, except her hands trembled on the table.

"Do you want to hear the rest?" Part of him hoped she'd say no, but she nodded the smallest assent. Fine. If this conversation was part of his punishment, he'd take it.

"Ashleigh worked with Patterson at the hospital, and they hand-picked the ones we sold. We had so much paperwork. It all looked legit." A pang pushed him. "I knew it wasn't, though. Just to be clear on that.

"Meanwhile, I was still dealing on the side. It's not like my supplier would take two weeks' notice. There was a girl, Hailey. Cute little meth head. She had a crush on me, but I treated her like a kid sister. I was with Ashleigh, and weird as it sounds compared to everything else, messing with underage girls was not my kind of trouble."

Stop stalling. He rubbed his temples.

"Then one day she turned up at the crematorium."

Solveig glanced up, frowning. "She wanted drugs?"

"She was dead."

Her eyes widened and filmed with tears.

"It was bound to happen eventually. When I wasn't looking, I had turned into a monster. Ashleigh had already sent over the forms from the hospital where she was pronounced. Hailey's body was scheduled to ship that day to the Finley Plateau College of Medicine."

Solveig covered her eyes with her hand. He was in for a long night, camping on the cavern's bedrock.

"I had excuses for everything. That jock had it coming. Addicts would find their fix, regardless. And the stolen cadavers were already dead. Victimless crime. Until Hailey."

His voice cracked. The image of her scabbed, silent face in the morgue would never, ever leave him.

"And then? There were no excuses. I'd sold her the drugs and had a buyer for her corpse. I might as well have killed her myself. For money."

Solveig's tears were rolling. One after the other. She just let them fall.

"I choked. I cremated her like I was supposed to, which left us short on the order. When Ashleigh got there, she panicked. Said Patterson would take her instead. I gave her the cash I had on me, three thousand bucks, and told her to hole up in a motel. Said I'd meet up with her.

"But I went to the feds. Named names. Struck a deal. Paid court fines and restitution. Long story short, I got whistleblower immunity on the cadaver trafficking but couldn't dodge all the drug charges." He coughed. "But I didn't give them Ashleigh. She was the only link to Patterson."

War waged on Solveig's face. He could almost read the thoughts as they formed. Disbelief. A faint smidgen of compassion. Horror. "You kept her photo."

His face burned. "I did."

"And you called her."

He shook his head. "I wrote letters until the prison mailroom informed me they all came back undeliverable. I figured she got caught or skipped the country. Who knows, maybe she's dead." The old ache stirred, but he squelched it. "Eight years at Sterling Correctional Facility gave me lots of time to wonder. I had a job in the prison laundry and other than that, I stared at steel and concrete and a cruddy latrine every day."

He paused, remembering. There was plenty to say about the awfulness of those years, but the point was made.

"One day, this volunteer shows up asking how I want to spend eternity. Got my attention. They offered chapel service at three thirty, Sunday afternoons. I figured it'd make me look good when I went up for parole. But when Brother Mike said I could leave the man I was for dead and be a new creation in Christ? Sounded like the plea deal of a lifetime."

His throat stung more with every word, but the tale was almost done. "By the time I got out, Keith was finally clean. He stayed with Mom and Dad, got a job, went to meetings, found a church. He painted constantly. I told you about his show. He set that up himself.

"Nine years to the day after I rolled on Patterson, Keith was found in his car at an art gallery. Asphyxiation, caused by an overdose."

She gasped. "That's like the man who was killed here recently."

"You noticed that too, huh?" He hung his head. "I knew Patterson did it but couldn't prove anything. Mom and Dad blamed me. Thought I gave Keith the drugs or that I rocked him after he was finally stable. The police didn't even try. Another lapsed junkie, case closed.

"We were heading for a blowout, so I applied for a parole transfer. It wasn't a sure thing, but I read about your grandfather online. He gave me the job, sponsored me.

"But Patterson followed me here, and the cops won't listen—" The rest hung in his throat. Trevor Roberts in his cabin, the meeting with Maxwell Fischer. The shortcuts he'd taken looking for justice, the fact he was most likely going back to prison in the not-too-distant future. *I'm not that guy anymore*, he wanted to say, but he was. He was.

When he looked up to finish his confession, her shoulders heaved and her lips clamped so tight they all but disappeared.

"Solveig—"

She pushed back her chair and fled. The door to the guest room slammed. He followed to the hall, but a loud sob carried from within. The message was clear. She'd heard enough.

He retreated to the living room and stared into the fire. If a tear or two escaped, so what? If nothing else, prison had taught him how to cry so no one but God would ever know.

Thirty-Nine

Solveig didn't mean to slam the door. It did slam, though. No pretending otherwise.

She wanted to be as accepting as Kyle had been, equally strong and in all the same ways. As with the sofa bed—and here she was, dropping her end of the burden again. His story overwhelmed with too much to take in, too much to grieve. She cried for Hailey, for Keith. For the lost years and lost innocence of a boy who wanted to save his brother.

He'd even given her a practice run in the hospital vestibule—*a prostitute, a thief, a drug dealer?*

I still don't want to leave them lost in the dark.

A fresh wave shook her. Indicted by her own words. She had to get herself under control and tell him Ashleigh had been here, because in spite of herself, she believed him. It made no sense to tell such a horrendous story only to lie about Ashleigh when she directly asked. Like Gussie's signature, his confession flowed from a place of brokenness and remorse.

She shuddered. This afternoon, Ashleigh hadn't seemed broken at all.

Her mobile chimed from the nightstand, still in its endless charge cycle. She resisted the temptation to ignore the message. When she reached for her phone, she wished she hadn't.

We have a cash offer! Full asking price, close ASAP. Sign and return attached. Congratulations! PV

Dread twisted her belly. Good as her word, Ashleigh had sent in the offer, signed *A. Weisher* in all the right blanks. Whatever her scheme, Solveig refused to play along. She tapped out a response Ms. VanGorden wasn't going to appreciate. *Thank you, but please decline.*

At once, the email chime sounded on her mobile. The answer was brief but direct. *Kindly explain. PV*

So much inflection for such a short directive. Solveig hesitated over her reply. *May I call you?*

The response zinged back. *Kids are asleep. Email only. Please advise. PV*

Solveig closed her eyes. The one excuse that came to mind might send Ms. VanGorden into orbit. *I noticed a possible forgery on the deed. Probably need to straighten out before we sell, right?*

Five minutes elapsed. Fine. Solveig needed a break. A chance to think. And a clear path to the bathroom.

In spite of her dramatic exit an hour ago, she cracked the door softly and crept through the back hall. No wit in sneaking around, though. The stillness amplified every sound, from the creaky knob and groaning hardwoods to the sharp intake of breath when Kyle must have realized she had emerged.

He didn't call or come after her. Maybe he, too, needed time to let the confession scab over.

She made her way to the bathroom and back, and he never budged. The washing machine had finished, so she put his clothes in the dryer. Such a normal thing.

She dared to spy on him from the hallway. The cot was folded up where she'd set it out, and Kyle sat in Bestemamma's chair. His head leaned into one of the wings, and his eyes were closed, but his breath was too shallow for sleep. She stood, self-conscious that he probably sensed her, and watched him rest.

He'd done terrible things. And suffered for them. Watched people close to him suffer. Loved and lost. He'd destroyed his own life, one decision at a time. Then he'd come here, hoping it would be different, only to learn as she had that you can never outrun yourself.

"Kyle," she half whispered. "Are you asleep?"

"Do you want me to go?" He spoke without lifting his head.

"No. But can we—"

"In the morning," he murmured back, then looked up and tapped his ear. She nodded. He closed his eyes again.

She padded back to the bedroom, more confused than ever. Here they were together, yet both alone.

But was that bad? It had taken a night's rest before she recognized the relief of telling him her story. Maybe it would be the same for him.

She dressed for bed, murmured a short prayer for wisdom, and took a final glance at her mobile to check the clock.

Two missed calls and one email from Ms. VanGorden awaited. She read the message.

CALL ME. PV

She sighed and put the mobile away. Her eyes burned, and exhaustion crept over her as she climbed into bed. "I'm sorry, Ms. Van-Gorden," she mumbled into her pillow. "In Oslo, it's almost four in the morning."

Forty

Gussie sat wedged between her sister and Mrs. Engelwood in the back seat of Harvey's Buick. He and Daddy rode up front, of course. Her vantage point in the middle glimpsed one side of each man's face, their clenched jaws like mirror images.

Of their miserable crew, only Eloise had anything to say. She gushed over the Home Coming Day events as if life held nothing finer than picnic food and parades. As if she delighted in riding the apple-pickers' wagon and had never scoffed at a community sing. Tucked away at her feet was a small traveling case. Whether Harvey carried one as well, Gussie hadn't seen.

To her right, Mrs. Engelwood maintained a rigid posture and stern mien, but if she knew of the snare around her son, she gave no outward sign.

For her part, Gussie sat still as stone, her hands folded over the handbag that rested in her lap. An old and ugly thing, but her only one large enough to hold Ibsen's plays, matches, a stub of a candle, and the gun.

The weight of it shocked her. In the dark of night, she'd practiced holding it, but her hands shook and its heft made her arm flag.

When they reached Harrisonburg, Gussie fell in step with Mrs. Engelwood. Ladies Auxiliary volunteers were to meet at the high school, where they'd prepare for the county-wide banquet that came after the ceremonies. Harvey was supposed to accept Victor's medal, but he, Eloise, and Daddy would be Richmond-bound on the first train out. Her heart ached every time she thought of it.

Volunteers crawled the campus like ants. Mrs. Engelwood led her to the kitchen on the first floor and deposited Gussie by a sink full of potatoes. "You will wash, peel, and dice them for liberty potato salad, *ja?*"

"Yes, ma'am." Gussie reached for the paring knife, but Mrs. Engelwood arrested her with a glance.

"What are you holding secret?" she demanded. "And why does your sister prattle on like a *tosk* while the rest are silent?"

Gussie's lip quivered. "I don't know."

A scrap of conversation flitted to mind. *I've never told a lie in my whole life*, she had claimed to Harvey. Well, here was one.

Mrs. Engelwood's eyes narrowed. The woman wasn't fooled.

Gussie stopped her before she could move on. "Before I forget." She reached into her handbag carefully and withdrew the book. "Thank you for loaning me this. I'm sorry I kept it so long."

Mrs. Engelwood's frown tinged with confusion or perhaps concern. "Augusta, what are you twirling on about?"

A frisson fluttered through her and threatened to erupt in tears or laughter. "Never mind me. So much excitement today."

Mrs. Engelwood gave her a final appraisal and handed her an apron. "You have your assignment, then."

Indeed she did.

Gussie scrubbed potatoes until the commotion had grown enough to lend cover, then laid her apron aside and slipped away.

Amid the noise and number of the crowd, she slinked toward the stable across from the firehouse. Hundreds of voices became none. No one to ask what she was thinking or remember which way she went. No wise counsel or warnings. This time, there'd be no one to help if her ploy at the cavern soured.

Gussie pushed away the thought as she reached the stable. The apple-pickers' wagon would leave for Massanutten on the hour, and she intended to be on the next run.

Forty-One

The house was quiet and warm, and Kyle was eons past exhausted. He'd dozed once or twice, but when the sun spilled over the mountains, he was awake to see the room lighten. He could stoke the fire, but that meant getting up.

He tried to move and groaned. All night in a wing chair. Better than the Rockingham County Jail bunk, but two nights of spotty sleep had taken their toll. He had a kink in his back for every one of his thirty-two years.

The wee hours had convinced him they were his last as a free man, but everything looked different by morning. He had two things going for him. First, he hadn't killed Trevor Roberts, and second, he hadn't set his cabin on fire. The pendulum might swing anytime, but until then he intended to go forward as if he wasn't dead and wasn't going to prison.

The silence from the next room ran like sand through an hourglass. He dreaded the first light cough or gentle creak of a floorboard to signal she'd roused.

His phone buzzed. A different number appeared than before. He accepted the call and held the phone to his ear, silent.

A breath puffed over the line. "The boss will see you now." The call disconnected.

Stiffness and aches forgotten, he rose to his feet.

A long-buried stealth returned like a second skin. He slipped into his clothes, his stinking jacket. The situation was bad. He had no plan now that Dade suspected him. No backup. No weapon.

The man who murdered Keith was closer than he'd ever been. As much as Kyle wanted to look that snake in the eyes, he had to be smart. Yes. Sneak attack. He'd take kerosene from the barn. Match them jab for jab. Burn the annex, smoke them out, call it in. Tip off investigators about the drugs and the connection to the funeral home. Ditch his phone and disappear.

Not a great plan, but the best he could do. He grabbed his keys and paused.

Solveig.

What would she have said last night if he hadn't cut her off? Another lost chance wedged into his mountain of regrets.

He dashed off a note, pressed the paper to his lips, and weighted it with his lighter. One final disappointment.

He let himself out. If he hustled, he could make it to the annex inside twenty min—

A meaty fist clocked him in the jaw.

Kyle swung wildly. His fist connected with Danny's eye. He jabbed to the gut and attempted to sweep Danny's legs from under him. The larger man grunted but didn't go down.

He lobbed Kyle in the ribs. The taste of smoke rose in a fit of coughing. As Kyle struggled to catch his breath, Danny wrapped him in a choke hold and wrestled him to the porch planks.

"Late for work, Benton." Danny twisted Kyle's arms behind his back and secured them with handcuffs. "Gonna have to dock your pay."

Kyle swore and grappled for leverage, but Danny kept him pinned with a knee in the back.

"Better keep it down." He emptied Kyle's pockets into his own. "You don't want to drag your ladylove down with you."

"You wouldn't."

"You're right," Danny said. "Always liked good ol' Soph. Besides, I got what I wanted."

Kyle growled. "What's that s'posed to mean?"

"You'd like to know. But unless you want her implicated, too, you do what I say."

He huffed for breath. "Implicated in wha—?"

Danny dragged him to a semiupright stance and herded him toward his Ranger. He hoisted Kyle into the truck bed like a sack of cemetery refuse.

"You're under arrest, chump."

Solveig peeked through the blinds to check the weather.

Gone. Fresh tracks out. No sign of Kyle's truck.

Her heart sank. Maybe he had lied about Ashleigh. He might be with her. And if not, he may have left to avoid being thrown out.

The frigid air forced her to change quickly. She stuffed her pajamas in the packed suitcase and emerged from the room, looking for signs of him, regardless. He'd ditched the borrowed clothes in the washing machine and left a blanket half-draped over the arm of the chair and puddled to the floor.

Seriously? After everything, he left like this?

She grabbed her phone.

Where are you?

No answer. None needed. A note lay on the kitchen table, a pen beside it. He'd left his lighter on top, a paperweight.

She pocketed the lighter and picked up the note. Impressions bore through the scrap of paper, signs of stress or rush, but his slanted print-script was legible.

Solveig—

You're one in a zillion. Sorry for pulling a Harvey on you. (He is not here.) Even sorrier I won't ever be the guy you deserve.

—Kyle

She squelched the desire to set it aflame, and read the message again. "Won't ever be"? Had he not changed? Then, why tell her any of it? Why come to her for refuge? No need to pass the night in a wing chair when Ashleigh's arms were open.

An undercurrent moved beneath the torrent. A disconnect. Her brain wrestled with it while she straightened what little remained throughout the house. Something he said, something she said.

The airport shuttle was due in two hours. Her flight remained on schedule for midafternoon. What had she accomplished? The house was in limbo, her deal with Danny still in motion. She had come to cut ties and ended up hopelessly entangled.

The fact she'd never see Kyle again burned.

Her mobile trilled and she jumped, but it was only Ms. Van-Gorden. She might have guessed the agent wouldn't wait for the clock to strike eight.

"Please explain precisely what you meant by 'forgery.'" Icicles spiked her words.

Solveig folded the abandoned blanket and draped it on the wing chair as she awkwardly shouldered the mobile to her ear. "The transfer is dated 1971, but the previous owner had been dead for over fifty years. Or rather, he disappeared. Either way, he wasn't here to sign a deed."

He is not here. The empty place in her chest ached.

"I will order a title search," Ms. VanGorden said. "Normally, that's a line item in your closing costs, but if we don't sell, I'll send you a bill."

"Mr. Forrester already had one for me recently when the question first came up."

"Miss Borja!" Her frustration pealed. "If you had questions, why didn't you bring them to me?"

"I—" Her voice shook. "I'm sorry I've made a mess of it. I came here to settle an estate. It's a nice euphemism for picking apart bones, isn't it?"

The agent sighed heavily. "This is why I hate estate sales. Let's start over. I'm dropping my boys off at school, but I can be there in fifteen minutes. We'll review your documents and go from there."

Solveig stuttered her thanks. For all her faults, Ms. VanGorden seemed to know how to wipe a slate clean.

She hurried to make herself presentable, but the knock came sooner than expected.

"Be right there," she called out. The clock was five over eight. Plenty of time. Ms. VanGorden would see something she didn't. She might even provide the insight that solved Harvey's disappearance.

Solveig swung open the door. "Sorry, I—"

Leering at her was the angular, mocking face of Maxwell Fischer. The goatee lost definition under days-old scraggly whiskers, and he reeked of cigarettes.

More importantly, he held a manila envelope in his left hand and a pistol in his right. He shoved his way into the house. Fixed the barrel at her heart. Locked the door.

Solveig's stomach dropped.

"Get on the floor," he said.

Forty-Two

As a kid, Kyle had always begged to ride in the bed of his dad's truck. The reality fell short of the dream.

When the Ranger finally stopped, gold-tinged rays lit the morning. A glimpse of heaven. Or a road sign pointing at earth's off-ramp. Sure felt like he was near his exit.

This was no normal arrest. No badge. No rights. Plus, Danny had trussed him like a Sunday chicken. His face had ground into the ridges of the pickup bed, and his mouth kept welling blood. Each breath came with effort. Probably some combination of smoke inhalation, exhaust fumes, extreme cold, and oh, possibly a bruised rib from knocking into the wheel well a dozen times.

He lay on his chest, listening, breathing. Breezes, skittering branches. Air sweet with snow and pine. No road noise or honking, no beeping of the Friday trash trucks making their rounds. No people around.

Not good.

The tailgate opened. The clang drilled his ears.

"You lunkhead, I told you not to hurt him."

His stomach knotted. That voice.

Ashleigh. And Danny. Working together.

Danny is Patterson? How is that possible?

"He's fine." Danny sounded doubtful.

"I haven't been Mirandized." Kyle's words came out mush.

"Plenty of time for murderizing later," Ashleigh said. "Come on, get him out of there. I want to see his face."

Danny hoisted himself into the bed of the truck and slid Kyle off the tailgate. His legs buckled, and his knees cracked against the freezing asphalt.

Explosions. White halos blazed at the edges of his vision. A guttural cry tore from his lips.

"Oh, you poor thing." Ashleigh rested her hand against his cheek, then slapped him. The stinging in his mouth sharpened under the blow. She turned to Danny. "Deputy Calhoun, the State of Colorado thanks you." She fiddled and swiped on a phone and held it out. "Care to do the honors?"

He tapped the screen.

"Poof. Thirty thousand dollars. You earned it." She dipped her head toward Kyle with a sneer. "They really wanted this one."

Danny surrendered the phone, keys, and wallet he'd lifted from Kyle into Ashleigh's hands. "You sure you don't want me to wait till your backup—"

"It's fine. I'll take it from here."

A rising shiner distorted Danny's left eye, but his uncertain expression remained intact. He'd been conned, but whatever was worth thirty grand covered a multitude of sins.

Danny strode away, head high and snow crunching under his boots. His Buick stood ten yards away, off the side of the highway. Ashleigh smiled in Danny's direction and tossed him a thumbs-up as the engine growled and the car pulled away.

She knelt beside Kyle. "Hello, David."

"Hi, Ashleigh. Been a while, huh?" Soreness gripped his bare fingers. He'd be flirting with frostbite before long.

"'Ashleigh.'" She shook her head. "Such nostalgia. I suppose 'David' sounds strange to you now. But I can't get used to 'Kyle.' It's a terrible alias."

"It's my actual name."

"You're adorable, thinking that was ever a secret." She laughed. "I planned for us to take a walk, but it looks like we'll need to get creative."

Her boot connected with his right knee, and he howled. She walked away and left him thrashing in the snow. He managed to sit up, but his useless knees made it impossible to stand.

He gauged the landscape. They were at the trailhead of the same short hike he'd made with Solveig to reach Rice Caverns.

The door latch of his truck rattled. Muffled thumps followed, then the distinctive clang of the bed box lid coming off echoed over the hills. "This'll work, I think." She shook out the tarp from his emergency kit and looped through the eyelets the lengths of red-and-white cord from his glove box. "Ta-da. Makeshift sled. Can't say I planned to drag you through the mountains today, but sure. Why not?"

She pushed him into a prone position with a boot to the chest, then rolled him onto the tarp. He resisted, but fresh waves of pain crashed from the least movement to his knees.

He struggled to catch his breath. "What is this?"

"I came to see if we can bring you back into the fold." Her eyes glittered. "Your recent indiscretions give me hope. I was starting to think you'd burned up on reentry."

Whatever that meant. He shook his head. Endorphins washed over him, bringing incremental relief. "I don't—"

"Okay. Small words. Call this a job interview." When she smiled, lines and shadows appeared. Her youthful prettiness had morphed into a slightly haggard sophistication. "Let's discuss your place in the organization. I have a unique opportunity for an experienced criminal."

"You're back with Patterson? Ashleigh, why? You're brilliant. You don't have to answer to him. You can go anywhere, start over, be someone else."

"That's exactly what I had to do." Poison seeped through her words. "You went soft over your little groupie and ruined everything. The first and last time I've been dumped for a dead woman!"

He coughed, setting his whole chest aflame. "No. I loved you, Ashleigh."

"Sure, because your love is cheap and easy to get." She drew a phone from the front pocket of her coat. "Which reminds me. I've been dying to show you."

The brightness of sun and snow competed with the screen, but the image she flashed sent needles buzzing and prickling throughout his body. Solveig's face showed apprehension, and Ashleigh's, cunning. He spat a mouthful of blood and growled. "Leave her alone."

"Ooh. So alpha male of you. Rawr." She put the phone away. "I planned to bait you with it but decided I wanted to see your reaction. You never disappoint. Except for that time when you destroyed my life's work."

"I didn't. I never gave them your name."

"You say that like you did me some giant favor." She turned her back and pulled the cord. "Just when I was ready to make you a full partner, I had to start from nothing."

He shifted his weight and rolled from the tarp onto the crunchy white layer disguising the rocks. "I don't understand."

She stomped back and kicked him in the stomach. "Do that again, and I'll tie the cord around your neck. Worked like a charm on Trevor Roberts." She shoved him back onto the tarp.

He gasped and sputtered as she rerigged the setup. A realization took shape, developing in textures and colors like a Polaroid photo. Whatever she said, she did not intend to bring him back from wherever she was taking him.

When he tilted his head upward, she was holding his phone instead of her own.

"Speaking of your boring little snow rat, she's wondering where you are. I'd send a picture, but we don't need her in our business yet." She started tapping and muttered the message aloud. "Hate to leave you hanging, but it's better this way. You deserve someone . . ." She cast an appraising eye at Kyle. "Stronger? Smarter? What fits here, handsome?"

Kyle tested the sore lower cuspid with his tongue. It moved. "With all his teeth."

She snickered. "Oh, David. Stop reminding me how much fun you used to be."

"'Kay. Ah." He coughed for an extra moment to think. "Write, 'Go wake up in the future, beautiful.'"

Ashleigh narrowed her eyes. "What's that mean?"

"Norway's six hours ahead. She'll get it." *Lord, please let her get it.*

"'Beautiful' is a stretch." Ashleigh tapped in the message and slid her reddened fingers into a pair of gloves. "You've downgraded."

He said nothing. A trickle of coppery saliva leaked from the side of his mouth where Danny had struck him. He twisted his head to wipe it on his shoulder, and the handcuffs bit his wrists.

"I wasn't thrilled by your 'gift,' you know. Some random dried-out skeleton? What am I supposed to do with that? Sell it to a high school drama club? Not my racket, but thanks for playing."

His gift. The skeleton. For Hera's boss. But there was no boss. Or there was no Hera.

The truth landed with sickening clarity. *Ashleigh is Patterson.*

She watched him. "Did you just figure it out?"

His chest heaved painfully. "You killed Keith."

"Of course I did." The cord slackened. She crouched before him and patted his face. "You wasted so much of your life trying to save his. We're all going to die, baby. Some sooner than others."

Dawning horror gripped him. His old partner, his fallen star, his brother's killer. His throat tightened.

"You've changed so much, it's like you already died." She shook her head and stood again.

A schism formed, a terrible double vision. Things he'd once treasured about her were still there. The tough loveliness, the dark wit, the scheming genius. Her nature quivered with contradictions. He'd faced them in himself the day he called on Christ to give him new life.

Lord, I'm sorry for ever doubting You did exactly that.

Death. Not ideal, but at least he wasn't David Kyle. He had freedom in that, and peace. For so long he'd sought justice and courted revenge, but now, pity overshadowed it all. He couldn't even hate her. She stood gloating over her kills, not knowing she was the one who was dead.

"You're r-right." The cold worked its way inward. "Because of forgiveness."

"Oh, that's fun. Yes, let's hear you beg."

He didn't know how much blood he'd swallowed, but it gagged him. "No. I'm saying I forgive you."

"David. That's precious." She doubled the cord around her gloved hands, yanked hard, and the tarp-sled jerked back to life. "But you may want to hold off. We're not finished yet."

Kyle lifted his head. The entrance to the cavern was well in view.

Forty-Three

Gussie slipped away from the revelers, and the apple-pickers' wagon returned to town without her.

The road to the cavern was long and the footpath silent, and why not? Everyone in the county had joined the celebration. Philip ought to be there himself, standing tall to receive his medal. But the war had brought him low. Broken him.

"It's a mercy," Gussie whispered, as if to convince herself. What did she know of mercy? Or of anything at all?

As she approached the hollow entryway to the pit, she found the thing she did know.

Misery.

Her shoes pinched, and the handbag looped over her arm weighed a mint. Her lip was no longer tender to the touch, but the memory of that violent kiss still burned.

Philip wasn't here. She surveyed the litter around the ingress for signs of him.

The suit coat she'd lent him lay wadded up beside the remnant of a fire. She picked it up and slipped it on, not sure what else to do with it.

Harvey's electric flashlight lay smashed beside rotted food scraps. The stolen Esterbrook pen looked usable though abandoned among shards of glass. She collected it and took tentative steps into the dark.

"Philip?"

Her echo returned, full of doubt and longing. She lit the candle and pressed forward. *Misery. Mercy.* Her terrible conundrum.

The darkness and dripping water sped her heart. Maybe . . . yes. She should write on the prayer wall. A petition for Philip's soul.

She crept toward the alcove. A special place, her mother had once told her, although she didn't say why she thought so. Yet the lead, ink, and etching spoke for themselves.

An open spot was all she needed, and she found one just above waist level. She crouched low, held the candle, and poised the nub.

Words to God. The wax dripped as she struggled with what to say.

Harvey would write something beautiful, seasoned with Scripture and heartfelt supplications. And here she was, unable to think of any verse but one, and that pounding a drum inside her skull.

God be merciful to me a sinner.

Her hand shook. It was true. She had lied. Coveted. Wished ill on another. Stolen from her own father, for pity's sake. Did she presume to pray for Philip's soul when her own was in such peril?

The ink stood out against the tawny stone. She signed her name and added the date. "Sorry, Harvey," she whispered. "You were right about me."

She placed the pen in her handbag. Her heart thrummed like the engine of the Buick.

When she found Philip, she'd hand him the gun. Whether he turned it on her or himself didn't matter. Either option put an end to misery, but mercy wasn't hers to bestow. As she turned a corner and stepped across a small stream, the ambient glow of an oil lamp bid her to come near.

Forty-Four

Solveig's ribs ground into the hardwood floors. Ms. VanGorden was right. They were ugly.

Ms. VanGorden. She'd arrive in ten minutes or less. Maybe not soon enough.

Please, Far, don't let anyone else get hurt because of me.

"Heard you planned to leave without saying goodbye." Maxwell Fischer roved about the living room, exulting in his power trip. His boots tracked pellets of snow on the floor around her. "After all the good times we've had."

A clammy sweat covered her skin, and her breath came in gasps. Familiar words looped in her mind, a staccato beat.

Hold it together. Stay with me, now.

"While I've got your attention, I've been wondering about Reeve, and Jonathan, and Heather." He pronounced each name deliberately. "Ever wish you died instead of them?"

All the time, but she remained silent. Chills racked her to the core.

He opened the pistol's chamber, perused its contents, and snapped it back into place. "I asked you a question."

She fixed her eyes on a packed bit of snow melting in front of her face. "Yes."

"I figured." He paced the floor and circled out of Solveig's view. Her skin crawled as she imagined his eyes on her prostrate form. "So. Say you can trade your life for one of theirs. Who do you pick?"

"I can't." Stars pinged her vision. She starved for a deep breath. "None of them deserved to die."

"That's cute, but cop-out answers take a penalty." Fischer circled forward again and pinned her left hand with the toe of his boot, increasing the weight on it until she cried out.

"Heather. I'd pick Heather."

"Huh. I said your boy toy, Reeve. Guess I owe the boss twenty bucks." He let up the pressure. "She was real annoyed you rejected her offer."

She snatched her hand away. So, he worked for Ashleigh. Of course. The funeral home. Her new source. "What do you want?"

"Relax, ice queen. I'm here to buy your house." He tossed the large envelope to the floor. It swished as he slid it in front of her and spread the dot of snowmelt. "Better grab that. Don't need the ink to smear."

She propped herself on her elbows and reached slowly for the envelope. The flap wasn't sealed. Shaking hands belied her calm facade as she drew out the documents.

The top sheet was a quitclaim deed form. Unsigned, but already notarized. The flourishing signature at the bottom said, *Hera Wise.*

The name from the sticky note. *Something Danny's working on.* She felt ill. A violent shudder rattled the pages.

Fischer crouched and leaned over her. "This is what you came for, right? To dump the farm and bounce? You play nice, we wire the money, and everything's smooth like silk." He shrugged. "And if you're a pain, you get more scars for your collection, and we take it anyway."

She blanched. "What do you want with my house?"

"What do you care? You don't belong here."

No, she didn't. Not here, not anywhere.

From the kitchen, a new-message alert chimed. Probably Ms. VanGorden, minutes away. And when she arrived and upset Fischer's weighted scales?

He might explode.

She couldn't let that happen. After all, Ms. VanGorden's boys needed their mother.

"Have you a pen?" she asked.

Fischer's grip on the pistol slackened. He felt his pocket and swore.

"There's one in the kitchen," she said. "I promise I won't move."

He glanced toward the back of the house, then scowled at her.

"Nice try," he said. "Get up."

She pushed herself up, grateful to take a full breath, and kept her hands out as he waved her along. If she slipped out the back—no. She'd end up shot. This time, her only way out was to face what lay ahead. She seated herself at the kitchen table. The pen Kyle had used lay beside his note.

The deed told her nothing. A simple one-page form, all blanks filled with typed details, except the signature lines. Inkjet blurs. Wetness at the edge of the page from Fischer's carelessness.

"Don't worry about the fine print, sweetheart." He tapped the table with the barrel. "We're on a schedule."

Indeed they were. She poised the pen over the signature line, but her eyes fell on Kyle's note. *He is not here.*

But Ashleigh—A. Weisher—*was* here.

Her ever-translating brain juggled letters into connections that, once found, she could not unsee.

> *a w e i s h e r*
> *w e i s h e r a*
> *w i s e h e r a*
> *h e r a w i s e*
> *h e r e w a s i*
> *I was here.*

The tracks in the snow had been hers. A taunt for Kyle. And then she came back, throwing out tidbits, baiting Solveig every step of the way. Why?

To find out who knew about the bones.

But no one else knew. Just her.

And Kyle.

The room spun. But he was safe, right? He'd gone on his own volition. He left the note.

Except for what had been gnawing at her. Ashleigh had lied. She hadn't contacted Kyle. But she knew about the fire.

Solveig turned to Fischer. "What will happen to Kyle?"

He smirked.

Her heart splintered, but she pressed on. "You'll end up the same. Whatever she's promised you is a lie. Ashleigh Weisher . . . Hera

Wise . . . she cares only for herself."

"Look at you, putting it all together." He pointed the gun at her head. "Too bad. We were having fun."

No darkness compared to staring into his aim. But maybe this was the clean slate she'd prayed for. The forgetfulness of death and then . . . heaven. Home at last.

The only words that came out were Christ's, spoken in the language of her heart. *"Hvad du gjør, det gjør snart." That thou doest, do quickly.*

"You makin' fun of me?" he asked, but then jerked his head to one side. "Did you hear something?"

"No," she answered honestly. *No, no, no.*

Fischer turned toward the living room. Ms. VanGorden charged forward from the front of the house, her right arm extended. Solveig threw her arms over her face an instant before Fischer started to scream.

"For future reference, young lady," Ms. VanGorden huffed, "this is a pepper spray scenario."

When Solveig dared to peek, Fischer lay writhing noisily on the kitchen floor, swearing and clawing his face. The gun lay a meter away. Solveig scrambled to retrieve it by the barrel and, for lack of a better idea, stuck it into the refrigerator for safekeeping.

Her whole body turned to melted wax. "I've never been so glad to see anyone."

"Here." Ms. VanGorden held out a mobile with one hand as she trained the pepper spray over Fischer with the other. "Look in my contacts and call Lenny."

Solveig did as requested. She would not die today. Today, she would live.

The line connected. "Dade speaking. Hey, Babe."

Or maybe, today, she would choke on her tongue.

Solveig coughed. "Sheriff Dade, this is Solveig Borja. Ms. Van-Gorden is here at my farm. We have an emergency."

"Is she—"

"We are both fine. She subdued the intruder, but—"

"On my way."

Wow. She laid the mobile on the table, unwilling to get closer to

Fischer than necessary. "Will he be all right?"

"The effects typically last an hour," she said. "But I can give him another blast if he gets cheeky."

Feral sounds of fear and pain rose from the floor.

Solveig stared in amazement. "How did you get in?"

"I used my lockbox code. There is a hearse parked outside, still running, blaring some dreadful excuse for music. Obviously, something was wrong."

Obviously. Light-headedness whooshed around Solveig, but passing out was not an option. "I need to see if my friend is all right."

"What about you?" Ms. VanGorden's concern didn't soften her stance against Fischer. What a comfort that was.

Solveig assured her and tapped her mobile. Dead.

⌒⌒⌒

At least Ms. VanGorden's designation as "Babe" came with the perk of a swift response time. Sheriff Dade arrived with all haste. He secured Fischer, who hadn't opened his eyes or stopped whimpering since Ms. VanGorden took him down, and then turned his attention to Solveig. "I need your statement."

She started from the ride in the hearse. By the time she finished, Ms. VanGorden's jaw went slack. "Miss Borja, why didn't you call the police before now?"

She stared at the floor. "Emergency lights give me panic attacks."

Bestepappa alone had known that secret. Next would come the sighs and ridicule.

But Ms. VanGorden surprised her again. She patted Solveig's shoulder and rubbed her upper arm. A motherly gesture. "I see."

Solveig swallowed a lump in the throat. Simple words to carry so much weight.

"We need to locate this Hera Wise." Dade tapped his stylus, signaling that their work was not done. "You haven't explained the struggle on the porch."

She collected herself. "I don't know what you mean."

All business, he led her to the front of the house and opened the

285

door. "Here. And here."

It took her a moment to spot the ground-out cigarette butt with green trim on the filter, and near it, a small red smear on the plank wood.

"Kyle." She choked on his name.

"Benton was here?" Dade asked. "When?"

"Last night. This morning he was gone. He left a note, and I thought that was rude, so I texted him." She blushed at how it sounded but then remembered the ill-timed notification and the blood left her face. "Excuse me. I need to see . . ."

She fled through the house ahead of them both and powered up the charging mobile. His was the only unread message.

Go wake up in the future, beautiful.

The incomplete reference whispered the missing words. *Come find me.*

"Oh." Her voice cracked. "Oh, no."

Dade strode in. "What's happening?" Solveig showed him the text.

"It's a standing joke, kind of." She explained the origin. "He's in trouble, Sheriff Dade. He would not have sent a veiled message if he was able to send a plain one."

"Agreed." Dade dialed as he continued speaking. "They probably chucked the phone used to send this, but we'll see which cell towers they pinged, to narrow down their location."

"The blood. What if he's—"

"He was alive at 8:09. I need you to focus on that and give me your description of the suspect."

Her heart raced. "I can do better. I have her photo. And if the cell tower agrees, I might know exactly where they are."

The handset squawked. "Dade speaking. Stand by." He was an entirely different category of frightening with his aggression directed at their enemies. "Get the photo. I have to deal with Fischer, but I'm calling backup. Pam, stay with her."

Forty-Five

Blackout darkness except where Ashleigh's flashlight led. Crushing silence apart from her footsteps and the drag of Kyle's not-quite-dead-weight. The cavern was like a nightmare of being trapped inside his skull, with waves of pain rushing in from the walls.

The tarp didn't glide over the rock as it had the snow. Ashleigh abandoned it and tied the cord to the ropes binding his feet.

She tugged. "Oh, yeah. That feels better."

Feeling better wasn't how he described it. Her pulling hyperextended his busted knees. In agony, he longed to walk toward death on his own power.

Solveig's voice echoed in his mind. *If I have to drag you by your feet, I'm not leaving you here.*

He grimaced. In spite of the pain, he'd cash in that promise if he could. The words had risen from the blur of semiconsciousness when he knocked his lights out. He might've imagined the whole thing, but since it didn't matter to anyone but him, he went with believing it.

Smoke-stinking leather shredded against the rock. If they didn't reach Ashleigh's destination by the time it wore through, the layers underneath would rag quickly to expose the skin of his back.

His body had precious little left to bring to this fight. Everything hurt, and he was running out of time. At least the warmer temperature in the cavern made breathing a speck easier. Talking was all he could do. "I'll pass on the job. It's tempting, no doubt."

She huffed a short laugh. "See, this is what I miss. It's not the same now."

"No? Fischer seems . . . teachable."

"You're kidding, right?" Ashleigh drew the words out in a groan. "He's not half as smart as he thinks he is, and he makes everything such a production. Do you know how annoying that is?"

"Yes, actually." Their voices sounded flat. A narrow corridor, then, not a big echoing chamber.

"And he can't sing. Not like you." The more she spoke, the slower she pulled. Whether that was any benefit, hard to say. "No long-term potential, but I can't get rid of him yet, so here we are."

He kept his chin tucked to save his scalp, but his neck muscles were spasming. The headache that had dogged him constantly since last Saturday ramped up, with the loose tooth throbbing in concert. His sides protested every breath. Rope burn, road rash. And his knees. If he got out of this, it'd be a while before he was whole again. A big if.

"Besides, after the fire at your place, there's no one else for this particular job."

His focus sharpened. "You need a fall guy."

"Exactly. The Bridgewater kill was for you. A few signature details, a smidgen of arson, and voilà." She puffed for breath. "They'll pin it on you. Keith's death, too, if we're lucky. Open-and-shut."

The shell of his coat snagged and ripped on a sharp stone. "I guess it's not going to trial."

"I guess not."

He closed his eyes. This darkness wasn't final. Pain had an end. He'd see his brother again.

"The beautiful part comes when your new squeeze calls to report the bones and they find you instead."

He opened his eyes and jerked against her grip, but she'd anticipated him and let the cord slacken. It whipped uselessly. "Still some kick left in you, I see. We'll take care of that in a minute."

"Ashleigh. Why?"

"I told you, because you ruined—"

"Yeah, but if you wanted me dead, why not put a bullet in my brain and be done? Why all this?"

She fell silent except for the huff of exertion, and when she finally did speak, the words dripped icicles. "If all you'd done was betray me, killing you would be enough. But you *fooled* me. That's the part I can't stand. I thought you were mine, David. Mind, body, and soul."

With a fresh burst of passion, she tugged hard on the cord, jarring every injury. He yowled.

"Poor baby. We're almost there. I brought you Tango and Cash, same as your brother liked."

The familiar street name made Kyle's stomach drop. "But I don't use. They won't believe it for me like they did him."

"That's true. And I hate to tell you, handsome, but we may have left signs of a struggle." Her voice rang, diffused by a trick of the tunnels. "That's why there's an extra vial from this same batch stashed at Snow Rat's house. After I buy the place, I'll be horrified to discover it and report it to the police promptly. And I love the graffiti confession idea. Totally stealing that."

He coughed weakly. "Solveig hasn't done anything to you."

"But she had the misfortune to get close to you, and she did furnish this lovely element to the plan. I was going to set up Danny for your murder, but this is better. More pizzazz."

"Danny'd actually do it," he muttered. Ridges in the stone pressed through his layers like dull knife edges.

Ashleigh ignored him. "You disappear. The evidence indicts you for the Bridgewater guy. Snow Rat—"

"Don't call her that."

"*Snow Rat* champions the poor, lost soul of the cavern and ends up a suspect in your murder. If Norway won't extradite her, I'll go there after her. Frame her for killing her mother too."

"She doesn't even—" He broke off to avoid giving Ashleigh ammo, but she seemed to know everything. Danny again, probably.

"Please. I already found her. Having a hacker on my payroll helps." She laughed. "Care to hear what I have planned for your parents?"

No. He had to find a way to stop her. Something, anything.

"What do you want?" All the force he could muster came to a pittance. "A pound of flesh? You're dragging a hundred and eighty-two of them into a pit. What does it get you?"

"A decent workout." She sighed. "What's confusing about this? You blew up everything I loved. I'm returning the favor."

"You loved money and control."

"Yes," she said. "And us. Dummy me. I thought we were the real thing."

Darkness settled over her admission. The time for reassurances and sweet words between them had long passed. And yet.

"Hey, Ash?"

She stopped pulling. "Yeah, D?"

"We were real. Okay? You don't have to hurt anyone besides me."

He read hope in her silence until it shattered.

"A smooth talker to the end." She made a slight leap.

A splash. A painful jerk. And *cold.*

Icy water soaked straight through his clothes, clean into his bones. She'd dragged him through some narrow stream. His breaths seared. Too shallow to satisfy. Too fast to pace. He couldn't slow them.

"H-huh-help. Help you."

She paused. "Help me, how?"

"I'll con . . . fess to . . . Trev-truh." He clenched his teeth to stop them chattering. "Confess to . . . m-murder."

"Oh. And in return, you want me to leave your parents and Solveig alone?" Her voice took a mocking turn. "Ooh, even abandon my life of depravity and get religion?"

"Y-y-yuh."

"Not interested. But here's my counteroffer." She sat cross-legged on the ground beside him. "You and me, like the last ten years never happened. If you forgive me, prove it. Can you get back in bed with Keith's killer?"

His heart thundered. The only dream he'd allowed himself while he served his sentence. That image he taped to the wall and tucked in his wallet, twisted and warped beyond recognition. Maybe it always had been. He'd been so blind.

But to save his parents? To protect Solveig? Was it possible to slip into David Kyle's skin one final, permanent time?

He waited for the temptation to ravage him, burn out the shell, and leave him to crack. Waited, but it didn't happen.

This battle he'd been fighting inside—how had he failed to notice it was already won? God promised he'd be a new man, and He delivered. Not in theory but in fact. Whatever pieces of him Ashleigh ever thought she'd owned, he'd turned over to Christ. Heart, mind, soul, and strength.

Though strength barely warranted mention at this point.

He shook his head, convinced. "N-no, Ashleigh. That g-guy you knew is d-dead."

"Not yet, but whatever. Can't blame a girl for trying." She withdrew a syringe and filled it from a vial. "Anyway, I'm going by Hera. Definitely my favorite alias. I think it fits me."

He curled his shoulders inward to shrink away from his wet clothes. No use. As he rolled on his side, shaking and on the verge of hyperventilating, the ambient glow of Ashleigh's flashlight spilled over the chilling lines of the bones.

Forty-Six

"Philip?"

Gussie stumbled as she groped toward the lamplight. She righted herself against the wall and called again. "Philip, are you there?"

A low groan sounded back. She was close. Whispered words parried and feinted in the stillness. "Lord . . . forgive . . . deliver . . ."

Was he praying?

She carefully approached another alcove, and finally, Philip came into view.

He leaned against the cavern wall, gaunt and poor. She clutched the little bag and approached cautiously. Should she give him the gun or say something first?

He groaned. "Who's there?"

She stepped closer. "It's me, Gussie." A stench hung around him. Sweat and filth.

"Send our relief." He coughed. "The bombs. Half our unit. They're gone."

"Philip, are you ill? What's happened?"

He squinted and appeared to notice the bag in her hands. "Sweet Gussie. Are you real? Say you have my medicine. One dose. One drop, just—"

He retched. She turned away, her own stomach churning.

"Philip, you're sick. Here, I can help you."

"Then give it to me." He grabbed the handbag.

Gussie froze.

He swore as he discovered the stolen gun. "Come to do me in, Darling?"

"No," she said. "Forgive me, Philip. I thought—"

"Thought you'd like to be rid of me." He stroked the stock and nodded slowly.

"I didn't want you to suffer anymore," she whispered. "I meant it for—" *For mercy*, she wanted to say, but an overpowering call echoed through the cavern.

"Gussie, where are you? I know you're here. Gussie!"

"No," she said.

Philip struggled to his feet. "Him. Did he put you up to this? Or did you plan it together?" The shadows over his eye sockets made him all the more terrifying.

Harvey called out again, closer, but winded. "Leave her alone."

"She was mine, Engelwood," he shouted. "You stole her from me."

Footfalls answered before words as Harvey stepped into view. "We've no time for this. Gussie, you must come with me immediately."

"I thought you were on the way to Richmond. With Eloise," she hastened to add.

"There's no route until tomorrow. I checked on Mother. She said you'd vanished." His breath heaved between phrases. "I knew you'd be here, but—"

"Because you sent her here to kill me." Philip's voice was hard as the stone walls. "Thought the deed would be done so soon, did you?"

"No one was trying—"

Philip pointed the revolver at Harvey. "Shut up."

"Be sensible, man. We've only tried to help you." He looked back over his shoulder. "We need to get out of here before—"

"Come out, Engelwood. Don't make me root you out like the snake you are."

"Daddy?" Gussie swiveled to locate the source of his voice.

A heavy splash accompanied the approaching light. He entered the corridor, his flashlight in one hand and the other at his hip. "What is the meaning of this? Skipping out on one of my daughters to meet the other? Stealing my profits, or did you think I'd miss the smashed bottles? On my own land, no less."

Harvey's words came out labored still. "Sir, I came to see that Gussie was safe."

"And that I was dead," Philip said.

Daddy started at the unexpected voice and aimed his beam at Philip. "You're that Marcus boy." The hand at his hip drew a gun. "One of you had better explain what you're doing here with my daughter."

The miserly lights glinted from the sweat on Philip's brow and left shadows on the furrow of Harvey's. Only the trickling stream answered.

"Well?" Daddy demanded. "Will it be two shotgun weddings instead of one?"

Oh. Gussie hoped the darkness covered the blush creeping up her neck. "Daddy, I—"

"Quiet!" He turned toward Harvey. "You. Answer me."

"I learned Gussie was missed and thought she may be here. She is, and we can all return to the Home Coming Day celebration." His voice, normally calm and sure, carried a waver.

"Ah, that's today, is it?" Philip maintained his stance. "Come to kill me in the middle of the big fete. Charming as ever, Darling."

"Don't speak to my girl that way, louse." Rage simmered in Daddy's voice.

"It's true, though," Gussie whispered. "And I stole the elixir. I'm sorry. So sorry."

"Don't worry your pretty head over that." Philip spoke over a dull metallic snap. "It's nothing but castor oil and a dash of menthol."

From there, everything happened like slides clicking through a magic lantern.

Daddy's face contorted. He raised his weapon.

Click.

Harvey yanked Gussie's arm. Her candle dropped and burned out against the rock.

Click.

A flash lit the alcove for an instant. Harvey's lips formed her name but made no sound.

Click.

No sound because the roar of gunfire keened in her ears, thoughts, soul and left deadly silence in its wake.

Forty-Seven

Solveig kept her eyes away from Dade's cruiser as he hauled Fischer away, but the flashing blue lights reflected off the snow.

Stay with me—

"So much excitement." Ms. VanGorden had never sounded so mellow and soothing as when she herded Solveig inside. "Why don't we—"

"They won't find him in time."

"They will." She picked up the scattered pages Fischer had brought. "Lenny is relentless."

"But so is Ashleigh." Solveig fought for calm. "And she is out for blood."

Ms. VanGorden tucked the unsigned contract into a folio and stowed it in her tote. "Very well. I have to be back for a closing at ten thirty, though."

Solveig stared at her. "What?"

"You heard me," she said. "Let's go."

Within minutes, the two of them were speeding down the sparsely traveled highway in Ms. VanGorden's Escalade. Solveig's stomach knotted.

"Rice Caverns, you said? Toward Massanutten?"

"Yes."

Ms. VanGorden cast a sideways glance at Solveig. "I assume there's a link to your property as the 'old Rice place.'"

Solveig bit back a huff. The woman wanted to talk real estate *now*? "Yes. The same family owned both at one time. Mr. Forrester assured

me our deed checks out, but the documents tie the house to the famous Engelwood mystery."

Ms. VanGorden nodded. "I'm familiar."

"I thought I had solved it. Kyle and I went hiking last weekend.
We found a skeleton."

Her brows arched into her hairline.

"I know I must report it," she rushed to say. "And I will. But there's
more." She explained the inscription to Gussie, the files from the genealogical society, and the rant Kyle had endured from Larry Tillman.

Ms. VanGorden accelerated past a slow-moving sedan. "Go on."

"Two men vied for Gussie Rice's heart. I believed the bones had
to be one of them, but they both left sketchy records after that date.
Harvey signed the property over to my grandfather unless it was a
forgery. Someone who claimed to be Philip was laid up in a hospital
two months after, but the news report is full of errors."

For a woman dating a policeman, Ms. VanGorden showed little
respect for the rules of the road. She took the route straight through
Harrisonburg and slowed only as much as necessary to maneuver the
city streets. At the Main Street square, she rolled through the four stop
out of turn and earned an angry honk. "If Harvey was assumed dead
when Mr. Borja filed the deed, he would have needed to legitimize his
claim to the property."

Solveig shivered as Danny's bitter voice invaded her head.

Squatting was and is legal if you do it right.

"I think I know how he did." She ran through Danny's insinuations.

"A reasonable solution if you're stuck with a deed signed by a dead
man," she mused. "But when did Harvey purchase it?"

Solveig's head spun. "He didn't, not really. Gussie's father, Caleb,
signed it over for a dollar in 1919. I have no idea why. He was to the
neck in debt."

She pursed her lips. "Trying to shelter his assets, sounds like."

Neon signs invited shoppers at some of the storefronts on Main,
but the window at Tillman's Fine Tobaccos remained dark. The art-
fully distressed shingle showed a logo stylized with old-fashioned
lettering, though the company's name had changed since its days as

Tillman's Patented Elixirs.

"Then the arrangement was never meant to be permanent." Chills raced over Solveig's skin. "If so, wouldn't Caleb have tried to get his land back when Harvey disappeared?"

Ms. VanGorden nodded slowly. "He could've claimed the transfer was fraudulent. Without Harvey there to contest it, he may have succeeded."

"Mr. Forrester didn't find evidence of a dispute, but—"

Evidence. The bottles in the barn. The ledger that went strangely silent. Assets that went from Harvey's hands to her grandfather's, then her own.

"But?" Ms. VanGorden prompted.

A buzzing sensation twinged at the base of Solveig's neck. "But that in itself raises the question: whatever happened to Caleb Rice?"

Despite the abrasive heat from the dashboard vents, Solveig shivered as the truth reached her core. "He was the one left in the cavern. Whatever happened, Gussie's prayer signaled her part in it. And Harvey loved her. He would have done anything for her."

"I doubt the history matters to Ashleigh." Ms. VanGorden accelerated as they breached the city limits.

"Likely not. Her history with Kyle, though." She swallowed hard. "He blew the whistle on her years ago. I don't know her plan, only what she said at the cavern. That if she wanted someone to suffer, she couldn't pick a better place."

"Tell me about him." An obvious distraction, but a welcome one.

Solveig pictured him on the porch the first time he'd come to her door, eyes glinting as if curious to hear what she'd say.

"He is hilarious," she said finally, "and so charming. And he understood some things I thought no one could. What was bitter is sweet and what was broken is—" *Healed*, she almost said, but that felt too revealing. "Fixed."

"You, dear child, are in love." Ms. VanGorden diagnosed her as if with a mildly regrettable disease. "Are we going as far north as Keezletown?"

"No. The turn is up ahead. We'll follow that road to the dead end." Solveig stole a peek at Ms. VanGorden's footwear. Low-heeled black boots. Fashionable, but more suited to salted walkways than mountain trails.

She groaned. No bad weather. Only bad clothing. She'd make the hike alone.

You are never alone.

Another problem reared up. "The snow tracks will lead to the cavern, but they won't know the way inside. Do you carry rope? Or chain? Anything I can use to leave a trail?"

"Just twenty-five feet of chain." Her eyes never lifted from the road as they made the fork. "Speaking of tracks. At least one vehicle has already been in and out ahead of us."

"Not good." She worried the fringe of her scarf. "I'm not sure how—" But the answer twirled and brushed between her fingers. She unlooped the scarf and tore its tassels until one started to unravel.

She kept winding the blue thread into a skein until they neared the dead end. The Escalade slowed as Ms. VanGorden negotiated the rougher part of the road, and barren branches scraped the windows. Solveig's heart rate surged. Nearly there.

What if she was wrong? If Kyle had been taken somewhere else or—

But the scene before them gave terrible confirmation.

"We'd best wait for Lenny," Ms. VanGorden said quietly.

Beyond the chain gate, Kyle's truck was parked off-road. Behind it were impressions in the snow. Scuffles, blood, and the disturbing trail of solitary footprints and something—

—someone—

—being dragged away.

Solveig let herself out of the vehicle. "You wait. Call the paramedics. Point the way."

"Miss Borja—"

She swung the door behind her. No time for argument.

Golden rays threw an illusion of warmth over the snowscape, but frigid temperatures belied the dawn. Solveig huffed over her bare fingers and started toward the cavern.

Even pace. Measured strides. She jogged carefully, grateful for every ski trip and winter hike she'd ever taken, breathing out single-word prayers. *Visdom. Hjelp. Mirakler.*

As she neared the entrance, she added one more. *Lys.*

She had not thought to bring a flashlight.

Her mobile? No. The screen didn't even light to the touch.

"Now what?" She glanced around. A short distance inside the stone walls lay a lump. She gasped and rushed over to find a discarded tarp with packed bits of snow clinging to the bottom.

She growled her frustration. Beyond this point, the uncompromising darkness left no options. She'd have to wait.

Unless.

She fished in her front pocket. Her hand curled around Kyle's silver flip-top lighter. She held it out and flicked its tiny light.

Takk, Jesus.

Solveig doubled back to tie the thread from her scarf to a knotty shrub beyond the stone entrance. She'd let the loose skein unravel with one hand as she held the lighter with the other.

So far as she knew, this was the only path in or out. No exit trail had marked the snow outside. What if she had to confront Ashleigh? Or subdue her? What if she was too late?

Useless thoughts. She measured her breaths. One foot ahead of the other.

She kept a careful pace inside the cavern. Kyle had learned that lesson for both of them. The way seemed easier, though the path was narrow and hard to find. Otherwise, the bones would have been discovered long ago.

Close. She was close.

The prayer wall's alcove stood apart from the way that led to the makeshift tomb, but the corridor funneled scraps of conversation into the chamber. She angled her right ear toward the sound and held her breath.

Two distinct voices. One chirpy and sharp. The other deeper, but weak.

Only bits of conversation came to her and from an uncertain distance, but *pris Herren*, Kyle was alive.

A grunt. Then silence.

She softened her steps. If Ashleigh detected her, Solveig would have no way to help Kyle. But if she waited too long—

A glow from the other direction gave warning. Solveig ducked into the dark of the prayer wall's recess and capped the lighter. She leaned into the wall and struggled to hear.

The steps were quick. Her muscles tensed. The woman's breaths were close. Uneven. Labored.

A shuddering sob echoed off the walls, followed by a short sniffle. She was *crying?*

Solveig gritted her teeth and forced herself to keep still for a count of ten. The footfalls and breathing receded, but even if Ashleigh turned back, Solveig had to get to Kyle. She would not leave him lost in the dark.

She flicked the lighter and abandoned her hiding spot. No other light. No time for stealth. Not if Ashleigh had walked away crying over what she had done.

Solveig hastened her steps. She remembered the path. The indignation she'd carried along it the first time. The apprehension on the return trip. Now she clung to hope as faint as the tiny flame at her fingertips.

She stepped over the stream and rounded the wall.

There, sagging against the limestone where she'd discovered the bones, lay Kyle. Smeared blood covered his face.

She rushed to his side, dropping the skein and nearly dousing the flame as she crouched next to him. "Hang on, all right? We're going to get help, and—can you hear me? Kyle?"

No response. She pressed two fingers under his jaw to feel for a pulse. His constricted pupils sat like flecks in glass marbles. She shook his shoulder. Nothing. Maybe if she could get him upright? The flame in her hand wobbled as she tried to wedge an arm under him. She couldn't get the leverage to move him and keep the tiny light burning. "Kyle, I need you to try."

Vague sounds registered. A scuffle. Someone—a woman—swearing. A splash.

"You again." Ashleigh's flashlight blinded her. "I guess Max failed his assignment."

Solveig flinched from the stronger light and caught sight of Kyle.

Knees wrenched to an odd angle. Wrists bound. Blood everywhere. She choked. "What did you do to him?"

"I reduced his odds of being the biggest disappointment of your stupid little life." No weakness in her voice. "You're welcome."

Solveig stepped between them.

Ashleigh snorted and aimed the beam at her eyes. Maybe because she had no other weapon? "Tell me this." Her tone rang with clinical detachment. "Why did they matter, the bones?"

"Because they belonged to a person." Footfalls and shouts echoed around them. Even her left ear registered indistinct sounds.

"A *dead* person. Wouldn't a sensitive soul like you care more about someone living? Like your mom?"

Solveig's breath caught. "You don't know anything about her."

"You're probably right." Ashleigh cocked her head toward the rising commotion and smiled. "You do favor her, though."

"Police!" Two uniformed officers wearing headlamps crowded the entrance of the alcove, and their high-powered flashlights flooded the cavern. Several more officers filed in behind them, each with a light, leaving darkness nowhere to hide.

Ashleigh raised her hands above her head. "All this for little me. I'm so flattered."

The taller of the first two officers called over his shoulder. "Paramedic, now!" He stepped forward. "Ashleigh Weisher, you're under arrest for aggravated assault and battery, conspiracy to distribute controlled substances, and attempted larceny."

Not the half, but never mind. Solveig knelt beside Kyle as they read Ashleigh her rights. He was still breathing. "It's all right now," she whispered. "Later we're going to sit on the porch swing and eat pizza and watch the snow fall, okay? You have to hold on till then."

Choking noises came from his throat. Then nothing.

They took Ashleigh away, and paramedics barreled in, negotiating the tight space with some grunts and a few sharp words. Solveig watched as they covered Kyle's bloodied nose and mouth with a mask and strapped him onto a stretcher.

Another officer approached her. "You did good," she said, "and they're going to do everything they can for him. Now, let's get you out of here."

As Solveig threw one last nervous glance at Kyle, Ashleigh's voice rang through the cavern. "Let's keep in touch, Solveig."

The words reverberated in her brain long after they died against the stone.

Forty-Eight

A laser beam of daylight infiltrated the heavy curtains that blocked Kyle's window. The dry-erase board said his RN's name was LaShonda, the med tech was Owen, and the date was February 4. He had awakened eleven hours ago to find five days of his life completely gone, as if they'd never existed.

For someone who had cooled his heels in prison for eight years, that was unacceptable.

"Look, I don't need anyone else to take my blood pressure or ask about my pain. What I need"—he nudged Solveig in the chair beside him—"is a bacon-egg-and-cheese bagel. Extra bacon."

LaShonda cuffed him anyway. "At one thirty-eight over eighty-eight, that is the last thing you need. How's your pain?"

"Painful." What you'd expect with two shattered kneecaps, a cracked rib, and chemical burns inside your lungs.

Solveig sat with her eyes closed. A hint of a smile graced an otherwise serene expression.

"Wake up, gorgeous. You're busting me out," he said.

LaShonda ripped off the blood pressure cuff and stowed it on her cart. "If you want to leave, we'll send a bill. You are not a prisoner."

Not a prisoner. Healing words on his roughed-up soul, but for some reason, he couldn't help himself. "Great, but see, I don't know how much trouble I'm in when I leave here. I'd rather not add indecent exposure to the list."

The nurse snorted. "I got shift change. Maybe your girlfriend can help you figure it out."

Solveig opened her eyes, looking too innocent. "It is tricky to access personal effects around here. You may be stuck awhile."

Kyle flopped back against the pillow, forgetting to baby his rib. *Ow.* "Did she just ask you to be my girlfriend? Because this is really not what I planned."

"Tell him no, sugar." LaShonda keyed notes into the computer on her med cart and rolled it toward the door. "You can do better."

"Yeah, she's aware!" Kyle shouted after her.

When they were alone again, Solveig patted his hand. "They said to expect some irritability. Not to cultivate it."

"Who's cultivating? Is it wrong to want more substantial nourishment than watered-down apple juice?"

"No, but if she puts in your chart you're belligerent, then the next nurse comes in defensive as well."

"Oh." He squinted his eyes and thought about it. "Nope, don't care."

"Okay." She stood, crossed the room, and opened the curtains. The morning sunlight sparkled through her hair, and her blue eyes arrested him. Since he met her, all she'd done was shine. Well, if she stuck through this, maybe he'd found himself a lifer. "Your parents will be here at nine," she said. "If you want, I'll find out if you can have a breakfast sandwich later and ask your mom to bring—"

"Forget it." His mouth went dry. "I'm not hungry."

"I see." She massaged her temples. He should cool it. Those lost five days were stamped on her face. "I wish you'd relax until your CT scan."

"My brain is great. Never better."

"Congratulations. Mine is wrung out, sleep-deprived, and anxious for someone to say you're going to be okay."

"I'm going to be—"

"Someone in a lab coat." Her lips curled in a sardonic smile. "Please, Kyle? For my heart, if not your brain?"

He tried to glare as if she weren't melting him. "Dirty pool," he muttered.

As an avoidance strategy, the shenanigans backfired hard, because he was completely unprepared when Sheriff Dade showed up. If speaking to the man across an interrogation table was bad, doing so while stuck in a hospital bed was a million times worse.

"I'll let you talk," Solveig said, but Dade stopped her.

"You can stay." The man towered, filling the tiny room. He addressed them both. "Came to let you know we have Ashleigh Weisher, a.k.a. Hera Wise, in custody. She's not cooperating, but Max Fischer's talking enough for two."

Looks like he can sing, after all, Ash. Kyle stuffed that thought down. "So I'm not a suspect anymore?"

"Not at the moment." Dade's relaxed jaw was probably as close as he came to smiling. "We'll keep you posted."

"She admitted that she killed my brother," Kyle said, "and Trevor Roberts. I don't know who lit the fire at my cabin, but it was her plan. She had a drug operation moving through the depot annex."

"Son, I want your statement." Dade wagged his head toward the door. "But your nurse gave me two minutes. Let's wait till you're on your feet."

Kyle nodded, unsure how long that might be. The surgery had him nervous. Recovery, terrified. Ashleigh's mix of heroin and fentanyl should have killed him, and in a way, still could. Plenty of his old clients had started on prescription painkillers. His hands shook just thinking about it.

Time for a diversion. "Sir, what about Danny Calhoun?"

"Turned himself in." Dade smirked. "Coughing up every detail he can, trying to get a plea deal."

Red splotches rose on Solveig's face. "What happened to him? I understand if you can't say, but I'm baffled. I used to know him."

Dade shrugged before answering. "He's been trying to get custody since his kid was born. Thought owning a business would help his case. He hired Fischer to scare you into making a deal and got sold up the river to Ashleigh. She dangled some story about a bounty on Benton, and Calhoun fell for it."

Solveig rubbed her arms. "I wish he'd told me. Now he has more trouble than before."

"Don't feel sorry for him. He decided on his own to play fast and loose with the law. As for you, if anyone else bothers you, call it in. We can't fix a situation we don't know about. Understand?"

She nodded quickly, biting her lip, so Kyle butted in. "All due respect, sir, but at the start of all this she told you—"

"Can it," Dade said mildly. "Now, Calhoun's confession connected the dots, except for the break-in. He didn't know about that. Any thoughts?"

There's an extra vial from this same batch stashed . . .

Longing stole Kyle's breath and burned at the now-healed pinprick in his neck. If he found it, bliss. Just once more. Just—

"Sir? Fischer again. He planted drugs in the house." He let the words out in an irretractable rush before the desire took root. "Meant to frame her for killing me."

Dade eyed Solveig. "And they tried to force the sale to speed that along."

"Because I rejected the offer she sent to Ms. VanGorden."

Dade nodded. "And the portrait of your mother?"

Solveig huffed. "I believe Fischer took it for meanness, and Ashleigh decided to make use of it."

"Makes sense," Dade said, satisfaction in his voice. "Sounds like enough rope to let Max hang himself."

"Sir? This may seem funny to ask." Solveig rubbed her arms. "But what about the bones?"

"Recovered them from Miss Weisher's satchel," he said. "They're with the pathologist for now. We'll run 'em against missing persons. If nothing turns up, they'll cremate."

"I see," she said faintly.

He checked his watch. "All right. I'll let you two be."

"Actually, sir, I have something else to tell you." Kyle glanced at Solveig. "Man to man."

Her surprised look shredded him. Eyes shining and lips tight, she nodded once and fled the room.

Smooth. Great job, weasel.

The arched lines of Dade's forehead plainly said he thought so too.

Kyle tried to swallow his nerves, but his throat constricted. "Sir, what you said about Danny and the law. Um. Not everything I've done since I came here has been by the book."

"Like your meetings with Max?"

Ouch. Should have guessed that tidbit had circled back on him.

"For starters."

Dade held up a hand. "Tell you what. Taking down a crime ring and a murderer has me in a pretty good mood, and I'll bet whatever's in that IV bag might give me problems with admissibility anyway."

A monitor beeped low-key support for that idea. Kyle held his breath.

"I'll make you a one-time deal, son. You tell her"—he gestured the direction Solveig had gone—"every word of it. If she turns you in, I'll open a file."

Kyle lowered his chin. "Thank you, sir."

"What's left on your parole term?"

"Less than two years, sir."

Dade nodded. "Don't get so much as a parking ticket. I'll be in touch."

After he strode out of the room, Kyle watched the door. Minutes ticked by, but Solveig didn't return. She probably needed a break. Coffee. Bathroom. A breather from his surliness.

If he blew his chance with her, he'd wear out those patella replacements praying for a way to make it right.

He covered his eyes and exhaled too hard, which set off a coughing fit. It ached his chest and jarred his knees and reminded him this patch job wasn't done. He was partly fixed, but still broken. A work in progress.

As the cough subsided, he leaned back and stared at the ceiling.

"I'm an idiot and I'm sorry." He spoke to the empty room, half practicing, half hoping she might be standing outside. "Forgive me."

"Enough of that, son."

He eased himself upright. That voice. The voice of the only man on earth he ever wanted to call him "son."

Dad.

Both he and Mom looked road weary and heartsore. His eyes were bloodshot and hers were swollen and glassy.

Kyle's face flamed. Not like this. Schemes, drugs, cops, consequences. Too much of the same old. They'd never see past that skin.

"Mom. Dad. I—"

Mom wrapped her arms around him and Dad, around her. "My boy. You're all right," she said. The words muffled against his head, and he had no argument against the tears spilling into his hair.

They all had much more to say, but it would wait.

⌢⌢⌢

After a full day of blood draws, brain scans, x-rays, impromptu police interviews, and family reunions, plus every single person in Rockingham County urging him to rest, Kyle was beat.

Even so, once his parents returned to their hotel, he fought sleep, hoping for a certain winter rose to appear in his doorway. Solveig had spent a half hour with him and his parents after the CT scan, but she barely spoke and otherwise made herself scarce. Maybe she'd already left for the night. Or for good. Or maybe—

"Kyle? May I come in?"

That beautiful lilt did more good than all the doctors, nurses, and techs combined. "You came back."

"Of course." The fear that he'd driven her off with his attitude melted away as she eased into the chair beside him. "I wanted you to have time with your parents. Did you think I'd let you go into surgery without a word?"

"Wouldn't blame you if you did."

"Neither would LaShonda, but here I am." The cute crinkle around her eyes gave way to a slight frown. "You had a long day."

"That obvious, huh?" He grazed his scratchy face. "I'll tell you, it's humbling when they need to check if your brain is healthy enough for knee surgery."

"You'll do great."

"I'm sorry I chased you out when Dade was here."

"Let me tell you a secret." She leaned close and mock whispered. "Sheriff Dade terrifies me. Still. So if I scampered like a scared rabbit at the first opportunity, that is on me."

The last of his tension evaporated. "At least you were dressed. Next time I talk to that guy, I hope I'm wearing pants."

A giggle tapered into a nervous look. "On the subject of clothing." She tugged her scarf until it fell away. "If we're—well, you should see—"

"Hey." He let his gaze linger, drinking her in. "I see a beautiful woman who's survived hard things. And saved my life. Twice."

Her shoulders loosened and she slipped her hand into his. "So long I wished God would erase those hard things. But the clean slate I wanted, He's already given in Jesus."

"Doesn't always feel like it, does it?"

She shook her head. "I didn't know how weak my faith was. Is. But it's stronger now than before."

"Mine too." Those crystalline eyes reflected the hope of new life that stirred in his soul. He traced infinity loops over her knuckles. "But I still have one problem."

"Ah." A playful note in her voice teased. "Can I help?"

"Hope so. See, I thought I understood koozley."

"Okay." She nodded.

"And this seems like the least koozley thing ever." He used the bed remote to straighten up. It whirred as if in pain. "Wires and beeping machines. Nurses prodding. Disinfectant."

She rocked the flexible backrest behind her. "Uncomfortable chairs. Hospital food. Fluorescent lighting."

"There's a dimmer for that, at least. Here." He passed her the remote, and she dialed the lights down to a peaceful glow. "Point is, I'm in the place I least want to be with the person I most want to be with, and things are gonna be okay, and maybe it's the pain meds, but if this isn't koozley, I don't get it at all."

"*Så koselig.* It's not the pain meds," she agreed. "I can't stay long, though. They'll soon run me off."

"Here. I'll hide you under the covers." That tickled her, apparently, but as peals of laughter stretched into hysterics, he grumbled. "Okay, come on. It wasn't that funny."

"I'm sorry." She wiped a tear. "But I started thinking of when they take you to surgery in the morning, and—" Another round of giggles.

"That's great." He sat up as she collected herself. "Listen, I want to kiss you now."

Unfortunately, she chose the same moment to speak. "Your folks are wonderful. I love your mom."

He groaned. "What? Solveig, you can't love my mom first. It's not right."

The roses in her cheeks were in full flower, and her eyes lit with a fever shine. "Tell me the right way, then."

"Okay, here it goes. 'The Love Song of Kyle D. Benton.'" He reached for her hand, and when she placed it in his, he kissed it. "When I'm pretty sure I'm a goner, I'll ask the lady to dance."

Palm to palm, he led their hands back and forth through the air to the music of monitors and the rattling heater. He held her gaze and finished the "dance" with a mock twirl above her head.

"If she seems amenable, I'll spoil her with cheesy lines from old sci-fi movies, because waking up in a future with her sounds more like a dream."

Solveig played along, shaking her head as if in a tragedy. "I don't even like that movie."

"If she doesn't even like that movie," he continued, "I'll resort to my best Springsteen parody and hope for the best. If everything's going well at that point—"

He stopped short and studied her closely, letting it seem like part of the theater, but honestly needing to know whether to go on. Because if she wasn't all in . . .

But she was. Her lashes were wet and there was nothing shy or reserved in that beautiful smile. He breathed deep, savoring the scent of pears. "Then, and only then, I'd let her see me at my rock-bottom lowest. If she sticks around after that, she'll find my heart exactly like an old sofa bed—hers if she's willing to take it."

She melted closer. "I want to hear the words," she whispered.

"*Jeg elsk-er deg*, Solveig." He puffed his chest. "I asked the x-ray tech to look it up for me."

She raised her eyebrows, all innocent, but a twitch at her mouth betrayed her. "I'm sorry, your accent . . ."

"Right." If he didn't spit it out, the stupid heart monitor would call in the cardiac cavalry. "Monolingual oaf that I am, I'm trying to say I love you."

Solveig brushed a lock of hair away from his forehead and let her chilly fingers trail and linger on his face. "*Jeg elsker deg også,* Kyle Benton. I love you too."

Footfalls interrupted. Visiting hours were over, but whoever came to see her out stepped back into the hall with a soft chuckle.

He tugged her hand, and when she leaned down to brush his lips, their kiss carried in it the power and hope of its newness, and along with that, the deep peace of coming home.

Forty-Nine

If the aphids got into the broccoli again this year, Gussie would have to marry Eddie Dade. Simple as that.

Mr. Bartoo's generous prices for produce came close to charity, but that wouldn't help if the crop failed. Their agreement was for her to buy what she couldn't grow and to pay Daddy's debts, a few cents at a time.

Daddy. Her heart squeezed.

The rows behind the barn looked all right, but those in front of the house wanted weeding. When Priscilla Dade's youngest son came by bursting to show off his new Moline tractor, Gussie'd been grateful for help with the plowing, but lately he spilled over with ideas that included both of them.

She ought to go along with him before he found a new target for his attention and a disappointing harvest buried her in bills. After all, Eloise had snared Wendell Marsdon during the search party for Harvey, near as she could tell.

Those who noticed at all, including her sister, thought Daddy had simply skipped town. Gussie sent an unsigned letter to the police captain about an accidental death at the cavern, but if they found him, the newspapers had never broken the story.

The cavern was like a tomb. Or so she told herself.

Ever since, Gussie had eked out an existence. She tried housekeeping until her employer's wife dismissed her in a huff. Two different elderly ladies hired her as a companion but then up and died. A stint as a Hello Girl ended in disaster. The switchboard simply baffled her. Her sewing skills were mediocre, the local laundress hadn't needed the help, and the hospital only wanted volunteers.

Harvey would tell her to trust the Lord. She did try. Thinking of him hurt her heart too.

She shook her head to clear it. No ragged leaves, no sign of bugs. Safe for now.

The mail truck rumbled in the distance. No small effort kept her from hiding in the barn as Stephen Locke drove up.

"Morning, Miss Gussie." He braked in front of the barn and shuffled a handful of envelopes. The idling motor whirred and clicked. "How's the prettiest girl in the county today?"

"I don't know." She brushed away wisps tickling her forehead. "You'll have to ask her."

You'd think that was the funniest thing he'd ever heard by his grin. "Ask her, eh? I'd like to, truth be told." He winked. "So long as I know your daddy won't shoot me."

Oh. She ought to have realized. Stephen liked to flirt now as much as he had as a patient at Rockingham Memorial, but the bill collector notices made it hard to look him in the face. She missed Mr. Wexler.

Gussie fought for an even tone. "Can't say. I don't know where he went."

In a spiritual sense that was true, so she tried to mean it that way whenever people asked. As easily as she might imagine him trying to sell silver-lined clouds to Saint Peter, she wasn't silly enough to believe it.

Fragmented memories intruded at will. Darkness. Twin blasts. Gunpowder and blood. Laying the soiled suit coat over Daddy's lifeless form. Helping Harvey carry a bleeding Philip to the Buick.

He had torn off for Richmond, for the nearest hospital where they stood a chance of moving about unknown, while she took the horse Daddy had left at the trailhead back to town. Philip's name quietly vanished from the newspaper's oft-published list of Valley Turnpike Company shareholders who hadn't cashed out. Otherwise, neither of them had been heard from since.

No, the cavern was never far from her thoughts.

Stephen must have sensed her doldrums. "Chin up. You've got a package today." He held up a bulky rectangular parcel.

"Goodness, it's big." She frowned. "I'm not expecting anything."

"Aw, don't break my heart and tell me you've got a secret admirer."

She shook her head, bewildered. "None I know of."

He placed it in her hands and tipped his cap. "That's all today. Fine seeing you, Miss Gussie."

"Likewise." Her attempted smile felt flat. She did think Stephen was a decent man. Just one who didn't *see* her at all.

As the mail truck puttered off, she took the package and the bills inside and set them on the sideboard. Their contents would wait, and the gardens wouldn't weed themselves.

On the brown-paper wrapping, the return address named Mrs. Nancy's Tailor Shop as the sender. Odd. She'd asked for work some months earlier but never patronized the shop.

Curiosity nibbled. Might as well satisfy it before it started to gnaw. She washed the dirt from her hands and fetched a knife to cut the strings—carefully, reserving them for reuse. When she lifted the carton lid, she gasped and cupped a hand to her mouth.

Inside lay the yellow tea dress, complete with the celadon drape and peacock-feather fan she'd seen in the Marcuses' shop on that long-ago day.

She ran her fingertips over the luxurious material and gingerly lifted it out. How?

In the bottom of the carton lay an envelope marked, *For Gussie.* Was she mistaken, or was that handwriting she knew?

She snatched it out and tore the envelope with her trembling.

Dearest Miss Rice,

For three years, I have written and rewritten this letter in my mind, only to struggle now, it seems. I pray you are well, in spite of the losses and hardships you've surely faced. I'm grieved to add to them, but it is my sad duty

*to report the boy you knew as Harvey Engelwood is no
more.*

Tears sprang up instantly. But the penmanship. It was uncanny.

*The enclosed gift, purchased for you by Harvey, regret-
tably languished with the tailor while he waited for the
right time to present it. Now can hardly be called that
time, and if it's gone out of fashion, please accept it nonetheless as a token of his high esteem.*

*You may wish to know Mr. Marcus, once weaned from
all poison, recovered from his wounds. However, Harvey
met with the unexpected misfortune of being accused of
inflicting them. To protect those he cared for, he offered
authorities a false name, a hasty decision he repented
of many times in the run of his arrest, trial, and prison
term.*

She read the statement three times. Harvey? Prison?

*Yet the Lord was faithful to do a work with this error.
Stripped of family and friends, home, freedom, possessions, and even his name, what has one to cling to but
his Savior? My spirit resounds with His words, crying,
"Remember ye not the former things, neither consider the
things of old. Behold, I will do a new thing; now it shall
spring forth; shall ye not know it?"*

*Miss Rice, I shall be given a new suit of clothes and de-
ported to Norway in three weeks, and there's nothing to
be done for it. I have sent word to my mother, and if you
retain some small measure of affection for me, I hope you
will travel with her to Baltimore to let me bid you both
goodbye.*

But if by God's grace you love me as I've loved you, and you'd be content to leave your home and walk through this life as my bride, come with me. Let the dress be your reply. Wear it to Baltimore, and even at a distance I'll see your heart and know from the first glimpse that your answer is yes.

What do you think, Gussie? Shall we go see the fjords?

Ever yours, I am,

Hans Aksel Borja, erstwhile known as Harvey

The fullness in her chest clamored for release. Something halfway between a laugh and a scream escaped as she ran upstairs to try on the dress.

Yet an hour later, she quaked before Mrs. Engelwood's front door, with the envelope in her pocket and a wrapped half loaf of soda bread in her hands. The weeding had gone unfinished while dreams and doubts wrestled, and now she was sorry she'd knocked on—

The door opened, and Mrs. Engelwood actually smiled. "Augusta, come in. I've been expecting you."

"Thank you," she stammered. "Here. For you." She thrust the bread away as if it were burning her hands.

"How kind of you. Come in. Shall I put on some coffee?"

She stepped over the threshold. "I got a letter from Harvey today."

"Yes. Mine came yesterday." Mrs. Engelwood remained serene and led her to the drawing room. "Have a seat, dear."

For a moment, Gussie froze. Mrs. Engelwood had never called her "dear" before.

When she found her feet, she took two steps toward her old place on the piano bench. Old habits, but this once, she perched on the settee instead. The calming green of the Imperial Artichoke wallpaper wasn't working at all. "I don't know where to begin."

"Then let me." Mrs. Engelwood took the Queen Anne chair beside the piano. "He's in Richmond, bound for Baltimore, then Norway, and he's proposed marriage. Correct?"

Gussie's cheeks flamed. "That's right," she said faintly.

"And will you accept?"

The mantel clock ticked while she considered her answer. "What right have I to go? My debts . . ."

"Your father's creditors are not your concern."

"But it's so far. Everyone I know is here."

Mrs. Engelwood's demeanor cooled. "It sounds as though you've decided."

"But I haven't," she cried. "I love Harvey. It took losing him for me to see it, but it's true. It's my fault he's in this predicament, and of all places, why would they send him to Norway?"

"Because the fool boy gave my father's name and nationality, and now he is presumed dead and has nothing to prove who he is and no means of appeal."

"Goodness. Sounds like something I'd do."

Their laughter cut the tension. Gussie patted her cheeks. "All this time, I thought you were from Germany."

"Did you?" Mrs. Engelwood stood and took an envelope from the writing desk. "I misjudged you, as well, Augusta."

Gussie composed herself and listened.

"I watched my son's puppy love mature and go unreturned for ten years. Your father and sister's behavior made it easy to believe you thought yourself too good for him and cared only for what you might get from him. Particularly when you were infatuated with that Marcus boy."

The mere mention set her cringing. "The truth is that I'm a dolt, and when I finally started to see, I couldn't admit how stupid—"

"Enough." Mrs. Engelwood used the stern face that governed the Ladies Auxiliary so well. "Let us not forget Harvey also lacked the courage to make himself clear. He has overcome and so have you."

She nodded, but her head spun. "What should I do about Daddy's property? I suppose Eloise should have it."

"Your sister came to me full of demands two years ago. She did not like to hear that the land comes with the debts." Mrs. Engelwood rolled up the shield of her writing desk and withdrew papers from within. "Here is the deed, if ever you should need it. Until then, I will find a tenant for you. That and arrange a small gift so you both can start your life."

Gussie pressed her lips together before speaking. "And what about you, Mrs. Engelwood? We've become closer and I'm glad of it, but isn't Harvey your only family?"

She lifted her chin. "I fully intend to visit for months at a time, and I shall expect long, interesting letters to come here regularly. Otherwise, I have friends and service work, and that will do."

All the proud words in the world couldn't hide the pain in the woman's eyes.

Mrs. Engelwood unfolded the letter in her hands to consult its details. "We travel on April 4. I will pay your way and handle the arrangements, but you must decide for yourself, Augusta, whether you will go or stay."

The decision in Gussie's heart and mind was made, and the breath she drew to speak of it felt like the first air she'd breathed in a long time.

Fifty

Fluffy snowflakes floated down from heaven, quickly erasing signs of the pizza delivery. They'd settled on a supreme, half with black olives, half without. Solveig peeked in the box. "Another piece?"

"I'm good."

She placed Kyle's empty plate with her own on the tray table she'd set up beside the porch swing. As soon as she settled, he rearranged the fleece blanket wrapped around them and slid his arm around her again. "Think this is like your nuclear-winter romance?"

Her heart warmed. "We are writing the alternate ending. The one where we can go in and sit by the fire anytime."

Which would be soon. The cold had to be bothering his new knees. He hadn't complained, though, so they'd whiled away the afternoon, sharing minor secrets, filling lapses with kisses, and studiously avoiding the subject of her impending flight.

Out on the highway, the mail truck stopped at her box. "Ah. We are not the only two left after all."

"So much for repopulating the earth."

She laughed and pecked his cheek. "You're bad."

"I know. Will you hand me my drink?"

She reached toward the tray again as he shook pills out of a miniature bottle. An antibiotic, a steroid, and an anti-inflammatory. He never filled the painkiller prescription. The way he threw them all down at once was both endearing and weirdly gross.

The snow had piled high atop the mailbox and everywhere else. She hated to spoil the moment, but one of them had to and she wouldn't leave it to him. Not after everything he'd endured in these last weeks. "I should get the mail. I wish I'd thought to start the hold today." A small interruption, but she'd gone over and over her list specifically to protect their day together. All the hard things—hiring a manager for Bestepappa's company and giving statements to police, rescheduling flights and arranging time with dozens of people she had to see—she'd made sure none of it would spill into these precious hours. His mom would arrive at six to take him back to the physical therapy center.

"I think I'm ready to go in anyway."

She stilled the swing, moved his walker, and held it steady while he stood. Since the surgery, he rehabbed as if he had something to prove. Considering his father's lack of interest in his progress, maybe he did.

Though she moved to hold the door for him, he waved her off. "Let me try. Meet you on the love seat in five."

"Race you." She winked and set out for the mailbox.

Minutes later, she bounded back to the house with her fist full of envelopes. Kyle had beaten her to the goal and looked ready to gloat when she burst through the door.

"What's the matter?" He straightened up and reached for the walker.

"Nothing," she said, breathless. She ripped open the envelope. "Richmond State Prison wrote me back."

Kyle recoiled. "Um. Question."

"Hopefully, answers too. I didn't expect anything so soon. 'Dear *Solving.*'" She rolled her eyes. "'Thank you for your inquiry,' blah blah . . . 'Happy to report, we located the case file you requested'!"

She skimmed pages, pulse thrumming while Kyle stared. "Solveig?"

"You'll never guess." She held up the pages, triumphant. "I found Harvey Engelwood."

"What? Just now?" He patted the cushion, and she slid beside him. They huddled over the pages for several seconds, and he shook his head. "Fill me in. This is about Hans Aksel Borja. A relative, I'm guessing?"

"Yes. His name surfaced when I searched online about Bestepappa's secrets. I wanted to find the connection. Especially when I finally looked at his Bible." She retrieved the volume labeled *Bibelen* that Kyle had brought over from the office. "Remember this? Look at the family section in the front."

As he studied the faded handwriting, she let the moment wash over her. A diffuser scented the room in Woodland Spice, her phone streamed a mellow instrumental playlist through a Bluetooth speaker, and a cheery fire licked at a few good-sized logs. In the mirror over the mantel, she spied that dreamworld she'd mused on weeks ago. The person sharing it, though, made her want to stay.

She marveled that shuffling pages should whisper their secrets across time. That love should link arms with sorrow. That out of the moments she'd longed to erase, God had brought these she wouldn't have missed.

"So, if I'm reading this right," he said finally, "Hans Aksel Borja and Augusta Rice were Mr. Borja's parents. And this is weird. They list two marriage dates. April 6 and September 30, both in 1922. But how do we get from them to Harvey?"

"Turn to the Births page." She held the prison records side by side with the Bible. "Compare Hans and Harvey. Both were born January 10, 1900, in Cross Keys, Virginia. Both show the mother's maiden name as Borja. Every detail matches except the names."

He nodded slowly. "He used an alias."

She flipped to the next photocopied page. "Here, it gives a physical description and discharge information. 'Released for deportation on April 5, 1922. Destination'—can you guess?—'Norway.'"

"So they got married practically the minute they boarded the boat. What's that second date?"

"A church wedding, I'd guess, after they settled in Stavanger." She paused over the list of names and dates. "Then children, grandchildren, and seeing many years before going to their rewards. All the stuff of happily ever afters."

"Wow." He shook his head. "So Harvey and Gussie are your great-grandparents."

"Yes. And when Bestepappa emigrated, Harvey signed over the land for one dollar, the same way he received it from Gussie's father."

"But how did this place sit here for fifty years?"

"I asked the same question of Mr. Forrester. He found that Mrs. Kristine Engelwood paid the taxes on it until 1970." She found Harvey's mother in the family record and pointed to her name. "The year she passed on. My grandparents came over the following year."

A pinch formed around his eyes. "Then Mr. Borja knew where Harvey had disappeared to all along. Why didn't he just tell you?"

She glanced at the picture she'd rehung after delisting the house. "I'd love to ask him," she said softly. "I can only guess that when it was simply an interesting question, he thought I should have the pleasure of answering it myself."

"Sounds like him." He perused the Bible again. "Here's you. Hey, cool. Our birthdays are exactly six months apart."

"How about that." She smiled and held out her hand, intending to put the volume away, but he lingered over its pages with his brow furrowed.

"Family changes things." A solemn tone matched his frown. Whatever troubled him sapped the room of its coziness.

"More problems with your parents?"

"Yeah, but that's not what I mean." He passed her the Bible and took a deep breath. "Solveig, if you find your mom and change your mind about us—"

"I'm not going to look for her." Finality nibbled her heart. "And if ever I do, she is not part of us."

"But Ashleigh found her. She's out there somewhere."

Resentment thrummed in her veins. How did that awful woman dig her claws into this, their one day to simply *be*? "Ashleigh lied to pull my strings."

"Are you sure? She told the truth to pull mine."

Her ire dissipated. When they'd finally won an undisturbed visit, he told her everything that led to the cavern and what he remembered from its depths. He spoke and she listened, and in the quiet hours between physical therapy and supper, she had held him tight as he grieved his brother.

She softened her voice. "Either way, her game fails because I refuse to play."

Silence stretched between them. "All I'm trying to say is, if anything changes while you're there, I want you to be happy."

"Strange. That is what I want for you." She leaned in and widened her eyes. "Let's first try being happy together and see how that goes."

He pulled her close, and strands of her hair slid through his fingers. "You are all kinds of beautiful when you're right."

Lingering kisses stripped their moment's discord to its essence. "Do you have to go?" he murmured beside her ear.

"It's not forever." Hadn't they discussed it enough? "There has to be some practicality somewhere in this."

"Hear me out," he said. "What's wrong with being Oslo's big mystery? Let them figure out in a hundred years you were with me the whole time."

She snuggled against his chest. "It's nice to hear I'll be missed."

"Extremely."

Yes, it would be a long two weeks. Exhausting, too, by the time she packed her things, sublet her flat, and drank farewell coffees with her closest friends. But at the end of it, she'd come home.

Headlamps flashed in the front window. She glanced at the clock. Anita Benton was right on time.

The inevitable heaviness of goodbye fell fast over her. She stirred, but Kyle didn't loosen his embrace. "One more minute," he said.

Solveig closed her eyes and let this *koselig* moment carry the sadness away. What a marvel. She and Kyle had pursued an unsolved death and arrived in a mystery of life, one curious and vast, unhindered by what lay behind and generous with the hope of new beginnings.

THE END

Beloved Reader,

Everyone has a unique way to engage with stories. Some readers let stories wash over them, accepting and absorbing what comes as it is presented. Others like to ruminate, ask questions, and even challenge the material. I admit I'm usually in the first group, but for those who'd like to dig into the Scriptures quoted and alluded to in *Like Honey for the Bones*, you'll find them listed here in the translation referenced.

Blessings,
Brandy

ENGELWOOD MEMORIAL

He is not here: for he is risen, as he said. Come, see the place where the Lord lay. (Matthew 28:6 KJV)

And thine ears shall hear a word behind thee, saying, This is the way, walk ye in it, when ye turn to the right hand, and when ye turn to the left. (Isaiah 30:21 KJV)

How sweet are thy words unto my taste! yea, sweeter than honey to my mouth! (Psalms 119:103 KJV; see Solveig's Prayer below)

KYLE'S SELF-ENCOURAGEMENT

Do not lie to one another, since you laid aside the old self with its evil practices, and have put on the new self who is being renewed to a true knowledge according to the image of the One who created him—a renewal in which there is no distinction between Greek and Jew, circumcised and uncircumcised, barbarian, Scythian, slave and freeman, but Christ is all, and in all. (Colossians 3:9–11 NASB)

HARVEY'S MESSAGES TO GUSSIE

For all have sinned, and come short of the glory of God. (Romans 3:23 KJV)

A virtuous woman is a crown to her husband: but she that maketh ashamed is as rottenness in his bones. (Proverbs 12:4 KJV)

A merry heart doeth good like a medicine: but a broken spirit drieth the bones. (Proverbs 17:22 KJV)

Remember ye not the former things, neither consider the things of old. Behold, I will do a new thing; now it shall spring forth; shall ye not know it? I will even make a way in the wilderness, and rivers in the desert. (Isaiah 43:18–19 KJV)

SOLVEIG'S PRAYER

For the kingdom of God is not in word, but in power. (1 Corinthians 4:20 KJV)

The Lord is my light and my salvation; whom shall I fear? the Lord is the strength of my life; of whom shall I be afraid? (Psalm 27:1 KJV)

The people that walked in darkness have seen a great light: they that dwell in the land of the shadow of death, upon them hath the light shined. (Isaiah 9:2 KJV)

Come unto me, all ye that labour and are heavy laden, and I will give you rest. (Matthew 11:28 KJV)

In all your ways acknowledge Him, And He will make your paths straight. (Proverbs 3:6 NASB)

You prepare a table before me in the presence of my enemies; You have anointed my head with oil; My cup overflows. (Psalm 23:5 NASB)

Who may ascend onto the hill of the Lord?
And who may stand in His holy place?
One who has clean hands and a pure heart,
Who has not lifted up his soul to deceit
And has not sworn deceitfully. (Psalm 24:3–4 NASB)

How sweet are thy words unto my taste! yea, sweeter than honey to my mouth! (Psalms 119:103 KJV)

And Simon Peter answered and said, Thou art the Christ, the Son of the living God. (Matthew 16:16 KJV)

Looking unto Jesus the author and finisher of our faith; who for the joy that was set before him endured the cross, despising the shame, and is set down at the right hand of the throne of God. (Hebrews 12:2 KJV)

En sang ved festreisene. Jeg løfter mine øine op til fjellene; hvor skal min hjelp komme fra? (Salmenes 121:1 DNB1930)

Translated: {A Song of degrees.} I will lift up mine eyes unto the hills, from whence cometh my help. (Psalm 121:1 KJV)

When I am afraid, I will put my trust in You. (Psalm 56:3 NASB)

The fear of the Lord is the beginning of wisdom, And the knowledge of the Holy One is understanding. (Proverbs 9:10 NASB)

Jesus Christ is the same yesterday and today, and forever. (Hebrews 13:8 NASB)

I cried out to You, Lord; I said, "You are my refuge, My portion in the land of the living." (Psalm 142:5 NASB)

Search me, God, and know my heart; Put me to the test and know my anxious thoughts. (Psalm 139:23 NASB)

Bestepappa's Interview

Remember the prisoners, as though in prison with them, and those who are badly treated, since you yourselves also are in the body. (Hebrews 13:3 NASB)

And the King will answer and say to them, "Truly I say to you, to the extent that you did it for one of the least of these brothers or sisters of Mine, you did it for Me." (Matthew 25:40 NASB)

Gussie's Prayer

And the publican, standing afar off, would not lift up so much as his eyes unto heaven, but smote upon his breast, saying, God be merciful to me a sinner. (Luke 18:13 KJV)

Solveig's Words to Fischer

Og efterat han hadde fått stykket, fór Satan inn i ham. Jesus sier da til ham: Hvad du gjør, det gjør snart! (Johannes 13:27 DNB1930)

Translated: And after the sop Satan entered into him. Then said Jesus unto him, That thou doest, do quickly. (John 13:27 KJV)

GLOSSARY OF NORWEGIAN WORDS AND PHRASES

Akvavit—Strong Scandinavian liquor.

Både—Both.

Barn—Child.

Bestepappa—Special family name for Solveig's grandfather based on the Norwegian word *bestefar* (grandfather).

Bestemamma—Special family name for Solveig's grandmother based on the Norwegian word *bestemor* (grandmother).

Bibelen—The Bible.

Bokmål—"Book language"; an official written language standard in Norway used by the majority of the population.

Den mørke vinteren—The Dark Winter.

Det finnes ikke dårlig vær, bare dårlige klær.—Common expression meaning, "There is no bad weather, only bad clothing."

Det tomme mausoleet—The empty mausoleum.

Direktør, Statsarkivet i Oslo—Director, the State Archive in Oslo.

Er du våken? Ring meg!—Are you awake? Call me!

Fantastisk—Fantastic.

Far—Father.

Gratulerer og velkommen!—Congratulations and welcome!

Hallo—Hello.

Hallo, søta—Hello, sweetie.

Hei—Hi.

Herr—Mr.

Herre—Lord.

Herre Gud—Lord God.

Herren—The Lord.

Hjelp—Help.

Hodestups—Headlong.

Husk å vise dette til Solveig.—Remember to show this to Solveig.

I øyeblikket—In the blink of an eye.

Ikke sant?—Expression similar to "right?" or "isn't it?" at the end of a statement.

Ja—Yes.

Jeg elsker deg også.—I love you too.

Jente—Girl; can be used as address between girlfriends, as in English.

Kjære godjenta mi—My dear, sweet girl.

Kjære Gud, tilgi meg.—Dear God, forgive me.

Kjempekjekk—Enormously handsome; literally, "giant" (*kjempe*) + "handsome" (*kjekk*).

Koselig—Cozy; a Norwegian way of life.

Lys—Light.

Mirakler—Miracles.

Nei—No.

Noe på norsk—Literally, "something in Norwegian."

Norefjell—A place name; a good destination for a ski weekend.

Nynorsk—"New Norwegian"; an official written language standard in Norway.

På norsk—In Norwegian.

Perfekt—Perfect.

Pris Herren—Praise the Lord.

Rett og slett—Expression equivalent to "plain and simple."

Så koselig—So cozy.

Søte Sol—Sweet Sol (shortened form of Solveig).

Takk for maten, Herre.—Thank You for the food, Lord.

Takk, Jesus—Thank You, Jesus.

Til vi møtes igjen—Until we meet again.

Tosk—Fool.

Trofaste—Faithful.

Uff—Oof.

Å høre hjemme—Expression for belonging; literally, "hearing" (*å høre*) + "at home" (*hjemme*).

Ørret—Trout.

ACKNOWLEDGMENTS

Among the myriad disadvantages of taking *so* long to finish a novel is this: the certainty of forgetting to thank people who helped along the way. To those I've missed, I'm sorry and I owe you a coffee.

My Savior, Jesus, thank You for the greatest story and for loving us enough to invite us into it. For the trials, blessings, and twists of imagination that shaped this one, Yours is the glory.

To my wonderful husband, Michael: thank you for sharing this journey of faith with me, always encouraging me in it, and reading my stories. What other novelist has her own dedicated QA?

To my awesome parents: Mom and Dad, thanks for always modeling what it looks like to pursue big dreams. To Isy, Valerie, and Jenny: no one could ask for better sisters!

Christy Gill, your amazing friendship is a gift. Thank you for the initial seed that grew into this story, opening your home for my research trip, brainstorming with me, reading multiple drafts, and being Kyle's biggest fan.

JoAnn Nolley, Beth Baxter, and Lisa Gerald, thank you for praying me through all my books. I hope you're ready for the next one!

Sherri Wilson Johnson, Lindi Peterson, Karen Nolan, Hope Welborn, Kristi Hunter, Lindsey Brackett, Jennifer Slattery, Sylvia Dorris, Loni Finley, Deanna Davis, and all my ACFW North Georgia friends, thank you for countless times you've come to my rescue with encouragement, ideas, critiques, advice, and beta reads.

Joanna Collins, thank you for answering my medical questions. (Any mistakes are mine alone!)

Mari Klingen Sørheim and Ingvild Horne Hauge, thank you for the inspiration! I'm so grateful for the time we shared, and I'm still hoping to visit your beautiful country. Mari, special thanks for your guidance on Norwegian language and culture questions. *Jeg setter pris på det.*

Tusen takk!

Jim Hart, thank you for believing in me and in this story. I hope you're enjoying your retirement!

Irene Chambers, I learned so much from working with you. You made this a better book and helped me grow as a writer in the process, and I appreciate you tremendously!

Every one of you has enriched my life far beyond what these few words can describe, and I thank you.

Also by Brandy Heineman

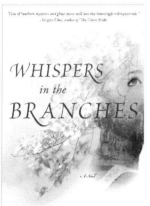

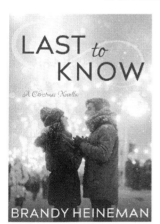

ABOUT THE AUTHOR

BRANDY HEINEMAN is a Jesus-follower, word nerd and storyteller who brings a fascination with family history to her dual timeline novels. She has been a member of the American Christian Fiction Writers since 2013 and has served as president of the ACFW North Georgia chapter. She is an alumna of Wesleyan College and a native of the Metro Atlanta area, where she makes her home with her husband, Michael. Visit her online at brandyheineman.com.

Made in the USA
Columbia, SC
01 August 2023